THE FOREST OF ANCIENTS

Fabled Quest Chronicles

Book Four

AUSTIN DRAGON

Published by Well-Tailored Books, California

The Forest of Ancients
(Fabled Quest Chronicles, Book 4)

978-1-946590-09-1 (paperback)
978-1-946590-04-6 (ebook)

http://www.austindragon.com

Book cover design by Humbert Glaffo

Printed in the United States of America

CONTENTS

INTRODUCTION

Once upon a time...

Beyond the Lands of Man and its Seven Empires, there was the legendary marker known as Titan's Bridge--the sole legendary gateway created by the ancient Titans themselves to the realm of the Magical Lands. Men had passed through the gateway for a millennium since its discovery in search of adventure and, later, unimaginable riches. The destination was the fabled kingdom of Atlantea coveted by humans and fae alike.

Long ago, before the dawn of man, fae, and beasts of light and darkness, was the Age of the Titans. They were gigantic humanoid beings of such size that their heads reached high above the clouds into the heavens. According to myth, a Titan known as the Maker of All Mountains was so devastated by the death of his beloved, he walked the entire circumference of Pan-Earth, dragging his fabled weapon, the Star Slayer. He carved a massive valley before he killed himself by leaping off the world into the void of space. This valley, cut through not only the known world but every other realm, was known as Titan's Trail.

Every three years, the northwestern lands of Avalonia became the starting point of the Kings' Caravan. Twenty years ago, the Kings of Xenhelm began this royal ritual journey across the Trail, attracting men—royal, noble, and commoner, farmer and knight, apprentice and warrior—from every corner of the Lands of Man. It was a year-long journey like no other through unimaginable dangers, mortal and magical, by day and night, all for one reason—to obtain the limitless riches of its final destination—the magical kingdom of Atlantea. Most brave men would never risk such a venture filled with danger and death, even with the protection of the Caravan. However, there were plenty of men who would and gladly did so under the auspices of the Four Kings.

But the Kings' Caravan was no more, due to their own treachery. There remained only Titan's Caravan. Under the command of a human, a man called Traveler, was a caravan the likes of which none had seen before—humans, elves, sprites, fairies, giants, other fae races, many magical beasts, and a shape-shifter not from the world of Pan-Earth.

But can the unlikely caravan make it to Atlantea? The Kings' Caravan was no more but the Four Kings, with wretched evil hearts, and their dark allies lived on.

The *Fabled Quest Chronicles* continues...through the Great Forest.

THE GREAT FOREST

Between Faë-Land Major and the
Great Oceans

CHAPTER ONE

The Four Kings

The expanse of Faë-Land Major, with its vast lands of the elves in the west, goblins in the east, and domain of the centaurs and other hoofed fae in between, had reached the end of its border. On his winged unicorn, the elfin general sat as motionless as his steed, his wizards at his side and his army of elfin fighters in formation behind him. They waited at the threshold of the Great Forest. Bright-green-leaved trees towered more than one hundred feet above them with trunks of forty feet or more in diameter.

To human ears the ground had just begun to rumble. To their elfin ears, they had heard the approaching caravan hours earlier, even before they landed on the ground to take up position.

As the human caravan approached, a snarl of contempt grew on the pale face of the elfin general. His armor was of a golden hue, his head adorned with a plumed helmet. The long feathers flowed high, and his dark hair hung down his back. His battle attire was no different than his men's or his twin wizards'.

Then came the sounds of horses and marching human feet. The Kings' Caravan came into view from around the wooded path. Flags high, the first units of the arriving Kings' Caravan were armored knights in muted silver armor draped with sashes in the colors of Xenhelm—orange and white. All of them wore helmets and carried spiked polearms that rose at least ten feet in the air. The second wave was made up of archers with helmets and armored breastplates. They carried longbows and crossbows with quivers on their backs that went from their shoulders to their thighs. The third wave of armored knights carried massive silver shields emblazoned with the symbol of Xenhelm—a majestic griffin. With them was the contingent of standard bearers on horseback, seven on each flank, bearing the Xenhelm flags flying higher than any of their polearms. The fourth wave of warriors wore spiked helmets, chainmail armor, and battle axes, flanged or spiked maces, war hammers, morning stars, or pikes. The final wave consisted of armored horsemen with lances, spears, or swords followed by war wagons with cannons.

The eyes of the elfin general burned with rage. The Kings' Caravan was not a caravan but an endless army of lowly humans. The shrieks of hawks— hippogriffs--was constant. He had heard of the Xenhelmians' fondness for the beasts, beasts taken from their rightful domain in Faë-Land.

The Four Kings approached. The first knight was Prince Wuldricar the Savage. He was a huge, brawny man, and his armor was built to suit his frame. His hair was blond, but his beard was dyed orange. The second knight was Prince Renfrey the Wily, revered for his strategic war thinking. Prince Wuldricar could lead an army to destroy any enemy or threat. Prince Renfrey would devise the plan to do so. Prince Gervase the Fair was primarily known for his womanizing. However, he was as clever as his brother, Renfrey, and as gifted a swordsman as his brother, Wuldricar. Their beasts shrieked as they dug their front leg claws into the ground and flapped their wings. The brothers held their fantastic steeds at bay as they lined up, side by side.

King Oughtred of Xenhelm galloped in on a giant griffin, appearing from between the columns of knights and warriors, his red hair, mustache, and beard distinguishing him. An orange cape billowed out from his chest armor, and a crown of orange metal sat on his head. The griffin let out a guttural roar that echoed through the air.

King Oughtred dismounted. His sons did the same and followed him; all four men in their stunning silver armor. Dozens of guardsmen approached the beasts and held their reins as the kings neared the elves.

The elfin general remained seated on his steed, as did his wizards.

"Why do you not dismount, elf?" Prince Renfrey shouted.

His father quickly raised a hand, gesturing him to silence.

"I am not an elf, human. I am General Gael of the elfin kingdom of Griffinheart."

"And I am not a human," Renfrey snapped. "I am Prince Renfrey of the kingdom of Xenhelm."

"I know who you are. I know who all of you are."

"Yes, I know of you...and your father, the elfin wizard King Rael," King Oughtred said.

"I see your Kings' Caravan continues to grow and trample the magical lands despite warnings from my kingdom and others."

"I do not take orders from commoners," Oughtred said coldly.

"Commoners?" Gael yelled. He jumped down from his unicorn.

"General Gael!"

Gael hadn't seen her. She appeared from nowhere. A thin and very tall woman, wearing a shiny silver dress and a band across her forehead. Her silver hair was braided elaborately, indicative of royalty.

"Princess Ilirora! Is the kingdom of Magica part of this?"

"General Gael, my kingdom is in alliance with the kingdom of Xenhelm," she replied.

"Why would Magica, a high elf kingdom, ally with humans, and humans such as these?"

"General, neither my queen nor I need to explain ourselves to you or your king. Xenhelm carries our banner and many others for safe passage to Atlantea."

Gael turned his gaze to Oughtred's smirking face. He stepped closer to the man. Oughtred's sons stepped closer to Gael.

"How?"

King Oughtred stared at him. Gael broke his stare to notice the hooded human men sitting quietly on steeds behind the royals. His elfin eyes noticed their yellowish ones.

"I do not know how you've managed this," Gael said to Oughtred, "how you've enchanted high elves to ally with you, but we will learn the truth." He glanced at the elfin sorceress. "What is Magica gaining from this alliance?"

"General, as I have said, neither I nor Magica need to explain anything to you or Griffinheart."

"Move your elves out of our way!" the huge Prince Wuldricar yelled.

Gael tensed to strike him but felt a hand on his arm. It was Ilirora.

"You can go on your own, or I can make you go," she said. "Do you really wish to test my magical patience against your twin wizards at the breach of the Great Forest? Maybe I might enchant its trees to swallow you into the earth, never to be seen again."

"Magica would risk war with Griffinheart over humans?"

"It is Griffinheart that risks war with not only powerful high-elf kingdoms but those of wind, cloud, star, and celestial elfin kingdoms."

Gael swallowed hard.

"Your wizard king and father is very powerful but is he that powerful?" the elfin sorceress asked.

Gael turned and leaped back onto his winged unicorn. He gave her a dirty look.

"This is not the last of this, elfin witch," he said as he gestured his men to follow.

He ignored the laughter of the human princes. King Oughtred and the elfin sorceress remained silent as they watched the Griffinheart elves ride off.

Gael seethed with anger.

"General, this is impossible," one of his twin elfin wizards said. "Did you see her? She is subservient to him. No high elf or elfin royal would follow a human. They would never do such a thing."

"But they are," Gael said. "This is the third year their Kings' Caravan has crossed into our lands, and already they have amassed so much power. What will happen in years to come?"

"Humans have such a short life span compared to elves or other fae. Let them grow old and die, and we shall be done with them," the other elf wizard said.

Gael flashed him a look, then turned his gaze back to the road.

"What is it, General? What did I say?"

"Maybe nothing. Maybe everything. What I do know is that there should be no humans in our lands at all. They trespass where they do not belong and should pay dearly for it. The magic of the Lands Between must be renewed."

"General, the Lands Between were created not to keep the humans from our lands, though that was a benefit. It was meant to keep fae from their lands."

"The wisdom of fae from the time of the Titans. I wish I could have been alive in those times, when the Titans ruled and the skies were filled with dragons and avians. How far we fae have fallen. All because so many of us seek the kingdom of Atlantea as do the humans. So many have fallen so low that my elfin eyes behold the abomination of the sight of a high elf taking orders from human trespassers. Maybe Father can create a new Lands Between to keep both humans and their fae from that kingdom itself."

"That is madness, General."

"It is a madness much more preferable than this. Ride faster!"

The twin elfin sorcerers raised a hand each, and their party of three riders and running elves became transparent, then invisible as a strong gust of wind carried them away.

King Oughtred returned to his griffin as his sons mounted their hippogriff steeds.

"Lead the caravan forth," he commanded.

"Yes, Father," they said in unison.

His sons flew their beasts several feet in the air as Prince Wuldricar bellowed out the command for the caravan to cross into the Great Forest.

The elfin sorceress floated beside the king, her feet inches above the ground.

"I hope King Oughtred the All-Knowing is not troubled," she said.

"We enter the mouth of the Great Forest. There is much danger within its realm, both ancient and new. In another time, I would have relished the challenge to conquer all within it. But the destiny of Xenhelm, as I have fashioned it, is far greater than any Faë-land forest or even fabled kingdom we feign is our destination. There is much to be accomplished with my caravan."

"We should not tempt the Fates. Rather than every year, make it every three."

"Then it will continue every three years without fail as we build. I do not desire any outsider distraction. I believe that Griffinheart should suffer the same fate as all my enemies in the Lands of Man. They should die."

"The elfin wizard king of Griffinheart is not without incredible magical power."

"But he has a son who does not. My late grandfather, King Tol the Defiant, was a vicious man who lived by the code that enemies should be destroyed and allies watched carefully. He was hated by all, even my late father, but under his rule, Xenhelm went from a tower and handful of hamlet villages to become one of the great kingdoms in Avalonia. My late father was obsessed with being just and respected rather than feared. Under my father's rule, Xenhelm was nearly destroyed, under constant attack, and almost defeated many times by enemies and allies. It is my grandfather's blood that runs through me, not my father's. No enemy of Xenhelm, current or future, will live. Griffinheart will learn this. Gael will learn this, and so shall his wizardly father. He is your kind. See to it. It is why you are here."

"Yes, King Oughtred."

Oughtred's griffin took to the air to assume point with his sons.

The Kings' Caravan marched into the Great Forest feared by both fae and humans equally. The magical forest had been home to monsters and giant animals eons before fae and humans even existed on Pan-Earth. But there was no alternative. Its domain had to be crossed to continue the trek along Titan's Trail to

Atlantea except for the rare few wealthy enough to hire the means to fly above it or powerful enough to possess the sorcerers and sorceresses to magically portal through it.

Princess Ilirora closed her eyes for a moment. She knelt down to place a hand above the ground. The rich green flora that once covered the patch was gone but not from being worn away by marching feet or frequent passage of beasts. The green life was ripped away from the patch of ground by violent magic. She rose to her feet to join the Kings' Caravan. What had happened there had happened years ago.

CHAPTER TWO

At the Great Forest's Edge

The boy ran faster still, but his stamina was quickly waning. He had first seen the bright-green-leaved trees towering more than one hundred feet in the air over a week ago, when his caravan first came out of the valley from Faë-Land Major. But they were dead. He was all that was left, clothes in tatters, feet bare and raw, sweat and tears in his eyes.

In his mind, he had convinced himself that if only he could get to the threshold of the Great Forest, he might have a chance, a chance for life. He ignored the pain, the fatigue, the fear that the creature may be right at his back to throw himself, with one final burst of energy, into the Forest. He fought his own body, which wanted to lie prone on the ground and pass out, to crawl through the four-foot blades of grass. He saw it. He crawled and pulled himself across the greenish dirt to a single giant daisy at the foot of a giant tree with a trunk tens of feet wide. The daisy itself was at least nine feet high.

The boy reached it and threw his back against its stem—firm but he could almost make it sway if he had the strength. A dew droplet landed on his forehead, falling from one of the giant daisy's petals. There was no time to study the flora of the Great Forest, or wonder if any giant insects were nearby that might take offense at him finding temporary shelter under the canopy of its petals. Young Traveler stared at the giant blades of grass he had crawled through.

His eyes could make out a form slowly pushing nearer, first a vague shadow, then what appeared to be a man's face became more visible. The creature had a human face, but its eyes were as black as night. Its smile revealed not one but three rows of ragged, yellowed teeth. One of its clawed hands came through the giant grass to set on the ground.

There was no energy in the boy. There was no fear either. He was too tired to be afraid. Young Traveler was content to simply await his inevitable end. He had cheated fate so many times before. Caravans lost, but he was always one of the survivors. Not this time. He would join his caravan in the afterlife.

The creature's eyes widened as it noticed something behind him. Young Traveler was too weak to turn and look. A light of such intensity flashed. The boy yelled as he closed his own eyes tightly with all his might, but the light still was blinding. He heard the creature yell, too, but knew the yell marked its death.

Titan's Caravan had reached the natural border of the Great Forest with its one-hundred-foot trees. Once across, Faë-Land Major and known civilization would be behind them. Traveler knelt at the barren patch of ground. He was about to touch the earth but changed his mind. The dog watched over him from nearby in a slender, regal gray wolf-dog form.

The caravan had stopped, the vanguard with Pangolin in the lead and the rest of their nearly nine-thousand-member caravan behind them. The royals and Maiden Gwyness moved the vanguard to Pangolin's side with the giants, half-elves, and elaphine archers around them.

"You were here before, Mr. Traveler?" King Aereth asked.

"Yes, sire, I was." Traveler rose to his feet, rubbing his hands to remove any dirt.

"I sense strong magic within this spot," the drow sorceress Dr'amal said. She, too, had moved closer to the front columns. "Will you tell us what happened here, Mr. Traveler? I sense it was...more than ten years ago for certain, possibly more than twenty, but you cannot be as old as that."

"I was a boy at the time. Our caravan—five thousand-strong, humans, elves, the caravan master was a centaur—it was the first caravan I had been a part of where the humans and elves weren't always trying to kill each other, but it was more than simply that we were led by a centaur. There was good camaraderie among the men. They had worked together often and had a good reputation among the fae. I was proud to be a part of it.

"We had come through Faë-Land Major without incident. Then the creature came at us. I was the only one who survived. They fought it hopelessly to give me time to run. They told me to run into the Great Forest. That was my only chance. I made it here. I thought this was where I would die. In fact, I had already prepared myself in my mind for it. Unfortunately for the creature right behind that tree, a flying caravan, back from Atlantea, descended from the clouds on their way to the elfin kingdoms. The blast from their magic blinded me for days. Nothing will grow in this spot for decades or more. I met star and cloud elves for the first time."

"What was your notion of them?" Lyre, one of the elfin questing knights, asked. The woodland high elf joined them from the rearguard with his desert–elf comrade knight, Taylos.

Traveler looked up. "I prefer drows."

Dr'amal laughed. The elfin knights weren't amused.

"And present elves, of course," Traveler added with grin.

"I would say not to judge elfinkind by them, but you already know that," the desert elfin knight, Taylos, said.

"Why?" Lady Aylen asked. "What of star and celestial elves?"

"Princess, they are not as noble as they appear or pretend to be. Both you and King Aereth must know every elfin race fully before we get to Atlantea."

"That's the talk we like to hear," Lady Aylen said. "Atlantea."

"What was this creature?" Pangolin asked.

Traveler looked into the Great Forest. "The creature would be something of interest to Mr. Bragg, some form of wingless manticore."

The dwelf had also joined the vanguard. "Looked like a human, but when it chased its prey, its legs bent out, and it moved across the ground like a spider," Bragg said.

"Yes."

"I never encountered one, but I heard of them. Killed your entire caravan? They are not as powerful—despite their horrific appearance—as their winged cousins but no less quick and cunning."

"I suspect it had been observing us for days. It struck when we were at our most lax in security—gorging ourselves on the end-of-day's meal to the sounds of singing and laughter. It moved quickly enough to kill our best fighters first then simply struck the rest, one by one, in the panic."

"I'm sorry, Mr. Traveler," Aereth said.

"Fortunately for us, we have a more accomplished caravan master who does not allow lax security while the men have their nighttime meal or any other," Pangolin said.

Traveler grinned. "Mr. Hobbs."

"Yes, sir." The caravan's steward stepped forward.

"Let us make camp here." Traveler tossed him a folded pouch.

"Yes, sir." Hobbs turned and walked to the caravan with Tyfer, one of his bodyguards, following.

"Make camp for how long, Mr. Traveler?" King Aereth asked.

"Until we are ready, sire. While I map out our path, each one of you will have your prospective duties to perform. Also, we need to know before we begin, not during, how the magic of the forest will affect the lizards and Lady Aylen."

"Lizards and Lady Aylen? Why am I in the same sentence with lizards, Mr. Traveler?" Lady Aylen asked.

They could not help but laugh.

Within the protection of a pocket-realm, their camp sat under a magical dusk sky. Duties had not been assigned, so it was rest and relaxation for the men. At the center of camp were the four walking trees, all reaching upwards, branches out. Parties of about a dozen formed their own small camps encircling the walking trees in row after row outward. A separate camp of the giant lizards with their minders had been set up adjacent. A third camp of giants, all asleep, and berserkers, human and fae, loudly laughing with horseplay and chatter, was set up at the entrance to their pocket-realm. From the inside, it looked like the opening of a giant cave out to the sunny world of the Great Forest. From outside, the entrance to the pocket-realm was invisible.

The tents of the leadership were at one outer edge guarded by humans, half-elves, and drows.

King Aereth appeared at the entrance of the caravan master's tent. "Mr. Traveler, am I disturbing you?" the king asked, peeking in.

Traveler sat at his table, busy scribbling notes on parchments with many thick books opened or bookmarked. All had seen their caravan master prepare for each leg of their journey in this way. The dog sat on a rug near the entrance, vigilant at all times, watching the king.

"Not at all, sire. Please come in," Traveler said.

The king stepped into the tent and smiled at the dog. Traveler stood from his stool and found one for the king.

"Thank you, Mr. Traveler." The king took the stool and set it near the table to sit. "How are the preparations proceeding?"

"Slow but that is to be expected. When we do set out, it may be days or weeks before we reach the next official leg of the journey."

"Titan's Walk?"

"Yes, sire. Imagine it as a path made from the footprints of the Maker of All Mountains himself. Parts of it are quite visible, but most are not."

"How long will it take us to get to the edge of the oceans?"

"Months, sire, but we must take our time. We cannot rush."

"Of course. When we do arrive at the ocean, reaching Atlantea will be a simple matter, will it not?"

"Possibly, sire."

"Possibly? Why so?"

"If we are not expected, it will be a simple matter. If we are, it will not."

"The Four Kings."

"Yes."

King Aereth sighed as he thought. "As if we needed any more dangers on this journey."

"When I finish my preparations, we will convene a meeting so that I can inform our caravan leaders."

"Yes. The men, especially Mr. Hobbs, appreciate your efforts to keep them as informed as you do. It reassures them, keeps the gossiping to a minimum."

"Gossip leads to fear. Fear leads to loss of focus of one's duties. When that happens, people die."

"What happened to you, Mr. Traveler, when you ran from that creature? We all could see it in your face. The tragedy had a special edge to it. You were the sole survivor."

"I was. A little boy without so much as a dagger survived and eventually made it all the way to Atlantea when those far more worthy were slain."

"Do you believe you are unworthy, Mr. Traveler?"

"Then, yes. Now? No. I worked hard to become a caravan master of note. I only wish that many of the ones who helped me along the way had made it too."

"There is term for it, Mr. Traveler. Survivor's guilt."

"I know it well, sire, as a healer. A very bad affliction of the mind for any man, let alone one traveling on Titan's Trail. No, sire. I made my peace a long time ago. I made it to Atlantea the first time due to luck, the second time due to my dog, the third time on my own."

King Aereth smiled. "This will be your fourth full journey?"

"The sixth, sire."

King Aereth was surprised. "I hadn't realized you made the journey so many times. Should you not share that with the men?"

"No, sire. I do not want any of them to become overconfident or feel they do not need to be careful because my knowledge and experience will protect them from all dangers. Let them believe that I did the full journey only a couple of times and much of it due to the assistance of my dog. Sire, as you can see, I am the caravan master I am because, to me, success is not the dog and me crossing the bridge to Atlantea. The entire caravan must make it too."

"Yes, Mr. Traveler. I feel reassured on many points now. I will leave you to your work."

"How do your studies progress, sire?"

"Studying the customs and protocols of elfin royals is tedious, but I make daily progress. Should I not also learn a bit of elvish? It is clear that the language of a particular elfin race plays an integral part in these customs and protocols."

Traveler nodded. "Very good, sire. You are very correct."

"It is no different for us humans. I attended many a royal gathering with dignitaries of other empires. Language, religion, history, dress, the commerce of their lands are all part of it."

"True, sire. If there were time, I would have you trained in the elfin tongues, but it is very hard for humans to master even after years of intense study.

Your time is best spent learning everything there is to know about them. And if there is time, you can learn about others."

"Others?"

"Elementals. Fae of the air and clouds and seas and oceans especially."

"I look forward to my continued studies then, Mr. Traveler."

King Aereth moved to the entrance but stopped. "Mr. Traveler, should we not have one of our magic-makers stay with you? Maybe Mr. Frog-Dor?"

"No, sire. His place is at the center of the men where he can use his powers to protect us all. I think our drowess can at least try to protect the leadership here."

"It is good to hear you say a kind word about her. You said you spent time with drows and it was a positive experience, but your interactions with our drows have been mixed."

"Our drows are a valuable addition to the caravan, sire."

"Yes, they are."

The king nodded and left the caravan master's tent.

"Oh, and I'm especially looking forward to our dinner meal where you will answer the question: 'What do lizards and Lady Aylen have in common?'"

Traveler grinned. "Yes, sire. I will."

The new day dawned within their pocket-realm. The encampment awoke not to a magical dusk sky but many large openings to the real sky outside letting in the full sunlight of the lands of the Great Forest. However, that was not the only sight the men beheld as they stirred from their sleep within the warmth of their giant-slippers. Giant birds and giant insects flew and buzzed past. The many beautiful multi-colored birds drew smiles. The giant multi-colored hornets, some with stingers longer than their bodies, drew only fear.

"We can see them, men, but they cannot see us through the realm's invisible barrier," Hobbs said as he walked through the camp on his rounds. He had his morning pipe, so it was time to get the men to their chores for the day.

With nearly ten-thousand men, both human and fae, there were plenty to visit. Usually, the fae were already busy at work before the caravan's steward began his rounds, and his fellow humans didn't want to wake. Today, neither party did.

"Get up!" Hobbs yelled at a camp of pech. The halfling sprites with their wild, bushy eyebrows, big noses, and even bigger bulging forearms slept in their clothes--off-white tunics, dark trousers, and boots—but not their dark caps. They put them on when they grudgingly rose—all five hundred of them.

"Mr. Hobbs." He heard a familiar young voice.

He turned to see the caravan's chronicler, Mr. Quillen, a boy in his teens, always with his magical notebook given to him by Traveler. The boy drew all the fae races, fantastical beasts, and evil creatures he witnessed on their march. He would be very busy over their year-long journey.

"Yes, Mr. Quillen?"

"Do you see them?"

"See what?" Hobbs asked, stopping his advance.

"They're bigger."

"Our fae lizards? They've grown more?"

"Not only them."

The caravan's giant lizards of fifteen feet in length, not including their tails, needed two-man teams to manage them. But the blue, yellow, green, and orange reptiles, not clad in their own special armor, were not what Quillen meant.

Hobbs and the boy neared the royal tents. King Aereth's royal guardsman, the berserker Nirgund, sat on a stool near a fire polishing his favorite halberd.

"Ah, Mr. Hobbs and young Quillen." He noticed them looking at his pack of reptilian hounds. "Yes, gentlemen, my alphyns are a tad bigger this morning."

The fae reptilian hounds, with their black fur and knotted tails, ridge of knotted fur along their backs, and eagle-like forelimbs, lay on their lizard-like underbellies, uncharacteristically calm, all together, watching their master sharpen the blade of his weapon with a special rock.

"I believe all the fae animals we have may be somewhat larger in appearance," Nirgund said.

"Their fur seems to have a slight glow to it, too, Mr. Nirgund," Quillen said, slowly approaching the hounds with a smile. They watched the boy with playful eyes. Quillen petted one of them on the top of its head and, once he saw they were amenable, did the same for all.

"Aye, they are magical beasties, Mr. Quillen. This ancient forest is where all magical life came from. The forest is magic above all."

Hobbs perked up again, and Quillen's mouth hung open.

"What, may I ask, is wrong with you both?" Lady Aylen came from her tent in her warrior garb—pants rather than her dress. But it was not her dress that drew their attention and made Nirgund laugh at their reaction.

"Lady Aylen, you look more...elfish," Quillen said.

She laughed. "How can I look more elfish? I am an elf."

"But you seem different somehow," the boy said.

Before Lady Aylen had "become" an elf, her eyes had been blue. When she became elfin, one would have described her eyes as crystal blue. Now, they seemed to have a slight glow, so much so that the men imagined they would shine in the dark.

"Aye, lad, it's the magic of the Great Forest. It affects alphyns and elf alike," Nirgund said.

"Yes, Mr. Nirgund, it does. And lizards too. Speaking of which, where is our caravan master?"

"Mr. Traveler is meeting with some of the fae leaders, princess," Nirgund answered.

"As long as he hasn't run off with his dog, leaving the caravan on another dangerous errand."

"M'lady, he did say he would not do that again now that we're in the Great Forest."

"Let's hope that's true, Mr. Hobbs."

"You're bigger, princess. I mean, taller," Quillen noted.

"I am the same height, Mr. Quillen."

"No, m'lady, you are taller a bit, and your features, hand, and arms visibly tighter in tone. I would wager you are stronger and faster now that we are here," Nirgund said.

"And you have a glow," Quillen said, staring at her forehead and face.

"Mr. Quillen, staring at a royal is not permissible!" she said but then laughed. The men laughed. She pointed. "Look!"

Quillen dropped to the ground to sit and open his book to draw. The caravan's two fairy sisters flew in circles around the camp with their swarms of multicolored insects. Wildglow had always appeared two feet in height, and her sister, Sunpetal, half that, but both sisters were about four feet in height, giggling as they led their swarms. They flew farther into the pocket-realm and higher up into its sky.

"As long as this Great Forest shares its magical power with us too," Lady Aylen remarked. "We already know it has done so with every animal, plant, and creature within its domain."

The small-realm of the kilmoulis was not known to any others in the caravan, except for Traveler and the Tree Shepherds. The realm was a simple woodland area with lots of green foliage and a bright-blue sky filled with large, billowy white clouds. The sprites had their own quaint hamlet to enjoy each other's company. They always enjoyed speaking with the human named Traveler because he had no issues with their strange appearance and didn't inherently dislike them.

"Welcome again, Master Traveler," one said, often self-conscious to all others, as kilmoulis spoke through their large noses.

"Welcome." The caravan master stood in front of all sixteen of the sprites near one of their hamlet homes. "What do your powerful magical senses of smell have to report?"

The sprites smiled with their eyes.

"There are goblins."

"How far away?"

"Not far."

"But close? Remember I am a human. Far to a sprite and far to a human is quite different. From where we camp to where they are in Faë-Land Major, how far back are these goblins?"

"As far back as before the city of Fae-Wick."

"Not far at all," Traveler said.

The sprites smiled in their unique way again. "Traveling to or away from us?" Traveler asked.

"Away, but they have changed their course many times in the last few days."

"Maybe to confuse us. They may know you're with us."

"None of the goblins ever saw us in our encounters."

"True, but they may still know. Maybe a dark fairy saw you or any number of their animal allies. The goblins may know, but it's good that we know they are close. What others have your senses detected?"

"Two parties."

"Yes."

"One is strange, the other different."

"Tell me of the different one first."

"One is a party of fae. We believe, maybe elves and animals, maybe dogs, wolf-dogs, or wolves, but we are not certain. They seem to change as they move."

"How far?"

"Arion's Spear."

"Far. Why do you believe they seek us?"

"They follow our path exactly."

Traveler thought for a moment. "What of the strange party?"

"They smell like...us but not us."

"What does that mean?"

"We do not know. It's as if members of our own party are following us. They are as far away as Faë–Land Minor."

"Back in the land of the fairies. You can smell living things that far away?"

"We can."

"Maybe they're doppelgangers."

"Those dark fae do not travel together. Never."

"We've already seen things that are never supposed to happen, such as high elves working side by side with goblins and dark fairies, or battle elves taking orders from humans."

"Titan's Caravan is also unique."

"But we are a collection of equals."

"They are not doppelgangers, this strange party," another kilmoulis said. "We know how they smell. This party smells as we do. We cannot explain it. We have never experienced this before."

"We are sorry we could not be more helpful, Master Traveler."

"You've been very helpful," Traveler said.

"You could send a scout to know for sure. Maybe the fairies."

"No. Our fairy sisters are children at heart, and I promised to look after them to no less than their queen mother. She is not the kind of fairy I would ever wish to anger. Besides, that's too far for them to travel alone. No. We will stay together. Even I won't be traveling outside the caravan with my dog. I know of these two parties, and that is more than enough. They are so far back, they should never reach us, and once we get to the oceans, they can't catch us."

"Yes, Master Traveler. Your reasoning is sound."

"My primary concern is that goblin caravan."

"Goblins and more."

"Yes, I've seen goblin caravans in the past. They are always more than just goblins. You are to find me, no matter where I am, no matter what time of day or night, should you detect them nearing our caravan."

"Yes, Master Traveler," the sprites said in unison.

"We will find you immediately," one said.

It was true. When Hobbs reached the area where their two thousand warriors and four hundred Cut-throats—both under I'wulf's command--camped, he saw that their one hundred chamroshes were clearly larger and far more boisterous than normal. Most of the Cut-throats were boisterous berserkers, so it was a good match as they "played" fight with their war-flock—the affectionate name they gave their collective winged eagle hounds—equipped with wooden staffs and training shields near one of the largest crawling trees.

Nearby was the camp of the Antaean giants, all fast asleep. They were the only fae that he excluded from camp duties. For the longest time, the only two he knew by name were their leader, Grakdar, and his second-in-command, Barg, but he now knew Arteus, Aronir, Alceir, and Alebar by sight as well. Giants were good for marching and fighting but little else. When not in battle, the only thing they enjoyed more than eating was sleeping, which they did most of the time.

"Mr. I'wulf," Hobbs said as he reached their berserker leader, who stood with a few others, including the caravan's fae berserkers under the lionoid Hax.

The men roared with laughter as they watched a chamrosh claw at one of the men playfully, accidentally drawing blood. Hobbs winced, but none stopped laughing or playing.

"Yes, Mr. Hobbs, our fine steward," I'wulf said as he slapped Hobbs on back in greeting.

"Did Mr. Traveler already tell you?"

"Oh, yes. It's time to retire our goblin armor for ourselves and the beasts. I can't say that I like elfin armor all that much. It's lighter, but it's so shiny and always so clean. We berserkers like a bit of dirt and blood on our armor. It's a shame that dwarven armor is so heavy."

"Only giants can wear their armor with ease," Hax said. "Or our larger animals."

"Besides, Mr. Hobbs, we like to be different. The entire caravan is wearing elfin armor. We should wear something else."

"Intriguing idea, Mr. I'wulf. I'll ask Mr. Estus and see if he has any ideas."

"Very good, Mr. Hobbs."

"Not sure if any of it can live up to berserker dirty-and-bloody standards though."

"I am sure our weaponsmaster will surprise us."

The pocket-realm that the caravan's fifty darklings slept in was a thick black forested island floating in a lake. The perpetual night sky was filled with stars, other planets and shooting stars. Here was where Traveler met with the fae-bloods. Ursi was the sole fae-blood of a bear clan kingdom. The fifteen male fae-blood mercenaries were of a wolf clan kingdom. Their races had been mortal enemies for hundreds of centuries. They'd only agreed to meet because the caravan master demanded it. The two parties watched each other closely, not saying a word. Only the heavy breathing and cackling of the sleeping darklings in the distance rang through the air.

Traveler felt he'd drawn the moment of silence out long enough.

"Thank you for meeting me together."

"This is a very interesting small realm for your phooka allies," one of the fae-blood men said.

"They like the stars," Traveler said.

"What is it that you wish?" another fae-blood male asked.

"I'm moving the drow sorceress to the royal tents. Ursi, I want you to share her quarters."

"Me, Master Traveler?"

"Yes. No one should be alone on this caravan, and you did bring her and her drow clan into the caravan. You said your peoples were allies."

"We are, but my clan is a solitary one. That includes solitude from our allies."

Traveler shook his head. "You can make whatever private sleeping space you wish but within her sleeping tent. We cannot take chances. We all must have others with us at all times."

"I understand," Ursi said. "Then it will be so, Master Traveler."

"Good. Do so starting tonight. The reason I wanted to speak with both of you in each other's presence is I need to know now, not at Atlantea, what will happen when you arrive."

The fae-blood men smiled in unison. "So certain are you that we will arrive?"

"I am certain I will arrive and my dog. So I'm assuming at least one of your pack will as well. Ursi, too, I'm sure will make it. Both your parties are traveling a very long way from your lands on this journey. I ask my question again. Will there be any strife between your clans once we arrive at Atlantea?"

"None," Ursi answered.

"None," one of the fae-blood men answered. "Neither of us have any cause for violence against one another. We hate the elves, too, but there is no cause for concern there either. We are as focused on the destination as any human or fae within the caravan. That is our only mission. Our clans can make war against each other another time."

"Would there ever be a possibility of your clans becoming allies or, at least, no longer blood enemies as a result of this caravan?" Traveler asked.

The fae-blood men smiled in unison again. Their wolf-like eyes flickered in the light of the small realms many moons.

"Is our caravan master also a diplomat at heart? Seeking to bring warring factions together, as he has done in this caravan. We appreciate the words, Master Traveler. But even a year-long journey such as this won't unlikely undo the memories, hate, and wars of millennia between us."

"I mean no disrespect," Traveler said. "I am a human. I know nothing of the fae-blood races or their conflicts with one another. I'm not dismissing the reasons for your hatred for one another. I am simply wanting to present the idea to you. One day, someone must stand up and simply say: It ends here. What went before will no longer dictate what goes on afterwards. I have said the same to other humans and fae before. It's advice that I have even given myself. That is all. I will not speak of it again."

Both Ursi and the fae-blood men remained quiet for a while.

"Will you also be moving the sleeping camp of the elves, Master Traveler?" a fae-blood male asked.

"With our drowess at the leadership camp, I'll move all the drows nearby. The elves will choose to be at the other end, near Mr. Pangolin, the Cut-throats, and the giants. Maybe you can have your camp in the center, if you don't mind the other fae there."

"That will be what we do. The fauns and the other hoofed fae are quiet people, so that suits us."

"Good. I'm sure they will all welcome accomplished warriors amongst them."

"Elaphines are ferocious fighters, even without their long bows," another fae-blood male said.

"That they are."

"Master Traveler, what do you believe will happen when we arrive at Atlantea?" Ursi asked. "The Four Kings live."

"They do. Do either of your fae-blood clans have any relationship with nymphs, sylphs, or any other elementals?"

"None," Ursi answered.

The fae-blood men shook their heads. "No."

"Do any other fae-blood clans?" Traveler asked.

"Are you asking me to reveal the other clans of the fae-blood?" Ursi asked.

"I'm asking if any other fae-blood clans have attempted this or succeeded at getting to Atlantea."

"No," Ursi quickly replied.

"How many other fae-blood clans have ventured outside your lands for Atlantea?"

The fae-bloods stared at Traveler.

"The cat fae-bloods have no interest in such journeys outside our lands. The hawk clans tried. The chameleon and gazelle tried and failed."

Traveler felt that the fae-blood had given him the information, not to answer his question but to annoy Ursi, who was visibly angry.

"Have other fae-bloods done so before?" Traveler asked.

"Not that we know."

"But the hawk clan may have gotten to Atlantea?" Traveler asked.

"Possibly."

"It matters not, Master Traveler," Ursi said. "They are not allies of either of our clans."

"That is exactly my point," Traveler said. "Remember, I lived in Atlantea before. I have seen elves engage in treachery against other elves. Humans did the same against other humans, all to gain an advantage with the Atlanteans. Fae-bloods and dwelves are the only fae I am unaware of, and don't know of their history with the Atlanteans."

"Fae-bloods have no history with the kingdom of Atlantea," Ursi said.

"Then your clans will be the first. Consider that too."

"When do we leave?" a fae-blood male asked.

"When the magic of the Great Forest does all that it will do to our fae members, including you."

"We will not be growing in size or glowing in the night, if that's what you fear," he said.

Traveler decided not to reveal what Staric, the moon elf, told him about the fae-bloods: "The fae-blood kingdoms are on the rise. They used to be as prominent as elves, but forsook all that for obscurity from all the other fae races, even from other clans. Their group appearance is significant to us because they are a people of great magic. Some of that magic is immune to the magic of our own wizards."

"No, I'm not afraid of that," Traveler replied. "It is as I stated. I will speak more of our strategy of departure when I meet with the fae parties. You should attend. I promise it will not happen again too often—our human meetings."

"I will attend," Ursi said.

"We will attend."

Traveler nodded. "Good. Let us leave before our darklings get up." He raised his voice. "Even though I know they're only pretending to sleep."

Loud cackles erupted from within the dark forest.

As Hobbs moved to another part of the camp, he caught the melodic songs the caravan's musicians, the Brothers Brimm, played. It was another thing the humans and fae shared, a love of music and the five musicians relished playing their instruments with a variety of songs, each with their own story, history, and emotions.

The rear guard camped at one of the towering crawling trees. The Cut-throats, their beasts, and the giants, rested there when not on watch. There had also been one hundred fifty fae mercenaries, but after their encounter with a manticore, only eighty-six remained. Those men stayed close to I'wulf's Cut-throats.

A second magical tree was for mostly fae parties: the one hundred gnomes, who amused themselves with dancing, gossiping, and playing with the fae animals of the caravan; the four hundred fauns under the leadership of their chief, Ammon, a quiet bunch that loved music and storytelling; about fifty gnomes and horned gnomoids from other fae kingdoms; and nearly seven hundred humanoid animal men: frog men, lizard men, squirrel men, raccoon men, possum men, fox men, rabbit men, bird men, mouse men, and a mole man. Even with so many different races, the animal men always stayed together. It was their giant animals—giant crabs, turtles, porcupines, ducks, and cranes—that the gnomes loved to play with. Their fantastical beasts included a carnivorous moose, jackalopes—rabbit with antlers—and enfields—animals with the head of a fox, forelegs like an eagle, and the hindquarters and tail of a wolf. Both giant and fae animals were used as steeds or guard animals.

At the third were the hoofed fae herds. The fae were well shaded by the tree's leaves, but Hobbs could make out the silhouettes of the watching elaphines with their large antlers. There were five hundred of the powerful fae archers and fighters. The largest of them was their leader, Strag, who always sat in the center. All had their backs facing the crawling tree. Those without antlers were either the two hundred cervids or more than two hundred fifty rusines. The cervids protected the elaphines when they slept, and the rusines were the cooks and laborers for the camp. Hobbs looked above to the top of their crawling tree, but he didn't see any of the four Tree Shepherds. The leshy were the masters of the four crawling trees, and whenever they were to be seen, they resided in the tree of the hoofed fae. Greenwig was the leader, then there was Mossberry, Thornbeard, and the youngest, Little Root.

The last crawling tree was home base to the royals and their caravan master's tent, both guarded by Nirgund, his thirteen reptilian hounds—alphyns, and a half dozen sentries under his command. Lady Aylen's tent was always guarded by her seven half-elf guardswomen.

"All men accounted for, Mr. Hobbs?" Nirgund asked him as he approached.

"Have you seen our half-elf men, Mr. Nirgund?"

The berserker pointed up. Hobbs lifted his head to gaze at the top of their crawling tree. He could see them waving at him. Hobbs smiled.

"All eleven of them, Mr. Hobbs."

"Yes. Have you seen our fae-blood parties?"

"Them, I have not seen."

"Our drow parties seem to be absent, too, and Mr. Bragg and his party."

"Mr. Traveler is absent, so maybe they are meeting with him."

"That must be it. Mr. Gresham and Mr. Frog-Dor are in the healing tent. Mr. Estus and his men are in their pocket-realm, the brownies in theirs, the darklings in theirs, the väki in theirs. I never see the kilmoulis unless Mr. Traveler is present, and there are sixteen of them."

"You mean those sprites with huge noses that take up most of their face?"

"Yes."

Nirgund frowned. "I don't like them."

"Neither do the other fae but we need them."

"The fenodyree and the kirins are in theirs," Nirgund added.

"Yes. With all our human parties here." The steward gazed out across the many fires with men sitting and gossiping around them. He did a quick inspection. "Our one thousand servants for the king's weapons teams, Mr. Estus's seven hundred fifty men, our three hundred regular servants." He looked off in the distance and could see the two thousand lizard minders walking their giant lizard in two columns, something they tried to do four times a day when training. "Our lizard teams."

He also noticed his two guardsmen, Tyfer and Oeric, already leading the cooks, preparing the men's meal for the night.

Nirgund laugh. "Mr. Hobbs, you can't possibly count so many men so fast."

"It's an art form, Mr. Nirgund. I count groups of ten quickly. No need to be precise, just accurate enough. The men know their duties and to keep track of each other. Is the king sleeping?"

"No, Mr. Hobbs. He, Lady Aylen and Maiden Gwyness are gone too."

"Gone?" The steward stared at Nirgund. "Wait, I haven't seen Mr. Pangolin either."

Nirgund started to chuckle. "It will be okay, Mr. Hobbs. No meeting will begin without you."

The gathering was held in the tent of Chief Ethor, the rustic woodland elf leader. Woodland elves either lived simply in woodland villages or, like high elves, lived in large cities. Ethor commanded his three hundred rustic elves and also served as the elder leader of the elfin questing knights that joined the caravan, which included high elves, desert elves, woodland elves of the city, and moon elves. The elfin questing knight leaders, Lyre, Taylos, and Shadumun joined Ethor at the entrance as everyone arrived. Though not the original numbers of more than thirteen thousand, the caravan still had a force of six hundred experienced elfin questing knights.

"Tonight, you are our host, Chief Ethor," King Aereth said when he arrived with Lady Aylen and Maiden Gwyness.

Pangolin and I'wulf were already waiting. They arrived with Bragg, the dwelf and manticore hunter, and Bragg's seven-foot metal golem, Glog. Bragg commanded five hundred men himself, all barbarians, all elves—mountain, forest, and wild elves. The caravan's weaponsmaster, Mr. Estus, arrived dirty and dusty from a day of forging in his own small-realm.

"Come on, Mr. Hobbs." A smiling Nirgund arrived with the man rushing behind him into the tent. "I told you no meeting would start without our steward."

Nirgund joined Pangolin and I'wulf. Hobbs joined the royals. The drow leader, Dr'as and his sorceress daughter, Dr'amal, were also already waiting.

The caravan's healer, Mr. Gresham, arrived with Frog-Dog, still walking with metal braces on his legs and with the aid of a walking staff rather than being helped along.

A few carried on conversations while the group waited. Traveler arrived with his wolf-dog following. Right after, Ursi entered and so did all fifteen of the fae-blood men.

"Mr. Traveler, all are here," Hobbs announced.

"Thank you, Mr. Hobbs. Thank you Chief Ethor for allowing us to meet in your command tent."

The elfin leader nodded.

"I'll be quick about it. Even though we haven't begun our journey through the Great Forest, I wanted to let you know that when we emerge, we will not be at Oceans Omnis, the center of the Great Oceans. Instead, we will be at the Sirenic Seas."

The revelation drew gasps and expressions of shock from all the elves and other fae. None of the humans knew the significance.

"I take it that there is strong disagreement with our caravan master's choice," King Aereth said.

"It's madness," Lyre, the high elf knight, said. "Mr. Traveler, if we elves are not immune to the magic of sirens, then you humans surely are not. We are not simply speaking of one or several sirens. We are speaking of thousands of the creatures. They could overwhelm us no matter what magical barrier we find to shield ourselves or breach any pocket-realm we try to hide in."

"Neither the leshy, who are allies to their sister fae, nor the nymphs or the elemental väki would be able to help us," Chief Ethor said.

"The only one among us who would possibly be spared from their attack would be Lady Aylen," Taylos the elf said. "But once they saw she was not a real water elf, that would quickly change."

Lady Aylen's face contorted with anger. "I grow tired of the constant demeaning of my circumstances. I was taken from my elfin kingdom as an infant so that I would not be murdered. I had no say in the matter."

"My words were not to offend," Taylos said. "Only to emphasize the sheer danger to all of us."

"Our caravan master has not once led us astray, so it is doubtful he would do so now, when the danger increases every step we make toward to Atlantea. Let us ask the question. Mr. Traveler, especially for us humans who do not know of these Sirenic Seas, why do you choose this course for the caravan, despite the obvious danger?"

"Thank you, sire. Our fae colleague, again, forgets that I'm the only one in the caravan, save my dog, who has traveled from the Lands of Man to Atlantea and lived in the fabled kingdom. I have also had the great displeasure to be on a ship in Ocean Omnis that was attacked and destroyed by sirens. I know full well the enchanting power of siren screams.

"What do we know today? The Four Kings live. They know we have reached the Great Forest, either directly through magic or indirectly because of the battle we fought in Fae'el with their allies. We know there's a goblin caravan ahead of us. We know, or I know and you now know, that there are two other caravans behind us seeking us out."

"Two caravans?" Pangolin asked. "Who?"

"We don't know."

"How do you know this?" Lyre asked.

"The kilmoulis."

"Yes, they do have that ability. That is why our chief wizard hired them for our party," Lyre said.

"Then your plan is to go where they cannot possibly follow?" King Aereth asked.

"Yes, sire. We have too many dangers to contend within the Forest. We do not need more. Oceans Omnis is far more vast than Faë-Land itself, both Minor and Major, but there are a limited number of paths out of the Great Forest to its shores."

"They could lie in wait for us," Pangolin said.

"Yes. That's what I'm afraid of."

The group was silent for a moment. Some members looked at each. Others were in deep thought.

"Mr. Traveler," Dr'as said. "My people support your decision. However, I, too, have had the displeasure, as you say, of dealing with sirens. I cannot say that I won the exchange. We are a caravan of nearly a ten thousand, and our animals are far more sensitive to their powers than we are. How do you plan to protect the caravan through their waters? I assume you have already made arrangements."

"I have."

"As any true caravan master would."

"I have also traveled across the Sirenic Seas before...successfully. Not with a caravan of this size, but I know the waterways through it, waterways to sail clear of the regions they control."

"What regions do the sirens not control?" Shadu-mun, the elf knight, asked.

"The regions controlled by giant sea creatures."

Bragg the dwelf laughed. "I always enjoy our meetings, Mr. Traveler. You always know how to leave us with those precious notions to feed our nightmares as we sleep."

"Thank you for that, Mr. Traveler," Lady Aylen said. "Sirens and sea monsters. We are about to fight our way through the Great Forest, and that's what awaits us."

"Yes, princess, but after that leg of the journey will be Titan's Point."

She smiled. "Titan's Point. Atlantea."

"We are getting far, far, far ahead of ourselves. We haven't yet stepped through into the Forest to begin our march to Titan's Walk."

"When do we leave, Mr. Traveler?" Pangolin asked.

"Before we discuss that, should we not discuss what happened to the flying elfin caravan that we encountered?" Chief Ethor asked. "Victims of the

Four Kings sent to warn us not to proceed to Atlantea?"

"Chief Ethor, we won't abandon our quest to Atlantea. We know nothing of this flying elfin caravan for certain. They told Mr. Gresham that was their mission. How do we know? Maybe they were acting on the Xenhelmian's order to kill us rather than warn us as they claim—another of Oughtred's ploys to keep us from moving forward."

"But all those elves, agents of the Four Kings?" Lyre asked.

"Other elves have been sent by them to destroy this caravan before why not here?" Ethor asked.

"Blasphemy. Elves taking orders from a human," Shadu-mun said angrily. He caught himself and looked at Traveler.

Traveler smiled. "No offense taken."

"If they did tell the truth, who destroyed them?" Pangolin asked.

"We will never know," Dr'amal said. "Unless we wish to turn back to Fae'el to ask them."

"No," Lady Aylen said.

"We definitely won't be doing that," King Aereth said.

"Then there is nothing more to be said about it," Dr'amal said. "Move forward."

"Mr. Pangolin, we await three visitors and we will not move forward until they find us."

"Mr. Traveler, is one of them the servant from the white elfess queen?" Gwyness asked.

"Yes, Maiden Gwyness."

"What elfin queen?" Lyre asked.

"The Queen Mother Anelle of the Celestial Elves of Nimbus," Traveler answered.

"Celestial elves?" Shadu-mun asked. "They are allied with the Four Kings."

"Not all," Chief Ethor said. "Who is she sending to meet us?" the elf asked Traveler.

"A servant so old that I'm not sure the magic of any one in this tent, or any weapon or object, could harm him."

"An Old One," Ethor said. "They have the original magic, the same magic that flows through the ancient Great Forest."

"Yes, indeed. The other visitors we await have to do with our travel across the oceans, with our original plans changed, and our travel across the Great Forest. I do not know how long we will wait, only that we must until they arrive."

"There is plenty of training to do, to occupy our time while we wait," Pangolin said.

"Maybe my men and I could scout ahead for any game," a smiling Dwelf said.

Traveler wanted to respond but instead moved on. "Mr. Estus."

"Yes, sir."

"Have you categorized all the unknown magical weapons in our hoard?"

"I have, and there is much of value to us."

"Do we have magical armor that could be of interest to Mr. I'wulf and his men? They gave up their goblin armor but want something different from elfin or dwarven metal."

"I will see what I can find, but I must confess that we still have weapons in the hoard of unknown origin and ability."

"Maybe our Mr. Frog-Dor and Dr'amal should assist you," Traveler said. "And take our elfin questing knight leaders too. Combined, you should be able to figure out all that we have.

"Also, I want everyone to know that I have assigned myself the additional task of giving much thought to this 'mystery of the Great Forest' that has troubled the fae for so many centuries. Every land caravan I have ever been a part of has also weighed the question, though all of them knew the tangible dangers to contend with."

Lady Aylen asked, "Mystery?"

"The mysterious disappearances of large caravans traveling through the Great Forest," Traveler replied. "None have unraveled this mystery."

"Large caravans only?" Bragg asked.

"Yes," Traveler answered.

"Are we a large enough caravan?" Bragg asked.

"We are," Lyre replied. "Mr. Traveler, a wise assignment."

"Another reason for my decision to head toward the Sirenic Seas rather than Oceans Omnis is that far less disappearances have occurred in that direction over the centuries. But I admit, it's because no one knowingly travels that way through the Forest."

"You mean, Mr. Traveler, no one is that desperate or foolhardy," Lyre said.

"But we are neither, Mr. Lyre. We are Titan's Caravan," Traveler said.

"That would mean something if one of the ancient Titans were escorting us through the Forest, but then, that is not so."

"Pleasant dreams everyone," Bragg said with a laugh, already leaving the tent.

Everyone else looked at Traveler. "In closing, my final words are to remind all to report any strange dreams to Mr. Hobbs. Special attention should be taken with nightmares, especially those that you remember. Our meeting is concluded."

Lady Aylen walked to Hobbs as everyone exited the tent. "Oh, Mr. Hobbs, I can tell you my strange dream now. I don't have to wait until tomorrow morning. See, I had this dream about these sirens and horrific sea monsters." Humans and elves laughed. "What does it all mean, Mr. Hobbs?"

"I'll have to consult with Mr. Traveler, m'lady," Hobbs answered with a grin.

The man awoke to find himself dancing barefoot in a green glen of white trees with golden leaves. As he moved in a circular fashion to a tune in his mind, he realized he was not alone. Women danced all about him, transparent in form, but he could see them, their smiles, hear their laughter. He could see their long hair flowing behind them. He felt moisture splash on his face.

He stirred on his sleeping rug covering the ground. He could hear the crackle of the fire to his back. His eyes opened. *A dream.* But what woke him? He pulled down his blanket covering the top of his head and screamed at the sight of a giant eye almost on top of him.

The yell woke every man in the caravan's camp. Several brownies ran to him as the man jumped to his feet to run away. His human comrades grabbed him. The man looked again and stopped, ashamed.

A giant yellow lizard stared at him. The man jerked back as the lizard's long tongue almost brushed his face. Men laughed as Hobbs reached him.

"What is going on here, men?"

"Mr. Hobbs, this one was visited by our comely giant lizard there."

The man was embarrassed. Hobbs pointed at the lizard's minder. "Take charge of your lizard and return to your camp."

"Yes, Mr. Hobbs. Sorry, Mr. Hobbs. They've all been very restless these nights."

Hobbs looked at the growing group of onlooking brownies.

"May I humbly ask that you keep our giant lizards from the sleeping men as part of your nightly duties?"

"Yes, Mr. Hobbs. Of course." The brownies were always smiling and in good spirits.

"Men, return to sleep!" Hobbs yelled.

The steward realized that his duties for the day would begin that instant. He made his rounds to ensure that all returned to sleep rather than gossip for hours.

"We have work to do in the morning! Go to sleep! All is fine!"

Hobbs passed by the leadership tents. He could see Lady Aylen, Gwyness and the female half-elves peeking out. He saw something glimmering. Obviously, a blade of a weapon in one of the women's hands.

Hobbs was startled by the sudden presence of a drow on night duty appearing beside him.

"I apologize for alarming you, Mr. Hobbs. We fae know human eyesight at night is poor at best."

"Your dark-bluish skin doesn't help, sir."

"I suppose. You should know that some of the fae are already whispering that your human's scream could have awakened something in the Forest."

"How?" Hobbs asked. "We are in our pocket-realm. Even so we are in an open space."

"Mr. Hobbs, our realm is of magic, but the magic of this ancient Forest is supreme. The Forest knows we are here. There may be living things within it who heard or sensed his scream."

Hobbs didn't know what to say. "I will find Mr. Traveler. Hopefully, he isn't asleep."

Hobbs double-timed to the leadership tents. King Aereth and Nirgund stood in conversation just outside the entrance to the king's tent.

"All is fine, sire." The steward walked to Traveler's tent and peeked in. It was empty.

"Where's Mr. Traveler?" Lady Aylen was suddenly standing next to him.

"He's at the edge of camp...there." One of the male half-elves, Mr. Elman, pointed in the distance.

Hobbs shook his head.

"What, Mr. Hobbs?" Lady Aylen asked.

"Drows and elves and half-elves just popping up out of thin air next to me without warning."

"I do hope he isn't alone," King Aereth said, suddenly next to him.

"And humans too."

Hobbs ran off, leaving the royals and half-elves behind.

He didn't have to run far, as Traveler, his dog, and a small party were walking back from the camp's edge. As he neared them, he saw the others with their caravan master were the dwelf Mr. Bragg and a few moon elves. The moon elves worked night watch with the drows and darklings. Hobbs realized he hadn't seen the mischievous darklings that night yet.

"Where's the man who screamed, Mr. Hobbs?" Traveler asked.

"He was startled by one of the giant lizards, Mr. Traveler. Nothing more. I'll ensure the men get back to sleep."

"Very good."

"Is there any cause for concern, Mr. Traveler?"

"No, Mr. Hobbs. Mr. Bragg and I were simply taking a nightly stroll with the proper escorts."

"Mr. Traveler, the lizards are much bigger, are they not?"

"They are. Their minders need to make their heat pits larger."

"I will see to it tomorrow."

"Well, I shall leave you to your duties, but do not take too long to get the men back to sleep. You need yours too. We must be ready to set out at a moment's notice. Our three visitors may arrive all in the same day, for all we know."

"Yes, Mr. Traveler. Good night again." Hobbs ran back into the camp.

"The Great Forest," Bragg said with glee. "What massive prey can I add to my bag on this journey?"

"We still speak of hunting."

"I am a hunter, Mr. Traveler. My specialty is the manticore, but I hunt other prey of interest."

"Mr. Bragg, tomorrow morning we will make a brief detour before most of the men wake."

"I am always game for a new adventure, Mr. Traveler, even one called a small detour."

Bragg stared at the giant manticore skull in sheer astonishment. He was not a small dwelf by any means. His race was larger than elves, and he was larger still than most dwelfs. The weathered skull with the tell-tale triple mandible jaws towered over him with a rainbow sky above them.

The dwelf let himself fall buttocks first to the lush green ground. His eyes cast down and distant. He rubbed his thick forehead. The dwelfin hunter looked at the half buried giant skull again. He shook his head before looking up at the lone Traveler. Nearby, his dog lay on the ground keeping watch on the giant plant life and towering trees not too far away. His own metal golem, Glog, war hammer in each hand, also stood watch.

"What happened to you here? You said you were only a boy. No human boy could have traveled through the Great Forest with this alive."

"I never said I traveled through the Great Forest as a boy, Mr. Bragg. I said I survived it. Everyone else died. That's a big difference, but I did not show you this skull because I had anything to do with its demise. An elfin warrior pointed it out to me. He was a huge elf, a fierce warrior. He was one of the ones who died on the journey. I show you this for the same reason he did."

"I have hunted manticores for many ages, Mr. Traveler. No manticore can grow to the size this skull suggests."

"They did, and they do in these realms. Keep that in mind, great manticore hunter. The reason we do not know of them is because they never leave any survivors to tell the tale."

"Your point is made, Mr. Traveler. My men and I will not be venturing off to do any leisurely hunting."

"Even that is not why I showed this giant manticore's remains, though I welcome the added benefit of my lesson."

"Why, then?"

"This giant manticore did not die due to natural causes. It was killed."

"Killed? By magic?"

"No. Worse. Brute force."

"Manticores are evil, devious, and extremely intelligent. Normal manticores are terrible enough. I can only guess the added strength and dark magic power emanating from this foul body. To have the physical strength to stop such a thing with its whirlwind–like frenzy of flight, what could do such a thing?”

“I do not know, Mr. Bragg, and I don’t want to know.”

“Neither do I. You once told your fellow humans that there are thousands of fae races they have never seen.”

“And will never see.”

“And creatures.”

“Yes.”

Bragg got to his feet. “I shall definitely be remaining in the circle, Mr. Traveler.”

“The only solace we have is that such creatures do not want to be seen or known by any outside their own kind. We have so many different races and creatures that if they revealed themselves to kill us, they could not be certain they would destroy all of us.”

“That is what protects us from them, Mr. Traveler?”

“I would say yes.”

“That does not steady my pulse in the least.”

“It would be foolish to think it would for mortal beings such as ourselves.”

"Though it would be interesting to add even a piece of such a skull to my bag."

Traveler grabbed him before he could turn to step any closer to it.

"You did exactly what I did."

"And your elfin warrior friend stopped you too?"

"He did, and from the expression on his face, I got the notion that the skull might be booby-trapped."

Bragg stepped back on his own.

"Let the Great Forest claim the wretched skull naturally when it's ready, when all the evil magic from it falls to dust."

"Yes."

"We should return to the caravan."

"Immediately."

The dog transformed again to a giant bird with four arms. Traveler rode on its back while it deftly picked up Bragg and his golem and took flight.

"They return!" yelled the half-elf Mr. Elman.

"I still do not know how that half-elf can see farther than me," Lady Aylen said from her stool in front of her tent's campfire. She could hear the giggling of her half-elf guardswomen inside.

"They have magic, too, m'lady," Gwyness said, seated next to her.

"Just last night, our caravan master said he would not go off on errands, and yet he did so first thing this morning."

"They did not go far, and he was not alone."

"They should not have gone at all."

"You always get like this when you're frustrated."

"Yes, Gwyness, I am. We need to move forward, not backward or not at all."

Gwyness heard Traveler speak a strange language as he approached with his dog. Lady Aylen thought for a moment.

"No, Mr. Traveler. I am not being a child in front of my aide."

"When will you begin speaking elfish, too, princess?" he asked.

"When I am ready."

"You can visit with the Tree Shepherds and practice with them. Leshy speak many, many languages, human, fae, and animal."

"That I may do, Mr. Traveler."

Traveler stopped to look at the lizards.

"Do we have the food necessary to feed so many giant lizards on the Trail, Mr. Traveler? They look to be much bigger than what you originally told us."

"They've grown bigger than normal for their species. It may have to do with our encounter with the spriggans."

"The dark sprites that made them sick?"

"More than that, princess. Their dark magic made them diseased. The magic of the Great Forest is making them much stronger. A similar attack might not be as successful. But yes, you are correct, princess. That means they will eat more, and we may not have as much food as we thought."

"I thought our plan was to not stop."

"That's always the plan, but in all my travels on the Trail, that never is the case. We will stop somewhere. However, the food we'll gather for them is normal for traveling parties, so we won't draw undue attention to ourselves."

Traveler said something else in elvish to her.

"Yes, Mr. Traveler. Maiden Gwyness and I will get on with our training for the day. Women! Gather your weapons! Let's see who can reach the Cut-throats' pocket-realm first."

Lady Aylen was a blur into her tent and back out, racing to one side of the caravan. Five more blurs whisked past them. The flock of owl griffins flew after their new mistresses. They all disappeared through an invisible doorway.

"Well, Mr. Traveler. I will take my slow human body, gather my weapons, and join them in my own slow time," the maiden said.

"Don't feel bad, Maiden Gwyness. You and she have different roles. She is the slayer. You are the seer. Force versus magic, combined to fight as a unit."

"Yes, like your dog and you."

"Yes."

"Thank you, Mr. Traveler. Usually it's Mr. Hobbs with the reassuring words."

"I can manage it myself, too, when needed. Remember I began as a healer in life."

"Yes. Where you learned to tell your so-interesting stories." She moved quickly into the women's tent.

"Gwyness!" Lady Aylen's head popped out of the magical doorway.

"Reading each other mind's too."

Gwyness ran from the tent toward the small-realm doorway with her slender war hammers.

Lady Aylen broad jumped so far she astonished herself. Her focus wavered, and she lost her footing and tumbled down a hill but quickly jumped to look back at the training groups in the distance. Their training realm practiced in a woodland area encircled by green hills and mountains that came together to form an immense waterfall. The river it created went back around the entire mountain range then shot off in a different direction. Whenever she swam in any body of water, she would emerge completely dry. From those swims, she learned she also became stronger and her senses grew sharper.

She caught sight of the male half-elves standing near the magical doorway of their pocket-realm. The men were watching her female half-elves train. She grinned, then noticed Elman—the half-elf who could magically see farther than anyone else in the caravan, including all the elves—looking at her. He gave a wave with his fingers.

"Mr. Elman, stay away from my royal guardswomen."

Gwyness was getting used to training with the Cut-throats and their chamroshes. The drills always varied but were rigorous, and sometimes dangerous. Estus had created a wide variety of metal dummies able to stand with three legs for the men and beasts to attack. Gwyness had her own to practice her dual-weapon-style fighting on. Whether slashing or thrusting, she never felt at ease with the prospect of actual combat.

Pangolin usually joined the Cut-throats, but he was absent. King Aereth's weapons team was also hard at practice using their catapults and firing rocks at targets in the distance. They'd come a long way and could hit any stationary target with precision more than a mile away.

Gwyness stopped and grabbed the amulet around her neck. She could feel it glowing without looking. She nervously looked around. The glow disappeared. Lady Aylen had already reached her, running fast.

"Your amulet," she said.

"Yes, but its glow was brief."

"What does it mean? We're in a pocket-realm within another. How could it sense anything? Is it within the realms or outside?"

"It must be outside?"

The female half-elves joined them.

"What's wrong, m'lady?" one asked.

The pack of owl griffins flew to them from their play on top on of the hills.

"We are not sure," Lady Aylen replied.

"Did her amulet glow?" another asked.

"Doesn't that mean a fiend or creature of dark magic is nearby?" another half-elfess asked.

"We should not speculate," Gwyness said. "We should go back into the main realm and walk amongst the camp. No need to alarm the men without cause.”

“There is cause. Your amulet does not glow without reason,” Lady Aylen said.

“Whatever caused it to glow may have simply passed by.”

“Women, let’s go see for ourselves.” Lady Aylen looked at her royal guardswomen. “Will the men, or the male half-elves, be joining us?”

The female half-elves said nothing, but a few of them turned red.

The women returned to the main pocket-realm and walked through the men, but Gwyness’s amulet never glowed again.

At the pocket-realm’s entrance, a sentry of elfin questing knights stood guard, joined by Traveler and his dog. Pangolin approached with the half-elf and a few Cut-throats. The elves conversed with each other. Pangolin could not understand their elvish but instinctively knew what they were speaking about.

“Look!” Elman, the half-elf scout, cried out.

Everyone’s attention turned to the view outside the pocket-realm. Whatever it was cast a large, horrific shadow turning day to dusk.

Pangolin grabbed his axe-mace weapon from his back. "What is that?"

The elves had all drawn their weapons.

"Not everything that skulks through the Great Forest has a name," an elf said to Pangolin.

"It is some kind of chimeric monstrosity," one of the elves said. "Have you seen its kind before?"

"No," Traveler said. "It knows the entrance is here but not the exact spot. It will watch for a bit and then move on."

"What is that?"

It was young Quillen with his magic book in hand. The royals and Gwyness were with him. Nearing them were more Cut-throat warriors. I'wulf joined Pangolin.

"You returned with a friend," the fellow berserker said to Pangolin.

"Friend, indeed."

"Look at its shadow. Like a giant gorilla-cat-bird-wolf-stag creature. Seems as if it has multiple heads. Horns, wings, claws, hooves."

As Traveler had said, the creature moved on. Dusk returned to day.

The giants had also joined them.

Pangolin looked up at Grakdar. "Do you know what the creature is called?"

Grakdar shook his head. The other five giants did the same.

"To fight such a thing," Lady Aylen said aloud.

"That we surely would not have wanted," an elf said.

"Was your latest excursion a success, Mr. Traveler?" King Aereth asked.

"Yes, sire. When we exit the Great Forest, our means of transport over the oceans will be waiting."

"What if we do not make it?" an elf knight asked.

"We will make it," Lady Aylen interjected.

"Princess, we're glad you're so certain. We are not, especially," Lyre, the high elf, said. "We've met one of our visitors, which leaves two more. When will the last of our visitors be here, Mr. Traveler, so we can depart?"

"Not long," Traveler answered. "I had expected our land transport to arrive before the icarian, but..."

"Icarian?" Aereth asked.

"Yes, sire. They are a race of flying, bird-like humanoids who live in cloud cities."

"They're allied with cloud, star, and celestial elves," an elf said.

"And moon and most high elves," Traveler added. "We have nothing to fear. I've dealt with him in the past, and icarians have a high sense of honor and pride in their work. Our transport will be waiting, and no one else will know of it. Also, the kilmoulis told me they sensed those supplying us with our land transport en-route days ago. They're close."

"Sensed?" an elf asked. "You mean the kilmoulis smelt them. Are they not visible on your magical maps?"

"Magical maps do not work within the Forest. You know that."

"Why is that, Mr. Traveler?" Lady Aylen asked.

"Because the magical maps show all living things moving in a region. Every inch of the Great Forest is a living, moving thing. The magic of any fae map is rendered useless."

"Hence our great caravan master," Lyre, the elf, said.

"You say that with an edge of sarcasm," Lady Aylen said to him.

"No offense was meant, Lady Aylen. We elfin questing knights are here for the entire journey and will risk our lives to see that we reach Atlantea. Our leaders would not have sent us if they had any doubts about Mr. Traveler."

"Thank you, Mr. Lyre," Traveler said. "May I suggest we increase the guards at the entrance for the night and more sentries and patrols around the camp?"

"Agreed," the elves and berserkers said.

"Sorry, Mr. Quillen, that you don't have another creature to sketch in you book," Traveler said. "But you saw its shadow. That should be enough for your active imagination."

The boy smiled. "Yes, Mr. Traveler."

"Make sure you sleep through the night with no nightmares, and do not jump up screaming like that man the other night," Pangolin said.

"That was because one of the giant lizards was licking him and woke him up," Quillen said.

"That is an interesting dream," I'wulf said with a laugh.

"What does that mean?" Quillen asked.

The Cut-throats, elves, and giants laughed at him as the group dispersed for their duties.

"Lady Aylen, what did I say?" he asked her, following the royals and Gwyness back to their tents.

"Mr. Quillen, you're at a good age because you do not partake in the men's crude humor."

Quillen smiled. "Oh, I know why they're laughing."

"Mr. Quillen!" Hobbs voiced yelled out. Quillen sped away from them to see to his neglected duties.

Gwyness neared Traveler as the group walked back to the royal tents. "Mr. Traveler, I wanted to inform you of something."

"Yes?"

"My amulet was glowing earlier today."

"Where?"

"The princess and I were training in the Cut-throats' pocket-realm with our guardswomen. We exited the realm, but there was nothing to be seen. It didn't glow again. What does it mean? Are we not safe within the pocket-realm? And it's daytime."

"Mr. Traveler, we will patrol the camp as a precaution," Lady Aylen said.

"Yes, it is, Maiden Gwyness. It is daytime."

The day was winding down. Traveler normally walked faster than the average man, but this time he marched even more quickly toward the opening of the main pocket-realm. His dog followed alongside him as he noticed Gwyness leading the women slowly through the camp of men. His eyes met Lady Aylen's. The princess gave a slight nod as she blinked: All is fine, Mr. Traveler.

He continued to the realm's entrance with his dog. On guard was the caravan's master-at-arms, Mr.

Pangolin. The Cut-throats were training, so it was all the elfin questing knights who stood sentry with him.

"Mr. Traveler, you seem to be in a hurry," Pangolin said.

"Because I am, Mr. Pangolin. Join me with a contingent of our elfin knights."

"How far will we go from the realm door?" a high elf asked.

"Leave your axexs here. Bring weapons and falcons. We go about half a mile away to meet our visitor," Traveler said.

"How do you know your visitor is here?" Pangolin asked.

"I have looked each morning for his sign. This morning it was there with instructions of when to meet based on the sun's position in the sky."

With Pangolin on one side, and the dog on the other, Traveler led the group from the realm's magical opening into a wide-open area before the Great Forest. The dozen elfin questing knights following included high elves with their unicorn swords already drawn, desert elves with the fae falcons gripping the shoulders of their armor, turning their heads in every direction to observe, and woodland elves in green armor with their bows and arrows.

Traveler pointed up. Pangolin saw the "sign." A yellow ring of clouds hung in the sky without moving.

They waited at the base of a mammoth tree at the edge of the Great Forest. Pangolin's attention fixed on the army of soldier ants, larger than the dog, moving along the ground in front of another tree. The elfin knights stood in a circle around the men, eyes roving the terrain, weapons ready.

Traveler pointed to the sky again. They saw quite high in the distance a flying caravan moving over the Forest. The master-at-arms pulled his telescope from his armor to get a better view.

"Interesting flag," Pangolin said. "An eagle-winged fish."

"They head for Oceans Omnis."

Pangolin lowered his telescope. "Do you know the flag?"

"I believe I've seen it before. Nothing to concern us."

"If only we could travel by flying caravan," Pangolin said.

"Mr. Pangolin, for ten thousand and their animals, it would cost more money than even our kingdoms have," one of the high elves said. "The elfin kingdoms who run the flying caravans are by no means charitable, even to other elfin kingdoms, such as ours."

"That cannot be the real reason," Pangolin said.

"If you travel with their caravan, they are your masters," a desert elf said. "They can take any and all from you as further payment without warning."

"That does not sound very elfin friendly," Pangolin said.

"No, it's not," the elves said, some with a chuckle.

"Why not create a flying caravan?" Pangolin asked.

"Because the skies from here are the domain of the sylphs, or air elementals. The elfin kingdoms who travel it are under their banner. Those not under their banner and protection would meet a deadly fate," Traveler said.

"Also, the skies above the Great Forest and the oceans have their own kind of aerial creatures," a high elf said. "Many are invisible even to the eyes of elves."

"Which elfin races have alliances with the sylphs?" Pangolin asked.

"The cloud, star and celestial elves," an elf answered.

"I take it from the tone of your voice you aren't allies," Pangolin said.

"We are allies, Mr. Pangolin," the high elf said. "We simply do not talk to or trust them."

"Curious," Pangolin said.

"There were wars between the elfin races too," Traveler added.

"You elves sound more like humans every day," Pangolin said.

"Humans, elves, sprites, fairies, giants, all of us," the high elf said.

"The other reason is privacy," Traveler said. "To join a flying caravan means they—many, many people—know of you, your party, weapons, provisions, all your property, your wealth."

"Your magical abilities, weapons, and objects," the high elf said. "That's why one does not join a flying caravan. The star and celestial elves are sole caravan masters of the skies here. The cloud elves only benefit because they are the blood allies of the star elves."

"Why not the moon elves?" Pangolin asked.

"That is a story we will leave for the moon elves to tell, but you can imagine the story for yourself since they are with us and not with them," Lyre said.

"Mr. Pangolin, when our visitor arrives, do not be startled by any of his motions or behavior," Traveler said. "I give you fair warning. He is an icarian."

The wait was longer than Pangolin anticipated. The elves did not seem to mind, but in the time they waited, Pangolin saw giant birds—sparrows and wrens—giant bees, something that looked like a giant jellyfish floating in the air as if carried by the wind, giant millipedes, and he heard in the distance what sounded like a pack of giant monkeys.

"He is here," Traveler announced.

Their caravan had bird men. The animal men had their own guard animals of jackalopes and enfields. But the being that descended from the sky to them was a human with large eagle-like wings, large bird eyes, and feathers for hair. He was dressed like he was royalty, and his lips were pointed like a bird's beak.

The icarian cawed so loud that Pangolin instinctively grabbed his axe-mace, but Traveler put a hand on the man's shoulder to calm him. Pangolin was sure he could still hear the winged fae's cry echo through the Forest, which made him nervous.

Traveler said nothing. He handed the icarian a note. The fae grabbed it, fidgeted with clawed fingertips on his hands, then held the note up to his eyes. Suddenly, he crumpled up the note and swallowed it.

"You chose an unwise departure point," he said.

"It is the place we wish."

"It will be there."

"Our payment will be made there."

"I would say more, but the Forest has a thousand eyes and ears."

"It does, indeed. I am glad we're doing business again."

"You are the only human I have ever encountered to do business with and who has survived to do business with me more than once. I see your shape-shifter has remained at your side."

"Yes, he has."

"In the future, we shall conclude our business."

"Yes."

Caw! Once again, Pangolin was startled by the winged fae's call. Then the icarian shot up into the sky and when it was a dot, they could see its wings flapping.

Pangolin shook his head. "Why did you not tell me about its war cries?" he asked, even as he heard the elves laugh to themselves.

"Greetings, Mr. Pangolin, not war cries."

"That is how it says 'hello'?"

"Yes."

"Did you tell it that greeting a berserker like that is the surest way to get an axe buried in its chest."

Traveler smiled. "Different races have different customs."

Pangolin gave a dismissive grunt.

"We should return immediately," one of the elves said.

"Yes, we should," Traveler said, noticing the tops of the trees with their rich canopy of leaves were shaking and swaying.

"Father. Is that you? Help me, father."

The young man in sleeping clothes reached out from a ghostly white mist.

King Aereth's eyes opened. As he lay on his trussing bed, he could feel that he was drenched in sweat. He turned his head to look about his tent. Across the room, near the closed entrance, Nirgund, his guardsman, was fast asleep and snoring occasionally. He could see all the alphyns watching him from the low illumination of the sole candle on a table at the far end of the tent from the entrance. The reptilian hounds stared with suspicion. The king smiled at them and closed his eyes. He sighed, as he knew he would be unable to get back asleep.

Traveler stood at his work table in his tent. The dog sat near the entrance. The man Frog-Dor kept his braced-legs steady with his walking staff.

"I questioned him thoroughly, Mr. Traveler," Frog-Dor said. "An enchanted dream but common for any human this far into the realms of fae. There was no malevolent magic in his dream."

Frog-Dor was not in their caravan master's tent alone. Dr'amal, their drow sorceress, Lady Aylen, Maiden Gwyness, and Gresham, the healer, were with him.

"I agree," Dr'amal said.

"Are the five of us supposed to be the caravan's committee of dreams, Mr. Traveler?" Lady Aylen asked sarcastically.

"Actually, princess, that is an excellent idea, and that is what you all shall be. How is the king physically, Mr. Gresham?"

"The king is in fine health, Mr. Traveler. I would say it was more the shock of such a vivid dream."

"But Oughtred's threat, and my amulet glowing," Gwyness said.

"I detected no magic or any feeling of malevolence," Frog-Dor said.

"Dreams of this sort are common for humans and fae, even if not for Oughtred," Dr'amal said.

"Dreams in these lands can often be much more than dreams. Warnings of nearby magical beings—good or evil," Traveler said. "Or a way for an evil magical being to get control of the man—or woman—enchant them to do their bidding, or possess them to do evil. There are spell casters who specialize in nothing but dreams and dreaming."

"Dream catchers," Frog-Dor said.

"Yes," Traveler said.Traveler stood at his work table in his tent. The dog sat near the entrance. The man Frog-Dor kept his braced-legs steady with his walking staff.

"I questioned him thoroughly, Mr. Traveler," Frog-Dor said. "An enchanted dream but common for any human this far into the realms of fae. There was no malevolent magic in his dream."

Frog-Dor was not in their caravan master's tent alone. Dr'amal, their drow sorceress, Lady Aylen, Maiden Gwyness, and Gresham, the healer, were with him.

"I agree," Dr'amal said.

"Are the five of us supposed to be the caravan's committee of dreams, Mr. Traveler?" Lady Aylen asked sarcastically.

"Actually, princess, that is an excellent idea, and that is what you all shall be. How is the king physically, Mr. Gresham?"

"The king is in fine health, Mr. Traveler. I would say it was more the shock of such a vivid dream."

"But Oughtred's threat, and my amulet glowing," Gwyness said.

"I detected no magic or any feeling of malevolence," Frog-Dor said.

"Dreams of this sort are common for humans and fae, even if not for Oughtred," Dr'amal said.

"Dreams in these lands can often be much more than dreams. Warnings of nearby magical beings—good or evil," Traveler said. "Or a way for an evil magical being to get control of the man—or woman—enchant them to do their bidding, or possess them to do evil. There are spell casters who specialize in nothing but dreams and dreaming."

"Dream catchers," Frog-Dor said.

"Yes," Traveler said.

"I am unfamiliar with this. Do they exist in our human Lands?" Lady Aylen asked.

"Yes, princess, but of a benign nature. There are evil ones, too, which is why we're taking all dreams seriously on our journey. Even a simple dream can be a means of attack."

"We still don't know what awoke Maiden Gwyness's amulet," Dr'amal said.

"True. But if we stay in small groups and within the circle, all should be well. Mr. Gresham, I want you to personally check in with the king every morning for at least a few days."

"Yes, Mr. Traveler."

"Beyond that, there is nothing more to do. It was a dream."

No one believed that. It showed in their caravan master's face and theirs.

Four days more.

The pocket-realm looked like a full-fledged village. The pech by day and the brownies by night had built quaint huts for the men and stables for the animals. Gone were the tents. Overjoyed men had their own village to live in within the comfort of their pocket-realm. Even with the routine set by Hobbs and training for all the fighters, they had plenty of time for recreation. Humans and fae drank, danced to music from the Brothers Brimm, gossiped, and slept. The giants seemingly slept all day and night. Within the realm, the fairy sisters played with their swarms, day and night.

The royals sat at a table in a real tavern to enjoy their lunch. Their guards had already eaten and stood outside the tavern's entrance chatting and playing with the alphyns and owl griffins. Inside, the bar and tables were packed with men laughing, talking, enjoying their food and drink. The caravan had more than one tavern, and like the others, gnomes joined the men's merriment.

King Aereth dug into his food. "Lady Aylen, you do not seem all that pleased with our new accommodations."

She stayed quiet for a moment. Through the main door entered the three elfin knight leaders, Lyre, Taylos, and Shadu-mun.

"Sire, can we join you?" Lyre asked.

"By all means," King Aereth said.

The three elves sat across from the royals and Gwyness.

"I can guess what you're here to stay," Aereth said.

"Sire, we feel if we stay here much longer, we may never leave, as our feet will grow roots and bury into the earth," Taylos the desert elf said.

"Your sentiment is the same as our own master-at-arms' and the Cut-throats'," the king said.

"And all of the hoofed fae led by Chief Strag and Ammon," Taylos said.

"I've never seen Mr. Pangolin in such a morose mood," Gwyness said. "He's not even training anymore. He stays in his hut."

"Sire, we need to move on," Lyre said.

"We cannot, because our transport has not arrived," Aereth said.

"Where is it, then?" Taylos asked.

"Have you asked, Mr. Traveler?"

"We have," Lyre said.

"What is the saying? Our Mr. Traveler talks like an elf, whenever asked," Lady Aylen said.

"Indeed," Lyre said.

"I will speak to him again," King Aereth said. "I agree with you. I expected to be on our way sooner."

"The brownies will have time enough to build an entire city within this realm if we let them," Taylos said.

"We have another visitor, sire," Lady Aylen said, looking at the door.

"Mr. Elman," the king said to the approaching half-elf.

"Sire, some of the animal men are leaving the realm to scout the area."

"Why would they do that?" Lyre asked, standing from his chair.

"I don't know. They spoke of wanting to find some giant sweet fruits for the journey."

"They risk death and revealing our location because they want sweets for their meal?" Shadumun asked.

"Where's Mr. Traveler?" the king asked.

"He knows, but they won't listen to him."

Though the animal men were comprised of different races, they always traveled together. At the entrance of their pocket-realm, seemed to be all of them: frog, lizard, squirrel, raccoon, possum, fox, rabbit, bird, and mouse men. The royals, Gwyness and the elfin knight leaders could hear the heated argument from far away as they approached. The elfin questing knights on guard at the entrance were trying to keep more of them from crossing the threshold, but they were outnumbered by the animal men with their animals.

Traveler stood by watching, dog at his side, with Pangolin.

"Should you not do something, Mr. Traveler?" King Aereth asked when they reached him.

Traveler shook his head. "No, sire. Some fae, like some humans, must learn the hard way."

"That is hardly the proper approach, Mr. Traveler," Lady Aylen said.

"Are you not afraid that they could draw others to the realm's entrance?" an elf asked.

"They had already left when I arrived, the raccoon men with their giant porcupines and the bird men with their enfields."

Everyone heard the scream. The strange mole man jumped on his large carnivorous moose and ran through the crowd and out of the pocket-realm. Immediately, he was snatched from his mount by long black insect arms. He struggled in horror but was stuck. The giant hornet was struck with incredible force by something, and it plunged to the earth. The mole man screamed as he ripped his clothes and part of his flesh away to free himself. The giant hornet crashed to the ground. The mole man landed softly on the ground, bleeding.

His moose roared as it tried to bite at the swarm of attacking giant hornets. Pangolin ran to retrieve his axe-mace from the giant hornet dead on the ground and joined the fight. Elfin knights defended against the swarm with their swords and falcons, which grew in size to attack the hornets.

Almost fifty feet away, Traveler reached the other animal men with his sword drawn and his dog, now twice its usual size. A giant fly-trap had seized and crushed one of the animal men and two enfields. The other enfields ferociously clawed and bit the giant plant. Raccoon and bird men frantically tried to pry open the plant's mouth. The plant creature pulled itself away from the animal men and their enfields toward the thicker foliage of the Forest.

"Stop!" Traveler said and pulled the animal men off the giant plant. "He's dead. So are the animals. Let it go."

The raccoon and bird men sadly watched the giant fly-trap disappear into the Forest. The enfields wanted to follow, but the bird men called them back with special chirping sounds. The pack of enfields couldn't take their eyes off where the creature had gone. The fox hybrids were whimpering.

"Take them back to the camp now!" Traveler held his sword tight as he and his dog watched. Facing the Forest, they retreated backward into the pocket-realm. A giant vine shot out at Traveler, but he dodged it and cut it in half. It gave a muffled shriek, and not one but several of the giant flytraps pushed through the canopy of the Forest then disappeared.

When more than a dozen of the giant hornets were killed, the swarm flew away. They did so just before elfin archers ran through the pocket-realm entrance to join the battle. Pangolin studied the bodies of the giant hornets. Their stingers were five feet in length, and even dead, pulsated with their deadly poison.

Traveler and his dog moved with the animal men. The crying animal men appeared disoriented, and Traveler had to guide them to the realm entrance. Their enfields were in a terrible state—unable to stay still, whimpering, looking all around. Traveler went back out to grab the mole man, who was unconscious on the ground. Pangolin and the elfin knights struggled to keep his giant moose calm and from lashing out at everyone around him. They coaxed the animal back into the realm.

When the crying raccoon and bird men rapidly told the animal men gathered at the entrance what happened in their fae language, unintelligible to humans, everyone witnessed their entire party almost collapse with grief. Their animals, attune to the emotions of their masters, went wild.

"Mr. Gresham," Traveler said, carrying the mole man.

Their healer ran to him.

"Take him to your healing hut, but keep him by an open window. His animal will want to keep its eyes on him at all times."

"Yes, Mr. Traveler."

The healer took the unusual-looking mole fae from him. The elfin knights did their best to calm the giant moose and coax it to follow.

By then, everyone in the camp had left their huts and taverns to gather at the entrance. Fear and sadness filled the men's faces. Hobbs accompanied their caravan master. The royals and Gwyness joined him.

"Chief Ethor," Traveler said. The woodland elf had appeared for the first time in the day. "Can I leave the security of the entrance to your elves?"

The elf nodded. "We will not be able to stay here."

"I know."

The elfin chief moved to the three elfin knight leaders. All he had to do was point and the elfin questing knew what to do.

"Mr. Hobbs, please get all the men back to their huts. I will stay with the animal men to calm them, but it will likely take all night."

"Yes, Mr. Traveler."

"Can we do anything, Mr. Traveler?" King Aereth asked.

"For the moment, sire, no."

"Is this our first taste of what is to come, Mr. Traveler?" Pangolin asked.

"It is."

"At least the men got to enjoy themselves for a few days."

"Mr. Pangolin, get your vanguard ready to move out."

Pangolin was relieved, but he was happy only for the blink of an eye. He knew they were about to march into the Forest. Despite their eagerness, they might soon wish they had never begun their journey.

As their master-at-arms left them, Traveler looked into the crowd. His eyes found the drows as they approached.

"We are about to depart, Mr. Traveler?" Dr'as asked, his daughter, Dr'amal next to him.

"We have no choice."

"Yes, you are correct."

"Why can we not remain?" King Aereth asked. "What of our land transport?"

"Do you remember in Faë-Land Minor when it seemed that the birds and insects were watching us. That is because they were. They spread word amongst themselves to the sprites, to the fairies. That's why everyone knew we were in their realm long before seeing us in person. It's the same here in the Great Forest, but it isn't tiny birds, squirrels, and insects. It's giant ones and much more."

Traveler put a reassuring hand on the king's shoulder. "Sire, you and Lady Aylen should also ready yourself for departure sometime tomorrow."

"Yes, of course."

As the royals and Gwyness left for their huts, Traveler turned to the drows.

"Yes, Mr. Traveler. I know what you will ask," Dr'amal said.

"Our land transport is being delivered by a party of toad men. I need to know where they are and why they're not here, immediately."

"I will cast the spell."

"I know you can cast spells but—"

"It will work," she said.

"We are not keen to die here on edge of the Great Forest, Mr. Traveler. My daughter's spells will work," Dr'as said.

"Do you plan to leave the pocket-realm, Master Traveler?"

Traveler turned to see the fae-blood woman, Ursi.

"Why?"

"You must not leave this realm or its circle on your own for any reason. You promised your king," she said. "If you die, we die. If anyone else dies, the caravan can carry on."

"I see why fae-bloods and drows are allies. You both are very cold in your reasoning."

"But the reasoning is correct, nonetheless. You must not go off on your own again, even with your dog."

"Remember, I've been along Titan's Trail many times before."

"But not with a caravan of this size."

"The fae-blood speaks the truth, Mr. Traveler," Dr'as said. "If you must leave to find your toad people, go with an army. We have enough fae in the caravan to spare."

"Or your daughter can cast the spell we need and avoid that," Traveler said, staring at the drowess.

"Did I not help us in Fae'el?" the drow sorceress asked.

"Dr'amal, to perform at one's best is not a one-time occurrence. We are not even halfway to Atlantea. I agree with your father that you will be a powerful sorceress. We just need you to get there sooner rather than later. I need to speak with your father alone."

The drowess was not happy but walked away toward the drow huts in the camp. The drow leader moved his index finger in a small circular motion. A purple circle appeared around the men.

"Dr'as, who was meant to be your chief sorceress or sorcerer on this journey?"

"How long have you known?"

"When I saw what she did with Lady Aylen. Bringing out and magnifying her water elemental abilities. Your daughter can make others great in their magic, but her own is unclear and might be for many years to come. Dr'as, who was to be your chief sorcerer or sorceress?"

"Sorcerer."

"What happened to him?"

"He died."

"Why did you not tell me this before?" The caravan master turned around. "Ursi!"

"It was not her fault," the drow leader said.

The fae-blood woman appeared soon after. "Yes, Master Traveler?"

"She was following my directions."

"Did neither of you think to tell me about your chief sorcerer dying? How did he die?"

Traveler looked at both of them.

"He died in his sleep."

"When? How long before we met in Arion's Spear?"

"Six months."

Traveler sighed. "Dr'as, as a drow you know as well as any elf that a caravan needs magic-casters to cross Faë-Land. They are needed to cross the Great Forest, the Oceans Omnis, and Atlantea."

"We have the man you call Frog-Dor—"

"That was a chance encounter. What concerns me is when the caravan first set out from the Lands of Man, we had three sorcerers. We lost them. If not for the two of you, I would never have left Faë-Land because we did not have our own sorcerer. If I had known your own chief sorcerer died in his sleep, we wouldn't have left until we had at least another."

"What has brought on this sudden concern?"

"Dr'as, our land transport should have been here before the icarian arrived. Do you understand?"

"Yes."

"A true caravan master on the Trail plans out every step of the year-long journey. Above all, they ensure there are no surprises with the things they have direct control over because there are more than enough surprises from what they cannot control."

"My daughter will cast the spell to find out."

"Dr'as, this is serious."

"I know."

"We could be being led into a trap."

"I understand."

"We are sorry," Ursi said.

"My daughter will cast the spell."

Quillen sat at a campfire sketching in his magic book, but his heart wasn't in it. He and the men watched the brownies walk from hut to hut magically shrinking them so they were small enough to fit in a hand. One brownie would tap the structure with a magic staff and another would pick it up and place it in a cloth bag, then the brownies would move on to the next one. Hobbs had all the parties return to open camp with tents, torches, and campfires. No one objected. They had become too comfortable.

The enfields were still in distress. Their yelping could still be heard from time to time. Quillen had tried to enter their camp but was turned away by the fauns. All the animal men sat around their campfires, their animals close, overcome with the grief of the death of their comrades and animals.

"We have barely set foot in this Giant Forest," a man said, sitting across from the boy. "Giant bees, giant man-eating plants, giant shadow monstrosities. What else awaits us?"

"Mr. Traveler will get us through," Quillen said confidently.

"Aye, boy. We pray that he does."

Not too far away, Gresham's sole patient sat at a fire. The mole-looking humanoid was known for his surliness even among other fae. Not tonight though. He did not have facial features to reveal his mood, but Gresham could still sense his extreme sadness. Behind him lay his giant meat-eating moose. It lay on its belly, hind legs tucked in, front legs out with its head resting on them, its antlers covering and protecting its master.

"I want to return home," he said.

Gresham had been seated at a table just outside the healing tent reading by candlelight when he heard the mole man speak. He got up from his chair and walked to the fae. "Is there anything else I can do?" the healer asked.

The mole man stood and shook his head. The giant moose got to his feet. Gresham watched as the mole man walked toward the animal-man camp with his giant moose companion.

Quillen looked up again to see Gresham headed to the caravan master's tent. Normally, his curiosity would make him follow, but he felt overly lethargic. However, like the men in his circle around the campfire, he would observe.

"Mr. Traveler," Gresham called out as he reached the tent.

Mr. Pangolin appeared. "Come in, Mr. Gresham."

Inside were also Mr. Hobbs, the royals, and Maiden Gwyness. He did not see the dog.

"Sorry if I interrupted you."

"Not at all, Mr. Gresham," King Aereth said.

"What is it, Mr. Gresham?" Traveler asked, seated at his map table.

"I wanted to inform you, Mr. Traveler, that my patient is up and returned to his party, but he did express a desire to return home."

Hobbs glanced at Traveler. "You said, sir, that he's like their leader."

"The animal men have several leaders, but he is listened to more than the others. Yes, Mr. Gresham, the animal men will probably want to leave the caravan, and if we do not depart soon, others will want to follow."

"We should encourage them to go," Pangolin said. "Better here than in the center of the Forest."

"We need them, Mr. Pangolin," Traveler said. He stood and approached the healer. "Thank you, Mr. Gresham. We were discussing this very possibility. Even though he isn't in your care, check in with him daily. The animal men will let you into their camp freely."

"Very good, Mr. Traveler. I will see to it. Good night, all."

Gresham left the tent, then he noticed the dog sitting at the entrance, watching him.

"Why do we need them?" Pangolin asked inside the tent.

"You saw it yourself. Our mole man fae is allied with the water nymphs."

"We need them when we reach the ocean?" Lady Aylen asked.

"Yes. The other animal men are allied with others we may encounter on the way. I will speak to them."

"Poor animal men," Gwyness said. "The horror of such a thing."

"They should never have left the pocket-realm. They lost men over something as trivial as sweets."

"Don't be dismissive of them, Mr. Pangolin," Traveler said. "We all have our weaknesses to overcome. Theirs is no less trivial or less noble than our own. Yours is battle. Mine is no different than our young Mr. Quillen's—curiosity. Food is theirs. But our men learned the lesson in the Lands of Man. The fae have learned the lesson now."

"People had to die, Mr. Traveler, to learn this lesson?"

"Sadly, Lady Aylen, in all my travels along the Trail, no matter my warnings or those by other caravan masters of the true dangers, it is the only thing that makes everyone finally listen and heed."

Dr'amal hid in one of the mammoth trees of the Forest, barely visible, her face in shadows from the hood of her cloak. A giant white beetle jumped on top of her image then flew away. Dr'amal returned her attention to the ground below—many, many miles away. She saw at least four goblins in different locations hiding behind giant plants. Goblin warriors weren't known as stealthy warriors like elves could be. Goblins used their smaller hobgoblin cousins for that. But these goblins were unique—not a scouting party but a hunting one—with light armor, smaller axes, including throwing blades in quivers on their back, heads draped with hoods, quiet, disciplined. They were not the brutish goblins her people were accustomed to. They were the high goblins that they had heard of that were in the service of goblin royalty of the highest status. From the corner of her eye, she noticed movement in the mammoth tree across from hers, shadows of smaller humanoids—hobgoblins? She couldn't take the chance.

She opened her eyes and was in the drow's magic tent. Her father sat across from her on the ground, also cross-legged, both in a purple circle.

"Did you see them?" he asked.

"I saw those who keep them from us," she answered.

The royals waited. They glanced at Pangolin and all fifteen of the wolf fae-bloods always dressed in black.

"I do not like this at all," Lady Aylen said.

Traveler emerged from his tent with his dog. Their caravan master wore his elfin armor with a slight orange tint, his magic sword sheathed at his back, and one dagger of black metal tightly gripped in his left hand.

"Mr. Traveler, is this truly the only way?" King Aereth asked.

"Sire, we have no choice. If our land transport doesn't arrive, we don't leave."

The displeasure was obvious in the royals' faces. Ursi, the sole fae-blood of the bear clan was nearby looking on. Most of the men were on their feet watching. Mr. Elman ran to Mr. Pangolin.

"I can join you. I can see better than any other in the camp, even elves."

Traveler gave the young elf a smile. "Yes, Mr. Elman, you can, but we will have to manage."

"But the elaphine archers do not do well on their own."

"Elves have been known to strike a thing or two with an arrow every so often." Chief Ethor came through the men with two elfin archers. "Master Traveler, two for your war party, our best."

"Thank you, chief. However, all we need is for them to create maximum chaos. Are we ready?" Traveler looked at the small war party.

Pangolin, the fae-blood mercenaries, and the two archers stood together.

"We're not there to engage the goblins. We're there to move them on. Strike fast and never stop moving, not even to battle them."

"Do we not want to know where their goblin caravan is?" one of the fae-bloods asked.

"They won't tell us, and I would assume any information they gave us would be a trap," Traveler said.

"We could get the truth from them," a fae-blood said.

"We don't have the time. Our only mission is to move them along. If we fail in this, we could all die right at the edge of the Great Forest."

"Is it really that dire, Mr. Traveler?" King Aereth asked.

"It is, sire. We should have disappeared into the Forest days ago on our way. By now, word of our presence has spread throughout the Forest far and wide. Only the fae here have some sense of what that means. Caravans such as ours are not simply a source food to others but a source for slaves, a vault of riches—weapons, armor, money—a source of magic to steal." Traveler looked at Pangolin. "You and I will lead."

The berserker nodded and hoisted his axe-mace.

"One moment, gentlemen." Their weaponsmaster, Mr. Estus, ran to them. He clamped a band around each one of the men's forearms. The fae-blood men, at first, were resistant. "The goblins likely know you're in Titan's Caravan. The elfin archers took my magic arrows. You can take my magic shields. Both courtesy of the weapons hoard we took from the Four Kings."

Lady Aylen returned from her tent with her dual tridents. "Mr. Traveler, maybe I should go too."

"I thought you didn't want us to go, princess."

"You're going, and I should go."

"We already have elves."

"Neither one of them are me."

"Lady Aylen, I am not adding any more to the war party. We need you here, princess. For all we know, the goblins are keeping our land transport from arriving because they want to draw us out. You want to fight. When we leave, make sure no one breaches the realm."

The fae knew what he meant, but Traveler saw the confused faces of the humans.

"Yes, everyone, the magic of our pocket-realm is waning. If we do not leave here soon, it will disappear, and the caravan will find itself in the open air of the Great Forest. If that happens, we die."

The goblin assassin crouched on a branch of the same mammoth tree that he'd seen the shadowy figure in before. He had scaled the tree hours ago. There was no scent to the figure, but he'd certainly seen it. His pointed green ears began to fidget. The right one perked straight up. His fellow goblins, miles below on the ground, sensed it too.

One. Seven. Dozens of the arrows rained down from above. The first arrow hit the tree and, though the goblin easily dodged and leapt for another branch, the explosion of lightning ripped through his magical protection and armor. From the canopy of the trees to the ground below was now home to a growing, swirling black thunder cloud. Each arrow erupted into another cascade of violent lightning explosions as it landed.

The goblins could smell them but were helpless to do anything but retreat. They ran faster than the wind and could hear them closing in. They heard the yells of the hobgoblins left behind. Dozens of goblins burst through the dense foliage of the section of the Forest where they held their vigil. One goblin stopped to throw a magic blade. The axe-mace collided with his body with such force, he was dead before his body hit the ground.

The fae-bloods pursued them with eyes glowing blue, appearing as two images in one—a running human on two legs and a running wolf on all fours. More goblins turned to throw axes at them, but the weapons passed through them as if wisps of smoke. However, each goblin was mauled by the magical wolf image of the fae-blood.

All the remaining goblins moved in different directions, running deeper into the Forest and disappearing into invisibility. Traveler and Pangolin emerged. The berserker retrieved his axe-mace from the dead goblin. The elfin archers came out of invisibility and fired a flurry of magical arrows after the goblins. Lightning exploded. They heard a couple of screams, and the goblins were gone.

Traveler didn't waste any time. They ran back to the invisible entrance of their pocket-realm quickly. Their caravan master reached into a pouch from his belt and scattered herbs on the ground. Pangolin was intrigued.

"So the goblins or any of their evil beasts cannot get hold of our scent and follow us back to the caravan," one of the fae-bloods told Pangolin.

Just before they stepped through the realm door to the caravan, Traveler pulled something else from his belt. A yellow pebble. He threw it into the air, and it transformed into a bird made of light. The spell flew high into the sky.

Pangolin was the last to step through and the entrance was crowded with Cut-throats, elfin questing knights, the fae berserkers, pech, and surprisingly, the rarely seen väki.

"Any problems, Mr. Pangolin?" Lady Aylen asked. She and the king approached him from the crowd.

"Where's Mr. Traveler?" he asked.

"Our caravan master ran past and ignored us," Lady Aylen replied.

"No problems, m'lady. The goblins didn't stand a chance. All their hobgoblin attendants were vanquished easily. Most of the goblins scurried away."

"I hope this means we will be leaving soon," Lady Aylen said.

"Yes, m'lady. We must go. I cannot bear the wait any longer."

Traveler appeared again on the back of a furry horse with the head of a wolf-dog. He was speaking in a language the humans couldn't understand. Following him were several frog men with their giant crab and possum men, each riding a giant turtle.

"Leaving again, Mr. Traveler?" King Aereth asked.

"You just got back, Mr. Traveler," Lady Aylen said.

"No, sire. We await our land transport."

"Mr. Traveler, won't you need fighters other than the animal men?" Pangolin asked.

"All our business will be done in full view of the realm's entrance."

All the other animal men with their animals came forward. Their despair had been replaced with purpose. Everyone noticed the frenzy of conversation between them. Even the mole man and his moose joined them. The royals grinned to see Traveler speaking with the strange-looking sprite.

"We're happy to see our fine guardians," King Aereth said to the half dozen väki.

The sprites simply frowned at him, saying nothing. The humans watching the exchange laughed.

"Look!" Quillen yelled as he ran to the realm entrance.

One of the pech grabbed him. "Do not fall through the barrier until we know who they are."

Standing near the barrier were dozens of very thin, tall toad men. All were armed with spears that were a few feet taller than the toad men, and their green-and-orange bodies were covered with white symbols.

Traveler jumped down from his wolf-dog horse.

The frog men exited the pocket-realm first with their giant crabs. Everyone watched the frog and toad men rapidly speak to each other. One of the frog men gestured and the possum men came through on their giant turtles, and the giant crabs followed. Toad men surrounded them, touching the giant animals. The parley between the two groups went on for a long time. Finally, it stopped. A frog man gestured. Traveler stepped through the barrier with the dog. The toad men walked to him and began touching and patting both him and the dog.

"What are they doing?" Lady Aylen asked.

"It is how they greet each other," one of the fae berserkers replied.

The frog and toad men began chattering to each other again. One of the toad men raised his hand. Traveler pointed to one of the possum men, who dropped from his turtle mount, bag in hand. The toad men took it and threw it on the floor, and a few jumped into it, disappearing—another pocket-realm. The three toad men jumped back out. One grabbed the bag, and another raised his hand.

Before everyone's eyes, a giant turtle leg, wider than they thought possible, appeared out of invisibility.

"What is that?" a man asked.

"It's a giant turtle," Quillen answered, standing closest to the barrier. "I've never seen an animal so big. I think it's bigger even than that roc we saw." The boy jumped. "There's a caravan of them!"

Traveler patted one of the toad men on his arms and back. The toad man returned the gesture. The frog and toad men did the same to each other. The toad men assembled and ran off into the Forest.

Traveler stepped back through the realm entrance. "Mr. Hobbs, get the men ready to leave immediately."

CHAPTER THREE

Titan's Walk

"Atlas turtles," the giants told everyone when they finally rose from their slumber. No one could believe the size of the beasts towering fifty feet above on all fours. A frenzy had taken over the caravan to prepare to, at last, march into the Great Forest. The caravan's frog men stood together at the forefeet of the first ancient animal. The giant turtles stood still for the moment, lined up, one behind the other, but once the signal was given by their own frog men, the turtle caravan would march and not stop until they reached their own lands within the Forest.

A big smile came over the royals' faces. The kirins had finally appeared, just as Traveler said they would. "They'll appear when the caravan is set to march into the Great Forest." King Aereth's kirin stood at his side with its golden fur and scales, horse-like, powerful muscles, cloven hooves, a thick mane of hair, and dragon-like head.

Lady Aylen hugged her dragon horse with its lucent-blue fur and scales, single unicorn horn sprouting from its head, and catfish whiskers around its nose and mouth.

Gwyness had become very fond of her own kirin, bigger than the others, with black fur and scales, its head adorned with full antlers, and unlike the others, her kirin had a tail not unlike a lion.

"I need to give you a name," she said, stroking the side of its face.

Traveler, still in his armor, reached Pangolin and his vanguard. He handed the master-at-arms a large, gnarled staff. "From now on, as the vanguard moves, one of your men should carry it at all times."

One of the giants took it from Pangolin. "Where did you get this, Master Traveler?"

"What is it?" Pangolin asked.

Traveler took the staff from the giant. "As giants, your hands should be free for your powerful weapons. If we're attacked, by instinct, you would drop it. It would not serve its purpose on the ground."

Pangolin took the staff again. "What does it do?"

Elman took the staff from him. "It's a magic staff."

"A mirage staff," the giant Grakdar said. "Those who see you think you're ahead when you're behind, to one side when you're on the other."

Traveler took the staff from the half-elf. "Your task is to use those magical eyes of yours to see the danger before all others, not minding a staff."

One of the elaphine archers took the staff from their caravan master. "Master Traveler, we will mind the mirage staff."

"Very good."

Pangolin gestured, calling Traveler's attention behind him. He turned to see the front of the caravan watching, smiling, and laughing.

"Pass the staff to me, Mr. Traveler!" a man shouted.

"No, me, Mr. Traveler," said another.

"If only you could have seen how ridiculous you all looked," Lady Aylen said.

Traveler returned his attention to the vanguard men. "Since we've amused the men and will be the butt of their jokes for the noon meal, I'd say we can depart."

"Hear! Hear!" Pangolin said.

The caravan spilled out of the pocket-realm to form up under the Atlas turtles. All in the caravan were in awe except Traveler, the dog, and the giants. The caravan master had seen and traveled with the beasts in the past, along with his dog. For the giants, who stood with extreme pride, the beasts were prominent in all their ancient stories from the beginning of time.

Hobbs ran along the caravan for a final look. He wore his own armor, which he had never really liked at all. His two guardsmen, Tyfer and Oeric, followed. A caravan of humans, fae, and fantastical beasts of land and air with the cover of the Atlas turtles, they would not be seeing the Tree Shepherds or their crawling trees during the day. The caravan's fairy sisters and their swarms also would remain within the leshies' pocket-realm unless needed in battle.

The final part of the formation was the caravan's giant lizards and their human minders, both in armor, one thousand on the caravan's left flank, one thousand on the right flank, the main columns in between. Pangolin moved the vanguard to the head of the columns under the belly of the first Atlas turtle. Traveler waited until they were in position and gave the signal to the frog men and raccoon men on top their giant turtles. The frog men blew on ram horns. The ground shook as the first Atlas turtle stepped forward, starting the march of the Atlas turtles with the entire Titan's Caravan marching beneath them.

The frog and raccoon men returned to the animal-men section with their animals. Traveler joined the front of the columns.

"So it begins, Mr. Traveler," King Aereth said from his kirin mount.

"It does, sire." Traveler sat on top of his dog, its body more horse-like than that of a canine.

"An impressive caravan, Mr. Traveler," Lady Aylen said. "Far beyond anything my kingdom of Sirnegate or I could have imagined."

"Or any of the kingdoms of the Kings Elder: Helm Earldom, Strongbridge, or Eastmoor," King Aereth added.

"And this." Lady Aylen looked up at the belly of the Atlas turtle. "A caravan of gigantic turtles to shield us as we move through the Great Forest."

The high elf Lyre rode up alongside them from the rear of the caravan on a leopard axex.

"Master Traveler, a message from the Chief Ethor and all the elfin questing knights of Bravehowl, Falconbright, and Nightshade. Impressive, sir. You are a true caravan master worthy of the title."

"Many thanks, Mr. Lyre."

The elf touched his forehead in a gesture of extreme thanks and rode back to his section.

"Very impressive, indeed, Mr. Traveler," Lady Aylen said.

The two center columns were of not just humans, each equipped with fae gold and silver polearms, but also the pech. The brawny, big-nosed sprite halflings with their wild eyebrows carried large dwarven spiked shields and, in their other arm, an elfin weapon of choice. Also, in the center columns were the human domestics, servants, and, toward the front, laborers with pull carts, and one of the crawling trees in the center, with all the hoofed fae archers and servants following. Then came all the animal men and their animals. In the rear, were all the Cut-throat warriors and their chamroshes, flanked by an Antaean giant each. Mingling through the columns were the roving team of male half-elf warriors, the fae-blood men, Bragg and his party of golem, elves and Diomedian Mares on their flanks. At the extreme rear marched the entire elfin questing knights with their animals.

At point, Pangolin's vanguard consisted of himself, Mr. Elman, four of the giants, and two dozen of the elaphine archer hunters. Behind them, at the front of the columns, were the royals: King Aereth, with his royal guard of Mr. Nirgund the berserker and the reptilian fae hounds, as well as Lady Aylen and Maiden Gwyness, with their female half-elf royal guards. The two women walked alongside their dragon-horse kirins. Hobbs followed behind them at the head of the columns, with his two bodyguards, Mr. Tyfer and Mr. Oeric. Traveler and his dog led the caravan behind Pangolin's vanguard. Behind them was the fae-blood Ursi, and all the drows, including Dr'amal, their heads covered with cloaks.

"Mr. Traveler," Gwyness began.

"Yes, maiden," Traveler replied. Conversation among the caravan was light because of the heightened awareness that they had crossed into the Great Forest. No other giant animal or creature had been seen yet, but that would change. The other reason was the noise. The ground rumbled with every step the Atlas turtles took.

"You said we were waiting on three visitors."

"Yes, Maiden Gwyness, but we could wait no longer. Too dangerous. However, now that we're stepping into the Forest, he will find us. I am sure of it."

"That is what I am afraid of," Lady Aylen said.

"Why?" Gwyness asked her.

"All our lives, Gwyness, we've had many questions but no answers, plenty of dark dreams but no real memories. Perhaps ignorance of such things was best."

"Lady Aylen, I truly sympathize with your position. I even agree with it, in a way. But your destiny, yours and Maiden Gwyness's, will seek you out no matter how far away or how long you run."

"No escape for us then, Mr. Traveler?" the princess asked.

"We all have a destiny, Lady Aylen. I do not know any who have escaped it. You can ignore it, but you cannot escape it."

"Mr. Pangolin said the same," Gwyness said.

"Mr. Traveler, did someone tell you the same?" Lady Aylen asked.

"They did, princess. I did not ignore mine. I accepted it even when any rational person would have abandoned it long ago. I'm not one to quote goblins for inspiration, especially knowing that we are hunted by them even now, but I heard one say something to another when I was a healer that has always stuck with me: die or survive."

"Yes," King Aereth said. "Let us modify the story though. Say you heard it from a berserker rather than a goblin."

Traveler chuckled. "Yes, sire. Wise suggestion, especially in the company of elves."

They all laughed. Lady Aylen noticed they were avoiding eye contact.

"Wait, are you referring to me?" Lady Aylen asked.

"Aren't you an elf, princess?"

"Well. Yes. Of course, Mr. Traveler, but let me be. Sometimes I'd rather talk to your dog than you."

Traveler's dog glanced back at Lady Aylen and sneered.

"What do you see, Mr. Elman?" Pangolin asked, leading the vanguard.

"Too many things to name, Mr. Pangolin," he replied. "Mr. Traveler was correct in what he told us last night. The Forest is always changing."

"What do you mean?" one of the giants asked.

"I cannot explain it."

"Try," Pangolin said.

"It's as if the land itself is not fixed. Rather it shifts."

"The land is moving?" Pangolin asked.

"We should ask Mr. Traveler. He will know."

"We shall ask him when we rest for the noon meal, Mr. Elman," Pangolin said.

"Why rest? We should move until dark. If we rest, we could be attacked. We do not want to be attacked here," Grakdar said.

"Even I cannot march a full day to nightfall," Pangolin said.

"You could. Maybe even Master Traveler. Not your fellow humans, though. That is true."

"Let's keep our wits about us," Pangolin warned. "We don't want to be attacked here either." He looked up.

The lumbering form of the Atlas turtle moved fifty feet above him. Astounding.

"I wonder what I would be able to see from upon the back of the beast," a grinning Elman said to Pangolin.

"Nothing at all because you would quickly be dead," Grakdar said. "Under the beast's belly, we are safe. On its back, any manner of giant bird or insect would make a quick meal of you no matter how fast you believe you can move."

Elman laughed. "I can run fast, Mr. Grakdar."

The giant dragonfly flew so fast that it would have been impossible for any in the vanguard to react quickly enough. The magic of their mirage spell saved Elman. The six-foot-long monstrous dragonfly with an armored exoskeleton, eight wings, and many black thorny, clawed legs crashed into the front leg of the Atlas turtle. The mammoth beast was completely unaware, but the vanguard found itself in full battle.

All four Antaean giants attacked the giant insect with their maces, crushing its body to a pulp. A flurry of arrows flew past everyone from the elaphine archers. More giant dragonflies tumbled to the ground, cut down mid-flight. The rest of the swarm disappeared.

"Keep moving," Pangolin said.

The vanguard continued marching, glancing back for a quick moment.

Traveler steered the front column around the dead dragonflies. He pointed to two of the men. "Stand guard here around the carcasses. Keep the men and animals away from it, especially the lizards, and ensure their long tongues don't lick any part of the dragonflies," he directed. "Return to your post when the full caravan passes."

"Yes, Mr. Traveler."

"Are they poisonous, Mr. Traveler?" the king asked.

"Very, sire. This species has a retractable stinger. Once dead, the poison permeates every part of the body and seeps into the ground where they lie. Lady Aylen, you will soon see for yourself why one does not take horses into Faë–Land, and especially into the Great Forest.”

“How will we be protected?” she asked.

“The lizards, princess.”

Already they could see the lizards’ agitation at the flank, not frightened but eager. Their tongues flickered forth.

“Ow!” Quillen screamed, grabbing his ear. He tried to swat the insect, but it was too fast.

It disappeared at the end of a giant lizard’s tongue. The reptile turned its gaze behind to the flank, where it looked into the brush of the Forest.

Hobbs inspected the boy’s ear.

“It bit me,” Quillen said angrily. “That hurt.”

“You’ll be fine, Mr. Quillen,” Traveler said to him. “No poison or magic to worry about with that one.”

More insects appeared, and Quillen was eager to swat as many of them as possible.

“Mr. Quillen, you are fighting a losing battle.”

“They won’t stay away from me.”

Some of the men laughed.

“It’s that sweet meat, Mr. Quillen,” one said with a chuckle.

“It’s not funny, and I’m not getting bitten again. Ow!” He was able to grab the insect and throw it to the ground. He tried to stomp it, but it flew away. "That was a flying worm!"

"Another fantastic beast for your magical book," Tyfer said to him.

"It tried to fly into my ear." Quillen said no more. He disappeared into the caravan for the pull-carts carried by pech. When he returned, he had a hooded cloak over his armor. The hood was fastened securely around his ears.

He was not the only one bedeviled by insects. King Aereth tried to maintain his composure, but the insects were a nuisance to all the humans.

Lady Aylen looked at Gwyness. "You are immune to the pests, as is our caravan master. You are immune, Mr. Traveler, because you've been to the magical lands before. Gwyness is immune because of her magic amulet."

"Good guessing. Yes, princess."

"Mr. Pangolin, ahead there, because of his magic armor, but all the rest of our humans in the caravan, new to the lands, are not."

"Is there nothing that can be done, Mr. Traveler?" King Aereth asked.

"Sire, I have magical herbs, and so do the fauns, that could ward them off, but that would not be ultimately beneficial."

"We must get accustomed to it?"

"Yes, sire. As I had to. It's bothersome now, but it will pass."

"Ignore them all then?"

They all jumped in shock when Traveler sliced a two-foot round insect in half with his battle sword. It fell to the ground.

"What is that?" Lady Aylen asked.

"Something that would have tried to carry one of us away," Traveler answered.

"Eww. It looks like a fly with a humanoid head. That face is ugly." Quillen frowned and moved away from it. The advancing column moved around it.

"Sire, ignore the insects until it's foolish not to. Mr. Hobbs, instruct one of the pech to burn that."

"Yes, sir."

"How many days will it take to pass through the Great Forest, Mr. Traveler?"

Traveler laughed. "Princess, we have barely marched seven miles into the Forest."

"That's all?"

"We have well over two thousand miles to travel."

Lady Aylen closed her eyes and shook her head.

"Princess, it's called the Great Forest for a reason, and we're only moving through one of its narrowest edges. If one tried to travel through its center, the journey would take more than ten years. Be thankful we have only six months to endure on Titan's Walk."

Pangolin glanced again at the mirage staff in the hands of an elaphine archer. He glanced at the half-elf scout.

"I know, Mr. Pangolin. If not for our new magic object, the vanguard would be moving forward without me."

"But not without a proper burial," Grakdar said.

"Of course," the half-elf acknowledged. "My magic eyesight does not seem to work with things that move as fast as that insect of the Forest. The staff saved my life."

"Yes, it did. To know all the things our caravan master must know," Pangolin said.

"As a human, no less," Grakdar added. "But he must to be the caravan master he is. Our king would not have sent us if he wasn't convinced we would succeed in our quest. As are you, Master Pangolin. We benefit from the horrors he must have witnessed in the past."

"We benefit from his magic staff. We benefit from caravans past he walked among who did not have their own magic staff."

"But they would have had a proper burial," the giant leader said.

Pangolin glanced at the front column. "I cannot tell the time of day from the sky. We should find out when they plan to stop to feed the men."

"Are you tired?" Grakdar asked.

"Not me. The men. If they do plan to stop, we should find a defensible place."

The giants laughed in unison.

"What's funny?" Pangolin asked.

"Mr. Pangolin, Atlas turtles do not stop."

"What do you mean?"

"When they begin their march, they do not stop until they reach their breeding grounds."

"Do not stop?" Pangolin asked.

The giants shook their heads.

"If we leave the protection of their caravan march, we lose it for good," Grakdar said.

All the humans had the hoods of their cloaks over their heads to protect their ears. Quillen went further to wear a skull helmet with a chainmail head covering to protect his ears. He had to get used to the weight but was satisfied.

"Comfortable, Mr. Quillen?" Hobbs asked.

"Yes, Mr. Hobbs. I will not have any more insects biting me or flying in my ears." He waved the air around him. "Insects, giant dust in the air, these white specks. Are they pollen from the giant flowers?"

"Probably."

The front column noticed the approaching elaphine archers, the largest species of deer-like fae with deer noses, ears, eyes, and huge antlers sprouting from their heads. As warriors, they wore armor and chainmail. Their long bows were as tall as they—over six feet and made of smooth, immaculately polished white wood. They were fae archers as gifted as elves and centaurs.

"Is something wrong?" Traveler asked.

"No, Master Traveler. Mr. Pangolin wished to know when you plan to stop the caravan for the noon meal. They want to scout for the best location."

"No, my elaphine friend, tell Mr. Pangolin we will not be stopping at all."

The royals looked at Traveler.

"Atlas turtles do not cease their caravan march once they begin. They stop once they enter their own lands within the Forest. We will stay with them as long as we can to gain the benefit of their protection from all above us and most around us. However, that means we behave as they do. We will not stop.

"Tell Mr. Pangolin, we will take shifts for the noon meal. Your vanguard will be relieved for a time by the Tree Shepherds. We will all take our meals within one of our remaining pocket-realms. At night, the vanguard will be our moon elves, drows and brownies in the middle, the darklings on the flanks. This is how it will be for the next week to ten days. Maybe more."

The elaphine nodded and took long strides to return to the head of the vanguard.

"You should have told us, Mr. Traveler," Lady Aylen said.

"No need, princess. You know now. The protection of the Atlas turtles is extremely important. Without them we would be in a never-ending cycle of fighting, defending, and running."

"I do feel a deep sense of safety beneath their massive bodies," King Aereth said. "They seem to be docile beasts."

"Yes, sire. Ancient and wise are they. They were making their own caravan through the Great Forest before either the race of humans or elves were born."

"I can believe that."

"How old are they, Mr. Traveler?" Lady Aylen asked.

Traveler looked up. "My guess, princess, is a few thousand years. That was what the animal men told me."

"Helm Earldom did not even exist then," said the king.

"Nor Sirnegate," Lady Aylen said.

"I'll give it another hour then have Mr. Hobbs start his rounds to move men into the pocket-realm for their meal, one group at a time. We can still be attacked at any time, or have visitors."

Traveler was looking past them to their west flank. Others in the camp began to notice the mushroom men appearing from the Forest, eight-foot-tall cream-colored mushrooms moving on humanoid legs, with bowed humanoid arms, slits for eyes, and reddish-brown cap heads. One of the caravan's Tree Shepherds had already passed through the giant lizards, protecting the flanks, to greet the mushroom men. Two other Tree Shepherds stood near the caravan to watch. They were floating along with the moving caravan.

"Mr. Hobbs, keep the men moving."

"Yes, sir." The steward moved down the columns to tell the men to keep their pace.

"Should we join them, Mr. Traveler?" King Aereth asked.

"The Tree Shepherds will summon us if we're needed, but I don't think so. They will gather information and spread the word among friendly beings in the Forest that we're passing through."

"Did we not want to pass through the Forest with as few knowing as possible, Mr. Traveler?" Lady Aylen asked. "No need to answer. You already told us. The entire Forest knows we're here."

"Yes, princess. We were delayed too long. Anonymity for our caravan is gone, but no need to worry about it. I have already adjusted our path accordingly."

"Look," Gwyness said.

A pack of giant cù-sìths joined the mushroom men. The green wolf-like fae dogs were much larger than a horse, more like the height of two combined. They acted as guardians to the mushroom men, but one had already taken to the leshy, as the Tree Shepherd Mossberry stroked the beast's forehead.

They tried to watch the conversation among them as long as possible, but the caravan moved ahead.

"The Tree Shepherds will be fine," Traveler said. "They will not be separated from the caravan."

"I hope they will have good news for us," King Aereth said.

"If there's any news of importance, they will share it with us."

"Since we travel underneath a caravan of Atlas turtles, Mr. Traveler, couldn't other parties follow us with ease?" Lady Aylen asked.

Traveler shook his head. "Not so easily. The Atlas turtles are larger than most anything else we will see in our travel in the Great Forest, but they are still mere specks in its domain. Think of the Great Forest as a giant green sea of life. Different currents moving in different directions and different heights. The Great Forest to one standing still or moving slowly as we are is always changing."

"A giant green sea of life," King Aereth repeated.

"Above us," Traveler said, looking up.

Far away in the sky was a flying caravan.

"What do you see, Lady Aylen?" Traveler asked.

"Hundreds of elves on flying horses and flying unicorns, elves on griffins pulling winged wagons, flying fae archers on their flanks. I cannot tell the species, maybe icarians."

"Maybe, but more likely other kinds of flying fae," Traveler said.

"A caravan of thousands. Flying fast," Lady Aylen said. "A few of them are hovering above us, looking down. But I don't think they see us."

"Perhaps," Traveler said.

"They're rejoining their caravan. As much as I enjoy the safety of our Atlas turtles, if only we could have created our own flying caravan. Six weeks versus six months, Mr. Traveler. Surely we could outwit these sylphs or whatever fae have dominion over the sky."

"I'm glad you think I could outwit all the air elementals and sky elves so easily, princess. I cannot, however. Also, the skies have their own creatures."

"Invisible creatures, you said," Lady Aylen said.

"Invisible to humans and most elves. Every once in a while on the journey, you'll be able to see one yourself. A whisper of an image is the best way to describe it."

Lady Aylen stared up at something in the clear sky.

Gwyness had seen the expression before. "What do you see, m'lady?"

Lady Aylen returned her gaze to the vanguard. "Maybe it's best I don't look up at the sky."

"What did you see?"

"I'm not sure I want to describe it."

Gwyness heard a stifled laugh. The drowess, Dr'amal, had a devilish grin on her face.

"If there are flying creatures above our heads—"

"Maiden Gwyness, we should keep our attention on the Great Forest," Traveler said. "What exists above it, even if you could see it, is of no concern to us. If they enter the domain of the Forest, something will eventually snatch it from the sky. Besides, you are too small a meal to get even fleeting attention. The danger we face is within the Forest, not above it."

For most of the caravan, Estus and the men under his command labored within their small realm to fashion the armor for the growing giant lizards. The lizards had reached their full size, so Estus could somewhat relax and spend more time with the men. He'd been a weaponsmith all his life, but it was lonely work, and he was a gregarious man by nature.

He wanted to spend time with the elfin questing knights. Just as young Mr. Quillen wanted to know all about the fantastic beasts and races of the magical lands, Estus wanted to know all about the weapons of the land.

"What brings the caravan's human forge to us?" an elf knight asked.

Over four hundred elves marched at the very rear of the caravan with their leopard axex walking alongside them and their fae falcons resting on the shoulders of the group's soldiers.

"I wanted to take advantage of the time to inquire about weapons and armaments. The more I know, the more I can devise defensive and offensive weapons as needed. Our weapons vault is vast."

"Do you have a furnace capable of working the metals of these lands?" an elf asked.

"Yes, sir. And a working smithy to fashion them in any form we wish."

"Too bad you couldn't fashion weapons of pure magic."

"Very true, but we can always imbue our weapons with magic traits."

"Do you know how?"

"I'm learning, sir."

"Mr. Estus, is it?"

"Yes, sir."

"You should concentrate your efforts on fashioning defenses against elemental weapons. That's what concerns our knights."

"Such as the wind weapons we faced at Fae'el?"

"Yes. Those were one of—"

They had seen the men ahead of them looking back. Now they saw why. To the east flank was a mound of dirt infested with giant maggots, each the size of a full-grown human. As they wriggled upon the dirt their bodies made sounds similar to sloshing water. The elves and their animals did not take their eyes off the maggot pile as they passed.

"Are they dangerous?" Estus asked.

"One can never tell. Are they simply giant in size or are they magical in nature? Some with magic have been known to transform into the very thing they feed on."

"That's not a pleasant thought."

"We should burn them, but that would require us to move closer, which in itself might be a trap. We will let them be. The Forest can deal with them."

Suddenly a roar rang out from the head of the caravan, grabbing everyone's attention.

The Atlas turtles lumbered forward, but Pangolin gave the signal for the caravan to stop.

All within the vanguard were ready for battle. The elaphine archer-warriors had their long bows ready to fire multiple arrows of magic. The giants held their battle maces. Pangolin had his axe-mace in hand. Mr. Elman had a sword in one hand and a small shield in the other.

The giant Nemean lion, at least twenty feet in height, ran across their path about ten yards away. It reminded Pangolin of his encounter with the

Erymanthian boar—a giant boar with a monstrous body far unlike any other boar's. The Nemean lion's body was covered in a tangled mess of orange fur. Both the claws on its feet and its teeth had been naturally blackened over time. He had heard that the creature's claws could cut through any metal from the Lands of Man. He wondered if it was the same in the magical lands. The beast quickly disappeared back into the Forest. Fortunately for all, the beast had no interest in any of the vanguard, even their "tiny" giants. It looked like it was on the hunt for something none of them could see. The lion creature was fully aware of the Atlas turtles but didn't acknowledge the caravan.

"You can relax the grip on your weapon," Grakdar said to Pangolin. "Your weapon could not harm it. The fur on its body is impervious to all weapons."

"Even our magic weapons?"

"Yes. That's the legend of their kind. I don't think we want to test it."

"No, we do not."

Pangolin caught sight of Bragg from the corner of his eye. The dwelf stood nearby behind the vanguard. The manticore hunter was not alone. He had brought his metal golem, Glog, and a dozen of his elfin barbarian comrades: mountain, forest, and wild elves. The elves were not regal like the Elfin Quest Knights nor rustic like Chief Ethor and his elves. Bragg's elves were barbarians, the elfin version of the caravan's Cut-throats, but Pangolin did not like them or Bragg.

"Bragg wants to go hunting," Grakdar said.

"Bragg wants to get killed," Pangolin said.

From the front column, Traveler watched the dwelf and his men. His face expressed his displeasure.

"What is it, Mr. Traveler?" King Aereth asked.

"Within the blink of an eye, a lesson I gave to our Mr. Bragg has been wiped away, sire."

"What lesson, Mr. Traveler?" Lady Aylen asked.

"A giant manticore skull, princess. I had successfully made my point that this Forest contains creatures and beings that could kill even a manticore through sheer force."

"You don't think he'd run off from the caravan?"

"He's a hunter, sire."

"A manticore hunter."

"If that was all, princess, I would have no issue. We want and need his expertise in hunting those evil creatures. The problem is he likes to hunt other things too. The temptation may become too great for him to resist as we move along the Trail. We saw what happened when the fae mercenaries went off."

"They lost almost half their numbers," King Aereth said.

"It is worse than that, sire. Not only could he get himself and his men killed—I've seen it before—they might return to the caravan and lead something evil back to us."

The entrance to the caravan's new pocket-realm hung in mid-air under the second Atlas turtle. Nighttime brought the change in caravans—the day one replaced by the night one. Moon elves for the vanguard, drows and brownies in the front columns, the darklings on the flanks.

The pocket-realm was a simple golden field open under a bright moon. Men settled into their camps around large campfires. With only one rest per day and marching from sunrise to sunset, men spent no more than an hour with their night meal before turning in, falling fast asleep in their giant-slippers or sleeping rugs.

"Sire, he's here," Nirgund announced.

The guardsman motioned for the drow leader, Dr'as, to enter the king's tent. King Aereth remained awake a few hours each night for his reading.

"Mr. Dr'as." The king motioned to a stool near his table for the drow to sit.

"King Aereth."

Both sat. Dr'as noticed the king's reading—large volumes of ancient books on the table.

"Mr. Traveler's assignment for me. Large works on the history, protocols and customs of elfin royalty and kingdoms."

"I had the same studies as a child. I do not envy you. May I ask if this is wise? We are a disparate caravan of many races working together because we have a common goal and need each other, but ancient rivalries and enmity still exists. Some in the caravan may not be pleased you're meeting with a drow."

"Mr. Dr'as, I am meeting with all the caravan's fae leaders. I met with Chief Ethor of the elves, Chief Ammon of the fauns. I will meet with you."

The drow nodded in understanding.

"I'm not sure I can be of much help when it comes to elves."

"I've noticed that Mr. Traveler shares that apprehension both drows and elves—those represented in this caravan—have regarding the cloud, star, and celestial elves. I want to further understand this since we will inevitably encounter them."

"Mr. Traveler shares our disdain for them because he's seen them be their true selves without the pretense."

"My kingdom encountered star elves. The royal court was quite amazed. That was almost a century ago. Ironically, it led my kingdom, Helm Earldom, to the path of seeking a way to Atlantea."

"You were enchanted by them."

"We have sorcerers, so we weren't under any magic spell."

"Not enchanted by magic but their appearance and bearing, the beauty of their physique and their intellect. So impressive were they, it was similar to being enchanted."

"That I would agree with but comments from our Mr. Traveler, the elves here, and you tell me there is another story."

"They're not what they appear."

"You hint at a darker nature."

"It is the same with all others, human and fae, good and bad, light and dark. The star elves would have you believe they are all good and light. That is not true."

"What is the difference between these elves? I've been intrigued by the wide variety of descriptions."

"Cloud elves are similar to the wind elves we battled. They are also high elves with air elemental powers, but instead of control over the wind, their power is over the clouds. That makes them more powerful than their wind elf cousins. They live in cities on the clouds as they control the power of the clouds. They can call forth fog to blind and obscure, or storm clouds to create thunder, lightning, and hurricanes.

"Star elves have the power of the stars themselves, a magic of blinding starlight—the more powerful ones have starfire. They control the power of light.

"Celestial elves are their more powerful high-elf cousins with the power of the stars, planets, and the void that engulfs all that is. No elf is more powerful than they."

"What is the source of this rift between the elfin kingdoms?"

"The celestial elves wanted to take the heavens for themselves, away from humans, sprites, fairies, and even other elfin races."

"What happened?"

"The same as always. War. All the elfin races against them. The cloud and star elves betrayed all the others and joined with the celestial elves. This all happened eons ago. Have you not asked these questions of Mr. Traveler?"

"I have. I wanted to get the drow perspective. Though its more complicated than that."

"If you know the whole story, king, why ask me?"

"I was told all the elves made war on the Atlanteans."

"All fae made war on them."

"The fae lost?"

"You can ask twenty fae that question and get fifty answers. No one knows. What's true is the Atlanteans remain and all us fae seek out its kingdom. The cloud, star, and celestial elves have controlled the region that surrounds their kingdom ever since that war.

"King, we go to Atlantea for the same reason, to secure an alliance with their kingdom, an alliance that cannot be broken by any other. Others go there for riches. You and I, the elves, a few others see the wider picture."

"Yes, indeed. May I ask a question, Mr. Dr'as? I feel my studies must also include an understanding of the elementals."

"What can we drows do to help?"

"Do you have any works on the elementals?"

"Did Mr. Traveler tell you that we do?"

"He said you might."

Dr'as smirked. "But can you read drow?"

"With magic, I do not need to."

"A reading spell. We used them as children so the books would read to us while we trained in fighting. I may have a book or two in my personal library."

"No one says it directly, but my sense is that these elementals are more powerful than fae."

"You mean elves? They are allied with the celestial elves, and, therefore, the cloud and star elves too, but it's an alliance of convenience, nothing more. You ask about political intrigue among the races in the magical lands that may be far, far beyond your station. You are but a human far away from your lands. I am but a drow."

"True. But I'm a man of strategy. I seek knowledge to that end. Not for wealth or power, but to keep those I care about alive. It's what I did for my kingdom and its allies in the Lands of Man. It is what I must do for Titan's Caravan. The burden cannot rest solely on our caravan master's shoulders."

"I heard you're known as King Aereth the Wise in your lands."

"You wisely gather knowledge on me."

"You are the highest royal in the caravan."

"Not yourself?"

"Even if I were royalty with a crown, I would not reveal it. The story of the drows would only complicate matters. We must remain to the side."

"But only temporarily. Mr. Dr'as, I fully respect you and your people. You are valuable members to this caravan. Even though Mr. Traveler has been harsh with your daughter regarding her magic casting, he does value her abilities."

"It is kind of you to say, king. I understand, Mr. Traveler well. If he were truly vexed with my daughter, he would have asked us to leave. He does the same as I have tried to do but in a different way—get her to perform her best. We drows have a deep temper despite our outward calm most of the time. Mr. Traveler knows drows well. He seeks to use her own temper against her self-doubt to reach her full power."

"We are fortunate to have him leading the caravan, especially now. I feel our journey is truly beginning. Not when my party left the Lands of Man or you and your people joined us at Arion's Spear."

Dr'as nodded. "I will have those two books delivered for your studies, but I can save you some time. Sylphs are elementals of the air. Undines are of the water, salamanders of fire. Elementals of the earth have many names and many appearances of rock and earth. We thought Mr. Bragg's metal golem was an earth elemental when we first saw him. Oh, there are more than four elementals, a common human fallacy. And finally, just as you cannot kill water or the breeze with a sword, you cannot harm them either."

"How does one defend against them?"

"I suspect our Mr. Traveler would be better informed than either one of us. That armor he wears with the slight orange glow was forged to battle elementals. Elementals regard humans, drows, and elves alike as...lesser forms of life."

"I don't like the sound of that."

"I did not say my knowledge would bring you joy."

Mr. Gresham helped Frog-Dog set up his own tent. The hobbled man felt more at ease outside the gaze of the men. When they arrived at his tent, he was without his metal braces fashioned by Mr. Estus. Instead he slowly moved around with the aid of a walking staff in each hand.

Lady Aylen entered with both Maiden Gwyness and Dr'amal, the drow sorceress.

"Mr. Frog-Dor, have you summoned us for another meeting of the committee of dreams? Where's Mr. Gresham?"

The man forced a smile. Another entered the dimly lit tent, but it wasn't Gresham. It was the caravan's sole fauness.

"Zefea will join us," he said.

Like Dr'amal she had her hood draped over her head.

"So, this is our committee of dreams? Frog-Dor, is that even your name? I feel as is if I'm insulting you every time I speak it," Lady Aylen said.

"It is my name."

"But what's your real name? The name given to you at birth?"

Frog-Dor's brow furrowed, his eyes cast down. "I cannot remember. My memory of my past life is not complete, but Frog-Dor is not an insult to me. I've grown so accustomed to it over so many years, I would respond to no other name at this point. Frog-Dor is fine."

"If you say so, Mr. Frog-Dor," Lady Aylen said. "Why have we gathered?"

"M'lady, you stumbled upon an excellent idea."

"I have?"

"A committee. Master Traveler wanted one to read the dreams of the men, but I thought, to go maybe further. We need a committee of its magic-casters."

"Yes," Dr'amal said. "We are the caravan's wizards."

"What would be our purpose, Mr. Frog-Dor?" Lady Aylen asked. "We all have our own roles in the caravan. My magic is limited. The great power I exhibited I consider a one-off. My maiden's power is by means of her amulet."

"The only magic I possess is what I conjure through by herbs and plants," Zefea, the fauness, said.

"Only you and Dr'amal are the true wizards in the caravan," Lady Aylen continued.

"Mistress Zefea, your magic gifts extend beyond that. You are a healer of animals, both magical and not. Your knowledge surpasses all of us in that area."

"True."

"You can also sense the source of magic."

"You're correct again, though I don't know how you would know. I've only interacted with Master Traveler and Gresham."

"It seems that you can sense the magical abilities of those around you, Mr. Frog-Dor," Lady Aylen said.

"Your powers are that of a water elemental. Your maiden, I suspect does not need her amulet to ward off evil."

Maiden Gwyness gave a look of surprise.

"How do you know, Mr. Frog-Dor?"

"I do believe your amulet is a weapon not a beacon. I recollect something similar but cannot remember from when or where. Other wizards I believe. Mistress Dr'amal's magic is of mirages and illusions. She can also amplify the magical powers of others."

"And you, Mr. Frog-Dor?" Lady Aylen asked.

"I am a conjurer."

"The most powerful of all magic-casters," Dr'amal said. "Without your abilities, we might not have been as victorious as we were with our battle in Fae'el."

"What do you have in mind, Mr. Frog-Dor?"

"M'lady, if we are to battle war wizards or any being or beast of incredible magical power, we should have an agreement amongst ourselves to come to each other's aid for the sake of the caravan. Simply an agreement."

"As the fae berserkers have with the Cut-throats," Gwyness said.

"Yes. Come to each other's aid."

"Agreed, Mr. Frog-Dor," Lady Aylen. "Do you believe we will come across more of Oughtred's war wizards?"

"Others have war wizards, wizard assassins, and the like. I have also heard talk of this mystery of the Great Forest."

"Where powerful caravans with powerful wizards disappear without a trace," Lady Aylen said. "What are your theories, Mr. Frog-Dor? Mr. Traveler has none, but I know he's concerned."

"As are all the elves," Dr'amal said.

"I do not know. If the mystery has lasted for as many centuries as I'm told, they are overwhelmed by a power greater and faster than all."

"Then our committee of magic it is, Mr. Frog-Dor," Lady Aylen said. "Are all agreed?"

"Agreed," they all said.

The caravan was fast asleep. Brownies had made their rounds, tidied up camp, and sat in circles around campfires to keep watch over the men. However, all the brownies noticed that neither drow nor darkling patrols were on watch.

A black fox appeared and ran to the tents. A few of the brownies stood and followed after the phooka in its shape-shifted form.

"What are you up to, shape-shifter?" a brownie asked.

The fox glanced back with a smiling human mouth.

Ursi shared a tent with the drowess, Dr'amal. The fae-blood race was extremely solitary, but she'd put aside her discomfort to conform with Traveler's orders that no one should be alone at any time. The drowess had returned from her night meeting and fell asleep quickly. Ursi never fully fell asleep with another, not of her race so close. She had already sat up when the black fox entered her tent, a dagger in her hand.

The fox jumped on its hind legs and slowly transformed to a humanoid fox. The sprite beckoned.

When Ursi exited the tent, she saw the darkling clearly. Three brownies stood behind him.

"Sorry," the darkling said. "Please, please we must go quickly to the realm's entrance."

"Why?"

"Bring you best weapons with you but quietly. We must not wake the others."

Ursi followed the black fox, which ran quickly on elongated legs to the entrance. She saw that others were already waiting. She said nothing to them. The fifteen fae-blood men said nothing either.

"What is our purpose here, phooka?" a fae-blood male asked.

"Master Traveler said to guard the realm entrance. Nothing not of the caravan is to be allowed to enter."

Concern came over Ursi's face. "What is happening outside?" All they could see was pitch-black.

The darkling stepped in front of her.

"No peeking," it said, almost giggling. "I go back to join the fight. You must ensure it doesn't come in here. The men must have their sleep."

"Go on, dark one," a fae-blood scolded.

The darkling jumped across the realm threshold into the pitch-black.

The two fae-blood clans stared at each other.

The moment the darkling emerged from the other side of the realm entrance, the battle exploded around him. A myrmecoleon tried to bite off his head, but the darkling transformed from a black humanoid fox to a black fox-headed gorilla in moments and strangled the creature, throwing it at other of the creatures flying at him.

A myrmecoleon night swarm. The creatures were known as ant-lions in the magical lands—head of a full maned lion and the body of a giant winged ant. The myrmecoleons attacked the caravan's army of moon elves, drows, and darklings, with Traveler and his dog. The creatures also had stingers and three claws on each of their six legs.

The darklings enjoyed the frenzy of the battle, transforming from one hybrid creature to another to kill the ant-lion swarm. The moon elves wielded swords of pure magic moon light to cut the creatures apart. Drows fought with their swords or long two-edge daggers. Traveler killed so many with his magic sword that most of the ant-lion swarm avoided him.

The dog also transformed into different beasts to fight off the swarm. The dog transformed into an orange lizard the size of a small pony. It belched out a spray of fire, showering it far and wide. Ant-lions burned or fled. However, the dog, now in the form of a firedrake, was pounced on, from behind by dozen of the myrmecoleons, each biting with razor-sharp teeth. The dog turned into a two-headed firedrake with a rhinoceros hide and burned them alive.

Several of the moon elves ran to each other and struck their moon swords together. A blinding wave of white moon light exploded through the area. The ant-lion swarm finally relented and fled.

"As much as I would like to say our moon magic scared off the beasts, I'm not certain," Shadu-mun said to the others.

"We decimated enough of their swarm. They fled instinctively," Traveler said.

He looked around. "Are all your men accounted for?"

Shadu-mun glanced behind him as they all drew near. "Yes."

"Drows?" Traveler asked.

"Yes," a drow said.

Traveler looked at the sad faces of the darklings, now in the form of black rabbits. He ran to several fallen darklings on the ground. One looked up at them with weepy eyes.

"Master Traveler, we so wanted to join you in Atlantea, but now you must bury us and carry on."

"Stop that. I told you humans don't joke about death so casually as phookas."

Several darklings jumped to their feet and started cackling in unison.

"What evil creatures you keep company with, Mr. Traveler," a moon elf said.

"Do not embarrass me!" Traveler yelled at the darklings, and they quieted. "If you joke about death, how will I know when you're in true distress. We have spoken about this before. Joke about anything but that. And keep the joking to a minimum and to yourselves."

The smiles returned to the darklings' face.

"Yes, keep to themselves." Shadu-mun collapsed and was barely caught by his men before he hit the ground.

Other elves and drows fell to the ground.

"Get them into the pocket-realm immediately. To the healing tent!" Traveler yelled.

Above them the Atlas turtles lumbered on, completely disinterested in the battle of specks that had taken place beneath their bellies.

King Aereth often rose before Mr. Hobbs could peek in to wake him. Usually, the caravan steward's wake-up call would be for Nirgund. However, lately, the berserker guardsman was rising even before the king.

"A fine morning, sire," Nirgund said, already in his armor and marching attire, his alphyns playfully following after him.

The king sat in his trussing bed for a few moments. "Yes, it is, Mr. Nirgund. Though I may have spent an hour or two too long reading."

"A good meeting with the drow leader?"

"It was indeed. More to follow. I should get ready before our Mr. Hobbs makes me."

"Yes, he would, sire."

But Mr. Hobbs never did peek in.

King Aereth stepped from his tent. Nirgund waited outside with his reptile hounds. The pocket-realm's sky changed to a yellow when morning arrived. Most of the men preferred to have their meals on the march.

"There he is, sire," Nirgund said as Mr. Hobbs briskly moved to them.

Lady Aylen and Gwyness appeared from their tent.

"Sire, Mr. Nirgund, and company."

The alphyns yelped in joy at the princess's greeting.

"Morning all. Sire, I do have news of a change."

"Change, Mr. Hobbs?"

"You and Lady Aylen will lead the front column. Mr. Traveler will not be joining us."

"Why not, Mr. Hobbs?"

"M'lady, I can explain fully as we march. We have to change caravans."

"Yes, Mr. Hobbs. Let us not keep the men waiting."

"Has something happened, Mr. Hobbs?" Lady Aylen asked.

"We can speak on the march, m'lady."

The caravans changed places. Pangolin and his men replaced the Tree Shepherds for the vanguard. But when the royals and the men came out of the pocket-realm, only a small number of drows were on the march—no moon elves or darklings.

"What happened here last night?" Lady Aylen asked.

None of the drows answered as they passed for the entrance to the pocket-realm. The day caravan took its place under the Atlas turtle caravan. Hobbs moved through the men to ensure all were in their positions, including the lizards and their minders.

Pangolin joined the royals at the front column.

"Do you know what happened last night, Mr. Pangolin?"

"No, Lady Aylen. There must have been a battle of some significance. The elfin questing knights were not camped by us when I awoke."

"Where are they, Mr. Pangolin?"

"At the healing tent, sire."

They looked for Mr. Hobbs.

"Is Mr. Traveler in the healing tent?" Lady Aylen asked. "Mr. Hobbs, urgently."

The royals and Maiden Gwyness were not riding their mounts. Their kirins walked behind them. The steward joined them, rushing as fast as his short legs could carry him.

"Mr. Hobbs," Lady Aylen said impatiently.

"Yes, m'lady, I'm here. The night caravan was attacked by creatures," Hobbs said.

"Why were the warriors not called?" Pangolin asked.

"Traveler's decision. He did not want the day caravan impacted at all," Hobbs replied.

"Was anyone killed?" Pangolin asked.

"Fortunately, no, Mr. Pangolin. But many of the men were poisoned in the attack. Mr. Gresham is caring for them."

"Poisoned?" Lady Aylen asked.

"Have you heard of ant-lions?" Hobbs asked.

"Mr. Elman!" Pangolin cried.

"You do not need to call the half-elf," one of the pech called out. He gave his fellow pech his pull cart and walked forward. Elman arrived at the same time.

"Ant-lions are giant ants with the heads of a lion," the pech said.

"What manner of creature is that?" Lady Aylen asked. "How can such a thing exist?"

"How were they poisoned?" Pangolin asked.

"The ant-lions shot stingers at them in the battle."

Pangolin shook his head.

"They were attacked by a swarm," Hobbs said.

"How big of a swarm?"

"Night swarms can enshroud an entire city," the pech said. "Fairy swarms are the most dangerous, but any swarm, especially one of ant-lions, can be dangerous. Be thankful no one was mauled, carried away, or killed by poison.”

“What concerns me is whether we’ll have a defense for such an attack in the future,” Pangolin said.

“A sorcerer,” the pech said.

“The fairies would be the best defense against any swarm,” Elman said.

“But they’re not part of the night caravan,” King Aereth said.

“And Mr. Traveler?” Pangolin asked.

“He is resting and will join us at the noon meal,” Hobbs said.

“That is all I wish to know. I’ll return to my post, but we need a solution.”

“Yes, Mr. Pangolin. Our night caravan needs additional defenses.”

Pangolin moved to the front of the caravan.

“We travel underneath these mammoth beasts, but the danger remains,” Lady Aylen said, looking above. “What would have happened if we didn’t have their protection?”

Gresham’s long night had finally ended. He stepped from his healing tent for some air. Over fifty elves and nearly thirty drows. He had to expand the healing tent and have two separate sections as the two races didn't want to be in the same tent, even though they had fought a battle side by side. It was the way of things in the magical lands. Even allies wanted their own space.

When Traveler roused him from his sleep and rushed him to the healing tent, he'd expected he would be dealing with major wounds. Poisonous darts were nothing he had experience with. Fortunately, between the fauns, especially their fauness, and the animal men, they were able to treat moon elf and drow successfully.

"What is your name?" Gresham asked the fauness as she left the tent.

"Zefea," she said.

"Fine work, Zefea."

She nodded as she walked off to join the fauns waiting nearby.

One of the raccoon men came out and carefully handed him one of the stingers. Gresham still wore leather gloves.

"Thank you. For my studies."

The raccoon man scurried to join his people and the other animal men waiting.

"How did you get on, Mr. Gresham?" Estus arrived and took a look at the stinger. "Nasty thing."

"Yes," Gresham said. "I was told both the elves and drows have magic auras around them that normally protect them from such things. But when hundreds or thousands of these stingers are shot at one faster than the speed of an arrow, one or two are bound to get through."

Estus grunted. "Not good at all. All it takes is one to kill you."

"True. They were fortunate."

"Mr. Traveler fought with them?"

"He was there, along with the dog."

"Did you hear the description of these creatures? The magical lands have hybrid creatures, but a giant ant with the head of a lion? That makes the appearance of a griffin or hippogriff seem normal."

"Strange place, this Great Forest. We've seen things that not even the fae has seen before."

"And we are barely into the Great Forest. Six months is a long time to endure. You should join the day caravan when you can, Mr. Gresham."

"I will. I want to stay with my patients, see to their comfort, study this stinger."

"It would be nice if I could design a weapon to protect us from swarms."

"Fire, Mr. Estus. Fire scares away all insects, even these."

"I wonder if any of our magical weapons can shoot fire. I'll check. The only problem will be to set ablaze only the swarm and not ourselves, our animals, and our provisions."

"If it can be done, you'll find the weapon."

"I'll find our caravan master."

"He plans to join the day caravan at noon."

"I'll let him sleep then."

Shadu-mun, the moon elf, exited the healing tent.

"Where do you think you're going?" Gresham asked.

"I can rest in our camp."

"You can rest here. This is your camp." Gresham pointed into the tent.

Estus laughed.

"Your fellow moon elves are inside too. This is your camp. Go back and rest, please."

"I do not need any more of your healing services, human," the elf said.

Gresham extended his foot and tripped the elf. Shadu-mun glared up at him from the ground.

"In a hundred years I, a human, should not have been able to do that. You're not well. You were poisoned by a creature not native to your lands or mine. You could have died, elf. Get back to your resting bed. The caravan needs you back to full strength as quickly as possible. Mr. Traveler expects no less.”

“I will return to rest inside.”

“Good.”

Shadu-mun got to his feet and ambled back into the tent, where he’d lain before.

“You have everything under control, Mr. Gresham,” a smiling Estus said.

“For now, Mr. Estus. But my reign will be short-lived.”

“Enjoy it nonetheless, Mr. Gresham. You reign over elves and drows today.”

“No, he does not!” someone yelled from inside.

“Mr. Estus, elves have far superior hearing to us.”

“I keep forgetting that.”

Quillen showed Traveler his latest sketch in his magic book. The caravan master studied it.

“Looks too much like a wurm. A firedrake looks like a lizard the size of a dog. There are many species with different color markers, some with moist, smooth skin, others with ridged, rock-like skin, but they all breathe fire,” Traveler said.

“Breathe fire,” Quillen said, smiling. “Where do they live?”

“In the lands of the dwarves.”

"Where we will not be visiting for even an instant," Lady Aylen said.

The noon meal was underway in their pocket-realm. Half the day caravan had finished their meal and were making their way back outside to the march. The group with the royals had just arrived. Hobbs oversaw it all. At the moment, he was supervising the cooks. Traveler appeared from his tent, got food for the dog and himself, and sat with the royals and all those at the front of the column. He recited the story of the battle from the night before as the others eagerly listened.

"Why didn't the creatures fly away after such a defense, Mr. Traveler?" Nirgund asked, stuffing his mouth with food, not bothering with any utensils.

"Ant-lions are very much like gnolls. They attack until all are dead or there are so few left, they have no choice but to retreat. Their swarms can become quite thick with their numbers."

"I was wondering aloud earlier, Mr. Traveler, what would have been our state of affairs without these Atlas turtles for protection?"

"I can think of many different scenarios, princess. We could still be at the edge of the Great Forest. We could be five days ahead on the Trail, or we could be dead."

"That was not the answer I was expecting, Mr. Traveler," Lady Aylen said.

"The Great Forest is a fearsome place. If it weren't, the fae wouldn't need us, and we would not need them. One of the caravans I was a member of described the journey through the Forest as 'death by a thousand cuts.' Those cuts could be physical but often mental. We must push forward and enjoy our respite under the belly of the Atlas turtles."

Hobbs sat down to join them with his plate of food. "Sir, if I may inquire. How long will we have the Atlas turtles?"

"Are the men worried?" Traveler asked.

"More curious than worried, sir. They see the lands around them and the many giant animals. If we are to be here all six months of the journey, that would reassure them."

"Their caravan runs close to the shores of Ocean Omnis," Traveler said. "But we will part ways after ten days or so."

"Straight to the ocean, Mr. Traveler?" Lady Aylen asked.

"So if we didn't need to detour to the Sirenic Seas, we could travel with the Atlas turtles straight through to the next leg of the Trail?"

"Yes."

Everyone exchanged looks. Traveler smiled. He stood from his seat.

"Ten days will take us through the densest parts of the Forest. After that, we can manage. We will take different paths that crisscross Titan's Walk. Besides, our sea transport will be at the shores of the Sirenic Seas. Have you forgotten so quickly why we made the change?"

"No, Mr. Traveler, we remember well," King Aereth said. "But we've all grown quite accustomed to this land transport you arranged for us."

"I saw more of those cloud creatures in the distance," Lady Aylen said.

"Princess, I doubt you're seeing cloud creatures anymore. You are seeing clouds and imagining them as creatures. I should not have told you about them. Enough of this fear. We must travel with our wits about us, free of fear. When we do have to leave the protection of the Atlas turtles, we will return to our normal protection, that of the crawling trees under the command of our Tree Shepherds.

"And our crawling trees and lizards can be covered with our own swarms, that of our two fairies, if need be."

"You do know what you're doing, Mr. Traveler."

"Yes, I do, Mr. Nirgund. I have been on the Trail before."

"And lived in Atlantea," the berserker added.

"That too."

They waited for Hobbs to finish his meal then returned to the march. Moments of levity were welcome because, despite Traveler's admonishment, in the center of their deepest thoughts, they would never be free of fear. The Great Forest would not let them.

The burden of the constant march, switching between day and night caravans, had become routine. Several days had passed, and the Forest truly seemed endless. Many realized that the path the Atlas turtles traveled was likely carved through the Forests by generations of the beasts over many millennia.

Titan's Caravan moved through a sea of green. The flora, birds, and insects were not only of every size, but of every color, often multiple colors. Giant animals surrounded them at all times. They could also hear them: screams, chirps, roars, grunts and growls, singing, movement through the brush, jumping from tree to tree, chasing one another, fighting. Every so often, they would see them: many reptiles, such as toads, frogs, and snakes, many more birds, those that ate plants or insects, those that ate other birds or larger animals. Giant insects and mammals such as squirrels and monkeys were also seen. However, they had no repeat of an animal attack like the ant-lion swarm.

Traveler told them that the first ten days would be the toughest. Though they moved under the protection of the Atlas turtles along their own path, often the caravan would have to cut away blades of grass and flowers six feet to fifteen feet tall to continue their march. Sometimes the path was uneven or covered by a pond, which to them, would be the size of a small lake. They had seen a giant mosquito, but it flew away. One man thought he had saw a giant spider stalking them from the flanks, but there was nothing. All welcomed the lack of "excitement."

Pangolin raised his hand. The gesture was not to order a halt but to signal Traveler. The caravan master ran ahead with the dog to join the vanguard. Immediately, he saw what they wanted him for. The caravan had reached a region of the Forest where the ground was of stone, as if the beginning of a mountain.

"Titan's Footprint?" Pangolin asked with a grin.

"If it was a Titan, the footprint would be too massive for us to notice or even see from the backs of our Atlas turtles above. Possibly a giant or troll many centuries ago. Regardless, this footprint is a visible marker of Titan's Walk. We're seven days along. We will come across another set of markers, similar footprints, three of them, but then that will be the last visible sign of the Walk."

"How does a guide know the path then, Mr. Traveler?" Elman asked.

"Curious you would ask, Mr. Elman. Can you not see it?"

The half-elf looked ahead as they marched. "There is a path." He moved away from the men to the flank of the giant lizards and stuck out his head to see the sky beyond the Atlas turtle. He returned. "That cannot be possible. Can it?"

"Yes, Mr. Elman. The path is in the sky. Cut through the sky and clouds themselves, if you know it's there."

"One follows the clouds?" Pangolin asked.

"Yes," Traveler answered. "But you can see it only if you know it's there. What we're seeing is the aerial path created by the flying caravans. I was told that many, many millennia ago, the magic aerial path illuminated the night sky."

"When do we depart from the Turtles?" Pangolin asked.

"In a few days. You will know when. The thickness of the Forest will begin to recede a bit. We will reach a region of plains, where we will make camp. I'll chart our path from there."

"Master Traveler, are we likely to come across other caravans?" Grakdar, the giant, asked.

"We shouldn't, but we'll likely come across native nomads of the Forest."

"Isn't travel through the Great Forest so dangerous, humans and fae avoid it?"

"Mr. Grakdar, there are fae that live in the Forest," Traveler said. "Their caravans move ably through it."

"Are they friendly or dangerous?" Pangolin asked.

"Yes," Traveler answered.

The giants laughed.

The royals and Gwyness had grown closer to their kirins over the days traveling through the Forest.

"I need to give my kirin a name," Gwyness said aloud.

The kirins walked alongside their masters.

"What name do you have in mind, Maiden Gwyness?" King Aereth asked.

"I am not sure, sire."

Their caravan master and his dog walked ahead of them. They noticed both turn their attention to the side. A falcon landed on the ground about a few yards away sending some of the giant lizards into a frenzy. Their minders could barely hold them back.

A group of the caravan's bird men appeared with their enfields. Two approached the giant falcon while the other bird men restrained their flying fox hybrids. The bird men and the falcon exchange bird sounds loudly. The falcon shrieked then flew away. The bird men and their enfields walked back into the caravan.

"Is that why you insisted that our animal men were so important, Mr. Traveler?" Lady Aylen asked.

He nodded. "That's why we haven't been attacked as much, princess. The frog men speak to the giant amphibians. The lizard men speak to the giant lizards. The squirrel, raccoon, possum, rabbit, and mice men can speak to most of the similar giant animals. The fox men can speak to the meat-eating giant animals who are not vicious, and you saw the rabbit men. Our hoofed fae, including the fauns, are keeping the giant hoofed animals from us. Our own fairies sent out their swarms to tell the giant insects to leave us be. If we come across any giant water animals, the Tree Shepherds and that fae who looks like a mole man can speak to them."

The front of the column looked at him with disbelief.

"Are you being serious, Mr. Traveler?" King Aereth asked.

"I am, sire."

"We thought the Atlas turtles were keeping the giant animals away," the king said.

"No, sire. The animals of the Forest know the Atlas turtles well. The turtles protect us from giant animals and creatures attacking us from above and scare off most of the evil ones of a giant size. But it is our animal men, leshy, and fairies who are keeping most of the attacks away from us through words alone."

"You are saying if it weren't for them, we would be under constant attack by these giant animals, Mr. Traveler?"

"Yes."

Gwyness pointed out front with concern. Ahead of the caravan were thousands of mushroom men approaching them. They were of a different species as those before—white bodies with orange or bluish caps.

The caravan's four Tree Shepherds appeared out of invisibility. The white-skinned, green-bearded, hooded, and robed leshy walked out to meet the mushroom men. They moved out of the caravan then outside the foot path of the Atlas turtles.

The caravan watched the two races conversing, the six-foot Tree Shepherds, each with their thicker, wooden staffs, which curved at the top, and the mushroom men that stood almost ten feet tall.

"This is the second time the caravan has encountered these mushroom men," King Aereth said.

"I hope nothing's wrong," Lady Aylen said. "What do you think, Mr. Traveler?"

"I will ask them when we switch caravans tonight. Unlike the tree men we met in Faë-Land Minor, mushroom men do not like humans or most fae. They do not even speak to fairies. I will see what Greenwig tells me tonight."

"Not to be negative, Mr. Traveler, but what of this goblin caravan ahead of us?" Nirgund asked.

"Why do you ask, Mr. Nirgund?"

"I thought I heard the darklings talking about them the other night."

"Talking about them?" Aereth asked.

"The darklings found a hobgoblin corpse, dead weeks ago, the night prior. A victim of the Forest. I do need to scold them for being so careless in who overhears their ramblings."

"Mr. Traveler, we have not had our nightly meetings, but is this not something we should have been informed of?" Lady Aylen asked.

The caravan master looked at her. "No."

"No?"

"The darklings will handle it. I need your mind, especially, and Maiden Gwyness's uncluttered with extraneous issues, and I do not want the men gossiping about goblins or anything else. We need to keep our focus. In a few days, we will lose our Atlas turtle caravan. We know nothing, so there's nothing to discuss or gossip about. Mr. Hobbs, do you disagree?"

"I agree completely, sir," the steward said.

"We must focus on the here and now and what lies before us."

"Tell us, Mr. Traveler. Will we be able to avoid these goblins?"

"Hopefully the Forest will claim the rest of them so the answer to your question will be 'yes.'"

He noticed the mushroom men were dispersing and walking back into the Forest. The four Tree Shepherds, Greenwig, Mossberry, Thornbeard, and Little Root, walked to the front column.

"Mr. Hobbs, make your circle," Traveler told him.

The steward had gotten used to the practice back in Faë-Land. He removed the wand from his waist pouch and drew a circle in the air several times. A glowing circle appeared around the caravan of human, fae, and their animals. With the magic barrier encircling nearly ten thousand, Hobbs proceeded to have the caravan set up night camp.

He knew the work would be slow going, but he wouldn't get upset. The caravan's attention was on the Atlas turtle caravan lumbering along their path. Titan's Caravan had finally separated to set up camp in a sparsely wooden patch of the Forest. Many for the first time had a chance to fully appreciate the magnitude and splendor of the beasts. From head to foot, the entirety of their bodies were covered with armored shelled bodies. They looked ancient and magnificent. Their shells had a darkish-green rim, but the rest of the shells were patterned with golden blotches and spots of green. Their giant turtle heads slowly bobbed up and down, with large dark eyes and a horn on the tip of their noses. For the first time, the caravan also saw for themselves that the turtle caravan comprised of dozens of the beasts. They had marched under the first two alone, but there were many more.

Now that they weren't under the beasts' bellies, the ground rumbled but not violently as their feet landed on the earth in—a rolling movement. Traveler estimated that it would be well into midnight by the time the last sounds of their march passed by them.

"Mr. Hobbs, we have our circle. Now have the men set up camp within a pocket-realm." The caravan master handed the steward a cloth bag.

"Yes, sir," he said with a wide smile and strolled into the camp.

"Change your mind, Mr. Traveler?" the king asked.

"Best not to take any chances, sire. It would have been nice to be under the natural night sky, but this is still the Great Forest, albeit a quiet spot within it."

"The fresh air is nice, Mr. Traveler," Lady Aylen said. "We're close to one or more bodies of water."

"There's a river in the distance, princess, which should act as an additional barrier to keep giant animals from us. Once camp is set, we will meet to discuss the news from the Tree Shepherds."

"Other than the corpse, there has been no other indication of the goblin caravan ahead of us. In fact, our kilmoulis allies informed me the last time they sensed them, they were moving farther from us, and they haven't sensed them since our one encounter with that goblin scouting party," Traveler said.

Hobbs had the men set up a special meeting tent, where the leadership took their night meal.

"But we no longer have our land transport, Mr. Traveler," Lyre, the high elf, said.

The four elfin leaders, Chief Ethor, Lyre, Taylos, and Shadu-mun joined the meeting of the leadership, along with the drow leader and his sorceress daughter. The fae-blood, Ursi, also joined, standing quietly in the back of the tent. Bragg, the dwelf, wanted to attend, but he and his men provided additional security for the meeting outside the tent.

"No, we do not, Mr. Lyre. I believe the benefits far outweigh the dangers. Namely, we will travel along paths that no one will know of, enemies or allies, but that's not what we're here to discuss. We're here to talk about the news from the Tree Shepherds."

"It's interesting that what should seem to be amazing is just everyday here in the magical lands. Are these mushroom men trustworthy?" Lady Aylen asked. "We have come across untrustworthy humans, elves, fairies, and whatever else. Is it possible that they may not be allies or a disinterested party?"

"Master Traveler, I can answer."

The Tree Shepherd leader, Greenwig, stood at the entrance of the tent. Everyone turned.

"Lady Aylen, you are correct. There are as many species of mushroom men as there are mushrooms or insects or birds. These mushroom men are known to us. They are allies and we have shared good words between our peoples for centuries. They have no interest in seeing harm come to us."

"If you are satisfied, Mr. Greenwig, then I am," Lady Aylen said.

"Thank you, Greenwig," Traveler said.

The Tree Shepherd nodded and left the tent.

"If we have the opportunity, do we stop?" Traveler asked. "I told you there's no other vestige of civilization in the Great Forest. There are no towns or cities, as we're accustomed to, but there are occasionally chances to trade with other parties-- traveling merchants and nomads and the like. The Tree Shepherds can make the introductions with their allies."

"Mr. Traveler, every time we stop, whether in the Lands of Man or in Faë-Land, bad things happen. If at all possible, I would say we avoid any and every living thing we can," Pangolin said.

"Do we not have all we need, Mr. Traveler?" the king asked.

"Food, water, provisions, yes, sire. We do."

"But?"

"You can never have enough magic, and we should increase our water provisions as a precaution."

"And we will be in the Forest longer than intended?" Lady Aylen asked.

"Yes."

"I wish our kings had sent a few elfin wizards with us," Taylos, the desert elf, said.

"I say risk it," Lyre said.

"I say no," Pangolin said.

"If we do not risk it, then what we have is all we will have all the way to the gates of Atlantea itself. There will be no cities for us to take safe harbor in because all the cities in the Sirenic Seas will be full of sirens and their dark allies."

"If we went to the Oceans Omnis, there would be cities we could take port in?" Shadu-mun asked.

"Yes, but there I would be of the same mind as Mr. Pangolin. I would go nowhere near them. We've seen what happens when our enemies know we're coming."

"If I may suggest," Chief Ethor began. "Perhaps we do not have enough knowledge to make such a decision now. We should continue forth and if there is such an opportunity for trade, we can decide then.

Our mood today will undoubtedly be different tomorrow, based on what we've encountered."

"Agreed," King Aereth said.

"Agreed," the elfin knights said.

"That is the best middle ground position for us to take considering we've only traveled a fortnight of our six-month journey."

Bragg, the dwelf, stepped into the tent. "Pardon me, everyone. I believe something may be happening. Our Mr. Frog-Dor is doing his best to run to the tent."

Traveler stood from his stool.

"He seems very distressed," Bragg said.

A whirlwind of the spinning moon around and around in a center of darkness. The feeling of complete disorientation. Ever falling but floating at the same time. The fading of one's consciousness. Water. Submerged. Thunderous crashing. Pain of one's body slammed on the cold, soaking ground. Yelling. Screams. Fighting. Flashes of light. One's body being picked up. Voices. Fighting. Yelling. Balls of light. Fire. Running. Sleep.

Lady Aylen opened her eyes and instinctively sat up. The sky revealed it was early dawn. As her eyes focused, she stared around in complete shock. Bodies and animals everywhere. She remembered the similar sight when King Oughtred had transported all of their caravan before leaving the Lands of Man to that riverbank to be killed by marauder pirates. The sight before her was worse, and strange. The sight was of two worlds that had violently collided with one another and lay upon each other, with men and animals strewn about.

She noticed Gwyness nearby, and her female half–elf guardswomen, their owl griffin companions.

A brownie placed a hand on her shoulder, startling her.

"Have a warm broth, Lady," he said, smiling, handing her a metal cup.

"Thank you."

Her eyes studied the area. Drows stood closest, acting as sentries. Further on, she saw the elfin knights forming a sentry circle around the destroyed camp. In the distance, Pangolin and the Tree Shepherds stood around what looked like a fallen tree, but it was black, and its branches reminded her more of the tentacles of an octopus.

Brownies moved about, picking up men and animals to move them. She watched as they disappeared into an invisible entrance.

"Where is Mr. Traveler?" she asked a brownie.

"We attended to him first. His animal is watching over him."

"What happened to us?"

"One of the creatures of the Great Forest tried to run off with the pocket-realm," he said.

"I don't understand. I thought the doorway of a pocket-realm could not be moved."

"They can be. And there are some creatures that know how, even if it's by instinct."

"I don't understand what happened."

"All will be explained, but we must get human, fae, and animal back into the new pocket-realm. The one we were in was destroyed."

"Yes, of course." Lady Aylen got to her feet.

Another brownie seemed to appear next to her from nowhere and took the cup from her hand. She picked Gwyness up.

The new pocket-realm was a simple plain around a large lake. Humans were laid on their backs, side by side. It took every pech in the caravan to move each giant, still unconscious. They had moved two—four to go. The animal men, the deer-like people, and all the animals, including the giant lizards, were unconscious. The fauns seemed to be waking, but most were still prone on the ground. Lady Aylen saw in the distance a single body with a giant lion guarding it as it watched her, no doubt the dog not wanting anyone or anything near its master.

As Lady Aylen walked back out to carry the rest of her people into the realm, the metal golem, Glog, passed her carrying his master, Bragg. The dwelf wasn't passed out. He was seriously bleeding, his teeth clenched.

"Mr. Bragg," Lady Aylen said.

"I'll live, Lady Aylen. In this Forest, even the trees can kill you."

She exited the pocket-realm and noticed the drowess, Dr'amal sitting cross-legged in the center of the old camp. Her eyes were closed in deep thought. Lady Aylen let her be. The drow sorceress was casting some kind of magic spell. Brownies were passing her, each carrying one of the female half-elves.

"You can get the owl griffins," a brownie said.

"Yes, of course."

She reached the tiny animals. They wore looks of shock on their unconscious faces. She began to stack them in her arms, but—

"I can help you," a brownie appeared to help her carry the owl griffins.

"Do you know where King Aereth is?"

"Yes, I will take you to where he lies."

"Did anyone die?" she asked.

"Many men were wounded, some seriously. They fell on their own weapons."

As they walked back to the pocket-realm entrance, she looked out at the perimeter. Pangolin and the Tree Shepherds were still at the same spot near the fallen tree talking.

Now! The voice was in her head and startled her. The brownie saw her face. She quickened her pace to enter the pocket-realm first.

Maiden Gwyness was rising to her feet. Her head was a bit dizzy, but she steadied herself. She looked up at Lady Aylen approaching.

"Gwyness, are you injured?"

"I heard a voice inside my head."

"What did it say?"

"It said 'now.'"

"I heard the same."

Lady Aylen noticed in the distance, Traveler was on his feet and walking to them.

They waited, watching him and the dog following.

Traveler's hand dripped blood.

"You are wounded," Lady Aylen said.

"It can wait, but our visitor cannot."

"What visitor?" Lady Aylen asked.

"You both know," Traveler said. "The servant of the white elfess, the celestial queen. He is here and waiting. Waiting for us. Now."

When they exited the pocket-realm, all the elves and drows were ready for battle. In the distance, standing at the edge of the open plain, before the dense towering trees of the Forest, was a single black figure. Lady Aylen could already see him clearly, a giant in black clothes, his head concealed by a knight's helmet, and large, pale, clawed hands. As Traveler led them forward, Lady Aylen could make out the outline of the giant's broadsword under his full cloak.

Pangolin and the Tree Shepherds watched from their position. The berserker had his axe-mace in hand, ready to charge. Traveler gave him a simple hand gesture to assure him.

"Master Pangolin, Old Ones such as he are far too powerful for any of us in this caravan to harm in anyway. No weapon we have or magic we possess can touch him. His magic predates our own kingdoms," Greenwig said to Pangolin.

"We are helpless, then?"

"As an ancient being of incredible power, if he wanted to harm us, he would have," Mossberry said.

"His visit is expected. He is the servant of the white elfess we met in Druid Keep."

"The disappearing magic city filled with wizards, witches, and hags, where the fairies were almost killed?"

"Yes."

"Strange place for an elfin queen."

"I suspect she was only there to speak to those three, as her servant does now."

Pangolin noticed that the dog had stopped and sat on the ground as Traveler, Lady Aylen, and Gwyness continued forward to the giant.

"I was to meet you outside Fae'el but you infants were fighting amongst yourselves, as you often do," it said. "I did not wish for any to see me. Then you traveled with the Ancient turtles. I did not wish for any of them to see me either. Their words carry and are carried by the birds and insects throughout all Pan-Earth. My kind is supposed to be dead. So I waited. I do not like to wait but it gave me something different to do."

"Then we thank your queen for sending you," Traveler said.

"My queen made a promise. She keeps her promises."

Traveler nodded.

The giant lifted a hand, and a dark cloud rolled in above the entire area.

"Too many eyes. In the past, the Great Forest was known as the Forest of Infinite Eyes and Ears. No others need know our business."

The giant stepped closer to the women. Lady Aylen and Gwyness felt intense fear but they stood their ground.

"You both are the descendants of the kingdom of Rivermouth, where elves and elementals trained their mages and warrior clerics. The kingdom was destroyed. By whom does not matter anymore. It was so long ago. But the ones who did so are the ones who now seek to rebuild it through you—slayers and seers. The ones who were the kingdom's allies are now your enemies. I left you all the remaining volumes of works from Rivermouth from my queen— the secrets of their training of mages and warrior clerics, the weapons and methods. You do not have the benefit of their instruction, but you have all their knowledge. Guard these works well, for you are the only ones who possess it in all of Pan-Earth."

The giant pointed his clawed hand at Gwyness. "You are to be a warrior cleric. The amulet reflects your own inherent ability. You do not need it to detect evil and dark magic. You sense it from within.

The amulet is a weapon that you must master. But take care, as if you are not careful you could follow the same path that turned ancient high elves into drows, and your soul will be forever marked for all to see.

He pointed at Lady Aylen. "You've already had a taste of the incredible water elemental power you are capable of. Water is the liquid of life. It is a powerful weapon against those who cheat death to walk as if the liquid of life courses through their bodies when all that does is putrid dust and sand.

"But the decision of who is the slayer and who is the seer is up to you. It is not predetermined. Either of you can take either role, but you must choose and master one.

"There have been others who desired to rebuild the mages and warrior clerics of Faylen at Rivermouth. As your enemies know of you, so do they. These followers desperately pursue you. You must allow them to reach you somehow, as together you could be the beginnings of Rivermouth's rebirth. The legacy of Rivermouth is yours to shape for the future or to let die.

"My queen amends her words. Never speak of Faylen or Rivermouth again as the Great Forest's many eyes and ears could spread your existence immediately to those enemies who seek you out. If you ever do reach the oceans and speak those two words, you will never reach Atlantea. The oceans are ruled by the water kingdoms that once revered Rivermouth but now would build vast armies to stop even the possibility of its rebirth. The true reasons will be evident. Allies have become enemies, and enemies allies. Pan-Earth is only one world of realms that exists as your human male with a piece of a Titan sword knows."

"Was your queen an ally or enemy of Rivermouth when it existed?" Traveler asked.

"You direct your suspicions at the wrong being, human. But yes, we know so much about Rivermouth because we were among the ones who helped destroy it."

The women swallowed hard. Traveler kept his mind as calm as possible so as not to alert the dog.

"It is and isn't what you think. It is important you understand. Rivermouth was destroyed because they would have become too powerful, a threat to all elfinkind, a threat to the alliances of elves and elementals. They did not view dark magic as the danger all fae have been bred to believe from the very birth of all fae. We were wrong. Even Old Ones can be as infallible as you young ones. But my queen can help you no more. She is a queen but as she told you, she is only a figurehead in her end days. She could be killed if she was found to have defied the kingdom's wishes. We celestial elves and their servants can be ruthless even to our own kind when it comes to our kingdoms and its alliances. They are what matter above all, not mere individuals—even my queen, even me.

"My queen did not tell you all this in Druid Keep because she did not believe you would make it this far, but you have, so she will keep her promise. The books awaiting will begin your training which you were bred for but thought lost."

"May we ask a question?" Lady Aylen asked nervously.

"The followers of light that seek you are elves, faoladh, other fae, and humans. Doubtful they will ever reach you, but they will try."

Traveler glanced at Gwyness.

She looked at the Old One, teary-eyed. Despite her fear, she asked, "What is your name so my lady and I know whom to thank?"

The giant made a low, guttural belly laugh. "Your human tongue could not pronounce it. Ancient elfish is a struggle even for elves. You are one clearly suitable for your vocation. You have a sincere care for strangers without even knowing if they are benevolent or malevolent. A distasteful trait to me, but of value to others, I suppose.”

“May I ask a question?” Traveler asked.

“Be careful not to anger me, human. Neither your magic blade nor your shape–shifter from above would save you from me. If it is about the kingdom of Xenhelm, the Four Kings had nothing to do with destruction of Rivermouth, but their allies include those who did.”

“Since you’re a wizard more powerful than any of us will ever meet again and you admitted you had a hand in the death of the women’s parents and people, may I ask you to make full restitution with one magical act to help our entire caravan?”

“Certainly, you have more than one suggestion as to what that act could be. I could, but I will not. I delivered the books and the information. I have been told that you humans are fond of the number three but I am not here to perform a third thing for you infant ones. Since you all are mere moments away from being slaughtered by goblins, I will send you along the Walk so that my queen mistress’s promise is fulfilled. My only warning to the three of you is if you’re fortunate enough to ever gaze upon my queen again in your short lives, you are never to acknowledge her presence or her name. Also, I am no mere wizard. I am a spell-talker. My helmet prevents me from ever using my tongue. I speak to you in your minds."

The giant clapped his clawed hands. Traveler and the women felt an invisible wave of powerful magic blow through them.

CHAPTER FOUR

Realm of the Dead Skull

In the Great Forest, there were trees that stood but had died long ago, not yet claimed by the greater forest. Fixed upon one tree, high above, was an old, abandoned giant beehive that looked like a humanoid skull that had turned to stone rather than dust.

A high goblin emerged from the dense Forest on a single foot path. His mount was a vicious red-eyed black dire wolf. The green-skinned high goblin had refined facial features more similar to an elf's than a bulbous-nosed, thick-faced ordinary goblin. Several ordinary goblins jumped out of the forest behind him in full goblin armor with shields, battle axes, and war hammers. Behind them were more high goblins, mercenaries in light armor with crossbows, then the scorpion-tailed tarasque clawed its way through the trees. It had six clawed legs and long ridged snakelike tails ending in spiked balls. Hundreds of giggling hobgoblins stood on its rock-like turtled-shelled back.

"They have war animals too," Lyre the high elf said. "Tarasques."

"Likely they added them to their ranks because they saw we had them," Taylos, the desert elf, said.

The leadership of all the parties of the caravan stood at a magical window hovering in front of the entrance of their pocket-realm. Beyond the realm's entrance were two eye sockets of a giant skull-like beehive. The fae of the caravan called it a "dead skull." The entrance was inside the skull. However, all attention was on a magic window that was like the view of a telescope that followed the goblin party many miles away.

Traveler leaned over to Nirgund, the king's royal guardsman, handing him the long single handle of a metal bucket. The berserker saw charcoal inside and looked up at the caravan master.

"Treats for your hounds, but be sparing. No more than once a day. If they do something especially worthy, you can reward them with another, but be sparing," Traveler said to him.

"Treats?" Nirgund asked.

As the caravan master stepped back, Nirgund once again looked at the contents of the bucket. His alphyns were already trying to stick their noses in it, sniffing the bucket.

"Okay, lads. Let us wait until we return to the tents," Nirgund said. He calmed the alphyns down and made a signal with his index finger to his mouth.

"How much farther along are we on the Titan's Walk than the goblins, Mr. Traveler?" Pangolin asked.

"I am unsure. If the goblins traveled all night, as I suspect, and we see them from where we are here...we're two to three days ahead of them."

"Not much of an advantage," Taylos said.

"The benefit we have is that there is no scent for them to follow," Traveler said. "We need time to recover."

"If I may second what Mr. Traveler said," Gresham spoke up. "Not all of the men have recovered from the event we experienced last night."

"What did happen?" Gwyness asked.

"Mistress Gwyness, the Forest has creatures similar to our own crawling trees but primal and evil."

"They are called yateveos," Pangolin said. "Moving killing trees that hunt and feed on animals and humans."

"One found the entrance of our pocket-realm and seized it," Greenwig, the Tree Shepherd, said. "The creatures move very quickly, and it had started to scale one of the mammoth trees. My fellow leshy and I attacked, but it dropped the pocket-realm. When it hit the ground, the realm exploded and collapsed. The brownies joined in the battle."

"It was a horrific experience," Lady Aylen said.

"And then we were visited by a giant whose power was so great that even I could sense it from within our new realm," Lyre said.

"And he transported our entire camp and realm here with the clap of his hands," Shadu-mun said. "No matter how ancient he is, that is no celestial elf. He is something else."

Traveler, Lady Aylen, and Gwyness said nothing.

"What did he say?" Lyre asked.

"His words were for us alone," Lady Aylen said.

"Was it now," Lyre said, "and sent by a celestial elf?"

"But not an enemy," Traveler said.

"I am gladdened that you can be so sure of that," Lyre said.

"If the Ancient One wanted us dead, we would be," Greenwig said.

"We must rest here," Traveler repeated. "The men and all our animals must fully recover. Mr. Hobbs, how are the provisions?"

"Much was damaged, sir, but we'll manage."

"Mr. Estus?"

"Our weapons vault was a mess, Mr. Traveler. But the men and I will set it right again and lock everything down to prevent something like this from happening again."

"You would have had to do it anyway on the Trail." The caravan master saw Mr. Gresham's hand. "Yes, Mr. Gresham?"

"There were many men injured by their own weapons. Some severely."

"Not much can be done about that, unfortunately," Traveler said. "Many a time, their weapons must be in hand. How is our dwelf hunter?"

"He will recover fully, Mr. Traveler, likely join us for the noon meal."

"I need time to chart a new path for us, with the goblins so close. We know that what we see are only the scouts. Where is their full caravan?" Traveler asked aloud.

"There may come a time, Mr. Traveler, that we need to stand our ground and engage them. We cannot have them at our heels for our entire march," Shadu-mun said.

"Or we can lead them into a trap," Traveler said.

Grins came over the faces of the elfin leaders, including Chief Ethor.

"Better than fighting them," Pangolin said.

"Chief Ethor, I will leave it to the elves to keep guard at the entrance and keep an eye out for the goblins."

"What is their purpose, Mr. Traveler?" King Aereth asked. "Are they hunting us, or are they moving along the trail on their own? If they're hunting us, they would need a caravan."

"We upset their plan, king. They were all to march—they and the dark fairies—under the lead and banner of the wind elves of Fae'el," Lyre said.

"But that alliance is no more. Why continue? Their actions to me seem conflicted. They are clearly not focused on hunting us, as we would have encountered them sooner. They sent out a smaller party to delay or kill the toad men bringing us our land transport. Once they failed, they should have attacked. Is that not the way of goblins, even high goblins?"

"You are correct, king," Chief Ethor said.

"Maybe they are leaderless," Pangolin said. "Mr. Traveler did kill their beast lord king."

"More reason for them to return to their lands."

"Much to consider, sire," Traveler said. "For the moment, there is much work to do. We survived a carnivorous moving tree and we were fortunate to receive our third visitor. Nothing more remains to delay us."

"How long will we stay here, Mr. Traveler?" Lady Aylen asked.

"I will be ready with our new course the day after next. We can set out under the protection of our Tree Shepherd's crawling trees at that time. Mr. Estus, it will be your time to take command of your army."

The Old One sent the entire caravan—camp and pocket-realms—into what all thought was a cave at first. Once everyone got their bearings, they realized they were miles away within the "dead skull," not a cave.

Lady Aylen, Gwyness, and Traveler stepped into the forever dusk pocket-realm of the väki right after their meeting with the Old One the night before. A wall of black, volcanic rock encircled a black mountain with a cavernous interior. There the elemental sprites guarded the caravan's vaults of armor, weapons, and wealth. Other than Traveler and Estus, they allowed no one to enter their domain.

The three of them immediately noticed the giant chest of blackened wood with a dark metal lock. The väki alternated from looking at them and nervously watching the chest.

"How did the chest breach your magical barriers?" Traveler asked them.

"We looked one moment and it was there," one of the väki said.

"Did you open it?" Traveler asked.

"We were unable to pry it open."

"Lady Aylen, touch the lock with your hand," Traveler said.

Before her hand even rested on the metal it popped open. The chest was overflowing with huge leather-bound books. The women stepped closer and stared at the books. Traveler could see the sense of being overwhelming their faces.

"What language are they in?" Lady Aylen asked.

"Whatever language you read is the one they will be in when you open the first one."

Traveler looked at the väki. "We need the chest to remain under your protection. The women will come here to study every change they get."

The väki frowned in disgust.

"We do not want them here!" one said. "Humans, elves. No."

"What if we have the brownies bring in one of those huts they made into this realm for them to use?"

The väki stared at him, frowning.

"They will promise not to talk to you."

The väki shook their heads.

"Lady Aylen. Maiden Gwyness. Return to the main realm and let me speak to them privately."

The chest closed by itself as soon as the women stepped back. They headed for the magic doorway and disappeared.

"Should I be worried?" Traveler asked them sternly.

"The magic got into the realm, not the vaults. Worry not."

"The one who did it was an ancient being of extremely long life, the servant of a celestial elfin queen, also older than probably any elf I have ever met. The ancient told us that he was more than a wizard but a spell-talker."

"Helmet secured to his neck."

"You saw him."

"We see everything that could be a danger to our realm."

"Is this not the second spell-talker the caravan encountered?" another väki asked, but it wasn't a question.

"Yes, but he didn't come to kill us. He was sent to help."

"You have your answer."

"What answer?"

"Celestial elves sent the first one."

Traveler remained quiet.

"There are celestial elves at Atlantea."

"And their allies."

"Our service to the caravan ceases the moment we reach the borders of Atlantea."

"You will not remain with the caravan?"

"Väki are simple people. We go for treasure. You go there for other reasons. I have been in the world longer than ten generations of you humans and have never encountered a spell-talker. Then we meet you, human, and now we have encountered two."

"One."

"Two."

"He was an ally."

"Two! Spell-talkers are allies to only those they serve, no others. They are dangerous beings. My advice to you is to ensure you never meet one ever again in your life."

"You protect our weapons and wealth. I will get us to Atlantea."

"You humans, elves, drows, you play at dangerous games."

"No one is playing at games here."

"Go away. You are keeping us from our work. You can play your games outside our realm."

"The women will use your realm so they can study under your protection," Traveler said to them.

The väki left the caravan master there as they disappeared into their mountain cave for the castle within. Traveler sighed.

The Old One had summoned him from his rest, but he hadn't recovered fully from the attack on their pocket-realm. The Old One also hinted that they might see him again—if they survived their journey through Titan's Trail. It's curious that the ancient mentioned the number three. If they ever saw him again, it would be the third time they encountered a spell-talker, likely not a good thing.

Gresham walked through one row to another of men in large multiple tents. Humans in one set of tents, the hoofed fae—elaphines, cervids, and rusines—in another. He felt sad for the hoofed fae who did not do well with such stress. All the other fae had fully recovered. Most of the animals also hadn't recovered, but the fauns tended to them with the animal men.

"Mr. Gresham." Traveler stepped into the human tents. "How are you doing?"

"Mr. Traveler, all is under control. The men only need plenty of rest."

Traveler noticed that he had several more lads to assist him in the healing tents to serve water and light food when needed.

"Mr. Traveler, if I may suggest, you look to need some sleep yourself."

The dog was behind his master, watching carefully.

"Mr. Gresham, I will not argue. How are the hoofed fae?"

"Nervous and scared. Even the stronger elaphines."

"They need to be fully aware of their surroundings at all times. If not, they shut down."

Traveler walked back out and across to the tents with the hoofed fae. In the human tents, the men lay on the ground in their giant-slippers or sleeping rugs. By contrast, hoofed fae sat in small groups closely together. Inside, the large tent was dimly lit with only one torch hanging from the center of the tent, but that was how they preferred it. Most appeared as only silhouettes to the human eye, the elaphines with their antlers in the center, the cervids and rusines around them. All of their eyes were on him when he entered with the dog. The caravan master made eye contact with them, nodding.

"Strag, I need to rest," Traveler called out. "Can I rest here? My dog can guard the entrance."

After a moment, he saw the elaphine with his large antlers nod.

Traveler lay on the ground. He settled on his back and could already feel his eyes growing heavy. The dog moved his head close to Traveler's, watching him. As Traveler fell asleep, the dog lay down beside him and watched the entrance.

Gresham peeked in.

"Mr. Traveler, I was told about your healing technique of boiling vapor producing herbs and powders in a pot filled with water."

Traveler, eyes closed, smiled. "Have you been speaking to the princess?"

"Our fauness, Zefea. She said you are the resident expert."

"All we need is a full night of sleep, Mr. Gresham. Find our musicians. Their music playing in the distance will help, especially for our hoofed fae here."

"I'll have Mr. Hobbs get you your sleeping rug, too, if your dog will let me near you."

"Thank you, Mr. Gresham. You're settling into your healer duties nicely."

"I have a ways to go, but thank you for saying so, sir."

As the caravan's healer returned to the human tents, the dog transformed into a giant frog-like animal with large antlers. It sat in front of the door to block anyone else from entering. The fae whispered behind him, making the dog glance back at them. The hoofed fae were grinning at him.

Nirgund the king's guardsman, gestured for the two men to enter the royal tent. The entrance was larger than usual, so both Ethor, the woodland elf chieftain, and Dr'as, the drow leader, could step in at the same time. King Aereth stood in the center of his tent to greet the men with a nod.

"I do know that the protocol of your races makes this gathering inappropriate. So, we will talk amongst each other. You can speak to me. You both have knowledge I do not. It is not fair to our caravan master to shoulder the burden of all the dangers around us alone. We are leaders among our people with vast knowledge and experience. We must help. The behavior of these goblins concerns me.”

“Why, King Aereth?” Ethor asked.

“Mr. Traveler endeavors to lead them into a trap. I feel we may already be heading into a trap of these goblins’ making. His darklings found a weeks’ old hobgoblin corpse. Was it from the same goblin war party? A different one? Their allies?”

Dr’as nodded. “I agree fully with our vanguard leader. It’s not wise to have them about us. The Great Forest has danger enough without their additional plotting from the shadows.”

“It sounds as if you are suggesting we seek them out and attack,” the king said.

“I would never suggest something so bold when we know so little of these goblins’ forces, and fight in lands not our own. Drows are cautious and suspicious people. We would wait until we had the advantage. High goblins are not foolish.”

“We shouldn’t engage them at all,” Ethor said. “If Master Traveler can lead them into a trap or we can widen our lead from them, we should ignore them. A battle would risk loss of life we cannot afford. We’ve come too far.”

“I am nervous about them.”

"Because you do not understand," Ethor said.

"They're goblins," Dr'as said.

"Both your counsel is correct, of course. We do not know where they are, how many of them there are, what weapons they may have, what animals, what wizards. What gnaws at me is that they're not scared."

"What do mean?" Dr'as asked.

"Why are they not scared or even the least bit wary of the Forest? Our own Mr. Traveler has been here many times, but we observe his respect for the danger of the Forest, and he never lets us forget it. He carries with him the horrors of the friends and comrades he lost within this domain. These goblins move about within it without care."

"I understand your concern," Ethor said. "I will talk it over with my elves. They have had more dealings with goblins than my woodland elves."

"I will speak with the fae-bloods," Dr'as said. "They have a history and hatred for goblins deeper than any of us."

"Very good. With all of us working on the problem, we shall find the answers we seek."

Taylos, the desert elf, read from the journal. "Fear of the Forest among all fae dates back eons for just reason. To birth all the races of the fae, more numerous than could ever be counted, such a place would have to be the ultimate well of both life and death. We are not hunters here. We're the prey. The Great Forest is a place where every moment something is killing or being killed, something is eating prey or being eaten. The cycle of life in the Forest takes on titanic proportions. The horrific nature of the Great Forest is that every step forward condemns the elf to that unwavering fate. One becomes a part of the cosmic cycle of life without consent and without exception. The only way not to die is to kill and do so over and over. For that reason, no sane elf, or any sane being, can trespass through the Forest without going a bit mad or dying."

Taylos closed the journal.

The elves had gathered in Chief Ethor's tent—woodland, high, desert, and moon elves. Lyre, Taylos, and Shadu-mun, the leaders of the elfin questing knights, sat in chairs across from the chief. All other elves stood in a circle around them.

"Do you have doubts of our human caravan master?" Ethor asked.

"None at all," Lyre said. "You can see in his being the impact of this Great Forest on his soul. There is no lie in his words when he says he has been through more than once. I would say several times. We are in good hands with him as our guide. He not only has traveled through the Forest but knows a myriad of ways to ensure his caravan travels from end to end alive."

"What of your journal, Mr. Taylos?" Ethor asked Taylos.

"The last attempted caravan of my kingdom of Falconbright, the last time desert elves attempted the insane journey, my grandfather was its lead knight. He kept a journal of the experiences. They abandoned the journey only seven days in but lost nearly three fourths of the caravan's elves, some of our best knights in the kingdom at the time."

"You're concerned that we parted from the Atlas turtles," Ethor said.

"We have faith in our caravan master to lead us and faith in the ability of the Tree Shepherds' crawling trees to shield our elves on the march, but—" Taylos began.

"That giant," Lyre said, "was so powerful with magic that every elf in the caravan could feel his presence. He came all this way to seek out the one elf who is barely an elf. Why would he do that? We have nothing against the Lady Aylen, but it's obvious there are forces at work around us that we do not fully understand."

"The giant is a servant of the celestial elves," Shadu-mun said. "Our enemies."

"I met with the human king before," Ethor said.

"A human worthy of respect. Not like other human royals we have encountered. He does not regard himself above other humans, does not endlessly chase after human females for nightly liaisons, and is not shy about taking up a blade to join the battle. A true leader. I would say he is more elf than the princess," Lyre said.

The elves laughed to themselves.

"We should not discount the water elfess," Ethor said. "Her value will become clear after we leave the Forest."

"If we leave the Forest," Taylos said.

"The meeting I had with the human king was to discuss our joint suspicions about these goblins. I agree with him that their actions, their intentions are not clear."

"If our human caravan master cannot lead them into a trap, we may be forced to seek them out to destroy them," Shadu-mun said. "We cannot allow them to track us on the Trail."

"Ethor, do you not have any power with this forest?" Lyre asked.

"Woodland elves have some connection with jungles but it is limited. Within this Great Forest, it's more that it has influence over us than the reverse. Its magic power is like trying to stare at the sun without end. All that results in the end is blindness."

"That dwelf has forest elves," Taylos said.

"I see why our human berserker man-at-arms doesn't care for him and his own elves. Notice how his elves do not ever convene with us. There is a secrecy and selfishness to them all. They are here to benefit themselves only," Shadu-mun said.

"The dwelf chose wisely—the savage elves to cross through Faë-Land, the forest elves for the Great Forest, the mountain elves for the mountains outside Atlantea for their secret treasures," Ethor said. "But the dwelf's forest elves have been quiet because the advantage they thought they would have within the Forest has not manifested itself. The Great Forest is too powerful for any elf or fairy. Even the leshy cannot use their powers to speak to the trees. The trees here are too large and too old to even know the words of the leshy, if they can hear them at all. We must leave it to our human caravan master, but we must give him all the aid he needs."

The other elves nodded.

"The human berserker has been training his men hard. We should do the same," Taylos said.

"What of the humans' weaponsmaster?" Ethor asked. "We have great weapons, but perhaps there are weapons within his vault that may be of interest."

"The Xenhelmians did steal it from our lands," Shadu-mun said.

"The elfin questing knights will use our respite wisely," Lyre said.

Chief Ethor leaned forward in his chair and waved his hand. A magical map floated above his lap and grew out so the other elfin leaders could see it clearly.

"What I appreciate about our human caravan master is that he knows when to share and when not to. He keeps undo worry from the minds of us all."

"What do you mean, Chief Ethor? What else is there to worry the men about?" Taylos asked.

Ethor smiled. "We have yet to cross into the Great Forest."

The elves stared at him.

"We are in the Forest," Lyre said.

"We are in the outskirts of the Forest, not the Forest itself. That is ahead."

The elves looked at each other.

"Taylos, you should not have read your grandfather's journal to the elves aloud," Ethor said.

Estus's pocket-realm within the main one was a vast plain of golden grass. A small gray castle in the center, encircled by silvery water, housed his magical furnace and smithy. There the caravan master's weaponsmaster and forge worked with his men.

He led all six of the Antaean giants into one of the weapons vaults—Grakdar, their leader, Barg, his number two, and the other four, Arteus, Aronir, Alceir, and Alebar.

"We have weapons," Grakdar told him. "Our war hammers were forged by the dwarves."

"I only ask for you to inspect the weapons we have, a storehouse of weapons made of the best metals of Faë-Land," Estus said.

"As long as it's not goblin," Barg said.

"I will show you the dwarven-made weapons and others."

Estus lead the giants down a wide spiraling staircase from one level to another.

"Here we are," he said. "Watch your heads." The giants had to duck to enter the vault. Magical torches flamed on. The vault was larger, much larger than would seem from outside. Smiles came over the giants' faces.

"These are weapons made for giants," Grakdar said.

The giants slapped Estus on the back—meaning they almost knocked him over multiple times as they stepped into the many racks and tables of weapons larger than any a human male could carry or wield.

"There are so many weapons here to inspect," Grakdar said. "How long can we stay?"

"As long as you need," Estus said. "So the dwarven-forged weapons are closest to the door. Then we have these others, but I am not aware of the metal."

Barg lifted the axe to his teeth and bit down on it. "Elfin."

"Elves make weapons this large?" Estus asked.

"Star or celestial," Grakdar said. "But not for themselves. For their servants."

"Oh."

"They employ many giants too," Grakdar added.

"These here?"

The giants touched the shimmering blades of different colors—white, blue, translucent, dark silver.

"Elemental," Grakdar said.

The giants' complete focus was on the elemental weapons.

"Yes, we will need time to inspect these," the giant leader said.

"Do other fae forge weapons?" Estus asked.

"They do, but there's a reason only a handful are sought by all. They do it better and have been at it for eons."

"I'll leave you here to pick out a new or second weapon." Estus saw that the giants hadn't even heard them. They were already enchanted by the many gigantic weapons all around them.

Drows rarely had large gatherings. They preferred to share information in small groups or whisper magic to pass news amongst themselves. Several drows entered Dr'as's tent where the leader and his daughter waited.

The lead drow, the most accomplished warrior of the drow party, stepped closer.

"You met with the human and elf."

"I met with the human king," Dr'as said.

"We have no quarrel with the elves as long as we are in Titan's Caravan," Dr'amal said to the drow, standing at her father's side.

"Dr'as, we have no quarrel with you," the drow said. "We know that a gifted and renown warrior leader such as you would not pursue any childish drow-elfin alliance even if it included humans."

"We are here for Atlantea," Dr'as said.

The drow nodded.

"I have ancestors who were killed by elves too."

"As long as you do not forget."

"Why would I forget?"

"This is really about me, Father," Dr'amal said. "Out with it. Say what you really want to say."

"Will our great sorceress be aiding the water elf in the future?"

"I helped her use her water elemental powers to benefit us all." Dr'amal had to contain her growing anger.

"I can understand your apprehension about the elves, but hardly her," Dr'as said. "To be blunt, we are more elfin than she is."

"She was raised human," Dr'amal said.

"She's an elf. When we reach the oceans, she will come into the height of her power."

"Meaning what?" Dr'amal asked.

"I merely point out a fact."

"The fact, Dren, is that we have not even begun the journey through the Great Forest, yet you concern yourself with the oceans. Concern yourself with the here and now. Last night another of the Forest's foul creatures could have made a meal of us. There is plenty here for us to guard against. I could ask how such a thing could have happened with us drows on patrol. Did the oversight lie with our drow night patrols or the moon elf sentries?"

"The fault was neither."

"Yet the leshies, sprites, had to save the night."

"What's your point, Dr'as?"

"Maybe if drow and elf would concentrate less on how much they hate each other and more on the task at hand, such a thing would not have occurred. See that it does not reoccur in the future."

Dr'as stepped closer to Dren, face to face. "I care not about what others think of the elves. I do care about the reputation and honor of the D'Shar. When the D'Shar take on a duty, I do not expect for them to be rescued by sprites. You dare challenge me and talk of elves when drows bring shame to the D'Shar and, rather than acknowledge it, feebly try to deflect attention."

"We apologize, Dr'as. Never will it happen again."

"If you feel the night watch is beyond your capabilities, I can speak to the Tree Shepherds and ask if they can replace you."

"We were not the only ones on night watch, Dr'as," another drow said.

"Excuses, is it? In my day, D'Shar would never think to make up an excuse, any excuse, let alone utter one aloud. Not our fault. It was the elves. It was the brownies. It was the phookas. Yes, it was their fault. Maybe I should tell the humans my drows are no longer worthy of the caravan. We were all almost killed, our quest ended, because we were almost bested by some mindless carnivorous tree creature slithering through the Forest, with the first blow not delivered by a drow's blade but by pale-skinned green-bearded leshy! Get out of my tent!"

The drow leader's eyes were white with rage.

"We apologize, Dr'as."

The drows quickly left the tent.

Gwyness sat in the training pocket-realm. The woodland area was encircled by green hills and mountains that came together to form an immense waterfall. The river it created wound around the entire mountain range to shoot off in different directions. The sight of the waterfall gave her a sense of serenity. At her side rested her dual war hammers.

"Maiden Gwyness, no training today?" Pangolin, the berserker, asked.

"Rest was not my intention, Mr. Pangolin, but my body has a mind of its own. My heart is not in it."

"Do your weapons have names? Some warriors name their weapons."

"Soul Strikers. That is their name on a note in the box they were kept in. Me, a warrior."

"Maiden, you seem to be doubting yourself again. We had this discussion before."

"Mr. Pangolin, I am thoroughly overwhelmed. The answers to all our questions sit in a vault in the väki's realm. Book after book of a kingdom no more. Mages, warrior clerics, and seers. We are their legacy. Two women whisked away as infants. How pathetic."

"Not pathetic, maiden. Does Lady Aylen feel the same as you?"

"She pretends not to, but she is as fearful as I. What if we open one of those books and see our parents? Neither of us can remember their faces, their voices, anything about them. Our mothers. Our fathers. Did we have any siblings? It too much for me to handle."

"The books can wait until you're ready."

"That giant you saw."

"What of him?"

"He said he was a spell-talker."

The memory of the last encounter flashed in Pangolin's mind. His face was not happy.

"How was he able to speak to you then? I thought they were demons of a sort."

"He said he spoke in our minds. His helmet was fastened on his head so that he could not use his tongue, but he was not like the other we encountered. That was like an animal with a singular purpose. This one was a person."

"The giant was a servant of a celestial elfin queen. You know what that means. Mr. Traveler already put it to him directly. They had a hand in the death of our birth kingdom, both of them."

"But now they help you."

"He said to make up for their mistake."

"Mistake?"

"They've lived so long. Perhaps that's what happens when you live so long. The wiping out of an entire kingdom, people, families, children, it's all a mistake. But he also said he could not help us further. His queen could not go against the wishes of her kingdom."

"The celestial elves are our enemies then. I have heard our elves speak about them—the high, desert, and moon elves especially. I think they hate each other more than they hate the drows. These fae are as

Mr. Traveler told us—no different than humans. So many different wars against each other. One moment allies, the next blood enemies, but what you say concerns me, maiden."

"Why is that, Mr. Pangolin?"

"Will we not encounter these celestial elves again in Atlantea? With their allies the cloud and star elves."

"I believe Mr. Traveler hates them as much as the other elves, the star elves. He fought them."

"He did. There is much more to the story, and it involves his dog too. When we were in Druid Keep, where we met this celestial elfin queen, she said, 'There will be many who will try to involve us in their affairs.' That is why I am overwhelmed. I am a player in game created by others, rules created by others. I do not know all the other players. The ones I know of, I am absolutely terrified of. How can I battle these forces, Lady Aylen and I?"

"Train, maiden. Pick up your Soul Strikers and train. As warriors, that is why we do so. When the fear comes, as it often does, you will fight with instinct."

"I will train, Mr. Pangolin. But not today. I want to stare at the waterfall and hold to the woman I am for as long as I can before other, dark forces change me into something I do not wish to be."

"You do wish to be it, Maiden Gwyness. That is the fear speaking. You are afraid of failure. But neither you nor Lady Aylen will. I have every confidence in your ability."

Gwyness smiled. "We do not know what my abilities are, Mr. Pangolin. The lady is an elf. I am only a human."

"As am I, but look at all that I can do. You will be the same."

The darklings had left the pocket-realm the night before. All fifty had taken the form of spider monkeys with black eyes and spider legs. They had sensed something within the Forest and decided to investigate, though they also sensed the danger. The leshies had destroyed the killer crawling tree, of a size and form they had never seen before. They even saw the giant with the silver knight's helmet on his head. They watched him with Traveler and the two women. The giant clapped his hand, and a bluish whirlwind engulfed the camp, and they were gone. All that was left was the corpse of the blackish killing tree.

The darklings were ecstatic. A chance to explore the Great Forest on their own. First, to find out what they had sensed. Even at night, the Forest was teeming with life. Giant ants marched along the ground. Giant worms slithered near the base of a mammoth tree. A shriek from above drew their attention, but they did not see the giant bird that went with it—at first. The bird was in the mouth of some shadowy humanoid standing at the top of the trees in the distance. Glowing green eyes stared in their direction as it swallowed the bird.

They had a scent and jumped away after it as a group. They followed after the hobgoblin that disappeared into the brush. When they emerged, from the top of the trees in the night, they were blinded by light. The darklings jumped back into the dense foliage of the trees as darts ripped through the leaves. In moments, they dove for the ground below in the form of black flying squirrels with the heads of cats.

Running along the ground was dangerous. Giant insects and predatory plants were the obstacles they had to run around or jump over. The darklings ran in the night as black rabbit-headed gazelles. Their pursuers grew in number: hobgoblins and trows. The packs of hobgoblins with their razor-sharp teeth, beady eyes, green attire, and pointed green caps the darklings could see even in the night, hurled the darts at them. The trows-- small, ugly, human-sized, troll-like dark fae—followed after the hobgoblins. More and more of them appeared as the chase went on.

The darklings heard noise in the distance, the pounding of humanoid feet running to them, clanking of metal armor and weapons, the growls of giant dire wolfs, the flapping of leathery wings in the sky. The size of the unseen forces nearing was much larger than the hobgoblin and trows.

The darklings jumped off the precipice, transforming into flying black foxes. A giant arm barely missed grabbing them, followed by a roar. The giant forest troll plunged off the side. As the creature's scream abruptly ended with a splat, the darklings burst into cackles. They could see the growing goblin army standing, watching at the cliff's edge. A figure sat on a three-headed beast. A star of bright white light appeared in the goblin rider's hand. The darklings dove again.

The magic star bolt hit above their heads, and a blast blew apart trees all around them. Then the Forest roared. The darklings allowed themselves to fall into a river as it appeared to them that every living thing of the night stopped what it was doing—insect, bird, fish, reptile, amphibian, plant, creature—to attack the goblin army. As fifty black rabbit-headed fish swam away, all they heard were grunts, screams, and explosions behind them.

The darklings climbed ashore and huddled together within a forest of flowers. The night sky flashed with magic lightning. The ground rumbled with the sounds of gigantic creatures joining to the battle.

The entire sky flashed, then came a violent rumble of thunder. The sudden storm opened up with a downpour of stinging rain.

"Master Traveler will find us," one of the scared darklings said. "He will not leave us."

Traveler reached the royal tents. The female half-elves sat around the front of the women's tent chatting and playing with their pack of owl griffins.

"Is the princess in?" he asked.

"The lady does not wish to be disturbed. She's in a mood, Mr. Traveler," one of them said.

"She will have to get over it." He went straight into the women's tent before the guardswomen could object. The dog peeked in at first but decided to remain outside the tent. Lady Aylen lay on her trussing bed staring up at the ceiling of the tent.

"Princess."

"Mr. Traveler, I can recognize your footsteps from a mile away. Barging into the women's tent again?"

"Why are you brooding, princess?"

"I am not brooding. I'm resting."

"May I sit?" He didn't wait for her to answer. He pulled up one of the tent's chairs and sat. "We should talk about our encounter."

"Which one, Mr. Traveler?"

"The only one that matters, princess."

"What is there to talk about?" She sat up in her bed then started to laugh.

"What's funny?"

"I am a noblewoman sitting on top of my bed, talking to a common non-familial man, not in the presence of a female attendant. What will be people say?"

"I will let you worry about that gossip, princess."

"She killed my kingdom, didn't she? The white elfess."

"Likely."

Lady Aylen lay back down on her trussing bed. "Tell me about these celestial elves, these most powerful of all elves."

"Many elves, especially high elves, would strongly disagree."

"I will see to it that I know every elfin race there is before we leave the Great Forest."

"You read my mind. Celestial elves live on the clouds like their star and cloud elf cousins, but they travel beyond the realms of Pan-Earth itself."

"And they destroyed Rivermouth."

"Likely not alone."

"Who knows the full truth?"

"She told us—the air elementals and the Atlanteans. The first you did not know. The latter you did."

"Our simple fabled quest seems to be getting more and more complicated every step we make toward Atlantea."

"Yes, princess."

"Why are you doing this? You lived in Atlantea. You could have stayed there."

"I'm human. I could never live there forever. I stayed longer than I should have."

"Did you not enjoy it?"

"I did, but I wanted to explore more. It's a strange thing. You long to go to a place all your life, reach it, and even live there, and still it becomes commonplace after a time. Whether human or elf or other, it is not our home and never will be."

"I am beginning to feel that this place I have longed for all my life will only lead to my own destruction, just like my lost elfin kingdom."

"That will not happen, princess. You are a member of Titan's Caravan. We will not allow it."

"Thank you, Mr. Traveler. As always, I would never have been able to do this journey without you."

Traveler stood. "You're very welcome, princess. I do hope you and Maiden Gwyness read those books the giant left for you. The white elfess may not have been forthcoming with her entire story, but I do believe she gave you all the knowledge of your lost city of Rivermouth to help you. Whether out of guilt or selfish ulterior motive, it does not matter. It was sincere. I may not trust celestial elves but they do keep their promises when made. Know what lies within the book vault. It's in your care. Then, if you wish, you can lock it up and never look upon it ever again."

King Aereth stepped outside his tent, book in hand, to take a break from studies. Two fireflies appeared in front of him. The fairy sisters appeared in full form. Wildglow was a two-feet-tall fairy, and her younger sister, Sunpetal, was half her size. Both had two antennae poking out from their heads, the taller one with her short blondish hair, translucent insect wings from her back, and a muted ivory frock, the smaller one in her brown half-jacket that had the texture of a woolly caterpillar.

The king smiled at them. Nirgund and his alphyns were training. The women and the female half-elves were also gone from their tent. Hobbs sat outside, smoking his pipe.

"We are ready to fight!" Wildglow announced.

"Not yet. But maybe later on Titan's Walk in the Forest," King Aereth said.

"Forest? We aren't in the Great Forest yet. That's why we were sleeping."

"We aren't in the Great Forest yet?" Hobbs asked. "We've been marching through the Forest for ten days or so."

The fairies laughed. "You know nothing. We haven't reached the Forest yet. This isn't the Great Forest. This is the edge of the Forest only."

The men looked at each other.

"Is that so?" the king asked.

"We'll find Traveler," Wildglow said, and the fairies shrank to firefly form and disappeared as they flew away.

"We are not in the Great Forest, sire," Hobbs said, standing.

"I suppose it makes sense. Weeks to move through the edge of it."

"Sire, where is Mr. Traveler going?" Hobbs noticed the caravan master in the distance at the realm entrance.

King Aereth set his book inside his tent and ran to the commotion at the realm's entrance. Most of the men of the camp were on their feet, watching too. The king felt a presence and turned to see the fae-blood woman, Ursi walking toward him.

"Do you know what's happening, Maiden Ursi?"

"We are in the realm of the Great Forest, king. You must command him not to go."

They had reached the realm's entrance. The elfin knight leaders were yelling at Traveler, clad in his orange-tinged armor, the dog at his side.

"What is it with you and these creatures?" Taylos asked.

"Again, the only reason they were caught outside was because the giant transported us away."

"Life is not fair, Master Traveler. If members of my elfin knights were left behind, I would not expect you to jeopardize this entire caravan by trying to rescue them."

"It's too dangerous," Pangolin said.

"What's happening here?" the king asked.

"Our caravan master is about to leave the pocket-realm to find those disgusting black creatures," Lyre said.

"Master Traveler, you die, we die. You are not expendable!" Taylos said.

"Mr. Traveler, I must strongly concur with the elves. We spoke of this before. We all agreed. You would never leave the caravan again on one of your private excursions. Within the Lands of Man, fine. Within in Faë-Land, it could be forgiven. Not here, before we've even entered the Great Forest."

Many of them gave the king a look.

"We are in the Great Forest, sire," Pangolin said.

"Apparently, we're not, as I have been informed by our two fairy sisters."

"Who knew this?" Pangolin asked.

"We knew," Dr'as the drow said.

"We knew," Ursi said.

"So the drows and fae-blood but not us," Lyre the elf said.

"Master Traveler, you are not to leave here. Whatever you feel you owe these creatures, you must put it out of your mind and forget," Taylos said.

"Men and women!" Traveler's face was stern and unyielding. "We all have our fatal flaws. I am content with mine. As a caravan master, I do not leave behind any member to die—any. That is final!"

Before he could storm off through the barrier, a hand rested on his shoulder. "Then, Mr. Traveler, you should not go alone," Lady Aylen said. "Who among us could be of the most benefit to you and the dog?"

Pangolin looked around. "Mr. Bragg!"

The dwelf hunter stood among the crowd of men and animals. He stepped forward with his metal golem and his elfin hunters.

"What about your jungle elf comrades? If woodland elves are the best trackers in the woods, then would it not be the same for jungle elves in a forest, even this one."

The dwelf and his elves looked at the berserker vanguard leader with hesitation.

"Is something wrong, Mr. Bragg?"

"No, Mr. Pangolin."

"I'm sorry it's not as exciting as hunting a manticore but they can pretend it is. Send them so Mr. Traveler can find the darklings and get back as quickly as possible."

Bragg was visibly not happy, but he glanced at the forest elves and gave them a nod.

Three of the forest elves walked forward. "We need something of theirs to get a scent," said one of the forest elves.

"My dog will do that," Traveler said. "Just watch my back."

The black mice hid in the giant grass, soaking wet and shivering. Their eyes were large watching for any sign of predators.

"Darklings!"

Human mouths appeared on the face of the mice. Big smiles appeared as they raced out. Traveler stood on the back of a giant flying elefantagriff—a griffin with an elephant's head and long tusks, its tough gray skin covered with bright multicolored feathers on the back, around its joint areas, and backside. Three jungle elves stood up too with ten-foot spears, anchoring their balance by holding onto the dog-beast's back.

The black mice transformed into black squirrels and climbed onto the elefantagriff.

"Something comes!" a jungle elf yelled.

The eyes of the jungle elves were fixed on the fast-approaching flock in the distance. Traveler knew that the area was more marshland than jungle and kept his eye on the water. The giant water snake struck so fast that not even the jungle elves had time to react but the creature only bit at the dirty water. The creature had wings. The jungle elves leapt back onto the elefantagriff's back, and they were in the air. Traveler held the mirage staff tight. More giant snakes jumped into the air and again were fooled by the mirage. A gust of wind and as a giant bird snatched one giant snake in mid-air, then grabbed another flying giant snake with its beak. The other flying snakes fled into the trees.

One of the jungle elves pointed toward a swarm of giant mosquitoes in one direction, a towering giant humanoid animal leaping into the sky to grab at a flock of giant birds in another. Flying bees. Flying flowers with tentacle like vines hanging. The jungle elves looked at each other in distress then at the caravan master.

Traveler glanced at the fifty darklings. The black squirrels with smiling human mouths beamed at him. He smiled at them.

CHAPTER FIVE

The Killing Tent

Jungle elves were an elfin race that did not do well in the open sky with their feet not on the ground. With their elfin sight and hearing, they saw every giant animal in sight and heard the sounds of every movement. Traveler let the elves be as he kept his own attention focused ahead. His dog, in its current form, began its descent. Traveler also kept his eyes on the clouds above for any sign of a cloud creature or flying caravan scouts. He saw none. The darklings, clustered together and smiling, remained quiet.

The dead skull hung on its petrified tree ahead. Traveler glanced back at the jungle elves, who were still nervously watching the Forest's life around them.

The caravan master whispered to the darklings. "We're here."

Inside the pocket-realm, most of the caravan waited at its entrance. The external construction of the giant petrified beehive was a lower half mandible that was curved to almost create a natural step up to the eye socket openings of the skull's eyes.

When Traveler appeared, he was covered in moving black armor. His dog followed him then the three jungle elves with their long spears.

Traveler stepped through the entrance first.

A smiling King Aereth greeted him with a firm handshake.

"Welcome back, Mr. Traveler."

"Thank you, sire."

"You found your creatures, Mr. Traveler," Pangolin said.

"I did, Mr. Pangolin." Traveler looked around. "Are we missing people?"

"Yes, Mr. Traveler," Lady Aylen said. "Chief Ethor and the elves decided to do their own scouting."

"Goblins, Mr. Traveler," King Aereth said. "An army of them."

"Where, sire?" Traveler asked.

"They were riding flying giant creatures that looked like bats."

"The elves call them rat-bats, but I have never seen species that are large enough to ride. Goblins use them as hunting swarms. Why did they leave?"

"They would not tell us, Mr. Traveler," Lady Aylen said. "But they seemed quite disturbed by them."

"I know why," Dr'as, the drow, said. "One of the creatures had people chained to their bodies. They looked like elves."

"Chained?" King Aereth asked.

"Captives?" Lady Aylen asked.

"Mr. Hobbs, anything to report?" Traveler asked.

"No, sir. Only the elves are gone from the caravan."

"What should we do, Mr. Traveler?" Pangolin asked.

"Keep your men here to watch for them, Mr. Pangolin. We cannot leave until they return."

"I believe we said that about you," King Aereth said.

"It was a quick excursion without incident, sire." Traveler looked at the jungle elves. "You three follow me to my tent. I want to speak with you."

"Mr. Traveler, did you see any giant animals or creatures?" a smiling Quillen asked.

"Always, Mr. Quillen."

"May I follow along with you to the tent, Mr. Traveler?"

"Do you not have duties to perform, Mr. Quillen?"

"Sir, Mr. Quillen has actually done his duties for the day but not for the night," Hobbs said.

"Oh, Mr. Hobbs, I won't stay long. I promise. I want to add what Mr. Traveler saw to my book."

"Yes, Mr. Quillen. Your bestiary of fantastic beasts, races, and creatures. You are excused, but do not pester Mr. Traveler too long."

The boy smiled.

"Mr. Quillen, you can stop by my tent in an hour. I want to speak with my elfin friends."

"Yes, Mr. Traveler."

"Why do you need to speak with us?" one of the jungle elves asked with a frown.

"Because I'm not happy with you," Traveler said to him. "Follow me."

Traveler led the jungle elves through the crowd of humans, fae, and animals at the caravan entrance for the royal tents. The dog was in his normal form but was larger and more feral in appearance.

"This is unnecessary, human," a jungle elf said. "If you have a quarrel with us, then we'll speak with Mr. Bragg."

"Where is Mr. Bragg?" another forest elf asked looking back at the crowd.

"Elves, no talking and eyes front," Traveler said.

No one was at the royal tents. Traveler stepped into his tent. As the jungle elves stepped in behind him, he moved to light the torch on his table.

"Close the flap please," Traveler said to them.

One of the jungle elves complied. They noticed the caravan master slowly scanning the entire tent with his eyes. After that, Traveler touched every item: the map table, the wooden chests on the ground, his sleeping things in a bundle, the inside of the tent wall, he poked the tent ceiling.

"What are you doing?" a jungle elf asked.

"Where is your dog?" another asked. The jungle elves looked around, but the shape-shifter was not to be seen.

Traveler stepped up close to them. "Listen to me closely. Anything that enters this tent, is to be killed, quickly and before it can yell out. Are jungle elves capable of stealth or are you as bumbling and clumsy as savage elves?"

The jungle elves stared at him without a word.

"You, human, will tell us what is happening this instant, or we will demonstrate our stealth of killing with you."

A smirk came over Traveler's face. "I have killed elves far more capable than the three of you, but I will answer your question."

The jungle elves had forgotten about the darklings until dozens of eyes appeared on Traveler's black armor staring at them. The ferocity in the faces of the elves faded.

"Mr. Traveler!" a smiling Quillen yelled running to Traveler's tent, holding his book with both hands. He burst in, and the flap closed.

"Do not take up all of Mr. Traveler's time!" Hobbs's voice rang out from the camp.

Hobbs made his final rounds through the men. Night camp was being set up ahead of the appearance of the brownies. The steward stood overseeing the lizard minders creating their heat pits for their giant lizards to sleep in. His bodyguards, Tyfer and Oeric joined him. All three men watched the lizard minders work then turned to glance at Traveler's tent.

At the other end of the caravan, Pangolin, the Cut-throats, the fae berserkers and the giants waited at the realm's entrance. The magical sky was changing from day to dusk.

The royals were not at their tents. They gathered with their guards—the female half-elves and Nirgund, with his alphyns—talking quietly. All the other groups of hoofed fae, fauns, and animal men were busy setting up camp. The brownies marched out of their small-realm into the camp, cheerful as always, and already helping tidy up and light the campfires and torches.

King Aereth and Lady Aylen walked to Hobbs.

"Mr. Hobbs."

"Yes, sire?"

"Is Mr. Quillen still in Mr. Traveler's tent?"

"Yes, sire."

"That's strange. I have heard not even a whisper from the tent since he entered."

"I will see, sire."

"No, Mr. Hobbs. Mr. Nirgund can do that. Continue with your duties."

"Yes, sire."

Nirgund reached Traveler's tent with his thirteen reptilian hounds. "Mr. Traveler?"

"Yes, Mr. Nirgund," Traveler's voice called out. "Please, come in."

The berserker royal guardsmen pushed back the flap of the tent. His hounds followed him into the dimly lit tent. Traveler sat at his map table with the three jungle elves on their feet. All of them were leaned over, studying.

"Yes, Mr. Nirgund?"

"Sorry for the intrusion, Mr. Traveler. Mr. Hobbs was inquiring about Mr. Quillen."

"Mr. Quillen? The lad left the tent some time ago. We gave him the descriptions of plenty of giant animals to add to his magic book."

Nirgund looked concerned. "Mr. Quillen has not been seen, sir."

"He did leave the tent, Mr. Nirgund. He's probably questioning someone else in the camp."

"Yes, sir. That must be it. I will let Mr. Hobbs know."

Nirgund excused himself and exited the tent with his reptilian hounds following. The berserker approached the royals, Gwyness, and Hobbs.

"Mr. Hobbs, Mr. Traveler said the boy left the tent already."

Hobbs looked at the others, confused. "Left already?"

Dr'amal, the drow sorceress, appeared. "The boy did not leave the tent," she said.

"Why would they lie?" King Aereth asked.

"What are they doing?" Lady Aylen asked.

"Studying one of the maps," Nirgund replied.

The drowess walked past them. "I will speak with him," she said.

Dr'amal stopped in front of their caravan master's tent. "Mr. Traveler, may I enter?"

"Come in, Dr'amal."

The drowess hesitated. Her face grew suspicious.

The flap of the tent opened. Traveler stood there.

"What do you need, Dr'amal?" he asked. "I need to prepare our path. When the elves return, I want us to be ready to set out. Can we speak in the morning?"

"Yes, of course."

"Good. Mr. Hobbs can tell me when you find Mr. Quillen. I will see you in the morning. I plan to work through the night to prepare."

"Yes."

Traveler disappeared as the tent's flap closed.

Only moments passed, before it was Hobbs standing at the tent again.

"Mr. Traveler."

"Yes, Hobbs," Traveler said from inside. "Did you find Mr. Quillen?"

"The men are still looking, sir. We'll find him, but—"

"Oh, Mr. Hobbs, the lad dropped his magic quill for the book. Here. You can give it to him when you find him."

The tent's flap opened and it was one of the jungle elves. He stepped to the side for the caravan's steward to enter. He saw Mr. Traveler at the map table with the two other jungle elves standing on either side.

"Here, Mr. Hobbs." Traveler held a quill pen in his hand.

Hobbs stepped in and approached. He heard the flap of the tent close, he glanced back. The jungle elf stood quietly at the entrance with a slight smirk on his face.

"Is something wrong, sir?" Hobbs turned his attention.

Hobbs had no time to even scream. Traveler sliced off his head with one stroke. The body fell to the ground. As a translucent fire engulfed the body, Traveler and the elves watched the corpse transform from Hobbs into a goblin.

"Elves, it begins," Traveler said. "I hope you can kill goblins as well as you can hunt creatures."

"Do not worry about us, human. Killing goblins is a skill all elves are born with."

"These are not normal goblins. I hope you sense that."

"We do."

"Darklings, are these the goblins you saw last night?" Traveler asked.

Mouths appeared in the shadows of the tent. "No, Master Traveler."

"Elves, that means those goblins are on their way to our real pocket-realm, if they aren't already there."

"They'll never find it," one jungle elf said.

"The fact that these goblins created this illusion in this pocket-realm proves they know exactly where it is."

"We need to get there," the jungle elf said.

"We need to get out of here first," Traveler said. "Do it now."

"Human, it could bring about the death of all of us."

"If we do not shatter this pocket-realm, we will be dead."

"We should never have left the pocket-realm for your creatures."

"Those creatures are about to save your lives, so shut your mouth, and do what we agreed upon."

As the illusion spell evaporated, giant lizards turned into giant black dire wolves, lizard minders turned into skinny armored goblins. Nirgund ran to the tent with his reptilian hounds. He crashed through the tent's walls slashing it apart with his halberd. He screamed, impaled on the spear of one of the jungle elves. The berserker guardsman body turned into a goblin. The alphyns turned into hobgoblins, immediately flying at the jungle elf, chomping with their razor teeth.

The sound was so loud, a cracking of the earth beneath the feet of everyone in the realm. The ground violently shook, and the sky literally began to fall like large pieces of glass. The one jungle elf was joined by several darklings in the form of human-sized black goblins. The darklings overwhelmed the hobgoblins. Another jungle elf launched his magic spear out of the tent. The one spear became twenty as it flew through the air. The projectiles hit their marks, ripping through the unprotected faces of the six giants standing near Pangolin at the realm's entrance. The giant goblins yelled out as they collapsed. The ground began to break apart. Pangolin roared like a lion, not a human. His eyes were blood-red, and he charged forward.

From within the tent, the single sound of a drum rippled through the realm.

"Stop that sound!" King Aereth yelled, his teeth more like fangs. A battle axe in hand, he led a charge of hundreds of men.

"Traveler!" Lady Aylen yelled.

The caravan master deflected her trident attack from her left hand and jumped back to avoid the thrust from the trident in her right.

"You will never leave here alive!" she yelled with fanged teeth.

Another drum beat rippled through the realm.

Traveler let loose a flurry of low and high cuts and thrusts. Lady Aylen blocked each attack with her dual tridents.

"Know that while we kill you here, we destroy your entire caravan elsewhere," she sneered.

Traveler sensed the presence and flung a dagger behind him. Dr'amal caught his dagger with ease in her hand. Her smile disappeared as an elfin spear burst through her chest. The third jungle elf jumped from the tent to join the fight. The fanged drowess punched the air, and the third jungle elf was knocked off his feet. She pulled the spear from her body and threw it back at the same elf. A black arm grabbed it from the air. Black insect-winged hobgoblins swarmed Dr'amal. She screamed.

Another drum beat rippled. Giant shrieks shook the realm from above. Everyone in the realm could see the shadows of giant flying birds circling.

The battle between Traveler and Lady Aylen intensified. The gobliness grew more frustrated, unable to land a blow.

King Aereth charged Traveler but slipped. Rather than falling down, he fell up.

The pocket-realm continued to disintegrate.

The three jungle elves were clad in living black armor. Lady Aylen and King Aereth were in their true high goblin forms, futilely trying to stay on the ground. Goblin Lady Aylen threw her trident at Traveler. A black hand grabbed it from the air and flung it back. Goblin Lady Aylen blocked it with her other trident. Traveler was also clad in living black armor.

"Why did you do it?" Traveler asked the Lady Aylen and Aereth goblins. "I have never known goblins to enslave themselves to any human. The human Oughtred has so much power over you."

"You killed our father!" goblin Lady Aylen yelled.

"Zem the Beast Lord," Traveler said. "All makes sense. Revenge. The black emotion that has brought about the end to human, elf, drow, and goblin alike."

"Human, I have a gift for you," Goblin Lady Aylen said.

The next drum beat rippled through with double the intensity of the previous ones.

"I have a gift for you too," Traveler said.

The illusion spell was gone. Fauns turned into bugganes, dark sprite shape-shifters that appeared as large humanoids with thick black hair, sharp tusks on the sides of their mouths, and glowing eyes. The deer-like hoofed fae turned into boggarts that looked like ugly hairy humanoids with arms so long they dragged along the ground. Brownies and pech turned into the dark sprites known as bugbears, ten-foot-tall black bears with humanoid noses and faces and blank white eyes. All the animals were dire wolves.

All were falling up in the realm except Traveler and the jungle elves. Swarms of hobgoblins came at them still.

"Ahh!" Pangolin goblin swung his glowing magic axe-mace at Traveler with all the rage magic within his body. The weapon passed through the mirage of Traveler, pulling the goblin to the ground on impact. The pocket-realm shattered.

All fell to the ground. The Pangolin goblin yelled as he got to his feet. A giant flying snake snatched him away and he disappeared into the sky. Goblins and dire wolves battled giant ants for their lives. Giant birds and insects swooped down from the sky to snatch goblins away.

The high goblin King Aereth lost focus for a second. Traveler hacked him apart.

Goblin Lady Aylen screamed at the sight. "Brother!" she called out in goblin.

Her rage grew, but before she could throw her spell at him, smiling black cats were all over her arm and closing her hand.

"What's in your hand?" they asked with cackles. "Is it an evil spell?"

"Off me, pookas!" She sliced at them with the trident in her other hand, but the darklings disappeared.

She turned. Traveler sliced the high gobliness. She fell and immediately was pulled into the ground by the weeds of the Forest.

Even the hobgoblin swarm was destroyed when a giant carnivorous flower swallowed all of them whole.

Traveler and the three jungle elves floated in the air in their living black armor of darklings. The entire goblin war party was gone. Traveler reached into his "armor" and pulled out a telescope. A giant flying ant flew through their mirage as Traveler peered through the telescope. He looked all around, his body turning in a circle.

He saw the goblin wizard floating before them. A high goblin in regal robes more fitting of an elf than a goblin. His eyes were black, and a white streak parted his hair.

"We may have failed, but the brother of Zem will not," the goblin wizard said.

"We are Titan's Caravan, so your failure is assured," Traveler said defiantly.

The goblin wizard stared at him. "Are you certain?"

"Your illusion spell was perfect, if only you knew how to mimic elves with your magic or knew of kirins. I know you've already fled and we're looking at another illusion spell."

"I know you have already fled too. After all, your dog is not here."

"I am going to remember you, goblin wizard. Make sure I never see you again in your wretched life, or you will join your masters in death. In fact, knowing the ways of goblins, I will not wait. Goblins have many, many enemies and unlike elves and drows, I have no qualms in tasking them to hunt you down, as you attempted to hunt us."

The goblin wizard laughed. "Our goblin lands are vast. You do not even know which is our kingdom, and we have many, many allies."

"When we get to Atlantea, I will tell them of the goblin kingdom of Fearlock. Maybe they will drop a star from the heavens onto your monstrous island stronghold and send it to the bottom of the Goblin Sea. Until then, goblin wizard Alwing."

The goblin wizard's eyes teared up as his illusion spell faded away.

Traveler and the elves had already blinked away. Nothing remained of the goblin camp—no goblin, creatures, weapon, or item. All was gone.

CHAPTER SIX

Green Illusions

"Traveler is here!" Elman, the half-elf, yelled out from his perch in the sole crawling tree at the realm's entrance.

Hobbs could hear, and feel, the excitement of the men in the pocket-realm grow at the news. He ran from where he, Tyfer, and Oeric had sat for a quick bite to eat. Men always liked to eat when waiting—or sleep. His short legs took him through human and pech, then the animal men, Cut-throats, and the elves, royals, and leadership right at the realm entrance. The drowess, with her cloak over her head, and the fae-blood, Ursi, hadn't left their sentry post there since Traveler, the dog, and the three jungle elves left.

"Right behind you, Mr. Hobbs." The steward turned to see the dwelf walking fast after him with Glog and his elves, following.

Traveler appeared, walking up the mandible step of the dead skull. The dog and three jungle elves followed. The realm entrance was invisible to the outside unless those inside wished it to be seen to visitors outside. Bragg reached it and smiled at his three jungle elf comrades walking with their long spears.

"Welcome back, Mr. Traveler," a smiling King Aereth greeted.

"Thank you, sire."

"Your creatures are not among you, Mr. Traveler," Lyre called out.

"Sadly, no," Traveler said. "We lost their trail. We had to abandon the search. It was too dangerous to continue."

Hobbs pulled a small wooden wand from his tunic's pocket and tapped the threshold of the realm doorway. A brief flash of yellow.

"Sir, I would not want you to say I was neglecting my duties."

Traveler seemed good natured as he neared the realm entrance. "You are the caravan's able steward,

Mr. Hobbs. No one would ever accuse you of not doing your duties. Invite us in."

Hobbs paused. "Sir, you know how to pass through."

Traveler stopped at the threshold. "Invite us in, Mr. Hobbs. I feel saddened that we couldn't find them. Darklings are resourceful though. They will find their way back to Faë-Land if they are unable to make their way to us before we set out."

Hobbs remained quiet.

Traveler and the elves stared back at him. The dog stood still like a statue.

"Come through, sir," Hobbs said.

Traveler looked up at the top of the entrance door. They seemed unable to move even an inch forward.

"Invite us in, Mr. Hobbs."

"I cannot do that, sir."

Traveler smiled. He looked at the opening and touched the invisible barrier. A muffled sound.

Lady Aylen's face went pale. She glanced at Gwyness next to her. The maiden was holding the amulet around her neck in her right hand. The princess could see the faint glow. Lady Aylen returned her attention to the realm entrance.

Traveler and the jungle elves stepped back. The dog followed them. Bragg the dwelf yelled something in elvish to the jungle elves, but they didn't respond.

"We are Valravn. When we kill a prey," Traveler said, "we absorb all that they are, their appearances, their abilities. They are dead, but we live instead. Hide in your realm. We will return shortly."

Traveler, the jungle elves, and the dog stepped over the edge of the dead skull beehive.

No one spoke, paralyzed by shock. Tears streamed down the faces of Lady Aylen, Hobbs, and many of the men. The enormity of the emotions, their caravan master was dead, the realization that none of them would continue with the quest, was too much for some. Hobbs felt his legs buckling and knelt to steady himself.

"What are Valravn?" Pangolin asked aloud.

"They were not valravn," Dr'amal replied.

"What is a valravn?"

"They are supernatural beings, often in the form of black ravens. They feed on corpses and are said to assume the form and knowledge of those that they feed on," the drowess said. "But they were not that."

"What were they?" Pangolin asked.

"Goblins," Lady Aylen, Lyre, the elf, and Dr'amal said at the same time.

"How did they find us?" King Aereth asked.

"Is it true what they said? They killed Mr. Traveler and the elves?" Lady Aylen asked.

"And the dog too? Impossible. No, they are lying," Pangolin said. "Mr. Traveler is alive and the dog and Bragg's elves."

"They are not my elves. They are my comrades," Bragg said.

"I apologize," Pangolin said.

"Wait here," Taylos said. He summoned one of his giant falcons. He said something in elvish to it and released it.

In the distance of the pocket-realm, they saw the silhouettes of a small party.

"Who are they?" King Aereth asked.

"The kilmoulis," Lyre replied.

The falcons landed near them and, after a moment, returned to Taylos. Elf and falcon spoke. Immediately there was a reaction from the elves and Bragg the dwelf.

"What?" King Aereth asked.

"The goblin caravan we knew was ahead us in the Forest, it is more than a caravan. It's an army. But not just of goblins. All their dark allies too. And below us, they wait," Taylos said.

"Can they breach our pocket-realm?" Pangolin asked.

"Possibly," Taylos said.

"Especially knowing we're here and, thanks to falling for their deception, exactly where the entrance is," Lyre said.

Pangolin pointed to the berserker, I'wulf. The man followed the vanguard leader as he stormed off in the direction of the sleeping giants. The Cut-throats and fae-berserkers followed en masse.

"We prepare for battle, king," Chief Ethor said to King Aereth. The woodland elf gathered his elves and the elfin questing knights.

"We have a serious problem," Dr'amal said. "If they attack the dead skull, dislodge us from this petrified tree, or destroy the tree from the base, we will fall more than one hundred feet."

"But we would be unaffected by that fall," Chief Ethor said.

"We do not know that for certain, chief. Remember what happened when that crawling tree creature attacked our pocket-realm. That was a fall from a far shorter distance, and look what it did to us, and it destroyed the pocket-realm."

The view outside the realm entrance shook, startling everyone.

"They've started," an elf said.

She saw it before everyone else. "What is that?" Gwyness called out.

A small black wren floated in front of the realm entrance. They all saw its smiling human mouth.

Traveler peered through his telescope then handed it to one of the jungle elves beside him. They all lay on their chests high above on the edge of a mammoth tree's giant branch. A quarter of a mile away on the ground, a ferocious tarasque, twice the size of an elephant, charged the tree. Another beast was held at bay by goblin warriors nearby.

"What are they doing?" the jungle elf asked. "The beast isn't powerful enough to knock the tree over, as petrified as it is."

"The goblins don't want to knock over the tree. They want our caravan to panic and do something foolish, like leave the pocket-realm."

"Yes, foolish. No one in our caravan is that foolish," the jungle elf said with deep sarcasm.

"You can make whatever snide comments you want, but I would have done the same, even if it were you out there, stranded in the Forest."

"You, don't like us much, human."

"I like jungle elves fine. I've met many noble clans in my travels, but I am sure all of them would have as much disdain for you, as I do. You are nothing more than marauders."

"We came to your aid, did we not?"

"Yes, you quickly volunteered for the duty. You should not feel slighted. I don't dislike you as much as star elves."

Traveler reached for his telescope from the jungle elves. He looked. "Their illusion spell fades." He handed it back to the elves. "That is not a goblin caravan. That is an army."

"They have Redcaps," the other jungle elf said.

"Goblin armies always have much more hidden from view," Traveler said.

"What is your plan, human?" the jungle elf asked.

"We need to avoid this battle."

"How? The battle is inevitable."

"Do you want to stay here and spend weeks and months in battle, attracting every giant animal and creature to us from leagues away? You saw what happened to the other goblins. If there is a battle, then it's highly possible none of us will walk away from here. We can defeat the goblins. We cannot defeat the Great Forest. No one can."

"We can agree to argue another time." The jungle elf handed the telescope to his comrade. "But we are not powerful enough to take on a goblin army of that size, even with your shape-shifter."

They took turns looking through it. "Human, if you know of a way to avoid this, then do it," one jungle elf said.

Now both tarasques butted the base of the mammoth petrified tree with their foreheads. Each time, decaying pieces fell to the ground. Once piece fell that was so large, it crushed two of the beasts' goblin minders.

"Move them away!" the goblin general said. He sat on his three-headed dire wolf.

Behind him, in the front column sat hooded high goblins on dire wolfs—assassins, warriors, and wizards. Around them stood four green ogre-like giants in full goblin armor, sledgehammers in their hands.

Thousands of brutish, green-skinned, muscle-bound goblin warriors with their big noses, and pointy ears. Heavily armed, they stood at attention with spiked maces, battle axes, and spiked war hammers, crushing axes, and short morning stars. Behind them were goblin crossbowmen on the backs of dire wolfs.

Behind them were Redcaps. Humanoids with long, sharp teeth, skinny fingers ending in talons like eagles, large fiery-red eyes, grisly hair streaming down their shoulders, iron boots, and a red cap on their heads. In their hands, were crimson-tipped pike poles.

Hundreds of dark sprites followed: bugganes, dark sprite shape-shifters that appeared as a large humanoids with thick black hair, sharp tusks on the sides of their mouths, and glowing eyes; boggarts that looked like ugly hairy humanoids with arms so long they dragged along the ground; and bugbears, ten-foot black bears with humanoid noses and faces, and blank white eyes.

Then were thousands of trows, the small, ugly troll-like creatures of short stature. Encircling the entire army were the diminutive hobgoblins in formation as far as one could see into the Forest.

The goblin front column noticed immediately. The general gave a signal, and the goblin minders stopped charging the tarasques at the petrified tree. The human, Traveler, sat on a gray dog-headed griffin. Encircling him were dozens of black goat-headed humanoids with long clawed fingers and glistening teeth similar to the hobgoblins.

One of the darklings appeared in front of the goblin general. Goblin warriors rushed forward, but the general raised a hand and they stopped.

"Do you command these goblins?" the darkling asked.

"I am General Gorg, animal."

"My master wishes to speak with you alone."

"Why should I?"

"Is a great goblin general such as you afraid to speak with a human?"

"A human who sits upon a shape-shifting animal."

"If you don't harm my master, his beast will not harm you. If he wanted to attack, he would have done so. A few words with my master would not hurt such a great goblin general like you."

"There are fae who say you animals are related to goblinkind. A disgusting notion."

"What should I tell my master, Great Goblin General? You can leave your beast here, and he can leave his there. You can meet in the middle for parley, Great Goblin General."

"Stop saying that. Your mocking tone."

"I do not mock you, Great Goblin General. I humbly revere your greatness."

The high goblin sneered and, in a huff, dismounted from his cerberus beast.

"No, General. You must not," one of his wizards said. "It's a trap."

The goblin general looked at him. "If it is, then free me when sprung. That's why you are alive, to serve me."

The goblin general approached. Traveler jumped down from his mount and walked to him as well. Human and goblin met in the middle.

"I would have said you're a brave human to do what you did, but there's no need. Your presence here means our little trick failed. Did any survive?"

"None."

"My father, my king. My sister and brother. Tell me, human, what do you think will happen here?"

"Your father, your king, tried to kill me. What did you think would happen? I am not here to speak about the past but of the future, the immediate future. As impressive as you think your forces are, you will never defeat Titan's Caravan. Yes, you could delay us a very long time, kill many, but win in the end? No. You know it, and I know it. All that would accomplish would be to give the Forest a chance to kill us all."

"I would be satisfied with that."

"You would begin a fight where you and all your men would be slaughtered? You must not be a good general. Since you do this out of blind revenge, you're a waste of my time. Turn back, take your men, your creatures, and return to your lands to fight another day. That is the only outcome where you can win."

"We are goblins and do not take commands from humans."

"I am a human. I am not the elves. You have no blood oath to make war on us without exception. Go home."

"My goblins would never agree. They would sooner kill me than turn from this battle to avenge their king."

"Then let them fight. Let those who wish to fight, do so. Lead the rest of your army back home to Faë-Land. Go home. I am giving you a way out. No elf, drow, or any other in my caravan would give you this consideration."

"Then why do you?"

"I have no interest in you, goblin. I am only interested in fighting real enemies to the death. You are keeping me from that."

"We must avenge our king."

"What was your king doing collaborating with elves?"

"He did no such thing!"

"Goblins, like elves, are not the big happy family they would like all humans to believe. What would happen if goblins, allies and enemies, learned of your collaboration with elves? Common goblins do not trust high goblins to begin with. If they were to learn of this, elves and your personal revenge against my caravan would be the least of your concerns. Do not make the same mistake a kingdom of star elves made with me. They crossed me, and I personally led their enemies to wipe them from existence. You already know I am no mere human. If you need a small gesture from me to save face, consider this. If you return to your homelands, with a bit of effort and treachery, I know you are more than capable of becoming its new king, General. Assuming you get there before your other chief goblin wizard."

"I thought you said no one survived."

"No one did survive but goblin wizards are always so slippery, sneaking away before the battle is done. Do I need to say any more?"

"No."

"What is your decision?"

"I cannot find fault with your argument. I will return."

"Then return to Fearlock."

The goblin general's face contorted.

"So you know our goblin kingdom too?"

"I do."

"You've won this round, human, but you will see my people again."

He swiftly turned and walked back to the front of his column. He leapt onto his three-headed wolf.

"We return to our lands!"

"General!" one of the goblin wizards yelled. "Has the human bewitched you?"

The general moved his beast closer to the wizard. "If you wish to fight the humans, then do so. I return to our lands." He looked around. "Those who wish to follow me back to the Goblin Sea, follow! Those who wish to destroy the human and their allies, remain! The wizard is your general!"

"Gorg!" a Redcap yelled. "What of us?"

The Redcap pounded his short pike pole on the ground.

"You will receive your compensation as promised, when you return to the kingdom," the goblin general sneered.

Gorg kicked his three-headed beast and rode off hard. Goblins and creatures looked at each other, then at the goblin leaders at the front of the war party. The army of hobgoblins raced after the goblin general. With their cousins abandoning the fight, all the trows followed too. Bugganes, boggarts, and bugbears ran after them.

"We must fight, or we will lose them all!" a remaining goblin warrior yelled to the front from his dire wolf. He looked at their chief wizard. "You must take command! Our king must be avenged!"

"Then we fight!" the goblin wizard yelled. He led his dire wolf to the Redcaps. "Destroy the human and his animals and I will double your payment!"

The Redcaps nodded.

The goblin warriors on dire wolves yelled out, their axes held high above their heads. Confused goblin warriors began to charge. The goblin minders of the tarasques still did not know which direction to go. The goblin wizard killed two of them with a red fireball from his hand. The remaining goblin warriors jumped on their tarasques and led the beasts into battle.

All the Redcaps were closest to Traveler and charged. Some humans called Redcaps the goblin version of berserkers as they fought with a homicidal rage unlike any average goblin. Traveler ran forth, his magic sword already drawn. He raced forward to meet the Redcaps with his own army of fifty darklings—goat-headed, four arms, razor claws as long as their forearms. The dog raced past them and dove into the ground.

Hobgoblins in the distance heard the goblin war-cries and started to slow down, wondering if they should go back into battle.

Traveler reached the first Redcaps and threw what the goblinoids thought was pixy dust. He slashed his way through them. Neither party struck a fatal blow against the other. Their pike poles were no match for his magic sword, but their clawed talon hands were as dangerous as any fae metal sword. He moved quickly, careful not to engage the Redcaps or the wave of goblin warriors after them. His target was the goblin leaders on their dire wolves. The darklings fought at his side.

"Come, human!" one of the goblin warriors said from his dire wolf.

"I will destroy him!" the goblin wizard raised his hand, red balls of fire growing in his palms. Several elfin spears ripped through his bare palms. He screamed as the magic red fire dropped to the ground and engulfed him and his dire wolf. The giant animal ran off with its goblin wizard rider screaming.

Traveler reached them and killed two goblin warriors before they could jump down from their dire wolf steeds. He was left to fight the dire wolves with his sword.

Giant tentacles pushed through the earth. The tentacles wrapped themselves tightly around the goblins' tarasques, picked them up from the ground, and threw them at the goblins. The goblin leaders were the first to be crushed by their tarasque beasts. The other tarasque was thrown in such a way as to sweep away most of the Redcaps.

Redcaps jumped to their feet, more engaged, but they stopped. Something was wrong. The blood from their caps was dissipating. They dropped their weapons and grabbed their caps, their faces in utter shock. Even with their iron boots, redcaps could run faster than any goblin; and they did, hysterically screaming as their blood–soaked caps disintegrated. The goblinoids ran away in the direction of the goblin general, unable to disappear into invisibility.

The hobgoblins turned back around in the same direction. Tentacles pushed through the ground seemingly everywhere. Goblins had to choose between fighting Traveler, the darklings, and the jungle elves who had joined the battle, be ripped apart or crushed by the land kraken's tentacles, or to flee. All the goblin leaders were dead. The chief goblin wizard was gone. They fled after their general.

The battle was over. Before any of them could relax even a moment, tentacles grabbed Traveler, the darklings, and the elves and pulled them into the ground. Bursting forth from the Forest were giant animal predators that struck fear into the bravest elf or giant. They had wiped away the goblins at fake Dead Skull pocket-realm and would repeat it here. Animals ten feet tall. Animals fifty feet tall. All closed in on the battle that had ended. Insects, reptiles, and birds raced each other for the goblin corpses. The remaining goblins, Redcaps, and dire wolves had no chance at all. The tarasques were mauled and pulled apart by more than one flying ant or bird. Then moving plants and giant mammals joined the frenzy of violence. Giant vultures swooped in.

Titan's Caravan stood at the realm's entrance as a bloodied Traveler stepped across the threshold with the dog. The darklings strolled in after him in the form of black rabbit-headed monkeys. The three dirt-covered jungle elves stepped through after them, immediately greeted by Bragg the dwelf and their mountain and savage elf comrades.

King Aereth greeted Traveler with a firm handshake then an embrace. Pangolin wrapped an arm around the caravan master. Lady Aylen wiped his face and planted a kiss on his cheek. Men applauded then applauded more when Hobbs hugged him.

Traveler looked around. The entire Titan's Caravan were in full battle gear—every human, elf, drow, fae, giant, animal. The two fairy sisters floated in the air with their swarms above them. The king's heavy weapons teams stood ready for battle, their catapults and giant crossbows fitted with new magic projectiles and arrows, courtesy of Mr. Estus.

"You saw it."

"A black wren told us," Lady Aylen said.

Traveler glanced at the smiling darklings.

"We saw all of it, Mr. Traveler," King Aereth said.

"Seems that you didn't need our help after all," Pangolin said with a grin.

Traveler looked at Ursi and nodded. She managed a smile.

"No more distractions or detours," he said. "Mr. Hobbs, we leave for the Great Forest at last."

CHAPTER SEVEN

In a Sea of Trees

Pangolin raised a hand to stop the march of the caravan. The giants stepped forward, and the vanguard leader could see the nervousness in their eyes. The path that they had been walking abruptly ended yards from them. All there was to the naked eye was a sea of green swaying back and forth.

"This is where the Great Forest truly begins," Grakdar said.

"Can you see anything, Mr. Elman?" Pangolin asked.

The half-elf shook his head. "Just green and nothing more, Mr. Pangolin."

Traveler and the royals reached them.

"Look at this sight," King Aereth said. "Magnificent. An ocean of green."

"But at the base of a cliff, sire," Pangolin said. "If this is the Great Forest, I expect it to be nearly as bottomless as the chasm under Titan's Bridge."

"Ah, the land bridge you humans must pass to reach Faë–Land," Grakdar said.

"I hope you aren't going to tell us that we have to scale down a cliff like we had to do back in the Lands of Man, Mr. Traveler," Lady Aylen said.

"We will not need the services of Mr. Estus for this, princess. Mr. Pangolin, lead your men over the edge. Do not slow your pace for an instant. Walk, do not think."

"Walk but do not think, Mr. Traveler? Sounds like another riddle from when we were in the Lands Between."

"The forest is magic, Mr. Pangolin. You will not fall as long as you walk. You will be as an insect crawling down the side of a wall."

"How long is the path, Mr. Traveler?" King Aereth asked.

"Our march will last a few hours to get to the ground below, sire."

"Hours?" Lady Aylen asked.

"Continue on when you're ready, Mr. Pangolin." Traveler turned and led the royals back to the front columns.

The sensation was unnerving at first, literally, walking upright down the side of a giant cliff face. Never was there a feeling of being pulled to the thousands of feet below. After not too long, all in the caravan got used to the cliff wall surface and green tree sky.

"We never got to fully thank you, Mr. Traveler, for using the power of word to avert battle," King Aereth said, his golden kirin walking behind him.

"I have experience speaking to goblins, sire."

"You have the makings of a royal diplomat."

"Hardly, sire. I simply know how to threaten with credibility."

"That is royal diplomacy at its heart. The important point is you averted battle and loss of life and time to allow us to set out on our journey unscathed. You were even able to rescue your...comrades."

Traveler held back a smile. "We will keep the caravan together and tight, sire. I will have Mr. Hobbs create not one circle for camp but a circle within a circle within a circle. The magic of the Forest is stronger than any place we have yet traveled together. The animals and races that live within it are of that powerful magic."

Lady Aylen looked up at the sky. "I can barely see the sky above us. These trees are so tall. We thought the trees before were gigantic. They were sickly saplings compared to these."

"Mr. Traveler," Gwyness began. "This is the real Great Forest?"

"It is all the Great Forest, Maiden Gwyness. We were at the edges of the Forest where most of the giant animals thrive. That is why their concentration is so great. Even they do not travel into the heart of the Forest. The animals are truly gigantic, as are the creatures. We will be able to march normally until we get to the edges again and be faced once again with the concentration of predatory life."

"Is this the most dangerous leg of our journey, Mr. Traveler?" Lady Aylen asked.

"Interesting question to ask, princess. It is all dangerous. That is the mindset you must keep at all times."

"If only it were possible to fly above it all."

"Pondering the flying caravan again, princess? For one, we do not have the money to hire such a flying caravan. It would consume the combined wealth of all of Avalonia. The caravan's money is for entry through Atlantea's gates. I have seen many a person and caravan not have that fee and be turned away without hesitation. Secondly, such flying caravans do not accept humans. For that matter, they don't accept giants, brownies, pech, or much of the fae of our caravan. And they would certainly not accept any elfess who does not speak elvish. They would likely think you to be some manner of shape-shifter or doppelgänger."

"My elvish is getting better, Mr. Traveler."

"We shall see when you speak to another elf rather than a magic book. But no, princess, we stay on the ground. Our journey will be longer, the danger is more, but we control our own affairs."

"Will we take on any other parties into the caravan, Mr. Traveler?"

"Other parties?" King Aereth asked.

The elfin knight leaders and the dwelf, Bragg, had joined the front column for the march down the cliff face.

"No, Mr. Lyre," Traveler replied.

"That is all that concerns us."

"Why not?" Bragg asked. "If we can add to our numbers with others who have made it this far..."

"No, Mr. Bragg. This is our caravan, and no other members will be admitted," Traveler said. "I learned the hard way never to do anything so foolish and deadly ever again. We've had a time together, traveled as a group. I know with certainty that all among us are who and what they say they are. Can we say so with any strangers we stumble upon along the way, Mr. Bragg? Would you allow such strangers to enter the comfort and safety of our pocket-realm? As you sleep soundly in your bed?"

"You do not need to keep talking, Mr. Traveler. As usual you have a great ability to stir fear in a person's gut. First you show me a giant manticore, four times the size of the largest one I've ever encountered. Now you hint at us being murdered in our sleep. No strangers will be admitted."

"I am glad we are all in agreement, human, elf, and dwelf alike."

"Giant manticore?" Quillen asked, hovering behind them with an expression of shock.

For the first time, two of the Tree Shepherds joined the vanguard. As soon as the caravan jumped down to the ground—a strange sensation because it felt like one was jumping up to fall forward—they marched upright on the lush green ground below, Gigantic trees towered above them, wider and taller than any had seen before in the Great Forest. All three of their crawling trees moved along with them—one in the front to shield the vanguard and front column, one in the center of the caravan, and one in the back to protect the rear guard.

"Do you not have any power at all with these trees, Shepherd?" Grakdar the giant asked a leshy.

Greenwig didn't answer immediately. His hoofed feet seemed to glide above the ground. "The trees here are older than my people. We do not know them."

"We giants have heard many stories about the Great Forest. Some good, most are not. Some of our giant kingdoms forbid their people from entering it. Giant creatures seek giants alone to devour."

"Children's stories, Grakdar, to frighten us as babies," Barg said.

"Perhaps."

"Our people have similar stories," Greenwig said. "Great trees of evil that sought out all fae of light and their protectors to destroy. The Forest also fills us with apprehension. Here, neither flora or fauna can hear our words, and we cannot hear theirs. Such a thing for any leshy is unnatural and frightful."

The front column marched a few yards behind the vanguard, noticing that the Tree Shepherds had joined them. The trees were so massive that all felt like ants beside them. Their bark and leaves appeared vibrant, as if new, but they had already been told that the trees had stood for centuries.

"Mr. Traveler," the king's guardsman said as his alphyns playfully walked behind him. "Do you believe the goblins are gone for good?"

"We could only wish," Taylos said under his breath.

"I doubt we will see any on the journey through the Great Forest," the caravan master answered.

"There's a serenity to this part of the Forest, Mr. Traveler. Peaceful," King Aereth said. "You informed us that the horrific predatory life we encountered only reigns along the edges of the Forest. Why do they not go farther? What prevents them?"

"The Forest, sire. It doesn't want them within, so it doesn't allow them."

"Magic, Mr. Traveler?"

"When I first entered the Great Forest as a lad, sire, I asked the same questions. The elves I traveled with wouldn't tell me when I asked, but I learned for myself. All the trees are still, quiet and sleeping."

"Sleeping?"

"Yes, sire. And we do not want to wake them. Let us move along and be gracious passersby without disturbing them."

The humans and elves looked at one another.

Lady Aylen looked at Ursi, the fae-blood, and Dr'amal.

"Do your people know this?" Lady Aylen asked Ursi.

"Yes, we do."

"Drows?"

"Yes, drow-kind do," Dr'amal said.

"Mr. Traveler, could that be the answer to our mystery of the Great Forest?" Lyre asked aloud. "The very trees rise up and smite trespassers."

Traveler shook his head. "The Forest trees are not evil. We are of no concern to them. They sense our presence in a general way, but we are nothing more than a common fly against the back of a roc. We travel in the Great Forest, or as I began to call it when I was here as a lad, the Great, Giant Forests of Horror, with many months to go."

"None of us would complain if our travels remained uneventful," Lady Aylen said.

"We will encounter many beasts, perhaps a fae caravan or two. Yes, there are fae races indigenous to the Great Forest. They hide when outsiders are near, but we may, at the very least, see them. Regardless, we must always be on guard for anything and everything."

Traveler spoke several words to Lady Aylen. The elves burst out laughing.

"Mr. Traveler, that was not funny!" Lady Aylen said. A shocked smile stretched across her face.

"Good, you're understanding common elvish slang, too, and not just the proper, royal phrases."

King Aereth looked at Nirgund and Gwyness. "Appears that we'll need to learn elvish, too, if we want to hear the good jokes."

Ursi lifted her head. She caught a scent in the air. After a moment it was gone.

Night arrived on the Trail, pitch-black all around, but high in the sky, the night peeked through the leaves of the towering trees with a display of stars, shooting stars, and a quarter moon.

More than a few in camp were apprehensive about returning to the pocket-realm, even after the long day's march, but night camp had to be set up. As well as the security of their realm, Hobbs took out his wand to create a circle around the entire camp—a magical barrier around the camp within a hidden pocket-realm. The glow of the circle was visible to all the men as they settled in for the night with their meals and conversations. Others were already fast asleep as the brownies appeared from the small-realm for their nightly duties in managing the camp as the caravan slept.

Quillen showed the two brownies his latest sketch in his magic book. They nodded.

"Redcap. You captured their likeness exactly," Tidycase, the brownie, said.

"Terrible cousin creatures to the goblins," Quietlight, the brownie, said.

"I never heard of them," Quillen said.

"Nor should you. They are a murderous lot. They dye the cloth caps they wear on the tops of their heads with the blood of their victims."

"Oh, no. What happened to them? Mr. Traveler did something to them."

"Our Master Traveler used magic dust to make the blood of their caps disappear into the wind. Without the blood of their caps, they have no power and will scurry away, as they did. Even with their iron boots they can run faster than any man."

"I'd rather fight goblins, then," Quillen said.

Chief Ethor of the woodland elves kept a tent at the opposite end of the night camp where the elfin questing knights, Cut-throats, and giants had their camp. Traveler was led in by a woodland elf with the elfin knight leaders, Lyre, Taylos, and Shadu-mun.

"Greetings, Chief Ethor," Traveler said.

"Master Traveler," said the elf as he stood from his chair, a long pipe in hand.

"Have goblins ever made it to Atlantea that you know of?"

Chief Ethor put his pipe to his lips to inhale. "No. You lived there. Did you ever see one?"

"No, but the goblin general said something to me before he rode off. He said we would see his people again."

"Do you think he plans to return to the Forest to ambush us ahead?" Taylos asked.

"No, he's returning to his goblin city as fast as he is able. No, I feel he is referring to others."

"What do you believe he meant?" Ethor asked Traveler.

"I don't believe he was bluffing or trying to sow confusion or misdirection with lies as goblins like to do. I believe him. There are goblins ahead, somewhere. I wanted you to know."

"Thank you, Master Traveler," Ethor said. "We will ponder the question ourselves too."

"Our kings were wise to send us ahead with your caravan," Lyre said. "If only we had our full army."

"No, we wouldn't want that. We would be denied entrance at Atlantea. We are ready to do battle with any armies and win, but we are not an army. That can never change."

"Yes, agreed," Ethor said.

"Would the Atlanteans allow a goblin...caravan entrance if they had the money?" Lyre asked.

"I would have said no without hesitation, but I'm not so sure now."

"If true, this could be a serious threat to elfinkind," Ethor said. "We do this to secure an alliance for our elfin kingdoms, separate from the sky elves."

"The celestial elves have kept all the elfin races from such an alliance for too long," Lyre said. "But if goblins are involved..."

"Remember what we saw," Shadu-mun said. "Wind elves and high goblins conspiring together."

"Disgusting," Lyre said.

"We appreciate you informing us, Mr. Traveler," Taylos said, extending a hand.

"I know how important this is to you," Traveler said.

"Do we still travel in the shadow of the Four Kings?" Ethor asked. "Or in the shadow of other kings, too, perhaps with celestial elfin blood or even goblin blood."

Quillen saw him and ran full speed to the caravan's vanguard leader.

Pangolin saw the boy and straightened up with his arms folded over his chest.

"No," Pangolin said.

"Mr. Pangolin, I didn't even ask anything."

"You have that infernal magic book in one hand and your sketching pencil in the other. You should be sleeping, not chasing me around in the camp."

"But I didn't have a chance to speak with you before, Mr. Pangolin."

"What is it, then?"

"That killer crawling tree—"

"There it is. You want to draw more creatures in your book. My people call them yateveo, man-eating trees that can move using their branches and roots like tentacles of an octopus. I never saw one so black as night and able to move so fast. Actually, I never saw one in real life before. I read about them in books as a child. No doubt written by people like you. The Tree Shepherds say they come in all sizes and some live in the water."

"In the water? Like oceans."

"Like lakes and rivers to snatch boys like you."

Quillen laughed.

"I'm glad you find this funny."

"I never leave the circle, and I always make sure I stand behind all the warriors."

"Do you now? Well, I'll speak to Mr. I'wulf and tell him that a certain boy will be joining the drills."

"But I have my chores for Mr. Hobbs."

"This certain boy will learn how to kill yateveos on his own."

"I cannot do that, Mr. Pangolin. I draw the creatures we encounter. I do not kill them."

"That's going to change. In fact, Mr. Hobbs needs to be in training."

"Oh, no. Don't do that, Mr. Pangolin. Mr. Hobbs will blame me for you pressing training."

"It will serve as a lesson not to ask me questions."

"You are not very friendly at night, Mr. Pangolin."

"Berserkers are not supposed to be friendly, Mr. Quillen."

When Traveler returned to his tent with his dog, the royals were waiting. All three of their large tents were next to each other. He gestured for them to follow him in. The dog let the royals pass, grudgingly and strolled in last.

"Your dog almost tolerates me now, Mr. Traveler. It occurs to me, when we first met back in the Lands of Man, why he did not like me. He doesn't like elves."

"No, princess, he doesn't like certain races of elves."

"So you've encountered water elves before?"

"It was not a positive experience, princess. Not at the level of star elves, but not much better. However, ignore that. You are not them."

"Thank goodness for that."

"Did the elves have anything to say to your news of the goblin's comment, Mr. Traveler?"

"No, sire. They are aware. If there is anything of value or interest we should know, they will tell us."

"Should we tell the drows?" King Aereth asked.

"No, sire. We don't want to appear to either party that everything said by elves is shared with drows and vice versa. They won't trust us then. If we want to say something to both, then we speak to both at the same time."

"Yes, of course. We must respect the protocol of people, especially when they are not allies."

"Mr. Traveler, should we be worried? We are not there yet, far from it, but it feels like we go to a place where enemies may be waiting," Lady Aylen said. "Possibly, at Atlantea's doors."

"No need to worry, princess. I know something they do not know."

"What is that, Mr. Traveler?"

"I would rather keep it secret for the moment."

"As long as the secret gets us into Atlantea. If we make it all that way, almost a year, and can't cross into Atlantea's gates, our enemies won't have to kill me. I'll simply die of disappointment," Lady Aylen said.

Hobbs made his final round through the camp. Brownies had already lit the camp's torches and magically made all campfires burn brighter. Humans slept in their giant-slippers, all others on their sleeping mats, rugs, or on the green grass of their realm of warm night breezes. Moon elves had already taken their sentry posts. Nearby they could hear the darklings chasing each other around the camp perimeter.

On one side of the camp, the lizard minders had to build large heat pits for their giant lizards. The task took them well into the night to complete before they could turn in themselves.

The male half-elves preferred to sleep in the crawling trees whenever they could. For an unknown reason, they couldn't fall into a normal deep sleep.

I'wulf woke up. He always slept wrapped up in his big bear rug. Immediately, he sat up. One of the nearby giants was grabbing the air above him while asleep. Other giants were mumbling in their sleep.

The entire camp was awoken by screaming—one of the animal men. Moon elves rushed in. Fauns and the deer-like fae were already awake.

Hobbs ran to the center of the camp. Brownies held torches high to add more light.

"What's happening here?" Hobbs asked.

"Who knew animal men had nightmares?" a moon elf said.

"Are they all right?"

"Only nightmares. Nothing more that we can see."

"Mr. Hobbs, get the men back to sleep." Traveler stood beside the steward.

"Yes, sir. Immediately."

The moon elves stepped to Traveler.

"Every elf and fae in the camp either cannot sleep or were having extremely disturbing nightmares. You have been here before. Is this part of the magic of the Great Forest?" a moon elf asked.

"No. This is not the Great Forest," Traveler replied.

"Then, what?"

"Maybe there is someone who can tell us."

Traveler did not need to walk far. At the women's tent, Gwyness stood just inside but he could see the glow of her amulet. He turned, and there was Dr'amal.

"Tomorrow, I want you and Mr. Gresham to gather all the magic-makers in the caravan."

Traveler noticed her father and other drows nearing them.

"Dr'as, is there something you want to tell me?"

"There is another caravan."

"Another?"

"Yes," Dr'as said. "They are passing. This won't happen again."

Traveler stared at them for a moment.

"Night drows."

Dr'as smiled. "You've encountered our cousins?"

"No, but I know of them. Are you in communication with them?"

"We have sent word to them. They travel from the Forest to Faë-Land."

"Why are night drows in the Forest?"

"They wouldn't tell us."

"Why were they using nightmare magic on us?"

"That was unintentional. They sensed elves nearby. Their spells affected all fae, unfortunately."

"For their spells to have worked, to have breached both our pocket-realm and the circle—"

"The problem has been dealt with and was not my daughter's fault, if that's what you were about to suggest."

"Dr'as, whether it was your daughter or your men, what would happen if the caravan was to learn that someone used your people to channel magic into the realm from outside to harm us?"

"The problem has been dealt with. Neither night drow nor drow wizards will be able to repeat the spell again."

"Since all my previous encounters with drows were positive and fruitful, I have to believe that my problems with your clan are unique to the D'Shar. So many levels of secrecy and ages of subterfuge, you have forgotten the simple trait of honesty even among allies. This is very serious."

"We know that," Dr'amal said. "We are also capable of channeling spells through other drow clans. Our point to them was made."

Traveler sighed.

"Maiden Gwyness's amulet was glowing."

"Not because of the night drows."

"Then there is nothing else to be said or done. I will return to my sleep."

The dog watched them, flashed its teeth, then followed after its master.

"The human has clearly lived with drows before," Dr'as said. "He speaks with us much differently than the others, even the elves."

"He talks to us like a drow would," Dr'amal said. "Always annoyed."

"Yes. We may need to have the night drows return so that he knows they were not the source of the human female's amulet glowing."

"The dwelf and the fae-blood, both clans, were the only fae that didn't experience the nightmares last night," Gresham said to Traveler.

Titan's Caravan had set out at first dawn.

"Any similarities among the dreams?"

"Only that they were fears unique to the individual or their race. Understandably, none of the fae were willing to describe the nightmares in detail, especially with a human."

"Thank you, Mr. Gresham."

"I will inform you if I find out anything more."

Gresham dropped back to his post near the center of the caravan.

"Maiden Gwyness, you said your amulet was glowing the same night humans had nightmares?"

"Yes, Mr. Traveler."

"But they weren't nightmares, per se. They were dreams that didn't frighten, at least for me. I cannot put my finger on it."

"More like someone in the dream was communicating with you," Lady Aylen said.

"Yes. That's it exactly, m'lady. What does it mean, Mr. Traveler?" Gwyness asked.

"I am not sure, but we will keep careful watch over them and leave the matter in Mr. Gresham's hands."

"Agreed,"Gresham said.

"We need our caravan master not to be the healer again. Our healer can be the caravan's dream watcher," Lady Aylen said. "Look at that view."

As the caravan marched down a slight incline, before the vibrancy and thickness of the giant leaves, the scene truly looked like a green sea. The leaves moved as waves in the wind, both up and down and from side to side, a splendid sight that went for hours. The passage of the day was hard to judge with the towering trees around them.

Pangolin frequently thought he saw shadows high above them. The Tree Shepherds, the elaphine archer-warriors, and Mr. Elman told him it was simply animals jumping or flying from tree to tree.

One of the four giants grunted as his leg went down into the ground. His fellow giants grabbed and pulled him out of the sinkhole.

"Careful," Grakdar said as he noticed the ground beneath another giant collapse.

The two Tree Shepherds used their walking staffs to tap the ground.

"Much of this ground is filled with depressions under the grass, some very deep. My staff will reveal them."

As the magic of the leshy's staff made the grass turn from green to yellow above each hidden sinkhole, Pangolin noticed the ears of the elaphines fluttering wildly as they looked back and around. They all stopped immediately. Mr. Elman almost yelled out when he saw it.

The giant, monstrous woodpecker hung several dozen feet above an especially pale tree. It had a black body with a muted green head and plumage that matched the color of the Forest. Both its long, sharp chisel-like beak and clawed four-toed feet looked more like leathery metal. When the giant bird resumed pecking the bark with its pointed beak it was at such an intensity that chunks of the tree disintegrated, raining down below and hitting the earth with great thuds. The animal saw them.

"Get away from the tree!" Traveler yelled, running to the vanguard with his sword drawn.

King Aereth took charge, sitting on the back of his golden kirin, moving the main columns away from the trees. The center crawling tree spread out its branches like outstretched hands. The giant woodpecker jumped off the tree and swooped down, ripping through the crawling tree and stabbing down at one of the men in armor. The beast's beak did not penetrate the elfin armor, but it did crush it. The man collapsed to the ground, unable to breathe.

Pech pulled the man away as others hurled boulders at the monstrous bird's head. Its body was impacted by hundreds of arrows, shot from the elaphine archers. Elfin archers joined the fight and fired their arrows at its head. The monstrous bird shook its head and let out a thunderous shriek. Everyone winced from the painful sound.

Dr'amal appeared and created a cloud of purple smoke around it to blind it, but the bird shrieked again and flew through the illusion. Drows appeared everywhere and threw their two–blades at them.

All the elves ceased their arrow attack and stepped back, as the drows fought the bird on top of them. They slashed at it with swords, but its claws, beak and feathers were as solid as elfin metal itself.

One moment the man was on the ground. The next instant he was in the air in clutches of a giant dragonfly. A lightning arrow blasted through it, but the man remained in its legs as the body fell back to the ground.

The caravan found itself surrounded by a swarm of gigantic dragonflies. Arrows were flying from elves, elaphines, and fauns at the giant dragonfly swarm and the giant woodpecker hovering above the men and drows. The Cut-throats joined Pangolin and the giants keeping the monstrous bird at bay.

Two points of light led a swarm of insects from one of the caravan's small-realms up to rescue the falling man. The swarm pulled him from the clutches of the dragonfly corpse and flew him back to the ground, letting the insect corpse fall away.

The fairy sisters grew to humanoid form and commanded their insect swarm into a cyclone to attack the giant woodpecker. The monstrous bird's thunderous shriek made the sisters lose their concentration. Giant dragonflies ate every fairy insect they could. Wildglow and Sunpetal yelled out and commanded their insects back into a solid swarm. For every giant dragonfly that the caravan shot down, two or three seemed to replace them.

Traveler yelled in elvish and another language to the elaphines. All the caravan's archers formed a ring around the caravan. The lizard minders moved their giant lizards in another ring around the caravan to provide cover for the archers and men. Never had humans seen such a display of archery. Elf and elaphine were almost in competition to see which team could fire the most arrows and hit the most targets. A dizzying rain of magic arrows began to decimate the swarm, though the insects kept coming. Each elfin and deer-like fae archer looked as if they were shooting one to two arrows each second, every arrow hitting their mark. The fauns had stopped their arrow assault and were content with watching with smiles. Everyone was amazed.

Lady Aylen wanted to join the battle, dual tridents in hand, but Gwyness and the half-elf guardswomen encircled her and would not let her pass to protect her. Nirgund and his pack of alphyns did the same with King Aereth. The fae humans, Tyfer and Oeric stood close to Hobbs to protect him with their swords in hand.

Outside the circle, Pangolin, the giants, and the Cut-throats continued their attack on the giant woodpecker. The giants struck at the giant woodpecker with their new elemental war hammers but the bird always flew out of reach to dodge the blows. Grakdar threw his. The weapon landed on the bird's head and sent out a blast of hurricane-powered wind that launched the beast into the pale titanic tree it had been pecking, but also hurled the giants farther in the distance. Pangolin only escaped the gust because he stood just below the wave. Before the beast bird had even a second to recover, Pangolin sailed through the air and landed his own blow with his axe-mace. The dead, pale tree shattered, and the monstrous bird fell through, revealing the hollow interior.

The branches of a crawling tree rescued the berserker. The dead tree crumbled and cracked into pieces. All saw why Traveler wanted them away from it. Out spilled giant crawling flies and giant slugs.

"Move!" Traveler yelled. At his side, his dog had taken the form of a hulking humanoid wild cat, whose entire body looked to be made of the same skin as the giant woodpecker's bill and clawed feet.

The living wall of giant lizards with their archers moved as a unit away from the growing filth of giant flies and slugs. Everyone within the circle moved with them.

The dragonfly swarm had flown away as quickly as they first arrived. As pieces of the dead tree crashed to the earth, a dust cloud billowed out. The Tree Shepherds used one crawling tree to carry the wounded one, and the other helped lift up the slowest members of the caravan—human, giant, and pech.

The man Frog-Dor stepped to the center of the caravan and looked up. He drew a line in the sky. The golden arrow that fell from the clouds was almost as large as one of the trees. When it hit the ground, the entire earth opened up and swallowed the giant flies, and slugs, the dead tree, and the giant bird. The dust subsided, and the ground closed up.

CHAPTER EIGHT

The Gaean Party

The man who had been taken by the giant dragonfly had to be submerged naked in a hot bath as his body was infested with large ticks that lived on the body of the insect. The second man who had his elfin armor crushed by the power of the giant woodpecker needed the help of the elves and giants to free him. Both humans were lucky, as was Dr'amal, the drow, who barely escaped the attacking monstrous bird. The humans would be spending their next days in Gresham's healing tent. Dr'amal retired to the drow tent for rest.

The caravan was at a stop. Hobbs had the men set up as if for night camp. They had moved miles away from the battle, but it was not too much after noon. Traveler decided that there would be no more marching for the day. The caravan needed to recover. No one objected.

"The elves and elaphines went through crates of arrows. Crates our giants would call large," Estus said to Traveler. "But they'll be fully replenished by the time we're ready to set out. I now understand how they do it. Their quivers are magic."

"Each is like its own pocket-realm filled with arrows," Traveler said.

"It was an amazing thing to behold. Even the fauns could not compete with the skill of the elves and elaphines in shooting arrows. Centaurs are the same?"

Traveler nodded.

"Do we need to discuss the elves and drows?" Pangolin asked. "The elves stood back when the drows were attacked. Everyone on Titan's Caravan must come to the aid of every other, no matter what discord or hatred their races or kingdoms may have for each other on the outside."

"They will, Mr. Pangolin, but on their own terms. We humans are not going to undo centuries' worth of mistrust and animosity. We will work around it."

"You speak more than just elvish, I see."

"I did live here for a bit."

"I'll see to the defenses. These giant dragonflies are quite the terror."

"The part of the Forest we're in has marshy areas in the region, which are their breeding grounds. We need fae archers ready throughout the camp. The creatures move too fast for the human eye, so any human archers will be useless."

"We were fortunate—no loss of life and no one had to leave the caravan to rescue others."

"Be thankful for our fortunate days."

"I think it's time to pull our poleaxes from the vault for the men, especially. In a giant forest, one doesn't want their enemy to be close enough to reach it with your sword or axe when that enemy is a giant beast," Estus said.

"Which elaphine was the one who shot the magic arrow that saved the man seized by the dragonfly?" Traveler asked.

"One of Strag's two best archers, Aron. Also, our fairy sisters assisted. We were wondering when they would appear."

"The Tree Shepherds have their hands full keeping them occupied. In the Great Forest, they cannot leave the camp to play and fly freely with their swarms. They are just children even though they were both born before our grandfathers."

Both men heard commotion outside.

Everyone in the caravan was looking into the Forest. The sound was that of a low wail. As it went on, it became clear it wasn't a wailing sound. The giant tree was yawning. Its mouth made a few chomping sounds with a visible cavernous mouth. When it closed, the mouth disappeared and the tree returned fully to a tree form rather than a humanoid one.

"Hobbs, the fae already know, but tell all the humans that there is nothing to fear. Seeing a tree yawn isn't unusual here," Traveler said.

Hobbs laughed to himself and moved into the camp to make his rounds and spread the word.

"Killing trees and yawning trees," Pangolin said. "How do you know good from bad trees in this Forest?"

"Well, it's not trying to eat us."

"Quite impressive," Traveler said to Frog-Dor, the wizard.

The man sat quietly in his small tent. Since becoming able to walk without aid, he often preferred to remain alone. He did visit with Gresham in the healing tent but no others. Traveler stepped inside, and he stood from his stool.

"No need to get up, Mr. Frog-Dor. The princess told me you took the initiative to assemble all the magic-makers in the caravan, but it would seem you are more powerful than all of them combined."

The man seemed uncomfortable by the words.

"I will do my best, but I have not used my powers in a long time. I no longer remember what my abilities were."

"No one here will make you do anything you do not want to do. Your curse is lifted, but I know it will remain a constant struggle within you. Whether you feel you are ready or worthy of the position, both human and fae of the caravan will look to you for leadership in matters of magic. It may not be fair to you in your current state, but there it is."

"I understand."

"Your privacy is important, but I don't want anyone to be alone. Would any of the fae camps be suitable for you to make camp with?"

"I will go where you wish."

"In this caravan, you have two extremes, chatty like the pech and silent like the mole-man. Which do you lean toward in terms of your own disposition?"

"I like the calmness of quietude."

"Then let's hide you among those so silent and unassertive that most of the caravan doesn't even remember they are here. Our minders of the kirins, the fenodyree. Very calm, good-natured people."

"Yes, I would like that."

"I know the healing tent with Mr. Gresham has been very busy of late. With the kirins spending more and more time with their masters, the fenodyree will welcome the company."

"Thank you, Mr. Traveler."

"No, thank you. You successfully defended Titan's Caravan again. You are a valued member and should be treated as such."

The women's large tent was for the princess, her maiden, and the female half-elves. One of the female half-elves counted out loud to make sure all the little owl griffins were inside the tent before she closed it. She saw the drowess, Dr'amal, at the entrance.

"May I speak to Lady Aylen before you turn in for the night?"

"Yes, Dr'amal," Lady Aylen said from her trussing bed, where she read from her magic teaching book.

"May I borrow your maiden for a moment."

"Borrow? Why?"

"It will not be long," Dr'amal said.

Gwyness looked at the princess then put on a robe. "I will go, m'lady."

"Will you not tell me where and why, Dr'amal?"

"I prefer, Lady Aylen, to allow my leader to inform you of that."

"You mean your father. My maiden is meeting your drow leader, but you will not tell me why."

"She will be well looked after."

Gwyness followed Dr'amal to the only drow tent set up. Drows were gathered in small groups around campfires. Gwyness followed as the drowess stepped inside. Inside, Dr'as stood with Traveler.

"Mr. Traveler," Gwyness said.

Dr'as approached her. "Before we begin, I must swear you to secrecy."

"Secrecy about what matter?" Gwyness asked the drow leader.

"About what you will see and learn here in the tent. Drowkind are very private people. We keep to ourselves, and we do not like to bring outsiders into our business. Do you know much about drows?"

"I know nothing about drows other than you have dark–bluish skin and we're never to call you elves if I want to live."

Dr'as laughed. Gwyness saw that there were other drows besides Dr'amal in the tent with them.

"Very simplistic understanding, but it will do." Dr'as walked to the fire in the center of the tent.

"Maiden, there many, many clans in drowkind. There are even different races among the drow. One prominent race are night drows."

"The ones responsible for the nightmare spell on the fae?" Gwyness asked.

"The very same ones."

"The spell did not work on Mr. Bragg or the fae-bloods."

"They are fae separated from general fae races long, long time ago. I am going to summon the night drows so we may speak with them."

"You can do that?"

"With magic, you can do most things. The important thing for you to remember is that night drows do not like or trust anyone, even drows. Many find them arrogant and duplicitous, and we do not disagree. They speak with us only because we are drow, but we can expect no other consideration from them. The reason for your presence will become evident."

The spell created a mirror of blue glass. Dr'amal stood on one side of Dr'as, Traveler on the other. Gwyness stood behind them. A purple flame flickered, then the image of a purple-skinned drow sitting crossed-legged appeared before them. His eyes were all white.

"Dr'as," the purple-skinned drow said.

"Vrinn," Dr'as said with a false smile.

"Why have you summoned me again? I thought we said everything we needed to last night."

"We never got a chance for a simple chat."

"Which was intentional."

Dr'as looked at Traveler. "Vrinn and I are longtime allies. Ask him your questions."

"What title should I address you with?" Traveler asked.

"First, a drow. Then a human. This conversation has no interest to me."

"Vrinn, I am a human with no interest in involving myself in the rivalry between your races. We travel to Atlantea and your clan travels the other way. My question is this. Do you return to your lands because you reached your destination or because you did not?"

"Do you know night drows, human?"

"Not directly, but the celestial and star elves I encountered seemed to have many conversations about you."

Vrinn grunted.

"Are you an ally to sky elves?" the night drow asked.

Traveler smirked. "I am not in any way."

"Yes, I can hear it in your voice. You know them for what they really are and not the mask of beauty they wear for onlookers. Who is the human female behind you?" he asked.

"Her name?"

"One human male with magic weapons. One human female with magic about her. I can see their auras even from here. I care not about her name or yours. Your answer is the latter, but what does that matter to you?"

"Did I not tell you that I learned of you from celestial and star elves?"

"Repeat not any of what you heard to the drows."

"I am intrigued," Dr'as said. "We will talk more," he said to Traveler.

"Vrinn, I will promise not to repeat it to the D'Shar or any drows if you are a bit more forthcoming with this talk. Lack of it is a trait that both drows and night drows share."

"The drows already revealed your concern. I understand why your human female is here. She should not touch whatever it is around her neck so often."

Traveler and Dr'as glanced at her. The amulet was not glowing.

"Whatever presence of evil you sensed was not my people. We sensed it, too, but there was nothing to be seen or heard. Though we were moving quickly," Vrinn said.

"What do you think it was?" Traveler asked.

"How would I know? Wizard, creature, object. The possibilities are endless."

"Will you return to Atlantea?"

"I did not say anything about Atlantea. Just because humans, drows, and elves seek it out does not mean night drows do."

"You moved along Titan's Walk of Titan's Trail but not to its ultimate destination."

"Unlike you and the drows, if we need to go to Atlantea, we do not need to travel through the Great Forest to get there. We would simply fly above it like all sky caravans. They travel and rule the day skies above it. We travel at night when the skies are free."

"The Great Forest possibly but not the skies above the oceans and Atlantea."

"True. But again, we have no interest in Atlantea. I have been as forthcoming as is possible in one day for a night drow with strangers. Good travels. Though I'm doubtful it will be anything but, human.

"Dr'as, if you live, I look forward to our next battle. I have to repay you for the finger you sliced from my hand."

"That was a very long time ago, and you have already grown it back."

"I will say the same to you when I cut something from your body. I would tell you, but we are in the presence of women and I am of noble blood."

The caravan marched an hour after dawn. Estus had equipped every lizard minder with a crossbow—all two thousand humans. The giants returned their elemental war hammers for their own Antaean war hammers, weapons they knew by touch and ability.

"How far away?" Pangolin asked.

Elman had his eyes locked on the pathway ahead for a moment.

"They disappeared so they will likely reappear when they are upon us," he replied.

"Are you certain they are fae of light?" Grakdar asked.

"Yes."

"And here they are," Pangolin said, gripping his axe-mace.

"Mr. Nirgund."

"Yes, Mr. Traveler?"

"Take your lads back to the center of the caravan. They may get startled."

"Startled, sir. That is no concern—"

"And spit fire."

"Spit fire?"

"Alphyns spit and breathe fire, Mr. Nirgund. Their goblin tormentors fed them food with anti-magic to prevent their natural abilities, but you are their master."

"And you've had me feeding them those rocks. Treats you said. I will take the lads away. Come, lads!"

Nirgund had the reptilian hounds chase him as he moved away from the vanguard.

The fae caravan appeared. A tall humanoid woman with greenish skin sat on a large stag, both in wood armor. She wore a crown of thorns. Around her marched armed fellow dryads in wood–armor with slender black-tipped spears. A pack of large green fae dogs—cù-sìths—guarded her with her warriors.

Riding up alongside them was a party of centaurs. The male centaurs in the lead all wore crowns, three in all. Their upper torsos were fully armored in fae metal, their heads fitted with crowned helmets without faceplates to allow both their face and hair to be free. Tall gnomes, six feet tall, appeared. Then large satyrs with a herd of giant bison and boars behind them.

What piqued Traveler's attention were the other fae that appeared, men and women in black with stones on their necklaces. They walked as one, but they were clearly two different species. Some had eyes of birds and were no shorter than six and a half feet. The other species had eyes like snakes.

Two of the Tree Shepherds stood with Traveler and his dog. Mossberry stepped forward and nodded.

"I am the Tree Shepherd, Mossberry. My leshy brother is Greenwig."

"I am Princess Lua of the dryads of Dew Forest," the fae said from her giant stag mount. "This is Prince Allegor of the centaurs of the White Golden Plains. We heard you yesterday and thought it best to determine who you might be. We never expected to see another caravan reach this far into the Great Forest. Are you their guide, Mossberry the Tree Shepherd?"

"I am merely a member of the caravan on its journey."

"What a mismatch of a caravan you travel with. What is it called?"

"We are the Caravan of the Green Wurm, a heralded home of all leshy."

"We call ourselves the Fae Caravan of Gaea. Introduce yourselves," Lua said.

"I am King Aereth of Helm Earldom."

"A human," Lua said.

"I am Lady Aylen of Sirnegate."

"You are a curious one."

"I am an elf who was raised in the Lands of Man."

"That explains much. I am certain your elves have told you that you are no more elf than your half-elves."

Lady Aylen ignored her.

"Does that anger you?" Lua asked her with a smirk.

"Why should it?"

"Who are the elves?"

"I am Lyre of the elfin kingdom of Bravehowl and my comrade Taylos of the elfin city of Falconbright."

"We giants are of Antaeus," Grakdar said.

The human-looking fae stepped closer, staring at Ursi.

"You are bear clan?" one of them asked.

Ursi remained silent.

One of them pointed in anger. "The others there, they are wolf clan. You travel in the same caravan?"

The front of the caravan glanced back and saw the fae-blood men trying to stay hidden behind the men—human and pech.

"Which bird clan are you?" Traveler asked the man, but he turned away.

"You did not introduce yourself," Lua said.

"I am the human called Traveler."

The dryad princess and the centaur prince smiled. The centaur prince said something in fae to her.

"Why do you say that?" Lyre, the high elf, asked.

"Because we do," Lua said.

"We are of the condor clan," the fae-blood finally said.

"The giant bird of our human lands," Traveler said. "Traveling with the snake clan. I was told you were enemies."

"Our clans have been allies for centuries. We divided up our realms. One for the sky. The other for the land."

"So wolves are not the allies of snakes and birds," Traveler said. "But bears are not necessarily enemies of snakes and birds. Do I have it correct? I know so little of fae-bloods."

"The fact that you know our names and clans means you know too much for a human," the fae-blood man of the condor clan said.

"He only knows what our chatty brownies and gnomes have told him," Mossberry said with a smile and nodded at the tall gnomes of the fae caravan.

The fae caravan was growing in numbers as both parties faced each other. Pangolin, the giants, and the elaphine archers grew uneasy. The royals noticed the Cut-throats were moving to the front with their chamroses, followed by Bragg and his elves.

"Interesting," Lua said. "Our caravan is one of age-old allies. You are one of blood enemies. Elves and drows, high elves and moon elves, giants and fairies, bears and wolves, humans everywhere. Are you mismatches about to fight us?"

"Not at all, Princess Lua," King Aereth said. "Green Wurm's Caravan has no quarrel with any. Our caravan travels under many banners. The human ones are unimportant but we carry the banners not just for the giants of Antaeus, but the fairies of Chrysa, and the centaurs of Chiron."

Shadu-mun appeared on the left next to King Aereth. "And the elfin kingdoms of Magica, Bravehowl, Falconbright, and Nightshade."

"The queen of Chrysa," Lua said. "Kingdom of Chiron." She looked at the centaur prince. Both fae royals had lost their swagger.

"We can show you the official banners," King Aereth said.

"That will not be necessary. Where do you depart the shores of the Great Forest? Titan's Fall?"

"Yes," Traveler said.

"We shall return to the Trail," Princess Lua said. "Possibly we will meet again."

Lua noticed Traveler's dog. It growled at her with long piranha teeth and black eyes. Her eyes met Traveler's for a moment. "We withdraw, so you can return to your slow march."

Her yell was like the chirps of a hundred birds as she turned her stag around. The centaurs, the fae, and animals all ran after her, and the fae caravan disappeared into invisibility.

"Mr. Hobbs."

"Yes, sir?"

"Make your circle here. Dr'amal, enshroud us in an illusion. Like any other fae forest, we are being watched at all times, but there's no reason to make it easy. In fact, we should make it an early meal and rest."

"And discuss what just occurred," Lady Aylen said.

"Then we should do so within a realm," Mossberry said.

"Mr. Mossberry, a fae told me that Tree Shepherds or leshy in general do not lie," King Aereth said.

The Tree Shepherd grinned. "King Aereth, the fae who told you that were lying."

"The Green Wurm Caravan?"

"We thought it best not to reveal our true name. If any inquiries are made about us within the Forest, and those inquiries come across the ears of any enemies, they will not know it is us."

"Should we be concerned about this Gaean Caravan?"

"Precaution only. Dryads are our allies. They would not knowingly do anything against us."

Lady Aylen had pulled Traveler aside and spoke in a whisper. "Mr. Traveler, how long will I have to endure this constant humiliation from elves and the like? I am being mocked for circumstances not of my doing."

"You will not endure it much longer. When we get to the oceans, you will see. No one will be offending you there."

"I hope there won't be any more transformations. I almost died from the last one."

"That is over. With the magic of the ocean around us, you will know your abilities, what it means to be a water elf. But again, we speak about something that is many months away. We must first get through the Walk."

They rejoined the others.

"Mr. Mossberry has confirmed that we are not in fact the Green Wurm Caravan," King Aereth said.

"Are there actually green wurms?" Pangolin asked.

"There are, but they don't live in forests," Traveler answered. The caravan master noticed the elves. "What is your assessment of this Gaean Caravan?"

"Nothing, Mr. Traveler," Lyre replied. "Dryads, centaurs, satyrs, gnomes are not enemies."

"The fae-bloods we know nothing about," Taylos said. "But then the same can be said of the fae-bloods for our caravan."

"Does anyone here know what I am getting at?" Traveler asked.

Ethor and Mr. Bragg had also joined. Men, pech, gnomes, fae-bloods, and drows of the caravan looked on.

"Ursi, why were the other fae-blood surprised to see you?" Traveler looked at the lone female fae-blood.

"I don't know. We are not allies."

"How likely is it that their caravan is actually a flying caravan, that they set down to pretend to be traveling on foot, a ruse to see us with their own eyes?"

"A flying caravan?"

"Master Traveler, there is nothing about them that could possibly lead us to that theory," Mossberry said. "As the elf said, they are allies, not enemies, even if there is a spirit of competition between us."

"They were in Fae-Wick," Traveler said. He could see the confusion in the faces of the fae and ignorance in the faces of the elves. "It is the first fae city one reaches in Faë-Land Minor on Titan's Trail."

"As a caravan master, your abilities of awareness, memory, and recall must be beyond the average human," Mossberry said. "But even you could not remember that with all the many fae you have encountered."

"It was them. Leaving the fae city was a flying caravan—fairies and other fae races much larger than they appeared and fae-bloods. I remember because they dressed identically to Ursi. I remarked on the point in my mind when she first approached us. I am almost positive they were also condor clan. I even remember their leader riding a giant majestic condor. The same fae-blood man we just saw."

"If they left then as a flying caravan, they would have already reached Atlantea."

"They're not going to Atlantea. They are coming back from the fabled city," Pangolin said.

"Night drows and this Gaean Caravan. Both returning from Atlantea."

"Master Traveler, we share your suspicions but we must continue forward. What else is there to do?" Lyre asked.

"Nothing at the moment. The only bright spot for us, is that they believe we march to Titan's Fall for the Oceans Omnis. Dr'amal."

The drowess sorceress appeared beside him.

"Every night that you can, I want you to cast random dream spells. Not to affect the men, but to hang in the air. Images of anticipation of arriving at Titan's Fall. From this day forward, you are to speak only of us marching to Titan's Fall. Hobbs, spread the word among the men. I want the Forest itself to believe we march there."

"The spells will be cast starting tonight," Dr'amal said.

CHAPTER NINE

Safari Plains

Days became weeks on Titan's Walk. They saw no more signs of Titan footprints but they marched on a worn path, which meant it had been used many times before, possibly over many, many years. As they marched on, the nature of the Forest changed again. The density of the towering trees waned. The sky above was not as obstructed as before. The Forest was still gigantic but less so as they progressed.

Several days had passed since they'd seen their last sign of life, other than the trees. No giant birds, insects, or any animal. No more yawning trees. No creatures. No diversions at all. It reminded some of the humans of the Dark Forest in Faë–Land Minor but without the darkness. Many hours could pass on the march with no conversation at all.

"Mr. Traveler, would I be considered mad to wish for an attack?" Lady Aylen asked.

"Not at all, princess. It's normal. People recoil from boredom."

"How long have we been marching through this region, Mr. Traveler?" King Aereth asked.

"More than a month, sire."

"We've been on this Trail for a month?" Lady Aylen asked, exasperated.

"Princess, that means less than five months to go," Traveler said.

A smile flashed on her face. Gwyness chuckled.

"The Forest here seems to be thinning, Mr. Traveler."

"Yes, sire. We will reach the Plains in a day or so. Then we can rest."

"Rest? For how long, Mr. Traveler?"

"Only a week, princess, but we must take the time. Everyone in the caravan will have many duties to occupy their days. Once we enter the forest again, we'll enter a region of the Forest where many races live."

"The fae of the Great Forest you spoke of?"

"Yes, sire."

As the caravan master had done before, he ended the march early so they could set up night camp in the most defensible area they could find. The pocket-realm's entrance was hidden in a dense patch of giant dandelions and weeds. People and animals had to be led in single file.

"Mr. Hobbs, another leisurely night for the men," Traveler said when the last man stepped inside. "But it'll be a hard day tomorrow."

"Yes, sir."

"However, post additional security at the realm's entrance," Traveler said to Pangolin and the elfin knight leaders.

"We've seen neither beast nor creature in many days. Are you expecting trouble?" Lyre asked.

"I expect a very quiet night for the men inside our realm. Outside, the night could be quite different."

"What giant night animals frequent this region?" Shadu-mun asked.

"The only ones the night sentries may see are giant snakes, bears, owls, rodents, and the like."

"Nothing humanoid or of evil intelligence?" Taylos asked.

"Neither are likely."

"Good, but like Lady Aylen and certainly Mr. Pangolin and the Cut-throats, if this peacefulness continues much longer, we elfin knights may forget how to hold a sword in battle."

Traveler looked up from his map desk. A shadowy figure stood at the tent's entrance. The dog sat in front of it, barring his path.

"Come in, Dr'as."

The dog let him pass.

"I've been expecting you." Traveler returned his eyes to his maps.

"What are your suspicions exactly about what awaits us at Atlantea?"

"Why ask me? You know the night drows are lying to you."

"Night drows always lie to those who are not night drows. The key is to keep them talking. A truth or two is bound to slip out."

"Dr'as, let's speak honestly. I've been in many caravans. All is not right with this one. You know that. Why are you protecting the night drows?"

"What do you want me to say? We tolerate each other, but we're not allies. I know they're lying, but I don't about what or why."

"We all have secrets, but sooner or later, they come into the light. I knew Lady Aylen was an elf before she did and knew she and her maiden weren't seeking treasure for their kingdom of Sirnegate. In fact, no one in this caravan is going to the fabled kingdom of Atlantea for untold riches except for the human men. None of us."

"Why are you going to Atlantea? Or why are you returning?"

"That is my secret, but needless to say, humans cannot live in Atlantea forever. We are too short-lived. Neither can drows or elves. Their lives are also too short, but there are exceptions."

"Sky elves and night drows. Is that what you're saying?"

"Very few races can live there. Even though this caravan is led by humans, drows joining one with elves, and vice versa, speaks of desperation, Dr'as. But we can all keep our secrets until we cross the bridge into Atlantea. I can't burden myself with everyone's secrets. What I must concern myself with, as the caravan master, is getting the caravan to its destination. Everyone says we'll make it, but very few really believe it in their hearts. A caravan where so many of its leaders believe they will die along the Trail often will find a way to make it come true. I've been on such caravans, and I will not allow any caravan I command to become that. Dying on the Trail is not a pleasant thing. I don't care why you and your people are going to Atlantea. I do care that you prevent me from doing my job as caravan master. My job is to get all of us to Atlantea alive. My dog is very protective. He'll whisk me away and leave you all here, were it to come to that. Think about that when you keep information from me that could jeopardize the caravan's success."

"If Titan's Caravan, does not reach Atlantea, then neither would we. We know this, and everything I've done from the time we joined this caravan is to ensure it succeeds."

"Dr'as, I know that. What I need from you and your people is to be contrary to drowkind nature for our entire quest. I've been to Atlantea. You haven't. Drows have excellent instincts. Any suspicions, any whisper in your mind of something strange or unusual, you must share with me. That's how we stay alive and get to Atlantea. As a drow, you should understand this better than most in the caravan. Scouts and spies are integral parts of drow culture. Why? To keep your people alive."

"Vrinn is still in the Forest."

Traveler stopped. "How do you know?"

"A spell. We wanted to track their path."

"To spy."

"To know. We expected them to be back in our lands in Faë–Land."

Traveler stood from his chair.

"Dr'as, do the night drows live in the Great Forest?"

"What? In the Great Forest? Night drows live in the high mountains of our drow lands. Why would you ask that?"

"Drows live in the Great Forest."

"There are no drows in the Great Forest. The races in Faë-Land migrated out of the Great Forest eons ago. No drow races remain."

"If the night drows are here in the Forest..." Traveler said no more.

A restlessness came over Dr'as, confusion, anger, panic—too many emotions at once. He rubbed his forehead as he closed his eyes.

"Where do they live? If you believe night drows live in the Forest, where do they live?"

"Neither you nor I would ever find them. If they've been here for eons, no magic you could ever possess would find them. Only an Old One, something of ancient magic, could."

"I don't believe it."

"Dr'as this is very important. If night drows remain in the Great Forest when they told you they would return to Drow-Land, then maybe you can reason why."

"My people and I will. Night drows can be a very dangerous, though they would never hunt us."

"True. They view us as beneath them."

"Yes." Dr'as's mind raced with contemplation as he rubbed his chin.

"Why are they here, then?"

"There must be more though, more for you to mention ancient drows."

"Dr'as, the darklings saw them the other night."

Traveler marched with the vanguard. Both his dog and Elman noticed something ahead.

"What do you see, Mr. Elman?" Pangolin asked.

"One of my previous caravans called it the Giant Monster Plains," Traveler said.

"Giant monster?" one of the giants asked.

"Monsters as in giant animals."

"We'll wait here for a week?" Pangolin asked. "With giant monsters or animals about?"

"At least none of them will be able to sneak up on us."

The herd of giant zebra-striped ibexes—goat-like animals with large recurved horns—casually grazed on the yellow-green fields that stretched to the horizon. One of the giant beasts had its head to the grass and was chewing. It watched them with large eyes but was not nervous. The grass was twice the size of the giants. From the ridge of its forehead to the base of its nose was longer than the grass. Beyond it, the other ibex did the same but hadn't seen the tiny caravan yet.

Traveler and Pangolin noticed them. A smiling Bragg, with his metal golem, Glogg, then his elfin fellow hunters had joined the vanguard.

"What amazing beasts," Bragg said.

"I thought you only hunt manticores," Pangolin said.

"I specialize in the manticore, but I hunt all, Mr. Pangolin."

"Forgotten our conversation from a month ago already, Mr. Bragg?" Mr. Traveler asked.

"No, Mr. Traveler. You won't need to leave the caravan to fly off and rescue me."

"Good of you to realize. Mr. Pangolin, move the caravan forward but do not disturb our grazing friends. We'll find a place to camp."

"I see a plateaued hill in the distance," Grakdar said, craning his head. "Or is that the back of another beast?"

The animal men with their animals and the elfin questing knights with the other two Antaean giants were the last to climb up the grassy hill. The fauns used their scythes to cut the grass so they could set up camp. Hobbs took charge of the camp setup. Everyone noticed the agitation of the giant lizards.

"Mr. Hobbs, have the minders gather their fae lizards to the side," Traveler instructed.

As Hobbs moved off, Pangolin approached.

"Mr. Pangolin, we will not be in the pocket-realm," Traveler informed him.

"Is that wise?"

"Necessary."

"Our lizards seem to be in a state."

The royals had joined them.

"Mr. Traveler, what is wrong with our lizards?" Lady Aylen asked. "They seem as if they want to run away."

The caravan's lizard minders struggled to keep their lizards together. Estus had fitted the lizards' armor with metal chains so the minders could guide them.

"Men, remove your lizards' armor as quickly as possible."

The men were nervous but did as Traveler directed. Unfastening the armor from each lizard was no easy task. Each lizard had one human minder, but it took two or more to remove their animal armor. The first giant lizard free of its armor raced away. Soon, it was followed by others.

"Continue removing their armor," Traveler directed.

They did until every lizard was freed and gone. The lizard minders ran to the edge of the plateau. They were not alone as everyone watched the lizards run as a pack across the plains, avoiding the grazing giant animals.

"Do not worry, men. They'll be back."

"What's happening, Mr. Traveler, sir?" one of the distressed minders asked.

All of them were in shock or on the verge of tears.

"Men! We are close to Vivaria which is the birth lands of many giant animals, including your giant lizards. Once a year, they need to go on their own caravan. Don't laugh and please cover the ears of our young lads. Mr. Quillen."

"I am not here!" Quillen tried to hide among the men.

The men already knew what the caravan master was about to say.

"Men, our lizards are away for their annual breeding run," Traveler said.

Chief Ethor's rustic elves guarded the west end of the hill. They were at home within the wild forest. The open plains were in constant view with their herds of giant ibexes grazing. The elfin questing knights were of royal elfin cities. They sat in camps around fires, chatting and minding their falcons and leopard axexs but always ready for battle. Occasionally, a giant bird would appear high in the sky, bringing all to their feet, but none of the birds took any notice of their camp, possibly due to the three crawling trees stretched out over the entire caravan. The Tree Shepherds had the colors of the crawling trees change to match the yellow-green color of the plains.

The drows commanded the hill's east area. Their sentries all had their heads covered with their hoods. All of them carried six-foot spears. The Cut-throats, always joined by the fae berserkers, were spread across the entire northern area of the hill. They also kept a keen eye on their surroundings and their chamroshes resting in one of the crawling trees. Mr. Hobbs had open tents set up for not only the royals but most of the men, so something would be above their heads. The southern area was taken by the elaphine archer-warriors, cervids, and rusines. The hoofed fae seemed extremely comfortable in this part of the Forest. Nearby, camped the animal men with their animals.

All six of the giants were already sleeping, in camp near the Cut-throats. At the center of camp were all the humans, male half-elves, pech, fauns, and male fae-bloods. Brownies and darklings would not be seen until nightfall. All the camp rested within not one but three circles of white magic light only visible from a few feet away.

Traveler peered through his telescope across the Plains. He studied every giant animal in the distance.

"Mr. Traveler, you are doing what I was doing earlier?"

Traveler didn't take his eye from the telescope. "Mr. Bragg, my lesson with the giant manticore skull truly did not last long. Did you rehearse your argument enough times?"

"I think the men deserve some fresh meat of the Forest, even you humans."

"Are you certain eating such meat won't have a dangerous effect on the men?"

"Mr. Traveler, they are giant animals not magic ones. I would simply be hunting for food, and consuming one of them wouldn't be dangerous. The Forest wouldn't object."

"I won't waste my time trying to dissuade you. I would rather you get this hunting urge out of you here than later on when we head back into the thick of the Forest. Tomorrow morning, engage in your hunt when it's safe to do so."

"I was hoping to eat a hearty night meal."

"Mr. Bragg, would now be safe for your impromptu hunt?"

Bragg stared in the distance, his telescope gripped in his large hand. He put the scope to his eye.

"Hmm. A giant green leopard with yellow-green spots. No, two of them. I think one of their paws is larger than me. Tomorrow morning sounds acceptable to me, Mr. Traveler, after further consideration. A noon meal for the men sounds much more agreeable."

The sea of yellow-green tall grass swayed in the light breeze. For the animals that grazed within, the grass was short enough to still spot most predators. For Bragg and his men, the tall grass engulfed them, and the only senses they could rely on was their enhanced hearing. Bragg and his party of mountain, forest, and savage elves set out before the morning sun had fully risen. Already the men of the caravan were calling it Bragg's Hunt.

Bragg was not as stealthy as his elfin comrades. Dwelfs were called tall dwarves with elfin ears for a reason, but he was a lifetime hunter with the patience of a Titan, and though he was not as stealthy as an elf, as a dwelf, he moved quieter than most fae. As a dwelf, he had the strength to surpass either elf or dwarf.

Bragg took with him a small team—two forest elves and a savage elf. The rest of his comrades hung back with his metal golem, Glogg, including their Diomedian Mares. Bragg and team would slay a giant animal, Glogg and the others would secure it in a net to return to camp.

Bragg winced and held his breath. The giant green aphid crawled across his back without stopping. His elfin comrades next to him grinned. The giant insect was larger than their caravan master's dog in its normal form and size. They lay on their chests on the ground and let their hearing paint a mental picture as to the location and motions of each nearby beast. Bragg had his crossbow in one hand, an arrow at the ready and, in the other hand, his walking staff weapon with the axe blade nearest him. His quiver of arrows was secured tightly to his back, over his standard brown leather attire with his belt of tiny skulls. His elfin hunters were in green tracking attire.

The forest elves had their longbows and full quivers on their backs. The one savage elf with braided brown hair, bigger pointed ears, fanged teeth, and clawed hands hunted with multiple javelins and a belt lined with darts and knives.

The ibexes from the previous day were gone. Today it was a herd of giant yellow-green antelopes. They had seen a lone rhinoceros in the distance too. Its natural armored skin was more metal than flesh, but the rhino wasn't their quarry. The smallest of the giant antelopes was.

The waited for their moment.

"Mr. Traveler, this madness," Lady Aylen said.

"I have to agree," King Aereth said. "Mr. Traveler, why would you allow our dwelf hunter to leave the camp for this unnecessary activity? We have enough food for the entire quest."

"What if he causes a stampede?" Pangolin asked.

Traveler watched them through his telescope. The leadership had encircled him, including fae leaders, when news of Bragg's hunt spread through the camp.

"I learned the hard way, sire, that when a man on caravan has a particular compulsion, you either let him satisfy it or leave the man behind. If we hadn't stumbled upon a manticore, I would have chosen the latter option, but we did. Manticores are one of the creatures with a unique evil intelligence about them."

"You believe it still tracks us after all this time?" Pangolin asked.

"I don't know for sure, but I'm not about to leave behind an asset who specializes in killing them. Manticores are very hard to kill. Mr. Bragg says he's killed nineteen. I've killed none."

"How do we know his tall tales are true?" Pangolin asked.

"The tiny skulls on his belt are manticore skulls," Traveler revealed. "Magically shrunken."

"My people are hunters, too, but we detest displaying prey. It's deeply dishonorable and sacrilegious to us."

"Mr. Pangolin, many hunter kingdoms are the same, but many others are the opposite. They honor the prey by displaying it. I neither agree nor disagree. I am in no position to have an opinion on either age-old custom. We may not like everything about him and his men, but that's the story of most in Titan's Caravan. The point is that Bragg is needed. We all are. He's a real manticore hunter."

"Mr. Traveler, do not minimize your protection of this caravan from the one that we encountered.

Without you or your dog, the caravan could have been destroyed," King Aereth said.

"We scared it off, sire, but it came back to kill some of our men."

"Not our fault, not your fault, Mr. Traveler," Pangolin said.

"Let Mr. Bragg have his hunt. If he gets some of his men or animals killed, he will learn a lesson. If he succeeds, then we will have fresh meat for the men and animals—a treat they will be thankful for as we wait for our giant lizards to return."

"Hopefully, Mr. Bragg won't get himself killed," Pangolin said.

There was no warning. Suddenly, giant antelope were in the sky sailing above them. They heard thundering howls fast approaching. Bragg flipped on his back as he fired his crossbow at his prey. The body of the giant antelope crashed to the earth, sending a cloud of dust, particles, and grass fragments over Bragg and his men. Under the cover of the dust cloud, which quickly blew away, a metal sound fast approached as his elfin comrades leapt to their feet, already firing a blinding fury of arrows before even the first creature was seen.

As a hunter, Bragg had come across a wide variety of beasts called howlers. The giant ones that sailed through the air to pounce on them were giant monkeys with green fur and four arms, and they yelled with such a loud howl the air reverberated around them. Glogg appeared and crashed into the first creature before it landed on Bragg. Both automaton and howler fell to the ground with a loud thud. The pack of howlers held their hands over their faces to block the rain of arrows. A small red boulder struck another howler in the chest, and the projectile exploded in a ball of fire. The shocked howler picked itself up off the ground. The pack hopped away as fast as possible just as another projectile landed and exploded.

Bragg looked at the caravan's plateau camp to see that the projectile had come from one of their catapults. The dwelf looked at the fallen antelope he had shot, lying dead on the plain. "We shall have a good noon meal today, hunters!"

Bragg and his men had to drag the giant antelope body to the hill and use all their combined strength to carry it up to the plateau camp. The manticore hunter got the recognition he wanted as the men cheered. Hobbs had directed men after a hunt before but never for game of its size. The steward didn't even know how to begin.

"We will take charge, Mr. Hobbs," Mr. Oeric, one of his guards, said.

Tyfer followed, and both men had human and pech carry the dead antelope into one of the small-realms. It would take hours to prepare. In a short time, all in the caravan not on guard duty had followed the procession and disappeared into the small realm to watch.

"Mr. Traveler, can we humans eat food from the Great Forest?" Gwyness asked.

"Completely safe, maiden," Traveler said. "You actually should. We have food to last for our entire journey, but you will not likely eat food from the Lands of Man for years to come. You should get used to the taste."

"What she's asking, Mr. Traveler, is will we grow to the size of a Great Forest tree or shrink to the size an ant if we do?" Lady Aylen asked.

Traveler made a face as if seriously thinking. His expression suddenly changed to a smile. "No."

In the forever-dusk pocket-realm of the väki, its wall of black volcanic rock encircled a black mountain with a cavernous interior. The elemental sprites had allowed their nocturnal cousins, the brownies, to place a hut in their domain. Inside the magic hut was another realm—the book vault of the lost kingdom of Rivermouth.

"I cannot believe our Mr. Bragg would risk his life to hunt one of these giant animals, and Mr. Traveler let him," Lady Aylen said.

"Mr. Bragg will be popular with the men for some time."

"We'll see how long that lasts. I won't soon forget how we almost had to threaten him to get him send his men with Mr. Traveler."

"To rescue those things. Darklings. I hate them."

"Mr. Traveler will be even more popular with the creatures than he was before. He risked his life to save theirs."

"He would do the same for all of us."

"Yes, he would."

Lady Aylen and Gwyness opened the book vault's magic chest and spent more time viewing the ancient tomes with elfin symbols. The giant wooden chest of blackened wood and a dark metal lock opened with the touch of either of their hands.

"Can you read these markings?" Gwyness asked.

Lady Aylen shook head and ran her fingers over the ridged symbols.

"How old these must be."

"The väki said they would become whatever language we read," Gwyness said, opening a book.

Both of them sat on the ground of the hut at the front of the chest. The unrecognizable words in Gwyness's book transformed into her own language.

"We're the last of these warrior clerics," Lady Aylen said to herself, opening her own book. "After all these years, we have all the answers we've sought at our finger tips. I find that I am not so eager to know all as before."

"But we must," Gwyness said. "We have no choice in the matter."

"The Old One suggested that these warrior clerics were paired."

"Seer and slayer."

"He said we could each be either, though I am not certain he would know. I think we already have a comfort with our assumed roles. As the elf, I am the slayer. With your amulet, you are the seer."

"Yes." Gwyness turned the page and stopped. "Pictures."

Lady Aylen looked. "Pictures of what? I have never seen such creatures."

"The Old One said that the Four Kings had nothing to do with our birth kingdom's destruction but were allied with those who did," Gwyness said. "What bothers you about what he said?"

"The Old One, the white elfess, they were involved in the destruction of our birth kingdom."

"Do you think he was being untruthful with us? They gave us this chest. They told us about our origins. Why would they do that?"

"Who's to know? I'm moving toward Mr. Traveler's way of thinking in not being so ready to believe everything I am told by fae."

"If he was speaking in our minds, was he also able to read our thoughts?" Gwyness asked nervously.

"That, Gwyness, is a very disturbing thought considering he was actually a spell-talker. The fae swear they are demons of a sort."

"They say the same about Mr. Traveler's darklings."

"That they do, but I trust the darklings. I'm not certain about our Rivermouth benefactors. You asked the right question: Why would they help us? Why do they want the warrior clerics of the kingdom of Rivermouth to be reborn? So many questions."

"The pages go on for some length." Gwyness closed the book and handed it to Lady Aylen. "Yours."

"Mine?"

"You're the slayer."

"What about you? You need to see them for me to slay them."

Gwyness huffed and took the book back. "I don't like this."

"Get used to it, Gwyness. Look at the chest. It's larger on the inside than outside, filled with these huge books. We may spend all our free time in here and not even study a fraction of them."

"How could we? They said it was from the entire academy of these warrior clerics, of an entire elfin kingdom. Far larger than human kingdoms."

"We should organize the books first in stacks by subject. Know what we have. Then we can decide which to study first." Lady Aylen's mouth dropped open. She reached into the chest and rose to her feet as she pulled out a large case. Gwyness helped her open it and inside were dual tridents of a glimmering blue metal they had never seen.

"I know these," Lady Aylen said.

"They are familiar to me as well. These are—"

"Mine."

"Your mother's, but yours now."

"Do you remember her?"

"I think so."

"How could this celestial elfin queen have such a personal item? They had a direct role in the destruction of Rivermouth."

"And the murder of our parents and people."

Traveler touched the blade's metal with his hand. His dog stood up to sniff the metal himself.

"Sorry, Mr. Estus, my expertise does not extend much beyond the standard metals of the magical lands. How did our giants like their elemental weapons?"

Estus stood nearby, inside one of his many weapons vaults.

"They returned them for their original dwarven weapons. Air elemental weapons were not to their liking."

"Antaean giants are earthbound people. If you were able to find earth elemental weapons to their liking..."

"I tried, sir. I didn't know giants could be so choosy."

"Have you cataloged everything?"

"Not even close, sir."

"Make sure you go through all the weapons with your men, and have fae here with you, maybe the gnomes. They've been fairly quiet with the brownies about. They might like the idea of helping you tidy the weapons vault."

"I'll ask them, sir. Good idea. But I didn't ask you to visit for this. Lady Aylen and Maiden Gwyness have begun to look through that chest from that...whatever he was. Lady Aylen had an exquisite pair of long war tridents. Must be made of pure water elemental magic."

"The tridents she always carried were actually for training."

"Yes, that must be it, but there's more, sir. There was also a set of war hammers in there."

"For Maiden Gwyness."

"Yes. There are also many other weapons in there. It's an entire vault of weapons—enough to equip a small army."

"Interesting."

"Interesting, sir?"

"What's remarkable to you about this weapons vault within a chest of books? All magical weapons?"

"Yes, magical and possibly all of water elemental magic too. What's remarkable to me about all the weapons, including shields and armor, is how well-preserved they are, polished and cleaned. This celestial elfin queen found all their books and all their weapons—from this destroyed kingdom?"

"No, Mr. Estus. They destroyed the kingdom directly and took the weapons from the dead warriors and seized the books of knowledge for themselves."

"That's what I believe, sir. But why give them to Lady Aylen and Maiden Gwyness?"

"I do believe that part of the Old One's story. They had been enemies and believed they'd made a terrible mistake."

"You lived in Atlantea, sir. Any insight to all this from your stay then."

"I left Atlantea before the Kings Caravan began its triennial journeys there. I met many elves, including cloud and star elves, but never celestial elves in person. I don't want the women to search through either the chest or the vault inside without others nearby."

"Do you believe there might be danger within it?"

"I don't want to take any chances. The gnomes can help with your own weapons vault, but as for the Rivermouth chest, inform Lady Aylen of my concerns. Have her choose people she trusts to search the vault. A seeker spell should be cast to detect anything of malevolence."

"Yes, sir. We seem to have a few mysteries of our own to unravel on our quest."

"Not much of mysteries. We were told by our two fairy sisters' queen mother already. There are forces who want Titan's Caravan to get to Atlantea, and others that don't—both to involve us in affairs not of our own making."

"We have a lot of royalty in this caravan."

"I would say most. These fae-bloods. The gnomes."

"The gnomes?"

"Gnomes have kings."

"Makes sense. Fairies have queens."

"Our giant lizards will return in a few days. Their minders will need to be equipped to fight by their side."

"What weapons do you suggest?"

"Humans with bows and arrows in these lands is useless against the adversaries we are likely to face. Crossbows with special arrows. The magic arrows should be only for those who can hit a target."

"Our elves and elaphines. I have never seen such a display of archery. The monstrous howling monkeys didn't know what they had unleashed upon themselves. The men will be ready."

"I'll leave you to it."

"I won't tell anyone, but once we leave these Plains, where will we pass next?"

"A place with flying rivers, Mr. Estus."

In the training pocket-realm, King Aereth drilled with his heavy weapons teams.

"Men, we must adapt our tactics to the lands. We cannot solely rely on the magic power of our projectiles. We must employ superior stratagem."

It took twenty teams of five to manage each weapon and twenty teams of five to protect each team. Aereth had the men practice for hours. His golden kirin followed beside him, amused by the activity of hitting tables in the distance as targets. They would never be able to launch projectiles at the speed of the pech throwing their large rocks, but they were learning how to send multiple ones into the air in rapid succession.

Gwyness trained with her new war hammers. She practiced moves alone, away from the female half-elves training with their fighting staffs. The new slender war hammers felt strange in her hands. As she sliced through the air, it felt as if she was submerged in water—a force slowing their movement in the air.

She heard commotion in the distance and saw that is was the Cut-throats running into the realm for their own training sessions.

Pangolin followed after them and noticed her. He walked to her. "You have new weapons, maiden."

"I don't care for them."

He studied them. "Why not?"

"There is a strangeness to them. I can't explain it. They don't move freely through the air. I'll return them to Mr. Estus and retrieve my old ones that I'm accustomed to."

"That would be a mistake."

"Why? They're no use to me if I can't fight with them."

"You have not even used them a full day. It was nearly two years."

"Two years?"

"That's how long it took for Mr. Traveler to be able to use his magic sword effectively. Maiden, these are weapons of magic. You won't master them in a day. Time and patience are the twin friends of any fighter who uses a weapon. Give it time."

"Yes, Mr. Pangolin. You're right. I expect too much too soon. If I only I knew its full power."

"You've read nothing about it in your new book vault?"

"It may take Lady Aylen and me weeks or months to sort through all that we have."

"The answer is probably there, but practice every day with the new weapons. Some magic weapons need time to get used to their new owners as well, and trust you."

"Trust me? My weapon must trust me before it allows me to properly swing it. I'll take your advice, Mr. Pangolin."

"Good, fair maiden. I will rejoin my comrades."

As Pangolin returned to the Cut-throats, Gwyness heard giggling. She turned to see the female half-elves watching her and whispering.

"What are you saying about me there?" she asked.

They said nothing.

"Eyes everywhere. I can't even talk to someone without giggling and gossip. Ladies, don't spread any gossip about me."

"No, Maiden Gwyness," they said.

Gwyness resumed her practice drills with her dual weapons.

Bragg the dwelf stood at the plateau's edge scanning the plains with his telescope. He removed it from his eye and reached into one of his pockets with his other hand. The object looked like a large pearl.

He tossed it into the air through the magic barrier of the camp. The orb grew and sprouted eagle wings.

Men noticed the circular magic window opening above Bragg. The dwelf stood beneath it as the window expanded larger and larger. Inside was a whirling vortex of clouds then a bird's-eye view of the plains and its giant animals.

"What is it, Mr. Bragg?" Quillen asked him.

"It's my flying eye, lad. With it, I can see the terrain all around me."

Excitement spread through the camp as members gathered beneath the window to watch the birds-eye-view display. Bragg's magic eye had flown past where any could see from the plateau camp. Chatter grew as well as sounds of astonishment as giant greenish elephants with trees growing on their bodies appeared along with endless numbers of stags, gazelles, antelopes, ibexes, and zebras, giant ostrich-like birds and wildebeests. Herds of smaller monkeys roamed around, too, though the smallest was larger than five of their giant lizards combined.

In the distance they could see the Plains end and the dense trees of the Great Forest begin again. A pride of giant cheetahs lay at the threshold, some sleeping, others watching.

"That should be enough," Bragg said.

"No, Mr. Bragg, let it fly around more. We'll never have a chance to see the Plains again," Quillen said.

His comments were echoed by human and fae alike. Even the jovial gnomes gave Bragg dirty looks.

"Okay," he said chuckling.

Traveler stood with the royals at their tents.

"Do we have anything like Mr. Bragg's flying eye, Mr. Traveler?" King Aereth asked.

"I don't, sire, but some of the fae do, and others can cast spells that can do the same thing."

"Such a thing would come in handy, Mr. Traveler," Lady Aylen said.

"Possibly, princess, but a flying eye is not invisible. If it's seen, then others know its owner is not too far away."

"That should be easy to fix with another spell," Lady Aylen said.

They saw Bragg say something to the gathered crowd.

"What did he say?" Traveler asked.

"'Shall we see how high our flying eye can go?'" Lady Aylen repeated.

The image displayed by the magic window changed to the clouds above.

"Mr. Bragg, be very careful!" Traveler yelled.

The view was in the clouds then broke through. Men gasped.

The flying caravan was unlike anything they had ever seen before—armored riders on flying horses, flying chariots and wagons surrounded by griffins, flying warriors in armor. None of the faces of the men were visible. Their armor was a yellow gold. The flying eye moved its gaze to the front of the caravan, and they saw the caravan's flag. The symbol looked like a many-armed fairy.

At the front of the caravan were flying chariots filled with women with flowing hair, wearing translucent clothes. A face flashed on the magic window—a woman with pale, almost transparent skin, clear eyes, and long, flowing blue-white hair. She blew out a white gust of air.

The men heard Traveler yell out something. Bragg clenched his teeth and his fists, crushing his telescope, as a blast of freezing air punched through the magic window. Glogg tried to pull his master away, but both he and the dwelf were becoming frozen blocks. Men and animals ran away as the blast of frigid air turned the grass white with ice and a mist bellowed out. The warmth of the camp was gone, and cold air rippled out as men's eyebrows, facial hair, and body hair turned white. A flask shattered against the magic window, and it vanished. It had been thrown by the Tree Shepherd Mossberry.

Bragg fell to the ground, and Glogg was frozen solid. Men and animals backed away.

Bragg's elfin comrades ran to him. Already, fae grabbed torches as others set Bragg right next to a fire. The savage elves rubbed his body vigorously to remove the ice and get his circulation flowing. Another of Bragg's elves touched their torch on Glogg to melt away the ice. In moments, the metal golem was able to move.

Nirgund's alphyns jumped up and down and spat fire out. The royal guardsman smiled.

"They can breathe fire."

The reptilian hounds were trying to warm themselves up. Brownies emerged from their slumber in their realm and started throwing balls of fire into the camps. Blasts erupted temporarily then settled to roaring fires. Men quickly gathered around the fires and pulled their animals close too. The cold snap within the camp disappeared.

A grinning Bragg saw Traveler appear before him, the royals at his side.

"I guess sylphs do not like strangers spying on them," the dwelf said.

"No, they don't, Mr. Bragg. You're very fortunate they knew who we were."

"Knew who we were, Mr. Traveler?" King Aereth asked.

"Yes, sire. If they hadn't, Mr. Bragg would likely be dead. It's one of the downsides of flying eyes, which is why I never use them. An above-average spell-caster can send a spell through it straight to its master to cause mischief or worse."

"She had no intentions of killing me, Mr. Traveler. She was simply sending me a warning."

"Hopefully, she'll have a better chance of you listening to her warnings than I had with you listening to mine. Mr. Bragg, air elementals are not to be trifled with."

"I might as well get used to dealing with them here than when we reach Atlantea," Bragg said. "But do not be concerned, Mr. Traveler. They have no interest in us."

"I'm so glad the talk of reaching Atlantea has increased among the caravan when we haven't even gotten out of the Great Forest, but just because they have no interest in us doesn't mean they cannot fling a spell at us to do us harm out of spite."

"Mr. Traveler!" men called out.

They all saw it—images above their heads. One bright light from high above in the clouds falling down toward them.

"What is—" Lady Aylen began to ask.

"Why thank you, Mr. Bragg," Traveler said with annoyance. "The sylphs are about to shower us with a volley of magic shooting stars."

"Are they trying to destroy us?" Pangolin asked.

"No, but it will take all our effort and magic to fortify our magic barrier to keep from being killed."

"Killed?" Lady Aylen asked.

"Where's Grakdar?" Traveler called out.

"Here!" he boomed.

"We need the earth elemental power of our Antaean giants to hold up our barrier against the air elementals' attack."

"It will be done," Grakdar said. "Barg! Arteus! Aronir! Alceir! Alebar!"

The giant gathered his men.

"This is the sylphs not trying to kill us, Mr. Traveler?"

"Yes, sire. You don't ever want to see the opposite."

The intensity of yellow lights grew larger and larger, but it was becoming clear that it was more than a few shooting stars about to impact the camp's protective magic barrier.

"All this because the dwelf wanted to see some giant fae wildlife," Pangolin said under his breath.

The men got to see again the collective power of the six Antaean giants as they dropped their war hammers to the ground. They reached out their arms and pressed their palms against the magical barrier. The giants glowed yellow with magic from within, the light beaming from their eye sockets, ear canals, and mouths. Their size increased. A ghostly form took shape behind them, a composite of each of the giants, its size many times theirs. The form drew in its shoulders, lowered its head, chin to its chest, and held up the circle dome with its back and pushed out with its palms and forearms. The shooting stars crashed into the barrier but did no damage at all against the Antaean defense.

The men would have much to converse about for the rest of the day and night.

Traveler returned to the small-realm of the kilmoulis. He made his visits at night when most in the caravan were asleep and the kilmoulis in their small-realm were still awake. He stood in their simple woodland area with lots of green foliage and a bright blue sky filled with large billowy white clouds. The kilmoulis emerged from their own quaint hamlets to meet him.

"Welcome, Master Traveler," one said.

"Welcome," he greeted. "I saw your signal. You can always leave your realm to meet with me at my tent. My dog won't trouble you."

"We do not wish to trouble you, Master Traveler. You do not need to be burdened by us."

"You're no burden. You're valuable to Titan's Caravan. Have you sensed something we should be aware of?"

"Yes, Master Traveler. Ahead is a wet region of the Great Forest."

"Yes. Very dangerous. I am looking for the driest section for us to cross."

"There are many morgens and kelpies ahead. Do you know them?"

"Yes, I do. The morgens will be the problem. I have drilled into the men enough the danger of any stray horse outside the Lands of Man. If they cannot withstand them here, then we will have no chance once we get to the oceans. Have you sensed anything else?"

"Many others, Master Traveler. Water elves like our princess."

"Must be a water-going caravan of them. We should be fine, as long as they remain unaware of us. Any other creatures?"

"Many, many of them. None that seem to move to us from afar."

"I will keep us to a path free of them as best I can."

"You are a good caravan master, Master Traveler."

"Thank you. You know, you can join the rest of the caravan whenever you wish. Our Mr. Hobbs is an able steward and will not tolerate any ill will toward you from other fae."

"We will think on it, Master Traveler."

"You can even stay among the human men, if that makes you more comfortable. Some may look at you with aversion at first, but that would be replaced with curiosity. To my human race, you are fae, sprites, but do think upon it. Take your time. We have a long journey to go."

The kilmoulis smiled at him as they always did—with their noses.

Frog-Dor sat on the grass of the small-realm, shivering. With no fenodyree or kirins around, he was alone. He shut his eyes. He opened them and turned, continuing to shake, and saw a giant lime-green bullfrog larger than a man.

"No!"

He shut his eyes again and heard it croak. Then came the sound others, many others. He grabbed his ears.

His red eyes opened, and the grass of the small-realm was covered with normal-sized lime-green bullfrogs everywhere. They were all hopping toward him. He jumped to his feet in panic.

"No! No!"

He wanted to run but was surrounded. He screamed out. The sounds were gone. He slowly reopened his eyes. The bullfrogs were gone. Frog-Dor dropped to his knees in a whimpering mess. He curled up on the ground, sobbing.

"No. No more."

In the distance, the head of one of hairy fenodyree peeked in, watching with sad eyes, then disappeared through the realm's entrance.

With nightfall came the last meal of the day before sleep. That meant more of the meat from Bragg's hunt. The caravan had grown to crave the giant fae antelope meat. The humans who lived in Faë-Land for years remained the caravan's best cooks, and their seasoning of spices made an already mouth-watering meal heavenly. Hobbs's two guards, Tyfer and Oeric, were the best of the fae humans. They left their guard duties to take charge of the nightly meal preparation. So good was the meat, that the brownies started their rounds earlier to be in line for the dinner with the men.

The nightly leadership meetings had been discontinued. Each had too much to do even while they waited for the lizards to return. Traveler had the entire caravan take advantage of the respite. For most, it was about training for fighting or defending against attacks. Traveler gave human and fae scenarios. The human and fae leadership devised the methods to defeat it or defend the caravan from it.

The Cut-throats dragged themselves out of the training realm after another hard day of training. I'wulf walked alongside the fae berserker Hax.

"Can a human berserker beat an elf?" the lionoid Hax asked him.

"With our battle rage, we surely can," I'wulf bragged.

"Have you done so already?"

"Of course not."

The men laughed. Hax slapped him on the shoulder.

"My only advice to you is never let that elf get his hand on a bow. If the elf does, it's over. You saw what they did to that swarm."

"We berserkers can hold our own."

"What armor have you decided on with Mr. Estus?" Hax asked. "I was somewhat getting used to our goblin armor. It smells, but I have no qualms about it, and I care not if an elf hears me." He looked around.

"I wanted our Cut-throats to be different."

"We may not have much of a choice."

"I did not know there were more than four different elementals."

"Yes, you humans only know of the four, but there are many others."

"There are more kinds of weapons and armor in Mr. Estus's vault than even the fae can identify. He said he's been busy forging armor for us alone."

"What metal, then?"

"He said, 'Armor fitting a berserker.' In fact, Mr. Hax, since I was elevated to the leader of the Cut-throats after Mr. Nirgund abandoned us to be a lowly king's guardsmen," I'wulf said with a laugh, "I need a second-in-command. Why not you?"

"Second-in-command?"

"If something should happen to me—"

"Nothing will, Mr. I'wulf."

"But should it happen, I want someone to take my place who the men trust and respect and who can beat them handily in battle."

"If you put it that way, how can I refuse?"

The royals and Gwyness ate their night meal in Traveler's tent at the large map table. The dog chewed on his piece of giant stag bone.

"I'm not happy that Bragg did what he did, but this meat is very tasty," Lady Aylen said.

"And it will last for a month," Traveler said, watching the changes of the magical map.

"Mr. Traveler, how can you know what lies ahead with the Forest so huge and dense?" Gwyness asked.

"Too much life exists in the Forest for the map to show me, but it does show me clues—footprints or tracks in the dirt, a flash of a moving herd or swarm, a flash of shadow."

They all noticed it on the map.

"I see it now," Gwyness said.

"You can tell what a beast is from its shadow, Mr. Traveler?"

"I can, princess."

"Quite impressive," she said.

"Ahead we will cross a section of the Forest with much water, not quite a marsh. That will be farther on. Lady Aylen, you and I will march with the vanguard."

"Me?"

"Yes. It's Lady Aylen the water elf we will require, as we may encounter some dark fae that could decide not to bother with us if they see you."

"Which dark fae, Mr. Traveler?"

"The one I'm most concerned with are called morgens, evil nymphs who are fond of drowning people who cross into their domain. They're also capable of causing floods. The morgens of the Great Forest are far more powerful than their lesser cousins in Faë-Land Minor."

"Morgens," Lady Aylen said. "Their name doesn't sound evil enough."

"Mr. Traveler!" they heard men yell.

"Something's happening," Traveler said as he got up from his stool.

Suddenly, the dog increased in size, and a giant lizard's head rushed into the tent. King Aereth cried out as Gwyness screamed, trying to grab her weapons, but she had left them in her own tent. Lady Aylen stumbled back and fell to the floor. Traveler started laughing.

"Mr. Traveler, this is not funny!" Lady Aylen jumped to her feet.

"Our lizards are back," Traveler said.

CHAPTER TEN

Land of the Flying Rivers

When Hobbs began his rounds before dawn, the Cut-throats were already up and about. Mr. Estus was fitting both human and fae berserkers with their fellow warriors in new black metal.

"Mr. Estus found you new fae armor, I see," the caravan's steward said.

"No, Mr. Estus forged them new fae armor," Estus said.

Hobbs said no more. The metal, in his eyes, was...ugly, not smooth and shiny like elfin or dwarven metal. The finish was rough, with jagged edges and blotched spots of lighter or darker hue, but the Cut-throats loved their new armor made specially for them.

"We get back on the Trail, Mr. Hobbs?" I'wulf asked.

Hobbs noticed that each of the Cut-throats' armor was also etched with the individual man's tattoos.

"Yes, we do, Mr. I'wulf."

"At long last," Hax the fae berserker said. "Hopefully, we will have no more delays."

"On the Trail there are always delays, Mr. Hax, but we always manage."

Titan's Caravan set out two hours after dawn. Their giant lizards were back in their armor at the flanks. The giants kept their original Antaean war hammers slung to their backs but, with Estus's help, found massive dwarven-forged mauls for their main weapons. The giants couldn't stop smiling and couldn't wait to use them in battle. Estus even painted a dragon symbol on Barg's maul.

The caravan marched in the same formation out of the plains as they did into it. The rear guard consisted of the elfin questing knights, their animals, two Antaean giants, and before them, the Cut-throats in their new blacked armor and their chamroshes—especially frisky that morning—and one crawling tree to shield them all. The animal men and their animals marched before them with all the gnome races, the fauns, the majority of the hoofed fae, the fae blood men, and Bragg the dwelf and his men and their animals. The two center columns were made of humans, each equipped with fae gold and silver polearms, and the pech, carrying their large dwarven spiked shields and elfin weapons. There was another crawling tree then columns of the human domestics, servants, and laborers, the male half-elves, and the drows with Dr'amal and the fae-blood woman Ursi.

With a crawling tree at their back, the front consisted of King Aereth, with his royal guard of Mr. Nirgund the berserker and the reptilian fae hounds, alongside Lady Aylen and Maiden Gwyness, with their female half-elf royal guards. Their dragon-horse kirins walked beside them. Hobbs followed behind them at the head of the columns, with his two bodyguards, Mr. Tyfer and Mr. Oeric. Traveler and his dog led the caravan behind Pangolin's vanguard. At point, Pangolin's vanguard consisted of himself, Mr. Elman, four of the giants, and two dozen of the elaphine archer hunters.

A couple of hours into the march they could see the end of the plains and the beginning of the main Forest again.

"Mr. Traveler, most parties on land never make it past the edge of the Great Forest, I imagine," Lady Aylen said.

Traveler nodded. "That's why I first nicknamed it the Great Forest of Horrors as a boy. Such a concentration of predatory life that even the most accomplished of warrior caravans were simply worn down by the constant battle every step of the way. It's where one learns if the caravan master hired was any good. If you were killed, you knew you made an error in hiring."

The royals laughed at him.

"Mr. Traveler, we never had any doubts."

The front noticed the vanguard slowing to a stop.

"I hope we did not speak too soon, sire," Lady Aylen said.

As Traveler neared point, with his dog following, he saw what had caused the vanguard to stop the caravan—the shadow of the beast stood directly in their path just inside the tree line. A giant bear dozens of feet tall. Huge. They could see the outline of its massive claws. A giant bear waddling forward. Its mouth slowly opened as if to yawn, but instead it let out a roar so loud the trees seemed to shake.

"It's going to charge," Pangolin said, and he lifted his weapon.

All four Antaean giants gripped their war mauls tight.

Traveler noticed movement from the corner of his eye—Ursi.

The fae-blood woman walked toward the bear. Traveler raised a hand to signal to the vanguard to let her go forward.

The giant bear and the fae-blood woman met in the middle of the same path. The beast stared down at her. Then it crashed down on all fours. Pangolin and the giants were about to rush to her aid, but Traveler restrained them by simply raising his hand.

"It will not hurt her," he said.

They all watched.

"What do you see, Mr. Elman?" Pangolin asked.

"She has a hand on its snout. I think she's talking to it," the half-elf said.

"She is," an elaphine archer said. His eyes moved all around. "She speaks in its language."

The bear slowly turned and walked away into another part of the Forest.

Pangolin gave the signal, and the caravan moved forward. They stopped again when they reached Ursi, who waited for them on the path.

"A benefit of having a fae-blood of the bear clan amongst Titan's Caravan," Traveler said.

"He was not a threat. He was only curious about us," she said.

"That roar sounded like he was hungry," Grakdar said.

"If he wanted to make a meal of us, he would not have stood there watching us. He would have charged immediately. No matter. Either way I would have moved him on," she said.

"Thank you, Ursi," Traveler said.

"A simple matter," she said.

"Mr. Traveler, the lizards are spooked about something," Pangolin said.

The caravan master turned to see their giant fae lizards in a frenzy, looking at something in his direction. Traveler turned again to see the first spear burst through Ursi's stomach.

The human men known as the lizard minders took their duties deadly seriously. They were only human with no special abilities or magic but were tasked with guiding the caravan's two thousand nearly twenty-foot lizards in battle and protecting them however they could. The whole caravan knew of the lizards' uncanny ability to see invisible beings. They reacted to the invisible attackers before any of the other fae. The lizard minders pulled the metal ring from the walking chains of their lizards to let them move without restraint. The lizards swarmed out—

running on all fours then leaping at or spinning to strike with their tails.

Javelins came from nowhere. Ursi wasn't just impaled by one. She had two embedded in her shoulder, but she drew her sword and fought as if uninjured. She struck away another other javelin, but there was a flurry of them. The elaphine archers fired a frenetic volley in every direction. Lady Aylen instinctively caught one javelin in one hand and blocked another for Gwyness. She threw it back the way it came but all it did was hit the ground. Nirgund stood in front of King Aereth. His alphyns growled and jumped up and down on all fours, but they could not see the attackers.

The first crawling trees stretched out like a giant hand and swatted. Those at the front heard sounds of impact, but the giant lizards remained the caravan's chief defenders. Two thousand of the fae lizards attacked as a group, their armor blocking most of the spears thrown at them.

Then came the pech and Mr. Traveler. The caravan master threw what looked like a giant fruit. It exploded on something and the first attacker was revealed—a humanoid lizard man with four arms. But despite the yellow sap splashed on its upper body, it was disappearing. In moments the chameleon was gone again. Traveler slashed with his sword. A scream.

Pech ran forward and threw more fruit. More of the chameleon men were revealed. Now Pangolin and the giants could attack with their weapons.

More spears showered down upon them. The pech used their shields to protect themselves and others in the caravan. From the opposite direction, arrows sailed over their heads at the invisible chameleon men from the elfin questing knights at the rear. A wall of bluish smoke appeared before the caravan. Dr'amal made her wall spell grow taller into the air. The flying spears from the invisible chameleon man stopped.

"Heavy teams!" King Aereth yelled and ran to the men.

Catapults readied. Projectiles fired. One. Two. Five. More. The magic projectiles that landed exploded in lightning and thunder. Screams.

The giant lizards emerged from the bluish magic wall and ran to their masters.

"Dr'amal," Traveler said.

The magic wall dissipated.

"There," Grakdar said, pointing with his war maul.

Bodies of dead chameleon men were everywhere. Spears littered the ground.

The animal men also came to the front with their animals. The frog men, with their giant crabs, and the lizard men walked up to the fallen chameleon men. They touched a few bodies then seemed to be having an impromptu meeting. The animal men-- squirrel, raccoon, possum, fox, rabbit, bird and mice men all stood watch around their comrades. The possum men stood on their giant turtles, and the bird men's large jackalope and enfields guarded the group. The raccoon men's giant porcupines seemed to have the specific duty of protecting the giant ducks and cranes. The surly mole sat on the back of his giant carnivorous moose watching it all.

"Oh, no." Gwyness ran to Ursi.

Others noticed the spear embedded in Ursi's chest. She raised her hands and wouldn't let anyone touch her.

"Stay back from me," she said.

What was dripping from her chest wound was not blood. It looked like liquid light.

Gresham appeared. Some of the lizards had been wounded by javelins.

"Leave them to me," Zefea the fauness said to the caravan's healer. "I'll tend to the animals. You tend to the humans and humanoids."

Gresham ran to the group that surrounded Ursi.

"Everyone!" Traveler yelled. "Get into defensive formation. We're vulnerable!"

"Giants!" Pangolin yelled. The vanguard leader joined the animal men, and the giants took positions around all of them. Other than a few fae, no one knew what the caravan's frog and lizard men were debating, but it ended soon. The animal men moved back into the caravan with their animals.

Hobbs had already taken charge to restore order.

Ursi stood like a statue. She was hyperventilating, and her hands were like claws—bearlike. Her gaze had a far-off look.

"She will not let you move her," a gnome said to Gresham. The pack of fae-blood men stood at the front.

Traveler sheathed his sword. "Mr. Hobbs, Mr. Gresham, get me a tent. Everyone, move back into the caravan and away from her."

Traveler and the two men erected the tent over Ursi.

"You can both leave," he said.

"Shall I set up camp here, sir?" Hobbs asked.

"Temporary only, but heavy guard. We cannot stay long. The chameleon men will return."

Hobbs and Gresham left the tent. Traveler followed.

When the caravan master returned, he had his healing bag in hand.

"Ursi, I'm not supposed to be a healer anymore."

He dropped his bag on the ground. The dog ran inside the tent. Traveler got up and closed the tent. He took out one bowl and collected all the liquid light dripping from her in one. He used a large spoon to collect all the rest from the ground.

"Are you in pain?" Traveler asked.

"No."

"I'll remove the javelins from your shoulder first."

He gently pulled one out then the other.

"The fabric of your clothing is like armor, but it didn't protect you from these javelins. They must be made of material whose magic you have no defense against, not wood though. I would say they may be made of some magic insect beast."

She nodded. He pulled another bowl from his bag, and the dog, now in a humanoid form, gripped the javelin in her back.

"Pull," he said to the dog.

The dog yanked it out. Traveler collected all the liquid light spilling out from her back in the other bowl before plugging the hole with a clay-covered leaf. The front hole he already had his hand pressed against.

"Cover the front wound with your hands," he said to her.

She clasped both hands over his. He slid his out, and she grabbed at her skin to keep the hole closed.

"Do I need to sew the holes shut? Or can I have one of the fae do it?"

"No. You do it."

Ursi's skin was clammy and grayish. She shook slightly as she sweat, her eyes dark.

He did not ask if it would hurt her as he stitched all four wounds shut, sewing the skin together like fabric. He returned his instruments to his healing bag.

"I will return my healing bag to my things and be back."

The moment he stepped out of the tent, a small crowd waited for him.

"Is she all right, Mr. Traveler?" Gwyness asked.

"Yes."

"I can take that," Hobbs said as he took the healing bag from Traveler.

"Should I check on her?" Gresham asked.

"I will ask."

Traveler opened the flap of the tent and stepped inside.

She had her back to the entrance, her head tilted up. She drank the last contents of the bowl. Ursi turned to face him. In her hands, were all the bowls, one inside the other—all empty.

"I will need no further attention."

The fae-blood woman looked as she did before the attack, as she had always looked, as if she had never been attacked. The grayish tint to her skin, the sweats, were gone. Her solid bearing and demeanor had been restored.

There was not a single drop of the liquid light in any of the bowls. Traveler took them.

"You've treated fae-bloods before," she said.

"No, a sprite healer I knew did."

"As you're a healer, I can entrust my treatment will remain in absolute secrecy."

"Of course. I know you're an extremely private people."

"Deeply. Do not speak about this or me. No matter if asked. I healed myself is sufficient to say, if you must, but not in front of the elves."

"You should rest."

"No. I am whole. I am needed on the march. These lizard men were more than invisible."

"Chameleon men. Their skin is magic. Invisible and able to mimic the background around them to appear invisible even when seen."

"I did not hear them or sense them."

"Most fae don't, but they cannot fool our giant lizards. I'll have Hobbs strike camp, and we'll set out immediately. The chameleon men travel in large hunting parties and may return to attack us again."

Traveler marched with the vanguard. The dog trotted along, slightly changing its form to a fine coat of green fur. Pangolin glanced back at the elaphine with the mirage staff.

"Our magic staff did not have an effect on our invisible attackers," the vanguard leader said.

"It does not work on all inhabitants of the Forest," Traveler said. "Chameleon men are especially immune to magical defenses."

"Master Traveler, I'm not clear on their abilities," Mr. Elman began. "Were they invisible or in plain sight? My eyes could not tell."

"Mr. Elman, their skin has the ability to match perfectly with the environment they are in. Most living things are fooled by their magical ability. Most but not our giant lizards."

"How many were there?" Pangolin asked.

"Chameleon men travel in hunting parties of hundreds. Fortunately for us, their weapons are not exceptional, and they do not have the strength to throw with the speed and power of an elf or elaphine with an arrow."

"Fortunate, indeed," Grakdar said.

"They will return?" Pangolin asked Traveler.

"Likely, but not immediately. We should be long gone by the time they do. This part of the Forest is their domain along with many amphibian and water reptile humanoids."

"Is this why you said our animal men were important to the caravan?" Pangolin asked.

"You have already seen so yourself. The animal men in Faë-Land may not be acquainted with those of the Great Forest, but they speak the same languages. Hopefully, our animal men can talk us out of future battles."

"If all we have to contend with in these coming days are hordes of animal men rather than ferocious giant animals, then I would say we'll have a leisurely march," Grakdar said.

Traveler could see the vanguard team members looking for him to respond, but he did not.

"The Forest is changing," he finally said.

"Yes, Master Traveler. The giant trees are different, not tall and erect with their branches high above us. The branches sprout perpendicular to the ground and..."

"What do you see, Mr. Elman?" Pangolin asked, already grabbing his telescope from his armor.

"Frog men."

"Toad men, Mr. Elman," Traveler said. "We may have left behind us the structured civilization of human and fae with our cities and villages, but here, like all nomadic people, they carry their villages with them. Mr. Elman, look for their giant animals. That will tell us if they are hunter-gatherers and can be reasoned with or are hunter-destroyers like the marauders of our human lands and will need to be killed for us to move forward. Sorry, Mr. Grakdar and giants. No leisurely march for us."

A giant green net stretched out like a wall. That was the appearance of the Forest ahead. Others in the caravan described it as a spider's web woven with the branches of giant trees. Giant branches wound from their trees, stretching vertically to the ground covered in plants and vines, but the attention of the caravan was focused on the humanoids that waited in the trees before them. The toad men stood on branches, from the lowest, ten feet above the ground, to those branches, high up beyond clear view, enshrouded in deep shadows of the Forest canopy above into the sky. The trees were infested with the six-foot-tall bright-green amphibian men with orange stripes and white body tattoos. They carried spears covered in black spikes, which had main tips that looked like large hornet stingers.

Pangolin had already given the signal to stop. Before them was a sea of toad warriors. No giant animals were seen, but it didn't matter.

"They do not look so deadly to me," Bragg, the giant, said.

"But how many of them are there?" Grakdar asked. "We love to fight, but I don't want to be here all day."

"They're toad men, not gnolls or goblins. We wouldn't even need our war mauls to repel them. Their green skins are no thicker than parchment."

Traveler returned to the vanguard with the caravan's frog men and their giant crabs, the possum men on their giant turtles, and the lizard men, and they took the lead. The three different animal men races moved to the tree horde of toad warriors.

One of the frog men yelled out in some language. He spoke for a long time, and as he did toad warriors jumped down from the giant tree branches. The toad warriors walked to the animal men, at first using their spears as walking staffs, then they stopped to point them.

The caravan's frog men left their giant crabs behind and approached with the lizard men at their flanks. None of them drew their weapons. For the first time, those in the caravan noticed that all the frog men did not look alike. The frog man speaking was clearly the leader from his body markings. Some of the toad warriors yelled out, then one did the majority of the talking as he walked about three feet from the frog men's leader. The toad warrior raised his spear as if he was about to strike.

Pangolin signaled, and the elaphine archer warriors aimed arrows at the toad warrior, ready to fire. The entire horde of toad warriors on the ground and all the branches went into a frenzy, raising their spears and jumping in place.

"Lower your arrows," Traveler said.

The elaphine archers relaxed and pointed their nocked arrows toward the ground.

The animal men seemed upset that the vanguard had been about to defend them as they, pointed at the vanguard and yelled something. Pangolin looked at Traveler, confused. He saw the caravan master's grin.

The frog men ceased their yelling and returned their attention to the toad warrior leader. The parley went on for some time. The frog man leader motioned to Traveler. The caravan master approached but gestured for the dog to remain with the vanguard. When Traveler reached them, the frog men pointed at him, and the toad men studied at him and poked him with their hands.

"What are they doing?" Lady Aylen asked.

The royals joined the vanguard.

"The frog men are telling the toad men that Traveler is a friend." It was the first time that any of the animal men had spoken to them directly. The bird man was crouched down to keep the party's enfields calm, stroking their fox heads.

Finally, Traveler casually strolled back to them. Everyone watched as the frog men and lizard men moved through the toad men on the ground—each touching each other in their custom of greeting.

"Mr. Hobbs," Traveler said.

"Yes, sir?" The steward walked to him with his two guardsmen, Tyfer and Oeric.

"We will be trading with the toad men for passage through their territory. Have the pech help you. Let's give them some of our spices."

"Yes, sir. How much should we part with?"

"Between our animal men and the pech, work it out."

"Is there anything to be gained by this trade, Mr. Traveler?" King Aereth asked.

"Safe passage. Get used to it, sire. We're likely to be doing this type of trade often, paying people not to attack us. Personally, I find it more than fair compared to the alternatives."

"There are marauder clans that do the same, Mr. Traveler. 'Pay us to not rob you of everything,'" Lady Aylen said angrily.

"Yes, princess. It's exactly like that. Do you want to pay something or be robbed of everything? In this case, pay something or have to fight our way through the Forest, losing resources and lives. This is their home, princess. They have the advantage and they know it. Our advantage is they know we can kill them all if we're forced to. Let's make the trade, give them more so they are happy, maybe get a little information, and be on our way. This is why we brought so many supplies—not for us but to give away. Another mistake many a caravan in the past has made."

"It's the cost of doing business in someone else's lands, Lady Aylen. It's no different than in our lands," King Aereth said.

Lady Aylen sighed. "We leave civilization behind but not the corruption."

Traveler said, "I expect nothing but our best behavior. Join our frog and lizard men to be introduced to the toad warrior leaders."

"Our extortionists, you mean," Lady Aylen said.

"I'm surprised by your attitude, princess. As a royal, you should be schooling me on the ways of society."

"I was born into royalty. I did not choose it."

"I'm going to ignore you now, princess. You're in a mood. You've reminded me that this is how we first met in Caravan's Row. You felt the Four Kings were extorting money from those who wished to be paid members of their alliance, and you would have none of it. Though, if you had not done as you did, our caravan would not have you, Maiden Gwyness, or your men, but you must push this notion out of your mind. Sire, talk to her. What is our goal? To get to Atlantea as quickly as possible with the least number of lives lost. If we have to fight, we do so to win, but if we can avoid it by paying or running, then we pay or run. I see no dishonor in that. Many honorable people have been buried and swallowed up by the Forest. I buried many myself."

"Leave it to me, Mr. Traveler," King Aereth said. "Lady Aylen and I will meet these toad warriors."

"Yes, sire. Have a demeanor of graciousness with them. Think of it this way, princess. We're not giving away goods for nothing. We're paying for the privilege to not have to bury one of our men in the Forest."

"Hear! Hear!" Pangolin said.

"I understand, Mr. Traveler," Lady Aylen said.

King Aereth led her and their guardspeople toward the awaiting group of frog, lizard, and toad men.

"And, princess," Traveler said in a softer tone.

She turned. "Yes, Mr. Traveler."

"These toad warriors are distant allies of both water elves and water elementals. Something to keep in mind. Water elves are enemies to a race of dark fae called morgens."

She smiled. "Thank you, Mr. Traveler, for reminding me. I keep forgetting I'm a water elf."

The men of the camp were amazed. The frog, lizard, and toad men were still talking amongst one another even as the sun began to set. Crowds of the toad men had surrounded the caravan's frog and lizard men. Many asked Traveler what they could possibly be talking about nonstop for hours.

"They have a couple of centuries of history and gossip to catch up on between their clans," Traveler answered.

Hobbs had the full night camp set up. While most of the brownies carried on their nightly duties as usual, a contingent of them also watched the large parley of the reptile and amphibian men. Toad men appeared with spears, their tips engulfed in flames for illumination. The royals had been shown around by the toad men, but thankfully, they had been released to return to camp.

"Is there a race that can speak for as long and as rapidly as these animal men, Mr. Traveler?" Lady Aylen asked.

The leadership were gathered at the edge of the camp together. Mr. Quillen sat on the ground nearby, sketching an almost exact representation of the scene.

"Fairies are the same but speak much faster," he answered.

"We did not get a chance to ask them about the dark fae you mentioned, Mr. Traveler," King Aereth said.

"Do not worry, sire. The toad men will want to speak with you again. For you and the princess, it will be a long night."

"Why only us, Mr. Traveler? You're an equal leader," Lady Aylen said. "Besides, in reality, you're a royal, too, of an entire elfin kingdom."

"Nice attempt, princess, but if you remember, I relinquished any claim to that elfin kingdom."

"The king and I have had many opportunities to speak. We're on to you. I would not be surprised if you're actually a prince of some kingdom somewhere."

"Only a prince?" Traveler asked, smiling.

"Prince, king, emperor, if you like."

While the human members of the caravan remained wide awake, most of the day fae were fast asleep. The giants were always the first to bed. Traveler noticed both the moon elf leader, Shadu-mun, who was watching the animal men, and Dr'as, who stood with a small group of drows nearby. The two races never would stand next to one another.

"Do we have a new ally within the Great Forest, Mr. Traveler?" the moon elf knight asked.

"Possibly, Mr. Shadu-mun. Our frog men have made the introduction, Lady Aylen will hopefully make it official."

"Good. It would be desirable to count one race among this vast Forest as an ally."

"Our animal men speak our language. These toads do not seem to," Lady Aylen said.

"They do not speak our tongues, princess," Traveler said. "But their ears have heard elfish. You should speak to them. Even if they do not understand the words, they know the language. The frog men will translate for you."

"What are morgens, Mr. Traveler, this dark fae ahead?" King Aereth asked.

"Morgens?" Shadu-mun asked. "How far ahead?"

"Not far," Traveler said. "The day vanguard will encounter them first. Mr. Pangolin and I met last night. Sire, morgens are powerful water nymphs of evil that like to drown victims or wash them away with floods like their dark cousins, sirens. Do not be fooled by their beauty. We reach their domain by tomorrow."

"Look, sire," the king's guardsman, Mr. Nirgund said.

The frog men were gesturing to them wildly.

The night was indeed a long one for both the king and Lady Aylen as they had been brought in and were now a part of the conversation between the two groups.

"What can you tell us about the ones called morgens?" Lady Aylen asked. A frog man translated her words.

Suddenly the toad men on the ground and in all the branches above and around them went into an uproar. The warriors pounded their spears on the ground or trees.

"We can take that as confirmation of what Mr. Traveler said," King Aereth said.

"They are not allies," Lady Aylen said. "They're enemies."

"The morgens are bad. They steal toad clan territory, send creatures after them to kill their people and animals," a frog man said.

"Can the toad men help us in any way against the morgens?" Lady Aylen asked.

"No, they cannot help us. They do not want a war with them. They have a truce with the morgens and will not break it."

"Can they give us any information about the morgens?" Lady Aylen asked.

The frog man asked the toad men in their language.

The chatter went on for more than an hour. At times it seemed more like the frog men and toad men were yelling at each other and were moments from coming to blows.

"They can tell you something but they will want more spices," the frog man said.

"Why am I not surprised," an exasperated Lady Aylen said.

At daybreak, with the toad warriors absent from their perches in the netlike trees, the caravan was able to fully appreciate how many of the amphibian men must have been there the day before. They had thought the Forest before them was dense and thick with leaves. Now, they saw a clear view, all the way for as far as the eye could see.

Most of the men were still fast asleep. Traveler instructed Hobbs to let the camp sleep in late, including the royals who had only gone to bed an hour ago.

"Mr. Hobbs, with most of the men asleep, you will be working with our fauns." Traveler had led the steward to the center of the camp, where the caravan's gnome and horned gnomoid parties were all busy at work weaving what looked to Hobbs to be translucent fabric.

"What do you have there?" he asked them.

"Magic," a smiling gnome said.

"They're reweaving our pocket-realm that was destroyed by the moving killing tree," Traveler said. "The work requires many hours to remake it then to fortify it. Gnomes and brownies are well versed in the practice."

"Yes, we are, Master Traveler," a gnome said.

"You, Mr. Hobbs, will work with our fauns to create new charms for both humans and fae."

"Against these morgen creatures, sir?"

"Yes. Any nymph, whether of day or night, good or evil, has magic entrancing powers. It isn't only the humans of the caravan who are vulnerable. Ah, Zefea."

Hobbs turned and saw the caravan's sole fauness approaching.

"Mr. Hobbs will work with you and your fauns on the charms. When the men awake, he will see to it that all the humans replace them."

"The magic of these charms will need to be very strong. We can smell the water ahead. Magic water can weaken their power. Morgens may not be as powerful as sirens, but they are formidable nonetheless. They can also enchant water animals. The animal men have giant ducks, cranes, crabs, and turtles."

"They should be immune."

Zefea shook her head. "That is the true source of the enmity between the toad men and the morgens. The dark water nymphs enchant their animals and take them away from the toad men out of spite."

"We will watch them."

"Should I fetch Mr. Gresham, sir?"

"I have Mr. Gresham working on another task," Traveler replied.

Hobbs remembered when they first entered the magical lands and how he had been tasked with making their original charms of herbs and crystals to protect the men from enchantment spells from fairies and nymphs.

For much of the day, he sat with a group of the fauns, including Zefea, to fashion new charms—larger necklaces of herbs, vines, and crystals coated with clear magic liquids.

"The liquid will protect the charm as the charm protects its wearer," Zefea told him.

"Are you noble or royal, Zefea?" Hobbs asked.

The fauns laughed. "We are not elves or humans. We are simple people. We do not believe in kings and queens and the like. I am the daughter of the chief of our clan."

"How do I address you?"

"You elves and humans are very similar. My father is the only one with a title. My first name is sufficient, Mr. Hobbs."

The other fauns laughed.

With a smile, Hobbs asked, "Have you seen Mr. Frog-Dor?"

The steward could see the faun's face change from joyous to expressionless.

"Master Traveler should speak to him."

"Has something happened?"

"He's not doing well. The memories of his magical imprisonment are haunting him."

"I will speak to Mr. Traveler, then. I was hoping he could rise to be the caravan's chief sorcerer."

"He certainly has the magic to be, but his mind is damaged. He may never be whole, though his body is."

"Can magic heal him, his mind?"

"Perhaps. But it is magic I do not possess."

"I will stop by to see him when we're done."

"If you can find him."

"He's hiding?"

"Yes."

Hobbs was troubled by the news.

Hobbs entered the camp of the drows. Their sentries sat around campfires and barely acknowledged him. He was about to say something when the drow sorceress came out of her tent.

"Mistress Dr'amal, may I have a word?"

"Yes, Mr. Hobbs."

"It's regarding, Mr. Frog-Dor. The fauns told me he's hiding."

"He's being tormented by dreams."

"Dreams, but..."

"The dreams are not attacks on him. The dreams are from within himself. He is tormenting himself," Dr'amal said.

"But he's been doing so well," the steward said with sadness.

"It happens. Who is to say what brought it out in him? The man was cursed as a frog for many years of his life."

"But he's free of the curse."

"His body is, not his mind."

"Does this not seem strange to you, that it should happen now? It's happenings when others have had troubling dreams."

"It does, but I do not sense any magic at work," the drowess said.

"Might it be beyond your detection ability?" Hobbs asked.

"Possibly."

"Can you help me find him?"

"Mr. Hobbs, you should not go looking for him. He is in a state that makes him dangerous to himself and others. He must work it out on his own."

"Is that wise?"

"I recommend it."

"Thank you. I will inform Mr. Traveler."

Dr'amal nodded. Hobbs excused himself from the drow camp.

Traveler was not at his map table when Hobbs arrived. He sat on the ground playing with the dog, stroking his sides, playfully rubbing the dog's forehead and nose ridge.

"Come in, Mr. Hobbs," Traveler said, rising and gesturing Hobbs in.

"Hello, sir. The charms are ready for the men. I will pass them out at dinner. Should I exchange them with the old charms?"

"Have them wrap the old charm around the wrist of their fighting arm. You can never have too much magic here."

"Yes, sir. I wanted to tell you about Mr. Frog-Dor."

"Yes, I was told already by the fenodyree."

"Is he all right, sir?"

"He needs time alone for the moment."

"Is he dangerous, sir?"

"Only to himself, it would seem."

"I was saying to Mistress Dr'amal that these dreams seem to be afflicting the caravan all at the same time. She felt it was not an attack."

"She could be right. The Forest is of magic. All is heightened within it. A fleeting dream in Faë-Land becomes a vivid one indistinguishable from real life here, a simple nightmare becomes one of horrific proportions. I have already spoken to others in the caravan. He will be monitored."

"Good, sir. It's a shame. He was doing so well."

"He will come through it."

The female half-elves had risen from their beds hours ago, but Lady Aylen and Gwyness took advantage of the extra sleep. For the night meal, the female half-elves woke the women and had their food brought into the women's tent. The meat from Mr. Bragg's hunt was still being served to the caravan. They all ate watching the tiny owl griffins chase each other, running, jumping, and flying.

Watching the hybrid beasts always brought smiles to everyone's faces.

"I wonder if water elves eat meat like this," Lady Aylen said. "Or do they only eat fish?"

"You can ask them when you see one," Gwyness said.

"Or I can simply ask Mr. Traveler. He knows all about elves."

"Yes, he does, m'lady..."

Gwyness stopped eating. The seven half-elves noticed too. Lady Aylen was on her feet rubbing her forehead, her eyes closed tight. She dropped her hands. Her head jerked from side to side.

"What's wrong with her?"

Lady Aylen opened her eyes and they looked to be filled with water. Gwyness's mouth dropped open, and she jumped up from the ground and bolted from the tent.

The female half-elves were standing in a group, watching the princess, holding the tiny owl griffins, when Gwyness returned with Traveler. Lady Aylen was in a trance.

"What's wrong with her?" Gwyness asked Traveler.

"There are water elves nearby."

Shadu-mun, the moon elf, stepped into the tent too. Suddenly, Dr'as and Dr'amal entered too.

"Water elves?" Gwyness asked. "But why is she acting this way, Mr. Traveler?"

"She can sense them."

"We must break her out of the trance!" Dr'as yelled. "If she can sense them, they can sense us."

"In this case, I must agree with the drow," Shadu-mun said. "We don't know who these water elves may be. If they're allied with the sky elves, they are our enemies."

Traveler left the tent.

"How do we break the trance?" Gwyness called out.

"I could stab her," Shadu-mun said.

"Don't even think of it," Gwyness said angrily.

Traveler returned to the tent and threw a magic fireball at her. Lady Aylen's dress quickly became engulfed in flames. She yelled, and all the water in bowls and cups in the tent crashed in on her to extinguish the fire.

"You set me on fire!" she yelled.

"Gentlemen and sorceress, the princess is free from her trance. Let us leave these women be and go about our business. Good night, princess."

Traveler led Shadu-mun, Dr'as and Dr'amal from the tent.

"I should drown him!" Lady Aylen yelled.

The female half-elves turned so she couldn't see their faces.

"If I hear one laugh from anyone in this tent, I will drown you too!"

Gwyness ran from the tent.

Noon was about an hour away. From the time the caravan exited the entwined netlike trees and got back to the giant tree structures they were accustomed to, they noticed the change in the earth. The more they walked, the wetter the ground became. For more than an hour, the sloshing of nearly ten thousand feet echoed.

Pangolin especially did not like the caravan announcing its approach for all to hear. His hand rose to slow the caravan, then he brought it to a complete stop.

"A boulder, Mr. Elman?" he asked.

"No, a structure made of branches, Mr. Pangolin."

The dome-like structure blocked their path.

"What is that?" Grakdar asked.

A giant beaver rose on its hind legs behind the structure. It was twice the size of the giants. Traveler had reached them. The vanguard looked at him.

"The beaver has claimed our path as part of its abode," Traveler said.

"Can we go around?" Pangolin asked.

"We have to scout ahead," Traveler said.

"We can do that, Mr. Traveler," Pangolin said. "Archers, watch us closely and fire at anything that attacks us. Mr. Elman, behind me. Giants, we go."

Traveler watched as the vanguard moved slowly toward the—at the moment—docile giant beaver.

"We can pick up its tree house and throw it off the path," Grakdar said.

"Somehow I think it won't like that," Pangolin said.

"It can salvage it or make another one."

Pangolin gestured for them to wait. "I'll move ahead. It's less likely to attack if it's only me."

The vanguard leader stepped ahead slowly. The eyes of the giant beaver locked onto his. Pangolin had reached the structure and looked around. The beast's construction was attached to the giant tree with mud. He slowly reached toward it. The beaver made a sound. Pangolin returned his gaze to the beast. From the shaking of its body, he knew it was about to leap at him. He slowly stepped back to the vanguard.

"What do we want to do?" Pangolin asked. "We move forward, it attacks. We touch its home, it attacks."

"Are we seriously being stopped in our tracks by a beaver, a water rat?" Grakdar asked.

"A twenty-foot beaver," Pangolin said.

"It's a beaver, a water rodent that builds tree houses with mud and saliva. If our king were to learn of this, we would be thrown out of our kingdom," Grakdar said.

"Our children would disown us," Barg said. "Our wives would throw us out."

"We cannot kill it," Pangolin said. "This is its home. We're the trespassers."

"Cannot Mr. Traveler's dog turn into a giant cat and scare it away or pick it up and throw it and its tree house away?"

"No, Mr. Grakdar, my dog will not do that," Traveler said. "I learned the lesson a long time ago. Do not anger the Great Forest."

"What does that mean? The Forest will be mad if we push the rodent out of our way?"

"It means, Mr. Grakdar, to be humble when it's called for. Mr. Pangolin is right. We are better beings, so we will go around it," Traveler said.

"How long will that take? There's nowhere to go around."

"Look at this," Pangolin said.

The mole-looking fae rode up on his giant carnivorous moose. He yelled at the giant beaver several times. The beaver yelled back, almost like a roar, but got back down on four feet and ran off. The mole man gestured for them to move forward.

"How do we get through?" Grakdar asked.

The lead crawling tree became a bridge in front of them and over the giant beaver's structure. Three of the Tree Shepherds were suddenly standing with them. Greenwig extended a hand to signal them to start across the bridge.

"I say we should have smashed the water rodent's tree house," Grakdar said in a huff.

In Faë–Land Minor, the land of fairies and sprites, the caravan had seen a magical floating river. The moment they marched out from under the giant trees, they stood in awe at what was above them, not one but many floating rivers, each wider than most rivers any of the humans had seen. The speed of the rivers created tremendous gusts of wind across them. All of the rivers were saturated with life.

Someone yanked Pangolin back before he could react. From within the rushing river flowing past them, a giant green arm with claws as sharp as a sword almost grabbed him. Instead the claws slashed his chestplate. The gouges quickly disappeared from the magical earth elemental armor. The green arm pulled back into its waters in the distance. He glanced back. His savior had been Traveler.

"If you had not done that, Mr. Traveler, where would I have been off to?"

"You might have kept from being the sea serpent's meal but, unfortunately, you'd be on your way to the lands that even elementals never return from."

"Then I owe you my life."

"We all protect each other's lives on the Trail."

"Sea serpents and we're not even half way to the oceans," Pangolin said. "I would never have guessed I could be snatched away in the middle of the Great Forest by a sea serpent in a flying river."

"Your men must take extreme care," Traveler said. "We have the protection of our crawling trees, but they, too, can be snatched away by creatures within the flying rivers. We will stay for a moment, and I will find us the safest path."

"You're not scouting ahead alone," Pangolin said.

"All I need is my telescope. The rivers shift from side to side and up and down over time."

"In any of your previous caravans, Master Traveler, did you lose men at these flying rivers?" Grakdar asked.

"One of my previous caravans made the deadly mistake of believing that the flying rivers of the Great Forest were the same as the flying river in Faë-Land Minor. Men reached into the waters. Others ran under them in awe. A caravan of five thousand was reduced to less than twenty men in mere minutes. The giant fish and creatures within the rivers are also able to jump out and back to eat or grab prey."

Immediately, the vanguard stepped farther back.

Everyone in the caravan could see the fear in the faces of the Tree Shepherds upon hearing that their crawling trees could be grabbed by the water beasts of the flying rivers. The Tree Shepherds shrank all three of the crawling trees to the size of a palm and put them into the pockets of their robes.

Traveler left them to approach one of his pull-carts in the care of one of the pech. Everyone nervously looked at each other, even the fae. The life within the flying rivers were visible even moving by at their tremendous speeds. Most were giant fish of some type, but then there were creatures—some grotesque, some humanoid. More than a few reached out to grab at them but only grasped air. None of the caravan could see any path they could march cross to avoid the flying rivers.

Traveler returned to the vanguard with a broken curved-blade dagger.

"I will go first," he said as he made a circle with the dagger.

A portal appeared, and caravan master and dog stepped through. Swirling winds formed a circular doorway in mid-air just above the ground and large enough for their giants and widest animals.

"I see him," Elman said, pointing. "They're across."

Everyone gave a collective sigh of relief. The caravan marched through the tunnel, each human, fae, and animal stepping out on the other side of the valley, clear of all the flying rivers.

"I wondered when we would see our caravan master use portal magic on this journey," Lyre, the high elf, said. A few of the elfin questing knights had moved to the vanguard.

"Does that mean you believe me to be a true caravan master, Mr. Lyre?"

"We already knew that back at Fae'el, Mr. Traveler."

"Why can't you use the portal's magic to take us clear to…" Taylos saw Traveler's stern look. "Titan's Fall?"

"Do you wish to tell your elfin comrade, Mr. Lyre?" Traveler asked.

"The magic of the Forest prevents such long distances. None would arrive. The magic portal collapses, and we'd be scattered everywhere," Lyre said.

"If it were that simple, Mr. Taylos, you would not need a caravan master such as me. Besides, we are not a small group. We may not be as large as the numbers of the old Kings' Caravan, but we're nearly ten thousand not including our animals, our multiple pocket-realms, and our possessions, which would require more magic than most normal portal spells can manage."

Traveler pointed. "The ground river ahead should be safe. Greenwig, what do you see?"

The Tree Shepherd leader stared at it. "We will get a closer view."

Greenwig and Mossberry walked to the river.

"Lady Aylen, you should go with them."

The princess nodded and followed the Tree Shepherds. Her catfish-faced kirin appeared out of invisibility beside her, bringing a smile to her face.

Gwyness looked back to see her own kirin walking to her. "They came out."

"It is safe, then," Traveler said.

Their caravan master walked back to the main columns.

At the river, the Tree Shepherds released their crawling trees. All three trees grew to their normal size and stuck their roots into the magic river to drink. The trees grew larger. Out burst the fairy sisters and their butterfly swarms. The giggling sisters, two balls of lights, flew around the caravan as their swarms settled in the branches of the crawling trees.

Lady Aylen stared at the magic river and touched the surface with her hand.

"Did you sense other water elves, m'lady?"

"I did. Not anymore, but they were close. I think there were many of them."

"Another caravan."

"We seem to be encountering quite a few when it should only be us."

Traveler had the caravan's magic healing caladrius bird perched on his raised forearm. Gwyness drew closer to touch the magic bird's beautiful feathers.

"We're thankful that we haven't had to use your healing powers, as of late," she said.

The caravan master let it go, and the bird flew to the river and dove in and out, slowly, bathing in its waters. Pech followed with empty buckets, as did fauns and many of the animal men.

"We will gather as much water as possible," Traveler said.

The four hairy fenodyree appeared at the river, too, with buckets. They smiled at the royals and Gwyness as they collected water.

"Is this for us, Mr. Traveler, or for trade?" Lady Aylen asked.

"We have two thousand giant lizards and six giants who drink as much water as all the rest of us combined in the caravan. We collect for us and to trade."

"Are we going to set up camp, sir?" Hobbs asked.

"We might as well, Mr. Hobbs. It's relatively safe here. Once we cross the river, it will be quite the opposite."

"Those morgens?" Lady Aylen asked.

"Among other creatures."

On the opposite side of the ground river, a small herd of giant water buffalo stopped to drink. While many in the party collected water into the night, a few of the men took to using long polearms from Mr. Estus's weapons vault to try their hand at spear fishing. The water was clear enough to see the bottom, and the glowing fish were there, albeit the size of a man. The spear fishing became a contest between the human men with fae looking on.

The drow night guards had tripled their sentries and patrols. The moon elves did the same and were joined by their high elf and desert elf comrades.

The royals watched them from their tents.

"Are our elfin and drow friends expecting trouble?" Lady Aylen asked, more to herself.

"Sire?" Mr. Nirgund appeared at the entrance with Chief Ethor and Dr'as.

The berserker guardsman led the two fae into the king's tent. Lady Aylen and Gwyness joined them.

"I will summon, Mr. Traveler," Nirgund said.

"I am here." Traveler entered with his dog.

"Is this about me?" Lady Aylen asked.

"You did sense the presence of your kind," Chief Ethor said to her.

"This is a serious matter, Mr. Traveler. The water elves she sensed, were they part of another caravan?" Dr'as asked.

"Yes, they were," Traveler said.

"On the ground, at night?" Ethor asked, incredulously.

"Floating above us toward the oceans."

"I was not aware that water elves traveled at night unless they were in the company of sky elves—cloud, star, or celestial elves. Our enemies," Ethor said.

"They made no indication that they were even aware of us," Traveler said.

"Unless they also sensed our elfin royal here," Dr'as added.

"They're gone. They didn't stop. They flew by us, and that was it."

"This doesn't concern you, Master Traveler?" Chief Ethor asked.

"Many things concern me, chief. This least of all."

"What are your other concerns?" the woodland elf chieftain asked.

"We've encountered a few flying caravans on the Trail. Coincidence? Perhaps, perhaps not. Vivid dreams among the men. The väki told me that something fell to Pan-Earth from the sky far ahead of us. They are of fire elemental magic, and it was powerful enough for them to sense it from within their pocket-realm."

"How far ahead of us?" Ethor asked.

"A few weeks, a month away."

"Master Traveler, you had us leave the protection of the Atlas turtles. Do you still believe that was wise?"

"Chief Ethor, I do. These flying caravans were on a path directly over Titan's Fall."

"What does that mean, then?" Dr'as asked. "You believe others wait for us?"

"I don't know, Dr'as, but I do not want to chance it. The Great Forest is a vast, vast region, but still we've encountered other parties. One may be expected, but not more than one, especially ones aware of us."

"Do we need to abandon the Trail all together?" Ethor asked.

"I'm thinking we might."

"How would such a radical change affect our journey?" Dr'as asked.

"It would add more time and increase the danger."

"But increase the chances of survival and getting to our destination," Ethor said.

"Yes."

"Mr. Traveler, do what you must," King Aereth said. "We have full confidence in your decision."

Again, the Great Forest opened up into treeless plains, but instead of Safari Plains, as the men had dubbed it, it was water-logged brownish grass of vast marshy lands. The region was, in fact, another river to cross, shallow, choked with brown grass to give the appearance of solid ground.

All columns of the vanguard stood at the marshy river's edge. Traveler, Pangolin, Elman, and the giants stared through telescopes to survey the path across.

"How deep do you think it is?" Pangolin asked.

"There's no way to know for sure until we move across," Traveler replied, "but what I'm concerned about is what may live in its waters."

"A horse!"

The men turned.

A grayish horse galloped to the left flank of the giant lizards and their minders. The animal looked like an injured flying horse, its wings ripped from his body, leaving mere stumps. The men saw the indecision in Traveler's face.

"Do not allow the beast to get too close!" he finally yelled out.

The creature yelled out and ran at the flank.

"Archers!" Traveler yelled.

The creature changed from its equine form to a humanoid one covered in wet, shaggy hair similar to their own fenodyree, but its face was enraged with sharp teeth and white fish eyes. Down one of its arms went to grab the muddy earth and fling it at the faces of the men. It leapt over the giant lizards and, in a blink, landed and grabbed one of the minders. Multiple arrows struck. It yelled out and leapt back over the giant lizards but clutched the screaming lizard minder in its clawed hands. The human male was helpless. Rocks pummeled the creature's humanoid face—thrown by the pech—almost knocking its head off. More arrows landed. The crawling tree grabbed the man, but the creature would not let go despite the onslaught it was enduring.

Leaping over her kirin and landing, the ground giving way beneath her, Lady Aylen had to contort her body to steady her balance with one hand on the wet earth while she grabbed her weapon with the other. She reached the creature before Traveler, the drows, and the elves racing to it. She severed the creature's forearm with her new war trident. The creature yelled out and ran. It transformed into a horse and dove into the marshy river.

Three other kelpies rose from the marshy grounds, but they heard the growls. Bragg's Diomedian Mares rushed at them. The carnivorous mares attacked the equine shape-shifting sprites in a frenzy. The kelpies retreated but the Mares tried to dig up the ground after them. Bragg, the dwelf, reached them and pulled them back.

The injured lizard minder lay on the ground as his comrades surrounded him to give aid. One of them yelled for the healer, Mr. Gresham.

"Lady Aylen, for the first time, you moved like a true elf," Lyre the high elf said to her.

She nodded and looked in Traveler's direction. The caravan master was gone, back at the vanguard.

Lady Aylen looked at the drows. "We need more sword arms at the front. You drows cannot hide behind the front anymore."

"We do not hide, Lady Aylen," Dr'as said.

"Yes, you do. I know why and I understand why, but this is not the land of the elves. I say to you what I said to my half-elf guardswomen when they first came under my employ. Stand tall. If you cannot, then Mr. Lyre can fulfill the role."

"That will not be necessary," Dr'as said. "Mr. Lyre can return to the rear, where he belongs."

Lyre laughed. "Yes, we will return my drow comrade dog."

Lyre led his elfin knights with their axex beasts back to the rear guard. Dr'as gestured to his own drows, speaking to them in a language similar to elfish but different.

King Aereth stepped to Lady Aylen and whispered, "Very good, Lady Aylen."

"I must admit, sire, I do feel more powerful. Is it that simple? Proximity to water empowers me?"

"Mr. Traveler did say it would be so."

"He's quite right."

"M'lady, look at your hands," Gwyness said.

Lady Aylen noticed that her hands were webbed.

"Transforming from human to elf, now elf to fish. I'm not interested in turning into a fish."

"A frog, m'lady. Fish don't have webbed limbs."

"Fish, frog, gator. I want none of it. What are Mr. Traveler and the others looking at there?"

"That was a kelpie, Mr. Traveler?" Elman asked. All the men were back at point staring through their telescopes as if no attack had happened.

"Yes, Mr. Elman. The evil water sprites are fond of drowning unsuspecting travelers, but they can also rip a man to shreds."

"Do they only take the form of horses and humanoids?" Pangolin asked.

"And humanoid horses."

"In the water," Pangolin said.

"I see at least five of them," Traveler said. "We must assume there are more. The one here that attacked us was a diversion."

"Do these creatures have that kind of plotting intelligence?" Pangolin asked.

"Possibly, but the kilmoulis told me the kelpies and the morgens were together, which is what the toad warriors told us."

"We have been hearing so much about these morgens but they are only water nymphs," Grakdar said.

"We need to cross this marsh before more of the kelpies appear."

"I feel it's a trap," Pangolin said.

The wounded man was all right enough to continue the march, though Gresham put his right arm in a sling.

All four of the Tree Shepherds appeared. The men had not seen the youngest one, Little Root, for some time. He had the task of minding the fairy sisters. The three crawling trees moved together and entwined around each other as they grew larger and taller. The new combined magic tree stretched out across the marshy lands and became a living bridge.

"Dr'amal," Traveler said.

"Yes, Master Traveler?" The drow sorceress stood next to him with a grin.

"Kelpies cannot attack us if they cannot see us."

Bluish clouds encircled the bridge to form a rotating ring like formation. Traveler gave the signal as Pangolin led his vanguard across the bridge. The caravan moved across quickly in small groups. The caravan master directed the men from one end. Pangolin greeted them on the other end. When the last human, fae, and animal set foot across, the crawling tree picked up Traveler, his dog, and the Tree Shepherds to set them on the other end then pulling itself across too.

Pangolin and the vanguard watched the river closely. The muddy waters were filled with eyes watching them, submerged horses, only the tops of their heads visible.

"Come up here, beasts and we'll greet you with a smash to the head," Grakdar said, raising his war maul.

One by one, the kelpies disappeared into the marsh river.

"Why do they like to drown people?" Pangolin asked.

"They're sprites. Sprites bore easily and like to engage in mischief. Drowning men is the mischief they enjoy," Grakdar told him.

"Kelpies are not sprites!" the pech yelled at the giant.

"Evil sprites are sprites, like spriggans and bugbears."

The giant blocked a hail of rocks to his head.

"Giants and sprites! You can play like children at night, when we're through these lands!" Traveler yelled.

"How long will it take to get through these lands, Mr. Traveler?" King Aereth asked.

"Longer that I'd like, sire. Likely it will take us three days. Much of it will be marshlands like these."

Lady Aylen trotted forward on the back of her lucent-blue fish-scaled-and-furred kirin with its single unicorn-like horn on its head and catfish-like whiskers around its mouth. The princess had one of her new war tridents in her left hand resting across the animal's back, the other trident strapped to her back. Gwyness rode to one side of her large black-fur-and-scaled kirin with its antlers. On the Lady Aylen's other side was Dr'amal, her head obscured by her hood, riding one of Bragg's Diomedian Mares. The fae-blood woman, Ursi, also rode behind them on a leopard axex, its hawk head in constant motion as it watched ahead, its lion body sleek and slim.

They had heard so much about the morgens, but when they appeared before the caravan, they thought of the creatures as no better than ordinary. The beauty of their appearance gave a glow to their pale skin. Their long, curly black hair hung down almost to the ground. Their arms were bare, but they wore thin chest armor and helmets that covered the tops and sides of their heads. Their steeds were horselike, more like humanoid horses walking on all fours when they could walk on two, with front legs that were longer than their hind ones.

The caravan women found nothing remarkable about the dark nymphs, but Traveler told them of their dangerous power.

"Good day," Lady Aylen greeted. "I am Lady Aylen of the kingdom of Sirnegate. We are the Caravan of the Green Wurm."

"Are you?" the lead morgen asked. "The trees spoke of you to us, but they called your caravan by another name. Are you the successors to the Kings' Caravan?"

"We are not them."

"Obviously. Your men seem to be immune to our charms. We summon them, but they do not approach. Your magic is quite effective. Is it the doing of your leshies or others?"

The morgens before them were a caravan, too, hundreds of the nymphs on kelpie steeds. The women's own caravan quietly waited in columns several yards behind them.

"Your caravan blocks our way," Lady Aylen said.

"Yours blocks ours," the morgen said.

"I've never understood the need some find to blindly seek conflict with those they are unfamiliar with," Lady Aylen said.

"We are quite aware of you, elf. I see the drow at your side. Have the water elves and drows formed an alliance, or is the drowess a slave or servant?"

"I already tire of this conversation. Your childish words will not draw anger from either of us," Lady Aylen said. "What is your intention? Do you wish to battle? If so, let's get on with it so we can be done with it. My caravan has somewhere to go."

"Elfess, do you believe you could defeat us so easily as your false bravado suggests?"

"Nymph, your bravado suggests great power, but the only power I can see your fae have is splashing around in water or bed with men. No water, no beds, and no men here."

"Shall we demonstrate the true power of our caravan?"

"Yes, please get on with it. I'm so bored, I'm ready for a nap. You're as full of bluster as that man Oughtred of Xenhelm."

"The leader of the Kings' Caravan?"

"Yes. They annoyed us as well. Now the Kings' Caravan is no more."

"The caravan may be no more, for now, but the Four Kings live."

"We know that already. Are we fighting or talking about the Four Kings?"

"You have four women alone?"

Lady Aylen raised a hand. The fauness, Zefea walked forward with the seven female half-elves in full elfin armor. Two dots of yellow light set down next to Ursi. The fairy sisters appeared, not in their two-foot child-like forms but as young females of above-average human height wearing exoskeleton armor. Their childlike giggling remained. The morgens saw the swarms of the fairy sisters rise into the sky from the caravan.

A wall of water suddenly rose from the ground and crashed down upon the women. Lady Aylen, Ursi, and the kirins were unaffected. Gwyness, Dr'amal, the fairies, Zefea, the half-elves, and their steeds were blasted back toward the caravan.

Pangolin swung at the wall of water, smashing through it, and its power flooded around him and most of the vanguard. The crawling trees created their own wall of branches to shield the rest of the caravan.

A second wall of water rose to unleash another flood upon the caravan then disappeared. The morgen leader sat on her kelpie, trembling. She coughed up blood and gazed down at the war trident embedded in her stomach. The dark nymph slid to the side and dropped from her steed to the ground.

The morgens screamed, dismounting their steeds, and ran to their queen. Her own kelpie steed changed to a more humanoid form and knelt beside her. All the dark nymphs encircled her to console her. Morgens turned and rose to their feet, enraged with eyes glowing red. Others remained kneeling beside their queen.

Lady Aylen quietly stood there and reached out her hand. "My weapon, please."

A morgen, enraged, ripped the trident from her mistress, and launched it at the elfess. Lady Aylen caught it with ease. Morgens jumped to their feet, their eyes red with rage. The water all around them danced, hovering inches above the ground.

"We will drown you all and pound your bones into the earth!" one yelled.

The princess was unmoved, pulling her other war trident from her back. "You brought this fate upon yourselves. I warned you."

"We must attend to our queen, or she will die!" one of the morgens said, kneeling at their queen's side.

"Save your queen or battle on. You cannot do both," Lady Aylen said.

"You will pay for this, elf," a morgen snapped.

The morgens clustered together, their eyes pure red. The rage left their faces, and their eyes moved from Lady Aylen to someone nearing them. Traveler marched to them, his own face filled with anger, his magic sword in his hand, pointing toward the ground. Every morgen had their eyes locked on the sword. The morgens could see the blade's translucent flame. He stopped in front of the morgens, inches away. Their eyes had returned to normal to stare at him. There was a recognition of who he was.

"I would withdraw, morgen, or there will be none of you alive to save your queen."

Something slithered underneath the wet earth. Whatever the sea creature was, it made an unnerving growl, and multiple fins pierced the ground's surface as it encircled the entire morgen caravan.

"I don't know how long I can keep my companion from attacking," Traveler said. "Withdraw from us now!"

The morgens could feel the ground shake. The howls of the creature beneath the ground had a sickening quality and power. Fear replaced rage in the faces of the dark nymphs.

"Or my companion will kill you all."

"That is doubtful, human," a morgen said to him, unconvinced.

"I can do it too." Lady Aylen watched as she made water rise from the ground and dance around her.

"Leave them! We must save our queen! She will die if we battle on," one of the morgens at their leader's side yelled.

"Take her!" one of the morgens yelled.

Three of the morgens lifted the queen from the ground and floated into the air. Others ran and mounted their kelpies.

"You will never make it to Atlantea, Titan's Caravan!" one of the morgens yelled from her kelpie.

"When we do arrive, we will personally ensure that its gates will be closed to all morgens forever!" Traveler yelled back.

The words clearly upset the dark nymph. She turned her kelpie away.

The morgen caravan rode off east, following their three floating members, holding their queen as they, flew ahead. The caravan of dark nymphs disappeared into invisibility, but all could hear the echo of hooves in the watery ground for many miles.

CHAPTER ELEVEN

Merchant Realm of Abacus

A drenched Gwyness walked to her black kirin.

"I wish I had your powers." Gwyness noticed the fae-blood woman, Ursi nearby, also untouched by the flood attack. "You're immune to water attacks."

"I am immune to most magic attacks," Ursi said.

"But they commanded the water to rise from the ground and engulf us with it."

"The attack was more magic than water, or I would have been impacted too."

"I noticed that your fellow fae-bloods are absent."

"They are not my fellow fae-bloods."

"I apologize. I keep forgetting that though we all march as one in Titan's Caravan, we are not all one. Do you know why the fae-blood men are absent?"

"They hibernate."

"Hibernate? I thought only bears hibernate."

"Many animals hibernate besides bears, and I am not a bear. I'm fae-blood."

"Fae-bloods hibernate?"

"Yes."

"I learned a new thing today."

The fairy sisters sat on the wet ground spitting water.

"She tried to drown us, that nymph!" the older fairy, Wildglow yelled.

Her little sister, Sunpetal, walked to her, equally soaked. Wildglow stood and slapped her sister's back to help her cough out all the water. "Drown us! They tried to drown us! They had better have run away! Our swarms would have dealt with them good!"

Quillen nervously approached them. The fairies were startled.

"You appeared as big as human females."

"You humans are too big. When you're so big, you can be attacked more easily," Wildglow said. "You humans are like giants. Too big. We are not going to grow that big again. If we were our normal size, the nymphs would not have hit us with their water and made us fall. They tried to drown us! Fairies are not to be drowned!"

Quillen nodded, deciding not to ask the wound up fairies any more questions.

"Were you drawing my sister and me in your magic book?"

Quillen shook his head.

"We saw you! Do not draw us. We do not want you showing drawings of us to other humans."

Quillen nodded.

"We're watching you, human."

Quillen nodded.

"Where's Master Traveler? He's the only human we like."

Little Root, the Tree Shepherd, appeared and helped the older fairy to her feet with his fingers. "Please, we should not bother our caravan master. He has much work to do after those bad nymphs."

"Yes. They're bad! They tried to drown us! Did you see!"

"Yes, I did."

"We're going to swarm them. All three of our swarms would have gotten them. Bad nymphs! They're bad!"

"Let us return to our small-realm with the soul tree."

"Nymphs and fairies are friends. But not those bad nymphs!"

Little Root picked up the fairy sisters and set one on each of his shoulders. He walked into the caravan.

One of the pech threw a pebble at Quillen to get his attention. All the pech were watching him with big smiles.

"Human, do not engage the fairies in conversation. Master Traveler knows how to engage with them. You do not. Fairies can speak to you in one stream of talk, and when they're done, you'd be as old as Mr. Hobbs."

Quillen laughed. "That's not true."

"It is true. Leave them be."

Pangolin had the vanguard on watch as Hobbs made his rounds through the caravan and all got their bearings after the attack. Traveler and the dog joined them.

"We have to march on, don't we?" Pangolin asked.

"Yes. We can't wait here. I know it will be hard to focus everyone's attention away from the morgens and their kelpies, but if we march at a quick pace, we may be lucky and reach the end of these wetlands before nightfall."

"What's beyond this?"

"More trees but parts of the region ahead are unfamiliar. The Forest moves about within itself."

"I will get the vanguard ready to march."

The region of black rock was like a hard, dead scab on the living face of the Great Forest. There were no signs of life, no sounds, and the lands sloped downward, further slowing their march. The rock was so slippery that not even the crawling trees could get a proper footing. For the giants, all they did was slip. The humans thought the hoofed fae and fauns would have the most difficult time marching, but somehow, they had the easiest even with their cloven feet.

"What is this rock? We have no connection to the earth," Grakdar said. "It's as if we're floating in the air with no power."

Traveler had the caravan increase the distance between columns and men. It was worse for the animals, except for the kirins, who walked on the air.

Pangolin scanned ahead, nervous about the lack of defense of any kind. He held his axe-mace with a solid grip.

"I see the end of this ahead, Mr. Pangolin," Mr. Elman said.

The vanguard leader acknowledged him with a nod.

"I see trees again, but they're not giant trees."

The caravan finally made it off the black rock plains. What they thought were normal-sized trees were giant trees, too, but so close to the black rock they were starved of nutrients and stunted in growth. However, in every way, to the human men, it was as if they were back in a normal wooded area in the Lands of Man.

Traveler's dog took the form of a wolf-dog-headed horse and carried the caravan master to the vanguard.

"Mr. Pangolin, move forward a few miles. When you find a defensible open area, we can set up camp."

Gwyness walked alongside her kirin as the caravan moved farther into the wooded area. She felt uneasy but could not explain the reason. The caravan slowed ahead. She heard the voices then saw what it was about. The open area looked like a graveyard of weapons and armor. All were scattered as far as the eye could see through the area.

"Was it a battle?" Gwyness asked. Lady Aylen had joined her.

"If it was, the battle was a long time ago. Look at the weapons. Mr. Estus should be here. They look like elfin metal, but I didn't think elfin metal could rust and decay like that."

Traveler walked among the men. "Do not touch anything with your bare hands," he directed.

Someone heard Lady Aylen and called to Mr. Estus, the caravan's weaponsmaster. Pangolin had the men form a loose defensive ring around the caravan as men moved forward into the weapons' graveyard.

"There's too much activity. Keep close, men!" the vanguard leader yelled.

I'wulf arrived with his Cut-throats and headed to Pangolin.

"This is not good," I'wulf said.

"Yes, we need to keep the men close, tight circles. We're extremely vulnerable."

"The elves have the rear secure," I'wulf said.

"As secure as one can be in such lands," Pangolin said.

The royals stood together with their kirins and their guardspeople. Mr. Estus appeared with a few of his men.

"I don't think we should be here," Gwyness whispered to herself.

Lady Aylen heard and turned to her. "Why?" she asked aloud.

"I cannot explain, m'lady. I don't feel comfortable here."

They heard a man scream. People ran to the lizard minder. His giant lizard was flopping around. Lizard minders struggled to calm it while they tried to remove its armor. The custom-forged elfin metal was turning black and flaking.

"Get it off! Get it off!" the lizard's minder yelled.

A giant grabbed the lizard, and another held it down.

"Hurry!" Grakdar yelled.

More than one man ripped its armor from the giant lizard. When done, the lizard ran away then stopped and collapsed.

Estus reached the discarded armor at the same time Traveler did. The elfin armor had completely rusted black and continued to flake away.

"Mr. Traveler!"

The caravan master ran to the blue lizard lying on the ground. The lizard's skin was turning white.

"Fetch the fauns and animal men. The lizard is dying!"

The fauns arrived quickly, led by the fauness, Zefea. She already had her magic herbs.

Pangolin kept one eye on the perimeter guards and another on the growing chaos in the caravan about the lizard. He stopped and ran to Barg, the giant.

"Grakdar!" Pangolin yelled to the giants' leader. He pointed to Barg's armor.

Grakdar saw a black spot on Barg's dwarven armor growing.

"Barg! Wake up you, fool! Your armor!"

As Barg looked at his forearm armor first then lifted his arm to inspect the armor there, he winced. He stifled a yell in pain.

Grakdar reached him and helped him pull it off. The black spot was growing.

"Grakdar!" Pangolin yelled.

The giant's leader saw where Pangolin was pointing. The leader's armor, too, was infected.

"No!" Grakdar lifted his new war maul to see the growing black spot.

"Out of the forest!" Traveler yelled.

The caravan master ran to Pangolin. His dog transformed into a dog-headed, six-armed ape and picked the vanguard leader up. The dog ran and grabbed the royals, Gwyness, and Nirgund. Suddenly, he dropped the king's guardsman to the ground. Nirgund's armor was rusting away too.

The dog-ape sprouted wings to fly past the weapons graveyard into the giant trees and land on top of a gigantic branch. There he left Pangolin and the others. Then the dog flew away like a hurricane.

"Check my armor!" Pangolin told them.

Gwyness and Lady Aylen did so. The women checked each other's and then King Aereth's.

Pangolin stared at his axe-mace and fell to his knees. His axe-mace was pure white.

The Tree Shepherds led the ground caravan of hoofed fae, gnomes, gnomoids, pech, and brownies from the weapons' graveyard. The dog carried all the others in several trips to the giant branch. The titan tree many feet in the air would become their new campsite. They rested within another pocket-realm in three circles. Elfin archers stood guard, heeding Traveler's warning to keep an eye out for giant snakes or insects.

Hobbs had not set up a leadership meeting of this import in months. The mood was dire among the men. The caravan's steward had a special large tent erected for the night meeting. For the first time, Strag of the elaphines joined them, and the animal men, gnomes, and gnomoids watched from outside the tent.

"I consulted with all our fae. This infection..." Gresham began.

"It's a rust or mold that eats magic, especially metals of magic," Traveler said somberly.

"Yes, Mr. Traveler. I will leave talk of the weapons to Mr. Estus, but as for the men, all six giants and many of our pech, fauns, and elves are in the healing tent. Nearly one thousand men.”

“Any of your men, Dr’as?” Traveler asked.

“Fortunately, no.”

“Strag?”

“None of my people were affected,” the elaphine leader replied, a group of cervids standing behind him.

“Animals? Our giant lizard?”

Gresham looked at Zefea.

“More than half of them are deathly ill,” the fauness said.

“Mr. Estus, give us the worst news,” Traveler said.

“Mr. Traveler, we’ve lost a tremendous number of weapons and armor—all the armor of our giant lizards my men and I forged specifically for them. We’ll have to do it all over again. As for our lost weapons, I do apologize, but I didn’t think it was possible. My men and I went into the weapons vault and—”

“It’s okay, Mr. Estus,” Traveler said.

“I personally took it out of the direct guardianship of the väki. They yelled at me about it something fierce today in their pocket-realm, but all I did was exchange weapons and bring men into the vaults to look at weapons, back and forth. This spell or infection, whatever it is, followed us. The entire weapons vault with our best weapons is lost."

Gasps rippled through the group.

"We have no weapons cache at all, Mr. Estus?" Lady Aylen asked.

"That is correct, m'lady."

"Lady Aylen, your tridents?"

"They were unaffected, as were Gwyness's weapons."

"Mr. Pangolin?"

The sadness in Pangolin's face was obvious to all.

"My axe-mace was robbed of all its magic power. It is no better than a block of wood. My armor is not devoid of its magic but it has been substantially diminished."

"Chief Ethor?" Traveler asked.

"Master Traveler, most of my men's weapons are useless."

"For the elfin questing knights," Lyre, the high elf, said, "we lost half our weapons, including our arrows. Do you have your arrows?" he asked Strag.

"We have our arrows," the elaphine leader said.

"Chief Ammon?"

"Master Traveler, we lost armor and weapons, but it's minimal."

"Mr. I'wulf?"

"This is a calamity. We Cut-throats have lost armor and weapons. Also, our animals, our chamroshes, are not themselves. The fight in them is gone."

"Mr. Bragg?"

"My men and I were unaffected."

"Ursi, do you know if the other fae-blood clan was affected?"

"They were not."

"Titan's Caravan, there it is."

Everyone was silent.

"What do we do, Mr. Traveler?" King Aereth asked.

"We cannot move forward without weapons and armor," Lyre said. "We prepared so well. To lose all of it in a mere day in the middle of the Great Forest itself..."

"Mr. Traveler, there must be a solution," Lady Aylen said.

"There is, but none of us are going to like it."

"We must seek out merchants in the Forest," Chief Ethor said.

"Yes, chief. We literally have no choice. And as much as I hate to say, if we cannot make our caravan whole, we will have no choice but to abandon our quest."

Lady Aylen wasn't the only one overwhelmed by despair. She wanted to collapse.

"Master Traveler, have you encountered this magic-eating infection before?" Ursi asked.

"I hope you aren't suggesting this is the fault of our caravan master," King Aereth said.

"It's only a question."

"There are creatures called magic-eaters. Some are living. Others are golems."

"Yes, I know of those too," Bragg said.

"But like most caravan masters who travel the Trail by foot, I have heard the stories. This is the first I've encountered it directly. The stories always spoke of a strange mold that covered the weapons and armor and deprived both of their magical properties. We encountered one that is not visible to the eye and also affects living beings. Much different, much more powerful."

"My question, Master Traveler, was to ask if you felt this was a trap," Ursi said.

"For us?" Lyre asked her.

She waited for the caravan master to answer.

He sighed. "I have no answer. We can all speculate later. The urgency of the situation requires us to act quickly. We either make ourselves whole and replenish what we lost, or we return to Faë-Land immediately, otherwise, to be blunt, we die."

The royals sat in King Aereth's tent. Nirgund sat at entrance on the ground rubbing the heads and necks of his alphyns. The female half-elves sat at the back of the tent together, reading as the tiny owl griffins slept next to them or curled up in balls in their laps.

"A disaster, sire," Lady Aylen said. "We can't move forward without weapons and armor."

"No, we cannot," King Aereth said.

"We were making progress too. I could almost smell the oceans in my mind's eye. Turn back? Now? Never. I'd rather die."

"No, you wouldn't, Lady Aylen, not in the Great Forest."

Hobbs was at the entrance. "Sire, Lady Aylen."

"Come in, Mr. Hobbs," Lady Aylen said.

The steward entered.

"I thought you'd like to know the news. Mr. Traveler and his dog took some of the animal men out at dawn."

"They left the camp?" Lady Aylen asked with a look of distress.

"Yes, m'lady, but not alone. Ursi and the drows went with him."

"Good," King Aereth said.

"The Tree Shepherds also ventured out of the camp, but they are considerably closer. They travel among the giant trees around us. They also did not leave alone. Both rustic and knight woodland elves went with them."

"We must hope they all return safely," Lady Aylen said.

"I am not sure how long either will be, but we can watch for them, and the men will call out when they return. We, of course, are prepared to ensure that whomever returns is in fact truly them."

"Yes, Mr. Hobbs. We have you to thank for being so diligent in not allowing those goblins into our pocket-realm with their magical guise."

"That's why you're the caravan's steward," Lady Aylen said.

"Good of you to say."

"How are all our sick men, Mr. Hobbs?" King Aereth asked.

"Very sick still, sire. All is being done to help them and Mr. Gresham has all the help he needs from the fae. The brownies are in the healing tent to keep it orderly, and our Brothers Brimm are keeping all in good spirits."

"Thank goodness for our musicians," Lady Aylen said. "We too often forget about them."

"The mood of the men is the important thing to maintain," King Aereth said.

"I'm also keeping their duties light," Hobbs said. "They're not over the shock of it all."

"Neither are we, Mr. Hobbs," Lady Aylen said.

"Yes, m'lady."

"Where is Mr. Frog-Dor?" the princess asked.

Hobbs paused. "I've heard he's still hiding."

"That is unacceptable. Now more than ever we need his magic. I know something of transformations. I will find him and speak to him."

"Where is your maiden, Lady Aylen?"

"Gwyness is with the Cut-throats, sire, or, I should say, one in particular whose state of mind I'm also very concerned about."

"Mr. Pangolin?"

"Yes."

"We must make our master-at-arms whole."

"His weapon and armor are more than the trappings of a berserker, sire," Hobbs said. "They have been handed down through generations. He is the latest bearer, a high honor among his people."

"Mr. Hobbs, thank you for informing us."

"I will keep you both abreast of all news, sire."

In the Tree Shepherds' pocket-realm, Traveler met with all four of the leshies with the animal men leaders: frog, lizard, squirrel, raccoon, possum, fox, rabbit, bird, and mice men. While the other animal men left their animals outside the realm, the mole-looking fae came with his giant moose.

The magical fields were awash with new life. Plants of rainbow colors sprouted from the ground, and the sky filled with floating water lily-type flowers, only the breeze was their river. Their glowing soul tree stood in the distance.

"I will say it plainly. You here will likely be the saviors of Titan's Caravan," Traveler said.

"What can we do?" a mice man asked.

"Ask the animal men of the Great Forest. We need their help to locate the traveling merchant caravans."

"Master Traveler, can we really find what we need from these merchants?" Mossberry asked.

"No, but merchants here are no different than merchants in human and fae cities and towns. You find the people who can find what you need."

"Master Traveler, is that not dangerous?"

"Mr. Mossberry, we don't have a choice."

"Agreed."

"You want us to speak to the toad warriors?" a frog man asked.

"Yes. That's the best place for us to start."

"Master Traveler, have you heard of one called the Spice Market?" Little Root asked.

"Yes, I have. How do you know of it?"

"It's a place we've heard of from fairies, but you said there are no cities in the Great Forest," Little Root said.

"No cities, but there are moving pocket-realms that cater to the caravans. We civilized humans and fae use caravans for special journeys. For nomadic peoples, caravans are a daily part of life."

"Have you been to this Spice Market, Master Traveler?" Greenwig asked.

"I may have been. They change their names and often give false names to strangers, especially humans far from their native lands. We will search for these toad warriors again."

"We do not know the trees and fauna of the Great Forest but we will try to communicate with this tree we camp in. Maybe we can find a giant leshy," Mossberry said.

"To use your words, isn't that dangerous?" Traveler asked.

The Tree Shepherd smiled. "I am a leshy, Master Traveler. I know how dangerous leshies can be. I have been around them all my life."

Months had passed without any in the caravan ever seeing the väki. Only Mr. Traveler and Estus saw them regularly. The grumpy sprites of elemental fire magic in charred dark-brown and orange clothing emerged from their realm. Three of them in all marched past everyone without a greeting and exited the main realm's entrance. The elfin guards said nothing, but one sent word to inform Mr. Hobbs. The steward soon appeared, running to the entrance.

"They are gone already," an elfin archer said.

"Where?"

"Along the branch in the same direction as the Tree Shepherds this morning."

"Three different parties left the caravan."

"Hopefully, those will be three chances to save ourselves from our predicament."

"I hope so. We've come too far."

"Yes, we have. Too far indeed. For us, we either return to our elfin kingdom with treasure or an Atlantean alliance, or we do not return at all."

"That's harsh, is it not?"

"The stakes are very high, Mr. Hobbs, for all of us I would say. Correct?"

"Yes, you're correct. I never thought about that until now. I am part of Titan's Caravan to the end, no matter what befalls us. I have nothing to return to in my own lands. I will be in Mr. Traveler's service to the end. The thought of not continuing on to Atlantea is too terrible for me to think about. We must find a way."

"Mr. Traveler is resourceful. He does not strike us elves as a human who gives up. How else do we explain him learning how to defeat an elf with nothing but a dagger? If any in the caravan can find a way to make us whole to continue forward on the Trail, it is he."

The normally boisterous Cut-throats sat in their own camp away from the rest of the caravan. Dejected and quiet, they sat around campfires with drink. The berserker vanguard leader, Pangolin, sat apart from them. Gwyness had never seen him without his armor, helmet, and weapon at his side.

"Mr. Pangolin, am I disturbing you?"

"No, maiden," he said quietly, barely looking up.

"You have often built up my own confidence on this journey, so I wish to return the favor. Mr.

Traveler will see us through this, as he has before. I saw his demeanor when he left this morning, and there was no despair or sadness in his face. He would say quite relaxed, in fact. I took that to mean he has a solution to all this."

"What solution could restore the magic stolen from my weapon and armor of my birth land?"

"It is not lost. We travel in the land of magic. If it can be taken, it can be restored. One must simply know how."

"Our fae berserkers are well traveled, and they do not believe it can be done."

"Mr. Traveler is our caravan master for a reason. He knows more than we do."

"Perhaps."

"We will not have to return to our lands. We have come too far. We're almost there."

"I admire your encouragement, but we're not almost there. That reminds me. You knew that the graveyard was cursed."

"I am not sure how. I felt strange as we reached it. I knew something wasn't right, but I couldn't explain it."

"Maybe, like Lady Aylen, these magic lands are awakening your own inner power. The Old One said you didn't need your amulet to sense evil."

"Evil? If the magic-eating infection was evil, then it came from something evil."

"Or someone."

"Do you believe we will encounter the Four Kings?"

"He does not say it out aloud, but I know Mr. Traveler is certain of it. They're out there. Where? We do not know."

"I remember that remark Mr. Traveler made, which I thought was a jest, that the Four Kings would be waiting for us at Atlantea."

"Yes. But first we must make it through the Great Forest. My weapon's lost. All our best weapons in our vault gone. We were so well prepared. Now, all of it is gone."

"You will see, Mr. Pangolin. Mr. Traveler will come through for the caravan."

"Thank you, maiden, for trying to lift my spirits."

"I'm merely returning the favor, Mr. Pangolin. I will leave you to your rest. I expect a better day for us, today."

Swords drawn. The elves stood in a curved formation in front of the four Tree Shepherds. They had moved from one giant tree to the next, the elves leaping, the Tree Shepherds floating. The elves thought it was another tree before them, but then it moved. It wasn't a giant tree. It was a giant leshy.

The elves were aghast at the sight of him—a wild man with green skin and matted green vine hair hanging in front, covering most of his face. They saw his greenish teeth, the bottom teeth protruding up from his mouth.

His eyes glowed as he stared at them.

"Why do you bother me, insects?"

His breath was a gale warm but sickly-sweet wind across them.

Greenwig took a step forward, through the elves, his large staff in hand.

"Great leshy of the Great Forest, I am Greenwig," the Tree Shepherd said.

"I care not. You're all insects to me."

"Are your ways different here in the Great Forest? In our lands, insects are our allies, as are the birds and animals."

"Our ways were as they were long before your lands were seedlings."

"We tiny leshy children only ask for an audience with our great, older and wiser leshy."

"Your presence is not welcome."

The giant leshy jerked his head back. His eyes widened.

The elves and Tree Shepherds turned to see what had frightened him. Several väki stood on the giant branch behind them with magic balls of fire in their hands. The morose sprites then began to grow in size.

"Spritelings! To anger me is to bring your own death! To anger the Great Forest is to bring the death of all whom you know!"

"Giant leshy, you will give us an audience! If not, we will grow to a size to look down upon your head. We will rain down fire on your tree body!" the väki yelled.

"I will command the trees to pull up from their roots and smite all you trespassers!"

Mossberry held up his staff. "Silence!" The word echoed so loud that the air around them shook.

The Tree Shepherd angrily looked at the väki. The perpetually frowning men extinguished the fire in their hands and returned to their normal height.

"Great leshy, I apologize for the actions of my fellow travelers. They did not know what they were doing. Rather than an audience may I ask a question? Then I will remove us from your gaze immediately. We leshy are called Tree Shepherds, and we also command trees. We will command our trees to drag and remove all our fellow travelers from your forest."

"See to it that you do. If you command trees, then perhaps you are not insects. Perhaps you are distant relatives. What's your question?"

"My father told me of the power of great leshies and if one was kind and noble to them, one could ask to learn a secret of lost magic. He told me that great leshies know all that occurs in their forest. Nothing escapes their knowing. They know of all trespassers and the evil deeds they do, bringing dark magic into their forest, leaving it behind to kill and to suck the magic from their bodies, their clothes of metal, their weapons of protection, harming innocent animals of magic."

"I do not share my magic, but I will tell you where they do—for a price."

The single tent stood next to the large healing tents, almost hidden. Inside was pitch-black when Lady Aylen opened up the flap. She walked away but returned with a lit torch and opened it again.

"Where are you, Mr. Frog-Dor?" she asked as she stepped inside.

In the cornered behind a table the man sat on the floor. He had a disheveled appearance and was in an unwashed state.

"Mr. Frog-Dor, what's wrong with you?"

He stared at her from behind the table, not saying a word. She sighed.

"Mr. Frog-Dor, I have something in common with you. I was transformed from one thing to another, and I could do nothing about it. I could have died. My ordeal was nothing compared to yours, of course, but I can relate in a very small and fleeting way to what you must have endured for so long a time.

"Mr. Traveler saved you for a reason, Mr. Frog-Dor. You were doing so well. Why would you throw it all away to return to this state? Should Mr. Traveler have left you with your curse?"

"No." His voice sounded like a small child's.

"What brought this on?"

"The dreams. The dreams won't leave me alone."

"Dreams? What dreams?"

"They come at night. I can't stop them. They surround me. Crawl over me."

"What are you speaking of? Dreams?"

"The frogs."

"Frogs like the form you were cursed with?"

"They want to kill me. They will kill us all."

"What do you mean? Who will kill us?"

The man was silent again.

"Are the dreams so real that you don't know whether they're a dreams or reality?"

"Yes."

"The leader of our Committee of Dreams has been turned into a waste of a man by dreams. Tell me, Mr. Frog-Dor. Most of the camp have had flashes of these disturbing dreams, but it's worse for the leadership and, obviously, far worse for you. What does that tell you? Does that seem like chance or a deliberate act?"

"Deliberate?"

"Mr. Frog-Dor, I don't want Mr. Traveler to find you in this state. You're to leave this tent. Bathe and groom yourself. We have lost our weapons and now you."

"Lost our weapons?"

"You would know these things if you weren't hiding alone in a dark tent. I'm ordering you to do as I direct. Many have offered their aid, and you have refused. I am ordering you to accept that help. You choose who, but you will choose."

Lady Aylen marched up to the table. The man leaned back with frightened eyes.

"I will pick you up, carry you off, and leave you behind in the Great Forest."

"No."

"All of us, Mr. Frog-Dor, must contribute to the survival of the caravan. Otherwise, they are no longer members of Titan's Caravan. Are you a member of Titan's Caravan?"

"I am."

"Then do as I commanded. I do not want to see you in this tent again."

She knelt down near him. "Mr. Traveler helped me through my time of need. He would tell me stories. Mr. Traveler is a very gifted storyteller. Every day I would wait for him to visit and check up on me. I remember the fever, the shaking. I lived for those stories. He would talk, and I would listen. Then it was the reverse as I regained my strength. I would talk, and he would listen. I cannot remember what I talked about. Maybe about my kingdom, its people in the castle and in the surrounding towns, my favorite animals. Mr. Frog-Dor, find the person who can do the same for you here."

"Yes."

"Titan's Caravan needs you."

"Traveler's back!"

The voice was Elman's. Immediately, the men were on their feet, and a buzz erupted within the camp. The Tree Shepherds, elves, and väki had returned hours before, but they would not say a word until the caravan master returned. A giant winged snake—the dog—landed on the branch in front of the realm's entrance. Traveler, Ursi, the drows, and the frog and lizard men stepped down from its back. They stepped through the doorway, the dog in mid-transformation.

"How did you fare, Mr. Traveler?" King Aereth asked.

Crowds gathered at the entrance.

"We found the toad men, sire."

The Tree Shepherds stepped through the gathered men with Greenwig in the lead.

"Master Traveler, were you successful?" Greenwig asked.

"We were. How was your visit?" Traveler asked.

"Giant leshies are very ungracious beings. They prefer the company of trees and birds, but not insects or us tiny leshies. We are alike but so unalike at the same time. However, he did part with information of a traveling merchant caravan. He sent a giant bird to tell us the name after we left him. The merchant caravan is called Abacus. Both its merchant masters and its patrons are extremely dangerous, but they have existed for ages. We may find what we need there, but it will cost much silver and gold."

Traveler was quiet for a moment.

"What is it, Mr. Traveler? Is this not good news? A chance at least?" Lady Aylen asked.

"We spoke to the toad warriors. They were more than agreeable to receive our goods for a couple of words. They told us of many merchant caravans that travel the hidden paths of the Great Forest. The one they said was the most magical of them all in this region is called Abacus."

The caravan broke out in joy.

"Then why don't you seem especially overjoyed, Mr. Traveler?"

"Mr. Pangolin, one of the first lessons I learned as a caravan master is that, on Titan's Trail, you do not want strangers to know your path, and when those strangers tell you to go left, then maybe any direction but left would be the wisest course."

"Master Traveler, the toad warriors aside, a giant leshy would not partake in any kind of deception against us on behalf of any being. They do not care about our affairs. We bore them."

"You are correct, Mr. Greenwig, that the toad warriors could easily be manipulated to lead us astray or into danger, especially knowing what they can be bought with. But giant leshies can be manipulated, too, even if we are not aware of how. I have been to the Great Forest many times but have never heard of

Abacus. I'm sure that it does exist, and has existed for centuries, but why does everyone seem to know about it now, and by name?"

"Master Traveler is wise to be suspicious," Chief Ethor said.

"All this is a trap?" Lady Aylen asked.

"It doesn't have to be a trap necessarily, princess. We could simply be led to a place from where we are expected never to return."

"Mr. Traveler," someone called out.

The caravan turned to see four of the väki approaching him, the elemental sprites with deeply frowning faces, as always.

"I heard you accompanied our Tree Shepherds," Traveler said.

"We did not come to speak to you about that. You let your weapons be destroyed by anti-magic."

"Is that what's called?" someone asked.

One of the väki pointed at Estus. "If you hadn't take the vault from our guardianship, that would not have happened. All the vaults will remain in our care without exception until we reach Atlantea. We told you not to take it from us." The väki glared at Estus."

"Sorry, sirs, we had to inspect and choose from the weapons hoard," Estus said.

"Choose what? Humans, elves, and giants, posing with their weapons. It is a weapon, not shoes. Pick it, and be done with it. We will not have human and fae foolishness jeopardize our quest to Atlantea. What is your plan to regain your weapons?"

"We have a plan. Shall I tell you about it in great detail?" Traveler asked.

"No! As long as you have a plan and plan to continue the quest. We are uninterested in hearing anymore."

The väki turned to leave.

"I have one more thing to say."

The väki stopped to look back at him.

"For assisting the Tree Shepherds in their parley with the great leshy, thank you."

The väki grimaced and marched away as fast as they could to the laughter of the crowd.

"Master Traveler, I would not say the väki helped us with the giant leshy. They angered him greatly," Greenwig said.

"They helped. Trees, even those in the Great Forest, do not like fire."

"Yes, that is true."

Traveler looked out at the gathering.

"We have to do the very thing I endeavored to prevent from the time our caravan first set out from the Lands of Man, step into one of the ever-moving merchant caravans that travel the edges of the Great Forest."

"We are still at the edges of the Great Forest?" Bragg, the dwelf, asked. "Not even partly into its interiors."

"Mr. Bragg, the farther into the Great Forest you go, the older it is and the older and more powerful the magic. Caravans do not go there. Titan's Walk and its many branches cut through that interior. It does not take you into it."

"Imagine what beasts may live there," a grinning Bragg said.

"Yes, Mr. Bragg. I don't have to imagine. My dog and I saw for ourselves, flying high above it, and that still wasn't high enough. The creatures that live there can, and will, jump from Pan-Earth into the heavens with the stars to get at you. We did it once. We will never do it again. But why talk of this when we have a new mission before we can set out on the Trail again? One party will remain here to guard the camp within the pocket-realm. One will go. We must take great care in whom we choose for each. Our lives truly depend on it. Today, will be the most dangerous we have faced on the Trail so far."

Before them, the tree was so wide as a mountain that one could not see the end of it on either side. The bark was brown but coated in green moss. A cave-like opening seemed to be carved into the tree's trunk. Blocking the path was a guardian—a lone bald Cyclops fifteen feet tall, drinking from a golden mug. The moment they were in its view, its single eye was on them. His long-sleeved tunic appeared to be woven from plants, his pants from another fabric. His boots almost looked like leather, but as they neared, looked to be woven onto his feet and calves as if by a spider. His face had an expression of complete disinterest until he saw what came out of the bluish land cloud before him. Five of the caravan's väki stepped out—taller than the cyclops. The cyclops lowered his mug.

The bluish smoke dissipated to reveal the rest of the small caravan—two of the Antaean giants, two of the Tree Shepherds riding "tree" horses, the royals and Gwyness upon their kirins, the mole fae and Pangolin on the giant carnivorous moose, all the animal men, and their giant animals. At the rear, Traveler rode his own canine steed. On foot were Hobbs, his two fae human bodyguards plus three more men, Estus, a dozen of his men, a dozen pech, and a hundred of the gnomes and gnomoids. Dr'amal came out of invisibility with Ursi at her side.

"Good cyclops, a bird from a great leshy told us of this place where we can partake in trade with the best merchants of the Forest," Mossberry said to the cyclops.

"Trade?" the cyclops asked.

"Yes, my party and I have journeyed a great distance and will continue on from here. Good cyclops, will you allow us to pass?"

"The entrance of this tree goes nowhere. You were misinformed, leshy. It is my cave for my possessions and food."

"Is it not the way to a realm of merchant masters of the Great Forest?" Mossberry asked.

"No."

The five väki began to grow larger in size, and their beards and eyebrows blazed with fire. All five growled in anger.

"We command this caravan, not the leshy!"

"I beg forgiveness!" the cyclops yelled, looking up at the now twenty-foot-tall elemental fire sprites. "I did not know *tulen väki* requested entrance. Please, please enter the merchant caravan of Abacus without delay."

The cyclops pulled back the cave-like entrance like a hanging curtain. Beyond was a tunnel into a sunny inner forest.

When they exited the tunnel, everyone was truly in awe. It reminded Hobbs of Caravan Row back in the Lands of Man, but the open day markets went on as far as the eyes could see, littering the entirety of the wooded lands. In the distance, were green mountains, and they, too, were covered with merchant tents and wagons.

The five väki stood at the lead.

"What is your plan?" one asked Traveler.

"You command our small caravan as we journey through the merchant market."

"Why would we do that? We've never been here or to the Great Forest before. You are the only one in the caravan who has."

"I may have been to the Great Forest before, but I have never been here."

"You're the expert, not us. We will wait here. You go and do what you must. We expect you to acquire all that is needed, as we also expect to set out again tomorrow morning."

"Tomorrow morning?" Traveler asked. "You have never been concerned about our schedule before."

"We are now."

"When will you tell me why?"

"When we are on our way but not before."

"I have never seen a haltija anxious."

"Why not? We are capable of that emotion too. Go on, humans. All of you."

"Mr. Traveler, are those väki too?" Lady Aylen asked.

Both Traveler and the five väki saw them approaching—other väki clans.

"I understand now," Traveler said.

"We do too." The caravan's väki walked to them.

"We did not know metsän väki traveled so far from our lands," the caravan's väki said.

"We did not know tulen väki ever traveled this far into the Great Forest," one said back.

The metsän väki were väki of the forest, and all their many magic powers were of the forest. They, too, were frowning, full-bearded little men, but their pointy hats had their own foliaged branches like a tree, and all their clothing appeared as moving bark with a deep-brown hue. Their belts and the cuffs of their tops were leaves.

"What other väki are here in this realm?" a caravan väki asked.

"Many others."

"Any naisen väki here?"

"Yes. Do you seek wives?"

"We have wives. We seek magic. Point us to where they are."

All dozen or so of the metsän väki pointed in the distance. The caravan's väki grunted and nodded. The metsän väki all nodded too. Both groups walked away from each other—the metsän väki walked to the realm's entrance, and the caravan's väki pointed into the merchant market.

"They are a race of unfriendly elemental sprites," Lady Aylen said. "All of them are the same, no matter the clan."

"It is their way, princess," Traveler said.

"Master Traveler, this changes things," Greenwig said.

"Yes, it does."

"Why? We do not understand," King Aereth said.

"King, naisen väki are female väki with special magic powers. Some have been known to restore the magic of things," Greenwig told him.

"Did you hear, Mr. Pangolin?" Gwyness asked, looking up at the berserker on the back of the carnivorous moose with its mole man rider.

He was guardedly optimistic.

"We all have our tasks to complete," Traveler said. "But we must leave a group here for when the väki return."

"Look, there are more," Lady Aylen said.

She gestured to the full-bearded little men with dark dirt brown clothing. Their hats appeared more like mountain tops than anything.

"Vuoren väki. Väki of mountains and stones," Traveler said. "Mr. Greenwig, maybe we should engage their services."

"Our väki are of the same mind."

A member of the caravan's väki were already speaking with the half dozen mountain väki.

"Mr. Hobbs, create a circle here. You and your men, Mr. Estus, will remain here."

"Just us, alone, Mr. Traveler?" Estus asked.

"You will be safe here, in a circle. Observe. That is your mission."

Mr. Hobbs agreed as he began to create a circle on the patch of ground. "We should have brought Mr. Quillen. He is exceptional at observation."

"You and the men will manage. I don't know how long we'll be or when the väki will return, but be watchful of all."

"Yes, sir," Hobbs and Estus said.

Hobbs and Estus watched the small caravan move off and break into smaller groups as they moved through the open merchant market. Their gnomes and gnomoids were especially chatty, speaking to various Forest fae of the market. The fae were taller than they had been in Faë-Land, not quite the size of giants, but the shortest they saw was over six feet tall. The humanoid fae wore clothes made of leaves, roots, and flowers, very colorful and showy. They were many tall gnomes and the like. They saw tree people, flower people, and many types of plant people. There were also many types of animal people, many hybrids, too, of different animals—frogs, squirrels, newts, birds, monkeys. The caravan's animal men spoke with them and seemed to be the center of attention for many of the market's animal people.

Estus pointed to the large number of cù-sìths roaming the market. The greenish fae dogs were a favorite companion of the leshy. Here they were larger and covered with bright flowers. There were also cat, monkey, and bird species all around.

Like the gnomes and gnomoids, the animal men enjoyed meeting their counterparts in the Forest. Their animals of giant crabs, giant turtles, giant porcupines, jackalopes, and enfields were constantly surrounded by fae cats and cù-sìths wanting to play. For the animal men, it was a chance to learn of their Forest cousins and gather as much information of the journey ahead on the Trail.

"You!"

The animal had never seen such a beautiful humanoid animal before. Iguana men—warriors. Three of them stood at ten feet clad in green armor, with long axes on their belts, and a quiver of javelins. They held thick pike weapons in their clawed hands. Most exquisite of their appearance was a row of elongated yellow scales running from the top of their foreheads to their backs. Their tails were green, like the rest of their body, with a bright-yellow streak.

"You're of Kings Caravan!"

"We are not!" a frog man said. "We are—" One of the mice men hit him. "We are the Green Wurm Caravan."

"You are the Kings' Caravan," the iguana warrior repeated.

"How can we be the Kings' Caravan if we do not follow the Four Kings?" a bird man asked.

"All through the Forest, it is being said that the Kings' Caravan lives, led by a man with a magic sword and shape-shifter dog."

"Who spreads these lies?" a rabbit man asked.

"We are enemies of the Kings' Caravan," the iguana warrior said. The three warriors pointed their pikes at them, ready to strike.

The animal men's enfields jumped forward, and their giant crabs ran in front to protect them.

"Your animals are no match for us," said a reptilian warrior. "We will kill them and then you."

"You will not!" a mouse man said.

All the animal men drew their own meager daggers.

"We may not be powerful warriors, as you are, but we will hold our own. Maybe we will manage to kill one of you."

The iguana warriors turned and saw the mole man fae sitting on the back of his carnivorous moose, watching not too far away.

"His animal eats anything that threatens us," a lizard man said.

Patrons of the merchant market had moved back from the likely battle. The animal men divided up amongst themselves to encircle the three reptilian warriors, the bird men took to the air.

"Do not start a fight if you cannot afford to lose it," a bird man warned.

The iguana warrior attacked them. Enfields attacked him as a pack, flying at his upper torso. The jackalopes ran at his legs. A giant crab swung at him, catching him in the head.

Then came a roar. The giant moose charged with his mole-like rider. Two of the reptile men jumped high in the air to attack the moose. The mole man threw a ball of magic at them, and both reptile men screamed as they were carried away until they were distant specks in the sky, then disappeared into the far away clouds.

The sole remaining iguana man was surrounded. He dropped his pike weapon to the ground. The animal men stopped their attack and pulled back their animals.

"You are not so weak after all, but let us see how you do against an army of thousands of us," the reptile man said.

"We have defeated gnolls, goblins, trolls, and war wizards. Thousands of iguana men will be no challenge to us."

"We shall see, Kings' Caravan, thieves of the noble beasts and races of our land."

The mole-like fae jumped down from his giant moose and floated in front of the iguana man, unnerving him.

"He does not like you," a possum man said. "He says you lie and you should stop lying or else he will feed you to his moose."

The reptile lifted his chin high to the fae, picked up his weapon from the ground with his tail, and walked away into the market.

The animal men looked at the mole man, all smiles.

"Everyone believes you're a mole man, but you're not. You are a sprite of great magic who looks like a mole man," a fox man said.

"We are not weak. They do not know you are our chief sorcerer," said another fox man.

"And warrior," a lizard man added.

"But what of what the iguana said?" a toad man asked.

"We must tell Master Traveler," a mouse man said.

"Tell me, Mr. Hobbs, does it seem strange that Mr. Traveler would leave us here alone?" Estus asked.

"You are not alone, Mr. Estus. He left you with us," one of Hobbs's bodyguards said to him.

"Of course, Mr. Tyfer. We can defend ourselves, but we're not warriors and we are human. We can be defeated by a tiny fairy."

"Mr. Traveler knows what he's doing," Hobbs said.

"Mr. Hobbs. Mr. Estus. Look."

The men within the circle pointed to the ground around them. Several shiny gold coins lay unattended.

Hobbs gave the men a disapproving look.

"Do not give us humans a bad name, men. Golden coins lying on the ground, are you truly that feeble?"

"Maybe it's not a trick, Mr. Hobbs. This is a merchant market. People drop loose coins all the time."

"I have been to many markets in the Lands of Man, and I know of no buyer who freely drops their coin to the ground. I am certain that all those in Faë–Land and the Great Forest are no different. A buyer knows every last coin they have at all times. Men, you are to take your eyes off the coins and remain in the circle. I am not about to lose a man under my care, not matter how foolish and deserving he is of his fate," Hobbs said.

The steward glanced to the ground and more of the glittering coins appeared around their circle. One of the coins shook as if it wanted to jump from the ground into his hand.

"Mr. Hobbs."

"Yes?" Hobbs said to one of his bodyguard, Mr. Oeric, without taking his eyes off the coin.

"Mr. Hobbs, your eyes have a very wild look about them. If you do not take your gaze from the coin, I will have to assume you are enchanted, and Mr. Tyfer and I will have to restrain you."

"I am fine, Mr. Oeric, and I am not enchanted." Hobbs could not take his eyes off the coin.

The steward jumped. A hand covered his eyes. Hobbs calmed himself and gave a deep sigh. Oeric removed his hand. Hobbs was himself and looked at the men.

"How easy it is to be enchanted in these magic lands."

"Yes, it is, Mr. Hobbs. You can say the right words, and be of the right mind, but it can still happen," Oeric said with sad eyes. "I've seen it happen to many men over the years. It happened to me."

"Yes. Men, we were reminded of an important lesson. We see why Mr. Traveler insisted none of us are ever alone. We must keep an eye on our surroundings and keep an eye on each other at all times."

King Aereth led the group on horseback, with Lady Aylen then Gwyness on one side. On the other were Traveler and the two Tree Shepherds on their tree horses.

"What other väki are there, Mr. Traveler?" Lady Aylen asked their caravan master.

"There are väki of the water, princess."

"Is there?"

"They are of water elemental magic like you."

"But I'm not a frowning old man."

He grinned. "That's true, princess. There are väki of different metals, like iron, and elements like ice. There are probably many, many others since they're sprites. Their races and clans are endless."

"These women väki, Mr. Traveler, do you really think they can help us?" Gwyness asked.

"When something similar happened to my caravan in the past, they were the fae that restored us. It was the first time I met väki and how I learned of them, how I met our own väki. We should wait and see. We do not know what kind of magic was used in that weapon graveyard."

The market bustled with patrons and animals but overall was quiet compared to the markets that they encountered in either the lands of humans or fae. Conversations were hushed, and haggling for goods was reserved.

"I have never seen an open market so quiet," Lady Aylen said. "Do they not barter like we do?" She looked around and behind her magic steed.

Gwyness had a strange feeling. She noticed in the market an owl man watching them. Its neckless head seemed to be part of its body. Its large wings were tucked at its sides. She felt as if it wanted to approach them but didn't.

"What is our purpose here, Mr. Traveler?" the king asked.

"Distraction, sire."

"Distraction?" Lady Aylen asked.

"Yes, princess. We here on horseback are unimportant. It is the other members of our party that have the true work to accomplish. We will stop at as many merchant wagons as possible, though. Why not that large one ahead?"

The wagon ahead was more of a store on the back of a wagon. The merchants peeking out its windows looked like gnomes with red hair and had very tan skin, more like a dwarf's than a gnome's. The Forest fae saw them and waved them forward.

"Do we even know what they sell, Mr. Traveler?" Lady Aylen asked.

"We're about to find out, princess."

After visiting one merchant wagon hut after another, Traveler stopped his dog-horse. Something caught his eye in the merchant market.

"What is it, Mr. Traveler?" King Aereth asked.

The riders had all stopped.

Traveler stared at a group of hooded cyclops watching them.

"Princess, what do they remind you of?"

"Yellow eyes." Lady Aylen stared directly at them.

"Yellow eyes?" Gwyness asked as she clutched her amulet under her battle dress.

"Xenhelm. Here? That is not possible, is it?" King Aereth asked.

"We should conclude our business quickly," Traveler said, moving his dog-horse forward.

The others followed him, but glanced back at the cyclopes.

"What does it mean, Mr. Traveler?" Gwyness asked.

"I am not sure, maiden, but we shall move quickly nonetheless."

Traveler jumped down from the mount and walked to one of the merchant fae.

"Can you direct me to the caravan master for Abacus?" he asked.

"Why?" the thorned tree man asked.

"I am a fellow caravan master."

"You? A human?"

"Yes. I have traveled the Trail many times."

The tree man pointed. Recognition came over Traveler's face. "I know this place," he said to himself. He turned to the group.

"Wait there," he directed.

The dog had already turned to a hulking humanoid, dog-like creature to follow him. The royals and Gwyness waited on their kirins with two of the Antaean giants and two of the Tree Shepherds riding tree horses.

Traveler reached one of the merchant wagons. Their caravan master greeted a fae wearing a white hooded cloak. They could not see his fae face but noticed two antennae popping out of his cloak near the forehead area. The men spoke quietly. A group of fae jumped down from the back of the wagon to join the conversation.

"Can you hear what they're saying, Lady Aylen?" King Aereth asked.

"No, the words are being drowned out by a buzzing sound."

"They do not want you to hear them," Mossberry said. "The conversation among them is friendly. Master Traveler knows the man."

"Knows him?" Lady Aylen asked.

"Our Master Traveler seems to know a few of them. The fae shaking his hand now is one who Master Traveler saved when he was a healer."

"Thank the Fates that our Mr. Traveler was a healer—is a healer," Lady Aylen said. "They will help us, then?"

"Yes, they will," Mossberry said.

They watched as Traveler and the dog followed the men farther into the merchant market.

"I will create a circle around us for protection," Mossberry said. "I am sure there are many around us hiding."

The magic circle came from the feet of their tree horses to surround the group. All around them—on the ground and in the air—they heard sounds of annoyance or angry disgust.

Gwyness pointed to the ground as they saw many footprints of invisible beings running away from them.

The väki appeared and took Mr. Estus with them, leaving Hobbs as the sole member of leadership in the circle.

"Where are they taking him?" the men asked.

"I wish I knew," Hobbs answered. "We may be left here alone, but we have a task to complete. Men, take position as if we're sentries. Appear friendly, but do not step outside the circle, and keep your eyes off the coins."

"Mr. Hobbs," Oeric called out.

"What is it, Mr. Oeric?"

"I believe I know why we were left here."

The men looked where Oeric was staring, outside the realm's tunnel entrance. They could all see many figures gathering. Hobbs could see Tyfer and Oeric growing nervous.

"It will be all right, men. The last thing Mr. Traveler would allow is for us to be trapped by anyone in one of these magic realms. We have him, the dog, the Tree Shepherds, the giants, and the väki. We're more than a match."

"I hope so, Mr. Hobbs," Oeric said.

The figures were on horseback, and Hobbs could see them running forward into the tunnel.

One of the other men tapped Hobbs on the shoulder. The steward turned. Dr'amal and Ursi approached them. The men could not be more relieved.

"We are about to have visitors," Dr'amal said. "I believe they seek us out."

Ursi pulled her own sword from its sheath.

Dr'amal raised a hand.

"The animal men already had their battle. We should try to do better. I'll see if I can diffuse this before it comes to that."

The women noticed too late. One of the men within the circle had bent down and quickly grabbed one of the golden coins.

"No, human!" Dr'amal yelled.

The coin in the man's hand turned into a laughing, misshapen pixy-like humanoid with floppy bovine ears, hoofed hands and feet, and a tail. The man screamed as the sprite jumped onto him and into the circle. All the coins transformed into the pixy-like laughing creatures and rushed into the circle.

Dr'amal reached in and pulled Hobbs and all the men out. She tapped the circle near the ground with her hand.

"You wish to be in the circle, creatures? Be in the circle by yourselves, with no items or people to make mischief on."

The creatures jumped around in a collective tantrum, trying to get out, but they could not. As they yelled, they transformed into many different items—large pots, brooms, torches, rocks, pitchforks—the variety was endless.

"What are they?" Hobbs asked.

"Fae call them hedley kows, shape–shifting cousins to imps, but I didn't know they existed in the Forest," Dr'amal said.

"Because they don't." Traveler rode in on his dog. He jumped down. "Hedley kows are like imps and gremlins. They enter lands by stowing away in the possessions of others."

"They are but little thieves," Dr'amal said.

"Ignore them. Release the hedley kows. We will take shelter at the far end of the market."

Hobbs's circle disappeared and the strange imp–like creatures spilled out and disappeared into invisibility.

They followed Traveler and the dog.

"You know the fae in this realm?" Dr'amal asked.

"I know a few," Traveler said, glancing back at her.

"Then it is safe?"

Traveler did not answer, returning his attention ahead as they walked.

Traveler let them walk on as he stopped for the animal men chattering without pause, determined to speak with him. Hobbs led the men and the two women to a merchant wagon hut where the royals,

Gwyness, the two giants, and two Tree Shepherds waited.

"Mr. Hobbs," King Aereth said. "What happened?"

"Sire, what did we encounter is the question. Another race of impish fae, but I will save the story for the nighttime meal."

"Make sure you have a good account of it all for Mr. Quillen," Lady Aylen said. "What's wrong with our animal men? They're upset about something."

"Where are Mr. Pangolin, Estus, and the others?" Gwyness asked.

"I am still uncertain as to why we're really here," Lady Aylen said.

A party of fae had left through the realm's tunnel, creating a loud commotion. The realm's cyclops guardian ran through the entrance into the market. He reached for the first fae he came upon and grabbed his neck, strangling him. Another figure appeared, running through the tunnel—a woman. The hag of a woman appeared grayish with molting skin, ragged whitish hair to her knees, and a dress of decay. She yelled.

At the far end of the market, fae heard great commotion. People stopped and looked towards the realm entrance in the distance.

Traveler ran to Lady Aylen. "What do you see?"

"I wish I had Mr. Elman's magic sight, but I see people fighting." Lady Aylen had an expression of shock. "They're killing each other."

"Greenwig, your trees. Knock the men and Gwyness out now!"

Greenwig rose from his tree horse, and before any could react, branches shot out, knocking King Aereth, Hobbs, the men, and Gwyness to the ground unconscious. Gwyness recovered quickly. The crawling tree entangled her and Lady Aylen.

"Why are you doing this?" Lady Aylen yelled.

"Go!" Traveler yelled at the Tree Shepherds. He flew on the back of his winged dog to the animal men.

The Nemain hag ran through the market. Plant fae ran or flew away for their lives. Every other fae was gripped by a murderous rage and attacked each other. Many murdered, others killed themselves. Chaos erupted in every corner of the merchant market as fae were consumed by the murderous war cry of the Nemain. The demoness ran through the market as if floating on the winds. Some fae escaped to the pocket-realms of their own merchant wagons or rolling huts. Panicked animals—cù-sìths, fae cats, and others—stampeded from the market.

The ground reached up and seized the Nemain's lower torso. She was unable to move but yelled again. Väki appeared out of invisibility, many different clans, not frowning but enraged. Spikes of metal, rock, roots, and vines, ripped into her body. The earth swallowed her up until all that was visible was her head impaled with countless spikes. The demoness stopped moving.

Even from within the market, the Abacus väki felt the power of the giant portal outside the realm. Dozens and dozens of riders entered the realm's tunnel entrance. The shadowy riders sat upon black pegasi. They trampled the dead body of the cyclops guard in their path.

"Who dares unleash a Nemain demoness into our realm uninvited?" A loud voice rang from the sky.

The riders drew closer on their pitch-black winged horses. The center man was human. His riders were beast men, covered in thick black fur with pale monkey-like faces and razor teeth.

"I am King Prince Wuldricar the Savage of the Four Kings of Xenhelm," the huge, pale knight in black armor said. His hair, once blond was now white, his beard dyed orange.

"One of the Four Kings dares enter the realm of the Anemoi after a deed of such blackness?"

"I am not here for you. Give me whom I seek. And what of the name Abacus?" Wuldricar asked.

"We have had many names for outsiders through the millennia, but we are always the floating kingdom of Anemoi, and our realm is where you die!"

"But I am already dead." Wuldricar laughed.

"Yes, but you have not yet been burned and buried."

The entire realm shook with the force of an earthquake powerful enough to break Pan-Earth apart. The entrance vanished as the realm fell in on itself. Then the realm vanished.

CHAPTER TWELVE

The Great Caravan

Frog-Dor looked at his image in the long mirror of his tent. The brownies had made him a new set of clothes, and the fabric felt cool to the touch. He was pleased, as his metal braces were hidden.

"Mr. Frog-Dor," someone called from outside.

"Yes?"

He turned from the mirror to the entrance as the flap pulled back, and Traveler entered with his dog. The caravan master looked around.

"Mr. Frog-Dor, are you in this tent alone?"

"No, Mr. Traveler, the men gave me a moment to change."

"The brownies?"

"Yes. They made a longer coat for me."

Traveler nodded. "As long as you're not alone. I know you're still adjusting, but we cannot take any chances."

"Yes."

"Are the dreams gone?"

"They have not troubled me lately, but I may not be worthy to lead your 'dream' committee if I am also afflicted."

"My understanding is that most of the caravan has been afflicted."

"Is this normal for those within the Forest?"

"Normal is not the best way to describe it. It happens because of the magic of the Forest. However, nightmares are a signal of some other agent, but that is not why I came to speak with you."

"I heard what happened in the merchant realm of Abacus."

"No, that's not its name, and it's not merely a merchant caravan in a realm. It is a moving city called the kingdom of Anemoi. I was there once as part of another caravan. I did not recognize it because its great castles must have been hidden from sight. The merchant market we visited is outside its walls. The true market is within the city's walls. The leaders are a coalition of väki and elementals. I was suspicious that we were being led there for ill intentions, but now I know we were led there for the opposite. Such hidden magic cities can remain hidden forever. One does not learn of them or stumble upon them. They allow themselves to be found, otherwise no magic can locate them. The white elfess was right. There are forces who wish to aid us, as much as the one who wants to destroy us."

"Do you know why they wanted to aid us?"

"I'm forming a theory. I will know more when I speak with the leaders within the caravan, but even that is not why I've troubled you."

"No trouble, Mr. Traveler."

"When we were at the edges of the Great Forest, you said two parties followed after us. We escaped the merchant city before we could see who was arriving through a giant portal, but we could guess— agents of the Four Kings. Were either of those two parties your magic revealed at the merchant's realm?"

"No. They're not Xenhelm agents. I'm certain of it. One of them is strangely familiar. I cannot put it into words."

"Do you still sense them?"

"No. I'm not certain where they are. I believe they detected my seeker spell. I can speak with the other fae magic-casters in the caravan and we can see what happened at the merchant city."

"No. Let it be. Anemoi has existed for millennia and will exist for many more long after we have passed away. Seeker spells and seeing eyes can be traced back to their source. Xenhelm agents were in the merchant market, so they're in the Great Forest too. My goal is for us to sneak away into the night and back to Titan's Walk. The greater the distance we put between them, the more impossible it will be for them or any to track us."

Frog-Dor nodded. "You're correct in your thinking. I heard they sent a Nemain."

"They did. Another creature from the Lands of Darkness."

"Have you had any nightmares, Mr. Traveler?"

The caravan master grinned. "If I did and did not tell you all, then that would mean I am not following my own dictates to the caravan, but no, which is more reason to be concerned. Why not me? We have been made whole as a caravan, so we will leave as soon as it is wise to do so."

The last group meeting was one of despair. Mr. Hobbs arranged for the meeting to be outside on top of a small hill for all to see. Every human and fae gathered around. The mood was cautiously optimistic. Before the general meeting, Traveler asked to see the fae leaders privately. The royals and Gwyness waited at Traveler's tent, too, when they saw Pangolin walking toward them.

"Mr. Pangolin," Gwyness said with a big smile.

Their berserker vanguard leader was clad in his full earthen metal armor that looked like scales. They could see the handle of his giant weapon strapped on his back. There was a newness to his armor and renewed confidence in his face.

"Mr. Pangolin, the visit was successful," King Aereth said, greeting the man with a firm handshake.

"Yes, sire, it was. Apparently, the merchant market was where our Mr. Traveler got his own armor."

"He did?" Gwyness asked.

"The väki of steel forged his special armor. They do not do it often though. The väki brought me and Mr. Estus to their hidden city to a room of magic furnaces, but it was not of fire. It burned with magic. They threw my armor and weapon into it. When they removed it, they were more than restored. When I touched them, I could feel the power.

"They also knew my people," he said.

"Your people?" King Aereth asked.

"Mr. Traveler said they may have even helped my people's forgers create it. They told me that ages ago in one the many wars occurring between the fae, my people fought alongside their own warriors. I never knew that. I did know from my own elders that berserkers were some of the first humans to travel into Faë-Land because we are imbued with magic. It all makes sense to me now. My kingdom has also been strong with earth elemental influence. I saw the origin of it all."

"They fought alongside earth elementals? The väki too?" Gwyness asked.

"I believe so. They did not say it directly, but I believe so."

"You can say it, Mr. Pangolin. They spoke like an elf," Lady Aylen said.

"M'lady, you are always direct when you speak."

"Ah, here's our caravan master. Mr. Traveler, since we were not present ourselves, what do female väki look like?" Lady Aylen asked.

Traveler entered the tent with his dog.

"Princess, female väki don't have beards, but they frown a lot."

Inside the tent were gathered the leaders of the elves, the drows, both fae-blood clans, and the Tree Shepherds as well as Bragg the dwelf, the gnomes, the fauns, and a few of the animal men. Hobbs, Gresham, I'wulf, and the royals' guardspeople were also present.

"Mr. Hobbs, please close the tent," he said.

"We will be marching forward after our meeting with the men."

Near applause broke out among the gathering.

"Mr. Pangolin's armor and weapon have been restored. We secured all the magical treatments to cure our afflicted animals. Our stocks of magic arrows have been replenished and doubled. We do not have the vast weapons vault that we once had, which was filled with armor and weapons unused. We now have a true vault of spare weapons and armor while our best weapons are on hand."

The humans applauded.

"However!"

The gathering became quiet.

"I am not going to ask any of you to explain in this gathering, but sometime on the Trail you will. The merchant caravan was actually a merchant city. The city was magically hidden, but I was there on a previous occasion. It is also a place for caravan masters of the region to gather and exchange gossip for amusement and news of dangers and matter of interest.

He looked at the fae-bloods. "Insect fae-bloods. Are they not the rarest of the fae-blood clans?"

"They are," one of the fae-blood men said with a smirk.

"In all these centuries, no one, no fae, has even seen one fae-blood clan. On this one trip, we have seen not one but four different clans, two in our own caravan, and I heard of a fifth, all going to Atlantea. The question to ask is why? Why all these fae-blood clans, including those at war with each other, wanting to go to Atlantea?"

Traveler looked at the drows. "I have met the D'Shar before. You are D'Shar but do not dress or carry the weapons of their clan. Why? Then we encountered night drows. A race you hate more than the elves. All going to Atlantea."

He looked at the animal men.

"Why didn't you tell me the mole man fae was a sorcerer?"

"Master Traveler, no one asked," a bird man replied.

"Elves of city kingdoms sent their elfin questing knights to be under the command of rustic village elves, something they would never do. All this time, I thought the Four Kings were after us because of me, possible because of what Lady Aylen and Maiden

Gwyness may become, but I am starting to believe that the reason is not us but you.

"I realized at the outset that Lady Aylen and Maiden Gwyness were going to Atlantea for unstated reasons. When I first met the princess, I knew she was an elf because my dog knew. What I was unsure of was if she knew, which I soon realized she did not. But then there's the rest of you. Only you know your own unstated reasons. I brought the Tree Shepherds and väki to the caravan. The rest of you found us.

"When speaking to my caravan master comrades, they informed me that there were many, many caravans seeking a way to Atlantea, some led by, or including, fae that are beyond their lands they have never left before. Others are led by, or with, fae races no one has seen before. One that passed by months ago was led by a new caravan master who was a dwelf."

"A dwelf?" Mr. Bragg asked. "I am the only one outside our secret lands."

"It would seem that you are not."

"What are you telling us, Master Traveler?" Chief Ethor asked.

"Keep your secrets, but at some point you will have to tell us those secrets, as the ultimate success of our quest no longer lies with me, but you.

Everyone knows that we destroyed the Kings' Caravan, but how? We did not tell anyone. Someone made sure every interested party from here to Faë-Land Minor and beyond knows."

"Who, Mr. Traveler?" Lady Aylen asked.

"You met her, princess."

"The white elfess?" she asked.

"The celestial elf queen you met?" Lyre, the high elf, asked.

"She and her secret allies."

"Whom you say destroyed my birth nation," Lady Aylen reminded him.

"She did warn us that forces would try to involve us in their affairs."

"What was the creature that you protected us from, Mr. Traveler?" King Aereth asked.

"Sorry, sire, we had to hit a king."

"Seeing that it saved my life, Mr. Traveler, you will only receive utmost gratitude from me and those in the market."

"Sire, it's a demon whose battle cry causes men to be consumed by such a murderous lust that they will kill anyone around them, and if none are near, they kill themselves. The demon is a Nemain."

"Another demon, Mr. Traveler?" Pangolin said. "I thought they were rare in the magical lands. Yet we have encountered more than one on our journey."

"Actually, three if we count our 'friend' the Old One. Yes, Mr. Pangolin, they are rare, and the denizens of these lands will hunt and destroy them on sight. They seem to be frequently used by the Four Kings."

"But the iguana men in the merchant market said we were the Kings' Caravan of the Four Kings," one of the lizard men said.

"Our enemies. A lie spread to find out where we were, and they did, and our secret allies helped us to get to the secret merchant city. The väki there were expecting us. I have no more to say. We will give the men the good news that we travel on but I end on this: before we get to the oceans, I need to know your true reasons for going to Atlantea. I know the reason for the humans, Lady Aylen, the Tree Shepherds, the brownies, and the pech, even our fairy sisters. I'm not certain about the rest of you. It's certainly not for treasure. I believe if you revealed why, we would instantly know why Oughtred is so obsessed with keeping us from Atlantea. I thought he was mad, but there's a single-mindedness to it all. I thought maybe fear, fear of us from a being who knows no fear. But maybe there is a logic to his actions."

"Mr. Traveler, I can assure you I have no ulterior motives for the journey to Atlantea. I seek adventure along the way and untold riches at the end to pay for my hunting quests till my end days. What my fellow dwelves may or may not be doing, I have no idea. I am fervently disinterested in the politics of kingdoms, including my own. That's why I left. My people were becoming too elfin rather than dwarven for my tastes. No offenses to our present company of elves," Bragg said.

Lady Aylen and the other elves ignored him.

"Do you not trust us, Mr. Traveler?" Dr'as asked.

"Of course, I trust you. I would never have let you into the caravan if I didn't. It would simply be nice if you trusted me equally by trusting each other. After all, I am the one leading you to the fabled city and protecting our lives."

After the general announcements to the men, Hobbs had the spotlight for the night meal.

"The shape–shifting creatures are called Hedley kows, men."

Quillen planted himself right in front of the steward with his magic book open and his sketching pen ready.

"And yes, Mr. Quillen, I will give you an accurate description."

Hobbs's storytelling performance went on for a couple hours, including virtually every man wanting to add their own comments or ask their questions about the creatures, fae, and merchant market realm.

The men turned in a bit later, but it was hours before dawn when Traveler came into the king's tent.

"Mr. Nirgund, get up and get the sire up. We must be on the march before the hour."

The berserker got up from his bed. His alphyn hounds rose from the ground too, yawning, and as they did, flames came from their mouths.

Traveler walked into the women's tent. "Princess and ladies, rise. We march within the hour."

"March, Mr. Traveler? Dawn is hours away," Lady Aylen said.

"When luck smiles upon you unexpectedly and opens a door for you, you run through it with haste. We have new transport, princess. Not as good as the Atlas turtles but close." He left the tent with the dog.

"Where?"

Titan's Caravan hastily broke camp and marched. They had to run to follow their caravan master to the dawn sun barely peeking across the horizon. When they arrived, they could not believe what they saw. They marched but were far from alone. They had beheld a sea of trees weeks before. That early morning, they joined a sea of people. They became one of a great caravan moving along an open path through the giant trees.

Later, Traveler would explain that the years the Kings' Caravan chose for their triennial trek was not by accident. It was on the years that the Great Caravan of the Forest did not move. The path was always different and not known to outsiders, but it stretched all the way from one end of the Forest to the ocean's edge. Titan's Caravan had the blind luck to have been camped nearby as it passed.

As the day grew brighter, the men could get a better view of all the many fae around them. The sight was overwhelming. It was as if every inhabitant of Pan-Earth was with them, all marching as one. None had seen so many people moving as a unit, dozens of columns across, possibly hundreds. All were quiet, all watching their surroundings carefully for any sign of danger, all watching each other, the many, many parties that there were—mammal men, plant men, insect men, reptile and amphibian men, bird men. They had gnomoids, fae that looked like their own fenodyree, humanoids with yellow skin or green or albinos, fae with big ears, big noses, long necks, or no necks. Some wore hooded cloaks obscuring their faces. Others had armored helmets, faces unseen. There were many pull-carts and wagons, many beasts of burden—giant rodents, turtle-like mammals, feather-less land birds, bison-like animals, horse-sized dogs. All the fae had weapons, mostly long spears pointing many feet up. In the Forest, it was the weapon of choice to keep giant beasts at bay.

No one spoke at all. Among the countless tens or hundreds of thousands, not a word was said in any language.

Traveler walked with the vanguard. The dog was in the form of a hard-shelled canine. Otherwise, their caravan marched in usual formation with the giant lizards at the flanks.

"Ah!"

Near dawn a swarm of giant dragonflies attacked the Great Caravan. Two men were snatched away. One of the men managed to stab the creature and was dropped. The other was eaten in mid-air. Men stabbed at the swarm with their long pike staffs. Traveler nodded at Pangolin. The vanguard leader gave the signal, and the elaphine archers let loose a volley of arrows. Multiple dragonflies were hit and crashed to the ground. The swarm flew off.

The Great Caravan never stopped. No one said anything or thanked Titan's Caravan for their aid. The marching continued.

The men soon realized that there would be no stopping for the noon meal. Hobbs moved through the caravan to tell them to drink water if needed. The pech moved around to the humans and gave them snacks to eat, spicy or heavily sweet food, their choice, to relieve the tiredness.

The signal was given and the Great Caravan began to slow. Parties broke away and ran at breakneck speeds to defensive areas to make camp. Those who made it first to a spot claimed it. Already fights broke out, two parties or more claiming they seized an area first.

Traveler paid no attention to any of the chaos. He calmly led the vanguard and the main columns away. As they walked, all saw that however many they thought were in the Great Caravan was greatly underestimated. There was no end to the camps forming. Incredibly, they marched another two hours until they finally reached a spot Traveler was satisfied with, outside all others.

"Mr. Hobbs, we make camp here."

"Very good, sir." The steward ran off to oversee the quartering parties of the caravan.

"Mr. Pangolin, get your men to bed immediately. These are how our days will be for weeks."

"Good," the berserker said. "Daily movement means we get to our destination quicker."

He led his vanguard into camp. The four giants were already half asleep.

"Mr. Traveler, will you be up for the night meal or turning in as well?" King Aereth asked.

"I will join you, sire, if you'll be up."

"Princess?" the king asked.

"Gwyness and I will of course join the night meal. It's our ritual."

Brownies set the campfires up in their camp. The lizard minders dug the heat pits for their lizards with the help of the pech. Their work would take at least an hour. The moon elves were already on perimeter sentry.

As the royals, Gwyness, and Traveler sat around the campfire outside their tents, they could hear Dr'as speak to his drows then dismiss them to patrol the perimeter. Hobbs created four circles to protect the camp.

"Are we safe, Mr. Traveler?" Lady Aylen asked.

"Safety in numbers," Traveler said.

"I do feel more secure marching with such a large group," King Aereth said, "though they're not the friendliest or most sociable people I've ever encountered. However, their attitude is more than understandable."

"How often does this great caravan travel, Mr. Traveler, and what is its destination?"

"Princess, they follow paths winding in different directions than our Atlas turtles but arriving at a point near Titans Fall. Some in the caravan will depart from there. Others will continue their march across the shores to the many cities along it. True civilization begins again outside the Great Forests. From end to end, the full journey will take more than a year. These great caravans happen whenever they are needed. The fae just seem to know amongst themselves. Also, as you can see, they move fast, no stops, and no horseplay or gossip."

"A very serious-minded group," King Aereth said.

"They have to be. These great caravans will lose about ten percent of their people to the predators of the Forest."

"How many people are in this great caravan, Mr. Traveler?" Gwyness asked.

"Many hundreds of thousands. Ten times the size of the Kings Caravan with its five-hundred-thousand strong."

"That's a lot of people to die even at ten percent," Lady Aylen said.

"To them it is the way of life in the Forest. Night is even more dangerous because the caravan is not moving, and many more predators are waiting to pounce."

"Are our defenses adequate, Mr. Traveler?" King Aereth asked.

"They will be, sire. The moon elves and drows will be joined by our fae-blood men. We will be shielded by two of the crawling trees, each with a Tree Shepherd, during the night, and our brownies will be armed."

"Armed? Brownies can fight?" Lady Aylen asked.

"Brownies can fight quite well, princess."

The food servers arrived with the night meals. Gwyness called the royal guards. Both the female half-elves and Nirgund and all their animals joined them around the large campfire. Mr. Estus arrived with Mr. Gresham and Frog-Dor.

"Welcome, Mr. Frog-Dor," Lady Aylen said.

He nodded with a slight smile as he sat.

"Too bad we won't all be able to eat our night meals together," King Aereth said.

"This will be our new routine for a few months, sire. It's only temporary."

As with the Atlas turtles, moving with the Great Caravan meant they went without rest until sundown and moved faster. Men got used to eating while walking.

"Rain!"

The rain was a welcome change. Then it stopped and started again. It was not until Titan's Caravan came around the bend of the upward slope in the Forest that they could see why. A herd of giant greenish elephants covered with moss and trees played amongst themselves. A river—a stream to the elephants—roared by, and the play for the animals was sucking in water and spraying the Great Caravan. The adults had long pointing tusks, but none were hostile.

Days passed without an event until the week's end. They heard an attack ahead. They were too far back to see. They heard roars and screaming men, but the Great Caravan never stopped.

Another day, a giant stag came from nowhere in the giant trees, ran across the breadth of the caravan, trampling and killing dozens of men, and disappeared back into the Forest. Men, mangled but not dead, were swiftly killed where they lay with daggers or spears. Quick graves were dug, bodies tossed in, and dirt kicked back over. The emotionless calm of it shocked most in Titan's Caravan. Obviously, healers were not needed in the Great Caravan. If someone was injured and could not march on, they were killed. The Great Caravan surged forward without exception.

The Forest did not change. Trees all appeared the same. Days blended into one another. March, eat, sleep, repeat.

Eventually they reached the eleventh day.

Traveler had once told them that many of the creatures of the Great Forest defied explanation and bore no name. Men tried to fend off the monstrosity with their pike staffs but to no effect. At first glance, one would confuse its body with that of some type of wolf, but it was all tree like with green foliage and dark-brown bark. Its head was more like a flower with snapping vines. The creature roared but had no visible mouth. The sound was coming from the sides of its body. Men screamed as they were crushed under its feet or snapped apart or impaled with its head vines.

The entire attack was several dozen feet away from the tip of Titan's Caravan. The body of the Great Caravan continued moving forward while those directly ahead ran. Everyone else pulled back and ran away. Parties threw spears and fired arrows. Balls of magic light exploded on its body.

Traveler rushed forward with his sword, ready to attack. Pangolin led two of the giants. The human reached the creature before the giants. The caravan master slashed away at the creature's head vines. For every attacking vine he cut, seemingly two replaced it. Pangolin landed his blow with his axe-mace, and the creature broke in two. Two plant creatures attacked.

Traveler looked at Pangolin, shaking his head.

"This is not a fight for us! This is for the Antaeans!"

Grakdar yelled out. As the four other giants rallied around him, Traveler and Pangolin stepped back. Titan's Caravan's archers—elaphine, elfin, and faun—bombarded both creatures with arrows, slowing them down.

The six Antaean giants knelt to the ground in a circle, shoulder to shoulder. They glowed yellow with the magic from within. The light beamed from their eye sockets, ear canals, and mouths, and their size increased. A ghostly form took shape behind them, a composite of each of the giants, its size many times theirs. The form grabbed the two halves of the creature and, with a yell, threw them far, far into the Forest.

The Great Caravan had stopped in its tracks to watch.

Hobbs was the last to arrive for the night meal. Everyone seated around the campfire was already in conversation. The food servers passed out bowls of broth with healthy chunks of meat from Bragg's hunt weeks ago. No one could preserve food better than the fae. Hobbs took out his pipe and tapped it on the ground before he was handed his own bowl.

"Why didn't the dog attack, Mr. Traveler?" Lady Aylen asked.

"I told him not to, princess. Many of these plant creatures are covered with mold, ticks, and spores, some natural and some magical. Remember, neither my dog nor I are invincible."

"Maybe more of the magic–eating mold kind. We see what that did to Mr. Pangolin's magic armor, and I would have considered that invincible," she said.

"Mr. Traveler, it looks as if we have visitors," King Aereth said.

They could see a small party at the edge of the circle. Several moon elves stood watching from the other side, and brownies stood at their own campfires, ready to join them. When Traveler and the royals reached the perimeter, they could see the visitors were far taller than the average human male, gnome-like but with long elfin ears that pointed upward at least a foot. They wore battle garb of metal chest plates over tunics of thick leather. At their sides were greenish animals that looked like giant mongooses the size of horses.

"May we speak to whoever's in command?" one of the fae men asked.

"Mr. Traveler is our caravan master," King Aereth said.

The men were allowed to enter the circle. Two remained outside to mind their giant animals. Traveler led them to their campfire to sit. Gwyness, Nirgund, and the guardspeople moved back to allow the visitors a place to sit.

"We would have come sooner, but there were rumors that you were part of the old Kings' Caravan. We know that not to be true now," one of them said.

"I am glad you reasoned the truth without us having to tell you."

"The Kings' Caravan was fond of collecting things from across the magical lands, including allies of many different races."

"We are just a caravan on a quest. Our alliances are based on the simple fact that together, we can accomplish what none of us can accomplish alone."

"That is the philosophy of our great caravan, which has existed for centuries. We may never have the power of the sky elves or elementals, but we have our own way to travel the Forest."

"That you have."

"A human as a caravan master is also a rare thing. There was some discussion about that too, that you were a changeling of some kind, as no human could have acquired the knowledge needed to travel alone or lead a caravan through the Forest."

"I am certainly no shape-shifting cousin to the trolls. My knowledge is direct. I've been a member of countless caravans. My knowledge was acquired through trial and the many deaths of others."

"That is how all true caravan masters acquire their knowledge. Do you travel as far as the oceans?"

"Possibly. We will decide sometime in the days and weeks ahead. Thus far, we are very pleased with the progress we've made."

"Good, then. We would like to think that the Great Caravan is an efficient endeavor. Leave from one point and walk until you get to the end point. If you do decide to stay with us to the oceans and as far as Titan's Fall, we can talk further."

"Is there a problem?"

"There shouldn't be but the trees have told us that there's much activity along its shores. Undines, sylphs, mermaid war parties. The Great Caravan has never had problems with them in the past. We do not bother them. They do not bother us. It's an agreement we've had between each other over the ages, but we should be cautious. If you're with us, with the strength and magic of your party, it would be best that the strongest and best among us is at the front."

"That would be the best plan."

"It has also not gone unnoticed that your people are not averse to helping others even with no gain or monetary reward to yourselves. Such are the qualities of benevolent leaders."

"Very true. I'm Traveler."

"I am Thome of Gem Tree."

"The forest of gemstones."

"You know it?"

"I do."

"You're a well-traveled caravan master. Good. We can talk then if it should come to it. We, ourselves, may decide to change course if the trees warn us that we should avoid Titan's Fall altogether."

"Visit us at any time," Traveler said. "Where are my manners? Would you like to join us for our night meal?"

"We have already eaten, but if you have a good drink, we can remain to hear more about your caravan and your exploits so far."

"Mr. Hobbs, get some of the best ale we have for our visitors."

As the servers ran to get the beverages for everyone, many of them were thinking the same thing. Mr. Traveler was right—forces were gathering at Titan's Fall for them.

CHAPTER THIRTEEN

Nomads of Zingara

"Father."

King Aereth stood in a white robe at the edge of a river of pure, clear water. A simple green field surrounded him. The king turned. His hand grabbed at his own chest to calm an eruption of tears. His dead son, dressed similarly, stood at the base of the tall trees of the forest adjacent to the fields. The man was but a younger version of Aereth with the same facial hair and fairer hair.

"Father," his son said again as he reached for Aereth. "Please help me. I'm sorry I disappointed you."

"I was never disappointed in you," King Aereth said.

"Help me, father."

The king heard voices from the forest. His son stepped closer to him.

"Help you? How?" the king asked.

"They come for me, father. What do I do?"

"Come away from the forest!"

The king realized that he had a sword in his hand. He lifted it, and it dripped blood down his hands. He cried out. His son lay at his feet with eyes and mouth wide open, holding a bloody wound in his chest.

"Father, why did you not help me?"

The king dropped the sword and stumbled back.

"King!"

Aereth sat up in his trussing bed, drenched in sweat.

"Sire, are you all right?" Nirgund was at his side.

The king looked around, disoriented. Nirgund's reptilian hounds watched the man suspiciously.

"You were speaking in your sleep."

"Yes. My son."

"Sire?"

"I need to get up." The king pushed the covers from his body and turned to sit up straight as his feet rested on the ground.

"The nightmares are back," Nirgund said.

The king said nothing. He swallowed hard, still disturbed.

Titan's Caravan was no longer at the back of the Great Caravan. They were allowed to march near the front. Lady Aylen jokingly said they were once again "preferred" allies of a caravan, only this time no one was asking for payment. But the men were starting to recognize certain parties, races, and clans. They also realized that individuals and parties were constantly dropping out of the Great Caravan march or joining in.

One day a specific party drew their attention. Gwyness had a strange feeling about the new party—they were led by a woman with long, scraggly graying hair, but she was not elderly. Her party consisted of fae of different races, but they were similarly dressed, all their clothing made of the same fabrics and color patterns. She walked with a staff. Sometimes Gwyness felt the woman was watching them, or her in particular, but every time she looked, they were paying her no attention at all.

Gwyness looked over her other shoulder and saw him, the owl man she had seen in the merchant market who she was certain wanted to speak to them. He noticed her gaze and looked away. Gwyness looked over her other shoulder and, this time, caught the woman watching her.

"Mr. Traveler," Gwyness said, moving closer to the caravan master. "I wish to ask a question but no one speaks."

"The reason no one speaks on the march, Maiden Gwyness, is the beasts of the Forest may ignore the march of many feet upon the ground but not the spoken words of intelligent beings carried through the air," he whispered.

"Sorry," she said. "But who is that woman?"

"No need to point. We will talk at night camp."

Lady Aylen glanced back herself.

The Great Caravan never waited until sundown to stop. Always, they ended the day's march a few hours before nightfall, as it took that long for all the parties to select their areas, make camp, and set their defenses, and still it was not enough time for most. Those at the front of the caravan had the benefit of being able to select their camp area before the others.

Hobbs busily oversaw the camp's quartering duties. Gwyness appeared at their caravan master's tent. The dog lay at the entrance, always on watch.

"Mr. Traveler," she said.

"Come in, Maiden Gwyness."

"May I leave the camp to look for someone within the general caravan?"

Traveler rose from his seat behind his map table.

"This is not the place to be wandering around, maiden."

"I won't be wandering. I believe I know where to go."

"I thought we were going to talk about the woman you noticed when we sat for our night meal."

"Yes, I'll be back for that, but I need to find this fae. He is the owl man I saw in the merchant market realm. I had the impression that he wanted to speak with us. I feel I must find out why."

"Who will go with you?"

"Lady Aylen will accompany me, but as much as I despise the idea, I was thinking of your darklings. We haven't seen them."

"For them to behave themselves and stay within the circle of our own caravan is too much to ask of them. They remain in their realm. But yes, it's a good idea. It will give them a chance, in a limited way, to see the great caravan we travel among. I will get them."

"Please tell them to appear as something presentable."

"I'll be sure not to tell them that, as they would do the opposite."

The night sky above them had a quarter moon. Gwyness stopped in her tracks as something very large blocked it out for a moment.

"Gwyness, you do such a good job of scaring yourself sometimes," Lady Aylen said, walking at her side.

"What was that that flew above us?" she asked.

"What does it matter? We're in our protective circle, and every camp, look, is protected by their own circles."

"But we're not within any of them."

"This was your idea, Gwyness."

"It was a bat," one darkling said.

Their nighttime bodyguards were in the form of black rabbit-headed bears.

"No, it was a big, ugly, hairy flying goat," another said.

"I saw it. It was a big, disgusting, putrid, headless corpse with worms and—"

"You can say whatever foul words you wish, but I will not be unnerved by you this time," Gwyness said, staring at them with her hands on her hips.

The darklings smiled wide with human mouths of sparkling white teeth. Gwyness huffed and turned her attention to the front.

Lady Aylen laughed. "We follow our leader, creatures."

Walking through the camps was like moving through the void of space where every campfire was a star, but Gwyness was right to trust her instincts. Without consciously knowing where to go, her feet led the way. Before long they were at a campfire with a sole fae sitting, his eyes closed. He opened his eyes and turned his body to face them, as he had no neck. The owl man rose to his feet. He was almost seven feet tall.

Despite the fae's size, Gwyness walked right up to him.

"We see each other again," she said.

The fae stared at her with his large owl eyes but said nothing.

"I had the impression you wanted to speak with us. Am I mistaken?"

"You're not mistaken. I'm a messenger, but I will speak with you and the elfess alone."

"Our bodyguards stay," Lady Aylen said. "They have no interest in anything you say."

"Our memories are very bad," one darkling said.

"We forget all knowledge when the sun rises," said another.

"That's a lie, but whenever we see things that are big and disgusting and putrid and headless with worms, we forget everything we hear in the next hour."

Gwyness glared at the darklings. They smiled.

"Go on, owl man. Say what you have to say," Lady Aylen said.

"My message is brief. Your followers will be there at Titan's Teeth."

"Followers?" Gwyness asked.

"We don't know that place. We're traveling to Titan's Fall," Lady Aylen said.

"No need for deception. You don't understand, but you have told them where you will be already."

"We told them?" Gwyness asked.

"Who are these followers you speak of?" Lady Aylen asked.

"You know whom I speak of, followers of light elves, humans, faoladh, and other fae. My message is delivered to you. Be ready for them. Time will be short. Here is the message for your caravan master."

Gwyness took a small parchment from the fae's birdlike hands.

"May you arrive at the end of Titan's Walk to rebuild the warrior clerics and mages."

The owl man bowed and walked into the night. They looked on, but he was gone.

"You were right to seek him out," Lady Aylen said. "But he said much and nothing at the same time. This note, of course it's in some language I've never seen."

"Fine ladies, may I have a word?"

The voice came out of the night as the women walked back to their camp with their darkling guards. The woman of the new party, with long, scraggly graying hair, approached with her walking staff.

"I am with the nomads of Zingara," she said. "We joined the Great Caravan today."

"Yes, we saw you," Lady Aylen said.

"I could not help notice you meeting with the owl man. Nomads take advantage of situations placed before us. We are people of commerce, exchanging goods of interest and value, bartering for services or knowledge."

"What do you want?" Lady Aylen asked her directly.

"The trinket around the human female's neck."

"My amulet?" Gwyness asked.

"I've seen similar ones and would very much desire to acquire yours for a fair price."

"There is no price you could offer me to part with it."

"A magic doorway, perhaps? Here tonight, tomorrow morning at the gates of Atlantea."

The woman stood silent.

"You possess no such magic," Lady Aylen said.

"You sound unsure. Anything is possible in the lands of magic. Consider my offer with great care. The path to Atlantea is a deadly one. Even with a gifted and knowledgeable guide, success is not a certainty, especially when one has as many enemies as your party has."

"What enemies?" Gwyness asked.

"The Great Caravan may not know, but I know why the powerful Kings' Caravan of twenty human years no longer marches and its second city of Xenhelm in Faë-Land no longer stands, scorched from the earth, its lands still ablaze.

"You know much for a simple nomad," Lady Aylen said. "Why do you want my maiden's simple amulet, then?"

"That's my affair."

"No, our affair."

"I've given you more than a fair offer to part with it, one that could save the lives of you and every human and fae within your caravan. Live to step across into Atlantea or die on the Trail or oceans to it. To reject my offer is a great gamble on your part."

"We will consider your offer," Lady Aylen said.

"We will not!" Gwyness yelled.

Lady Aylen placed a hand on Gwyness's shoulder. "We will consider your offer," the princess said again.

"That is all I can ask," the woman said.

"What were the feelings of the nomads of Zingara toward the Kings' Caravan?" Lady Aylen asked.

"I am a fae of the Forest, elfess. Elves should be in Faë-Land Major, humans in the Lands of Man, giants and sprites in Faë-Land Minor. All should live and stay in their own lands and not invade others. Look at you, your caravan—elves, humans, drows, giants, and more—ancient enemies now allies to travel across my lands, trespass across my lands."

"We do not travel across your lands to cause any offense," Gwyness said.

"Ignore her," Lady Aylen said. "For all we know, the Great Forest considers her a trespasser since it has existed long before either our peoples were born."

"You don't understand nomad ways, and you never will. We are the ones who live here in union with the Great Forest, nurturing and being nurtured, never staying too long in an area but moving on to give the Forest time to renew. You cannot say the same, and trespassers bring others who do nothing good to these lands, only death and darkness."

"What others? What death and darkness?" Gwyness asked.

"You know what I speak of. Fiends of the night, walking evil in our lands of light."

"They are not our doing," Gwyness said.

"You're human, are you not? Humans brought them—and elves."

Lady Aylen touched her maiden's shoulder to keep her from responding. "What do you want with the amulet?"

"Possession of your human's trinket will help my people achieve the balance that used to exist in this world."

"She is not my human, but how?" Lady Aylen asked.

"My offer does not include explaining the reasons why we wish to acquire it."

"We have another long march tomorrow morning, so we will bid you good night," Lady Aylen said.

"Have a peaceful sleep, but consider my offer carefully. It may be your only true guarantee for the success of your quest."

Traveler looked up from his stool at his map table, the parchment in his hands. Lady Aylen and Gwyness faced him. The dog watched them both from his corner in the caravan master's tent.

"What language is that?" Lady Aylen asked.

"Ironically, one that I can read, which is interesting."

"But what language, Mr. Traveler?"

"Goblin."

"Goblin?" Gwyness asked.

"You speak goblin?" Lady Aylen asked. "Elfish, goblin."

"Please, princess, keep that fact to yourself. The other elves in our caravan would not be as complimentary."

"Maybe because I've only been an elf for a short period of time."

"What does the note say, Mr. Traveler?" Gwyness asked.

Traveler stood from his table and walked to the torch hanging from the center of his tent. He put the parchment in the fire and watched it burn.

"Why did you do that, Mr. Traveler?" Lady Aylen asked.

"What it said I will keep to myself for now since it was addressed to me. What will you say to this nomad woman?"

"Say? There is nothing to say but no," Lady Aylen said. "What else would you expect her answer to be, Mr. Traveler?"

"Why does she even want my amulet?" Gwyness asked.

"To destroy it, of course."

"What?"

"Yes. She would probably travel to the Land of the Dwarves and have them melt it to nothingness forevermore."

"She's an agent of the Xenhelmians," the princess said.

Traveler shook his head. "She's exactly what she suggested, a hater of all those who live outside the Great Forest. Her nomadic people have likely existed long before even the Great Caravan. I know you both will say no to her offer, but she will simply give her spell to someone else to use, or her people will use it."

"Such a spell exists?" Gwyness asked.

"Maiden Gwyness, there are portal spells that could take us to other worlds. It is of magic that is beyond most humans or fae, but not such beings as the Old One we met."

"What do we do, then?" Gwyness asked.

"Nothing. We stay with our plan, march forward until we need to separate. As for the nomad woman, she knows you will never accept her offer. She and her party will likely not even be in the Great Caravan tomorrow morning."

CHAPTER FOURTEEN

The Nether-Caravan

The front of the Great Caravan rumbled forward at dawn. The daily routine of wake, march, eat, sleep no longer seemed tedious to most in Titan's Caravan. Almost two weeks had passed, and the Forest was as infinite as always in breadth and distance. The one significant change noticed by all was that the land sloped upward at a slight incline, and both the trees and the few fauna they saw were getting bigger.

"One day we'll come across a giant ant that can swallow our entire caravan whole," Grakdar remarked.

However, chatter continued for the most part to be nonexistent on the march.

Every night at the campfire, the caravan leadership gathered for their only true meal of the day as they relaxed.

"Any thoughts of your kingdom, sire?" Lady Aylen asked before taking a drink from her mug.

The king sat next to her. All of them had their own short stools, courtesy of Mr. Hobbs.

"Often, Lady Aylen. I miss Kings Eothelm the Blessed and Sigbard the Humble and my own people of my own kingdom of Helm Earldom. but our sacrifice here on our quest will be rewarded. I'm certain of it. And all the people of the Kings Elder will be equally rewarded."

"Strangely, I almost feel my own kingdom of Sirnegate was but a dream. I cannot understand it. My feelings are so strong for my kingdom, the region, its kindly people, but I cannot clearly see their faces. I'm ashamed that I do not miss it as much as I should. Gwyness and I were raised there happily."

"Do not think of it that way," the king said. "There are obvious reasons why you would feel so detached from your kingdom."

"The magic of being an elf must be strong if it can almost erase the memories of my growing up in Sirnegate. The flashes of my childhood in my birth city are more vivid."

"Do not be troubled, princess," Traveler said, seated on the other side of the king. "You are closer to your birth kingdom than your human kingdom. That is all."

"I hope so. Sirnegate and its people should also be rewarded well for our quest."

"King Aereth," Gwyness asked, "do you believe your kingdoms defeated the armies of Xenhelm?"

"I have no doubt at all, Maiden Gwyness, that they did. No doubt."

"What of your home, Mr. Traveler?" Lady Aylen asked. "We already know you are elfin royalty," she said jokingly.

Those gathered around the campfire laughed.

"Princess, I am but a human."

"But I agree with King Aereth. I don't see you as a common man, a noble, perhaps, likely a wayward son of a royal family."

Traveler smiled. "If that were true, princess, certainly someone in the caravan would have recognized me. We do have men from virtually all the major kingdoms of Avalonia."

"Who said you were from the empire of Avalonia, Mr. Traveler?"

"My people were very much like the nomads of Zingara."

"Really?" Lady Aylen asked.

"You were right about them, Mr. Traveler," Gwyness said. "Gone without any trace of them the next morning."

"Your people were nomads, Mr. Traveler?" Lady Aylen asked.

"My ancestors were. They came across a kingdom and lands they fell in love with, and they stayed. I'm a descendant of wanderers."

"What will you do with your Atlantean riches, Mr. Traveler?"

"Have enough riches to continue my travels."

"More fabled quests, Mr. Traveler?" the king asked. "That would be tempting fate even for you, would it not?"

"Travels to the known realms, sire, in comfort and without danger."

"Sounds wonderful, sir," Mr. Hobbs said, smiling.

"May I say, Mr. Traveler, that this is the first time in a while where the men have not been stressed at all?" Mr. Gresham the healer observed. "They're more relaxed than even when we were traveling under the protection of the Atlas turtles. If only..."

"Yes, Mr. Gresham, if only. But then, that is the way of Titan's Trail. Peacefulness is not a permanent state of things."

Titan's Caravan had grown so accustomed to the safety of the Great Caravan, but one day, they readied themselves for the daily march, and instead, their caravan master led them away, down another path. The men watched the masses of fae and animals of the Great Caravan continue on. After an hour or so, they could no longer hear the millions of feet and hooves. They were nearly ten thousand stronger, but after traveling so many weeks with the Great Caravan, they felt tiny, insignificant, and alone in the vastness of the Forest.

The Tree Shepherds fetched their crawling trees as they marched. One shielded the front, another the center, and a third the rear guard, as it was before. Pangolin had a heightened vigilance. The path they walked changed from thick giant green blades of grass to green grass similar to the Lands of Man to dirt with no green at all. The giant trees shrank in size as the day passed and their collective appearance also lost their green vibrance. The trees were dark, black, and looked hollow and dead.

None of the men liked the change of the land. The air also lost its warmth. For the first time in many, many months, they felt a cold in the air. Hobbs took it upon himself to have the pech help him retrieve cloaks from the pull-carts for all who desired them for warmth. The rules were not the same as they were in the Great Caravan, but no one spoke at all as they marched.

"I do not like this place," Gwyness whispered to Lady Aylen.

Some of the men heard the sounds even before Pangolin gave the hand signal to stop the caravan. Traveler, the royals, and Gwyness rode to the vanguard.

"Another caravan, I believe," Mr. Elman said.

"I still don't know how a half-elf can see better than an elf." Lady Aylen squinted. "They look shorter than a man but stockier."

"Dwarves, m'lady," Elman said.

"Dwarves? Mr. Traveler, I thought you said we would come across no dwarves on our quest."

"Yes, princess. That's exactly what I said."

The caravan master jumped down from his dog-horse and walked forward.

"You should wait here," Pangolin said to the royals.

"Not likely, Mr. Pangolin. If they are dwarves, we have no quarrel with them and they should have none with us. Besides, I've never seen a dwarf before," the princess said.

The caravan was indeed made of dwarves but not just dwarves. It was a party of several hundred in thick dwarven non-reflective armor and armed with metal war mallets or piked double axes. They marched with many dozens of giant lizard beasts known as lindworms, in appearance like a snake the size of a horse with two large clawed legs and thick brown leathery skin, their tails ending in an arrow-shaped tip. Every one of the beasts were led by a single dwarven warrior, and everyone had a chain lock draped around their necks.

Behind the dwarves was another party, but all were hooded and cloaked, their faces completely hidden.

The lead dwarves were three feet tall but wide and bulky in frame. They eyed the members of Titan's Caravan approaching as they waited patiently.

"Good day," King Aereth greeted.

The dwarves simply nodded. They were especially interested in Traveler.

"Your armor, human, appears elfin, but it hides the star elemental metal beneath it. Only star elves know how to forge such dual metals, and they do not share with anyone, even their sky elfin allies."

"The star elf that gave it to me said he would not have any further use for it," Traveler said with a smirk.

"Did he?"

"Why are you here, so far from their lands?" Traveler asked.

"Why are you, human?" another dwarf asked.

"We travel on a quest."

"So do we."

"Why would you travel to the Nether-Lands?" Traveler asked.

"That is no business of yours."

"Of course. I asked only out of curiosity. Do you wish for our caravan to stand fast till you pass, or do you wish to wait for us to pass?"

The dwarves scanned the other members of the vanguard. They looked at Pangolin's armor.

"Earth elemental steel," one dwarf commented.

"Yes."

"Mountain rock and stone combined."

"You can see all that with the eye?" Pangolin asked.

"We are dwarves, human. Any dwarf knows the properties of any mountain or metal by sight. We are a magical people."

"I am too. A berserker," Pangolin said.

"A human berserker. Yes. Only such a human could bear such armor and wield such a weapon."

The dwarves turned to Traveler.

"You are a larger party. We will march forth first. Our beasts rouse easy and we would not want them to attack your feeble animals."

"I'm glad we had the chance to meet some dwarves on our journey," Traveler said. "Unexpected, but welcome. I've had good experiences with all dwarves I encountered in the past."

The dwarves did not know what to say, so they said nothing. Slowly they turned away to join their caravan and yelled to move it forward. The leaders nodded as they passed—the dwarves and their serpentine beasts. Then came the ones draped in their hooded cloaks. They were the same height as the dwarves but nowhere near as bulky, and their forms were slightly hunched. Only the faces of a few could be seen for brief moments—humanoid, oldish, ugly, gruff.

The Nether-caravan marched past—nearly eight hundred.

"Strange," Grakdar said. "Have you ever seen a dwarven party so large, Master Traveler?"

"Never. Dwarves travel in small parties, no more than a few dozen."

"Yes. Only armies travel in such numbers when it comes to dwarves," Grakdar said.

"An army, Mr. Grakdar?" the king asked.

"They are no caravan," the giant's leader said. "But the lindworms? Master Traveler, what are your thoughts?"

"Lindworms are beasts of burden. The locks around their necks are pocket-realms. Mining, perhaps?"

"Dwarves love to dig things up from the ground and caves for sure," Grakdar said.

"And then there are the kobolds," Traveler said.

"What race are they, Mr. Traveler?" Lady Aylen asked.

"Shape-shifting sprites. The ones that passed live underground."

"Dwarves and kobolds are the same to us. They're both always digging, shoveling, and carrying off rocks and gems like squirrels do with tree buds and nuts. Dwarves at least are productive and forge the best armor for all giantkind. Their cousins are like Master Traveler's phookas. When not digging and shoveling, they're changing into snakes and cats and chickens."

"Mr. Grakdar, that is very unfair," Traveler said. "They can be very helpful to fae and humans."

"If you mean they, too, can find veins of gems and metals in the ground, yes, but you have to pay them handsomely and pray that they're not leading you into a trap to be buried alive in some cave."

"So our Antaean giants do not like kobolds. Let us move forward."

"No." The elaphine archers never spoke except amongst each other. Strag, their leader, did the speaking for the deerlike fae.

"What do you see?" Mr. Elman asked the archer.

"We see a trick of the tracks," the elaphine said.

"What do you mean?" Pangolin asked.

"The dwarven party march from east to west, but they came from ahead us first."

"Ahead of us?" Pangolin asked. "Why would they want us to believe they came from east to west then? What is ahead of us?"

"The path we travel ahead is covered with earthen caves."

"Maybe they were mining there and don't want us to know, as they plan to come back," King Aereth said.

"Sire, take the front back to your station. The vanguard and I will scout ahead," Traveler said.

Traveler and the dog led, Pangolin, Elman, the four giants, and the elaphine archers.

"I will never be at ease in these situations," the king said.

Traveler stopped and took his telescope from his clothes. Pangolin did the same. Mr. Elman focused his sight ahead and scanned the area too.

"Do you see anything, Mr. Elman?" Traveler asked.

"No, Mr. Traveler. It appears clear of any danger, but the caves. I do not know how deep they truly are."

The path ahead was sparse of giant trees and dipped with mounds of giant earthen caves around it.

"The caves could have been caused naturally. However, they could have also been created by giant gophers, snakes, ground nesting birds, or even giant ants," Traveler said.

"Yes, Mr. Traveler," Elman said. "I do see tracks that could be giant animals."

"Mr. Pangolin, we can either risk marching forward, or we can spend an extra day going around this area all together. I say, since we cannot be certain what may be in those caves or why our dwarven friends would wish to deceive us as to where they marched from, we move away from here."

"An extra day is fine with me, Mr. Traveler," Pangolin said.

"Agreed," everyone else said.

At that moment, Elman said he thought he saw a figure peek out from one of the caves.

They all quickly returned to the caravan and led it away.

CHAPTER FIFTEEN

Caravan of Nightmares

As the caravan traveled away from the valley of caves, the air grew colder. Every human, fae, and animal felt it beneath their feet—the soil had a strange quality as they marched.

"I don't trust this path," Pangolin said. "Get me a sturdy polearm!" he yelled to the men behind them.

The weapon was retrieved from one of the pull-carts' small-realms by the men and taken to the vanguard. Pangolin tapped the soil as they continued on.

"What is this soil?" one of the giant's asked.

"It moves," Grakdar said.

"Moves?" Pangolin turned to the giants. He looked at the elaphine archers, who nodded.

At the front, Traveler gave him the signal to continue forward.

"Our caravan master signals it's safe," the vanguard leader said with a sigh. "So we move on and hope we don't fall through."

Everyone in the caravan nervously marched across the path.

"Mr. Traveler, this isn't right," Lady Aylen said to Traveler again. "Why won't you tell us what this soil is?"

"Soon, princess."

"Soon? Why not now?"

"Soon."

"I am having a very sickening thought at the moment," Nirgund, the king's guardsman, said.

"Please, Mr. Nirgund, keep it to yourself."

They were in barren lands, but at no time was the greater forest not visible to them. The giant trees appeared like a dark wall in the distance. Its green grew more visible as they neared after hours of marching.

Traveler and his dog waited outside the flank of the caravan as it moved past. The royals and Gwyness joined him.

"Is it safe for our caravan master to wait alone outside the protective cover?" Lady Aylen asked.

Traveler looked and grinned. "You will protect us."

"I doubt your dog would ever allow such a thing."

The dog sneered at her. King Aereth and Gwyness laughed. Nirgund with his beasts and the female half-elves and their owl griffins also waited. Gwyness's eyes and mouth opened wide as the last elf of the rear guard stepped past them.

The entire patch of the ground they walked upon rose up on a seemingly infinite number of feet, each leg many times wider than the length of their own giant lizards. Every elf of the rear guard drew their swords, startled. Their falcons tried to fly away, and their axex beasts tried to bolt but were restrained by their masters. The immense blob–like creature slowly moved away.

"What is that? A ground animal? An insect of some kind?" Lady Aylen asked.

"They are called behemoths," Traveler said.

"Behemoths?" the elves asked.

As the creature moved away, they watched incredulously. Trees rebounded and straightened themselves back up. Before their eyes, they realized there was no barren area after the valley of caves. The creature's immense size had flattened the entire region. Everyone in the caravan froze, staring up at the sky. The creature was flying. It soon disappeared as the trees resumed their normal height, blocking the caravan's view.

Everyone looked at Traveler.

"They are harmless. They have no teeth," he said. "We already made one detour to avoid the caves. No need to add to our journey by going around the creature. Besides, it didn't mind us walking along its back. It probably enjoyed it."

Within the magic hut, in the small-realm with the book vault of the lost kingdom of Rivermouth, sat Lady Aylen and Gwyness. The maiden's face was stern and focused on her giant book opened up on her lap. Lady Aylen had a book open but was anything but focused.

"Are you still in a huff, m'lady?" Gwyness asked, scanning one of her huge books.

She did not answer.

"Why be vexed with Mr. Traveler? He was right not to tell us."

"That we were marching on an animal larger than even that roc we encountered in Faë-Land?"

"Is that what vexes you or that he did not tell you?"

"What does that mean?" Lady looked at her suspiciously. "What are you insinuating?"

"Nothing at all, m'lady."

"Good. What do you think of Mr. Pangolin's renewed armor?"

Gwyness said nothing.

"Two can play at these games, Gwyness."

"M'lady, we have much reading to do. We will not be able to accomplish anything with distractions."

"I didn't like what Mr. Traveler said earlier. Things will be getting bigger in the Forest. I would say they are quite large enough already."

"That I would agree with."

"The giants knew of this behemoth creature. They said it's in the fabled stories their parents read to them as children. What a thing to do, read scary stories to children. Even giant children are children."

Gwyness laughed. "Do you hear yourself?"

"I have elfin ears, Gwyness. I can hear better than you."

"As children, if the stories weren't scary, we didn't want to hear them."

"Perhaps. Why didn't Mr. Traveler tell us we were walking on the back of a many-legged giant beast that can fly? And what manner of creature crashes down on the giant trees, wiping them from view. What animal does that?"

Gwyness closed her book and stood.

"Where are you going?"

"I'm taking my book and going to the tent. Even the owl griffins chasing each other around me will be far more peaceful than this. M'lady, read your book."

"Perhaps I shall speak to myself while you're not here."

"Perhaps, but I will not be here to hear it."

"What insolence for your princess."

"Read your book, m'lady. Mr. Traveler said we need to be as well versed as possible before we reach the oceans."

"Oh, Mr. Traveler said it. Then we must do it."

Gwyness shook her head and walked out of the book vault. Her book in hand was almost heavier than she was.

"Was it wise to exclude the women?" King Aereth asked Traveler.

"They are not being excluded, sire, by any means. They have important work to complete, and that takes precedence over any casual nightly meeting. We can inform them of anything important along the march."

The group gathered by Hobbs included all the human and fae leadership in a special meeting tent for Traveler. Included were the four elfin leaders, the drow leader and sorceress, the Tree Shepherd

Greenwig, Pangolin, the Cut-throats' leaders, I'wulf and Hax the lionoid, and Bragg, the dwelf. Besides Hobbs, the other humans were Traveler, the king, Nirgund, Estus, and Gresham. All the day fae, including the giants, and all the men were already asleep for the night.

"But like any elf, she is especially strong willed and likely to take offense to not being included," Lyre, the high elf, said.

"By now," Traveler said, "you know the full story of Lady Aylen on the Trail, her transformation, her lost kingdom, and Maiden Gwyness too. They've been given a storehouse of ancient knowledge by no less than a celestial elfin queen, delivered by an ancient one."

"A spell-talker," Pangolin said.

"Yes. We cannot minimize the significance of such a thing. The women must be allowed to take full stock of the legacy left to them. I believe it will be crucial to the entire caravan when we arrive at Atlantea."

"If we arrive," Dr'amal said sarcastically.

"I will arrive," Traveler said, "and my dog too. Whether you wish to join us is up to you."

"Celestial elves are rarely to be trusted," Chief Ethor said.

"Agreed, but in this, I see no reason to distrust the gesture."

"You have fought these sky elves," Shadu-mun, the moon, elf said. "You know their treachery."

"It is the star elves I've fought, not celestials."

"Sky elves are all the same. Cloud, star, and celestial," Shadu-mun said angrily.

"Obviously that's not true, as our caravan has moon elves."

"We are not of the sky elves," Shadu-mun said.

"We are not gathered here for elfin history. Dr'as, from every night forward, your drows on night guard are to be prepared for battle with full armor and fortified sentry posts, even though we are within the protection of many circles. The same for you, Shadu-mun, and your moon elves. Life within the Forest around us will continue to get bigger, and so will the danger. Especially at night. We sit like a bowl of dessert for many of the Forest's night beasts."

The drow leader exchanged words with his men, and two left the tent. Shadu-mun spoke in elfish to his men, and one of his questing knights exited the tent.

"Will we speak about the dwarves, Master Traveler?" Chief Ethor asked.

"Why were they here, in the Great Forest, so far from their lands? And if what the elaphines said was correct, they intended to lead us into a trap. We have never heard of such behavior from even the lowest of dwarven kind."

"I have been on many caravans. Encountering one party on the Trail is a rarity. With the vastness of the Great Forest, each caravan master mapping his own trail, we never should have encountered so many. If I did not know of the Great Caravan, it would have passed us by, and none in our caravan would have known.

"I spoke to fellow caravan masters in the merchant market. I had one suspicion but they told me the truth of it all. Apparently, we have ourselves somewhat to blame. We destroyed the Kings' Caravan, but we did not destroy all the many parties waiting to join them."

Everyone in the tent exchanged looks, almost shocked.

"That's not possible, Master Traveler," Greenwig said. "Dryads would never do so."

"Neither would dwarves," Bragg said. "We may be separate races, but our codes are the same. Never."

"I'm sorry, but it's true. The parties thought we were the Kings' Caravan or part of them. They all attempt to travel on, not together but separately. All of these parties, including the dwarven one, tried to hire caravan masters within the merchant market. Instead, all they got were maps. Unfortunately, many also received knowledge of us from Xenhelmian agents within the market."

King Aereth noticed the fae leaders glancing at each other.

"Secrets persist even within Titan's Caravan," Traveler said, noticing too.

"Yes, Mr. Traveler, such as humans who speak goblin," Bragg said.

Traveler had an expression not of anger but deep thought. He focused on the dwelf.

"Yes, Mr. Bragg, I speak goblin and elfish and other fae languages. I am human, not fae. Your ancient blood feuds are not mine. I came to Faë-Land and let each individual, not race, show me if they were friend or foe. If not for a particular goblin I encountered, I likely would not have survived my first encounter with the star elves, once they revealed their true nature. The goblin was not doing it to help me. I know. He did it out of his intense hatred for elves."

"They taught you how to use your magic sword," Taylos, the desert elf, said.

"Yes, until I got good enough to continue my training with elves. If not for that, I'd be dead. No elf would train a human to fight elves by swords—good or bad. Elves only would train me after I knew how to fight with it."

"Master Traveler speaks the truth," Chief Ethor said.

"As long as we never talk of bringing any goblin parties into the caravan," Lyre, the high elf, said.

"It's not likely since goblins hate every other race within our caravan. They view humans with indifference."

"Then who taught you how to use your magic sword concerns me not at all," Lyre said. "Only that you can use it to defeat enemies to this caravan."

"Tonight, you learned more secrets about me. Will you share some with us humans?"

"When we arrive at the oceans," Chief Ethor said. The three elfin questing knights said nothing, deferring to him.

All the other fae were also quiet.

"Thank you for revealing that fact to the group, Mr. Bragg," Traveler said.

"Why did you share that knowledge?" Pangolin asked Bragg.

"I thought it something we should know."

"I should knock you back into Faë-Land."

A big grin appeared on the dwelf's face. "Mr. Glog might not like that."

"Both of you, then!"

"Mr. Pangolin, it is quite all right. In fact, Mr. Bragg's action was a welcome one that answered a question for me."

"What question?" Pangolin asked.

"Really, it's not important."

"The creatures, Mr. Traveler, that the dwarves had," Nirgund said.

"Lindworms, Mr. Nirgund."

"I thought they had wings."

"Winged ones are wyverns. They still exist in the aerial cities of sky elves."

"Two-legged dragons," Nirgund said.

"They're not that," Bragg said. "Just pack animals and poor guard beasts. Not very intelligent creatures."

"Mine sprites," the mole-like fae said suddenly. The gathering looked at him. "Dwarves and mine sprites only combine forces to find something underground that neither could find alone. What could it be?"

"You tell us," Traveler said. "What do you think the dwarves and kobolds were searching for?"

"We saw elves, goblins, and giants allied together in Fae'el," Greenwig said. "Allied with the Four Kings. You tell us now that noble sprite and fairy races are allied with them. Master Traveler, is it not wise to ask the simple question?"

"What question is that, Tree Shepherd?" Chief Ethor asked.

"Whether it is wiser to return to our lands rather than continue on to Atlantea?"

Hobbs said it as the gatherers left the tent. "We should all be glad Lady Aylen wasn't in this meeting. Turn back? After all this?"

Everyone had quickly rejected the Tree Shepherd's words, but it had not been lost on Greenwig alone that the reflexive objections were not with the forcefulness one would have expected. They all felt the same whether they wished to speak it or think it. Ominous clouds of danger lay ahead for them somewhere. Of most importance was that their caravan master had rejected the Tree Shepherd's words.

"Mr. Greenwig, we continue onward. Do not be deluded to think that if not for the Four Kings, our quest to Atlantea would be uneventful and safe. Here at least we know who our adversaries are."

"But it would seem that their allies are far beyond what any of us would have thought possible," the Tree Shepherd said.

"True, but we have allies too. We simply need to get to them."

"Who might they be?" Greenwig asked.

"We likely have many but the most important of them I already spoke of, the Atlanteans."

The Tree Shepherd nodded. All were reassured, and with that, Hobbs ended the meeting.

Traveler remained awake, studying his magical maps. The dog, lying at the entrance, perked up at the arrival of visitors.

"Mr. Traveler." It was Lyre, the high elf.

Traveler stood and gestured the four elfin leaders, Lyre, Taylos, Shadu-mun, and Chief Ethor into his tent. This time Lyre took the lead with his two fellow elfin questing knights.

"I suspected that I'd be visited by at least someone before I turned in for the night."

"We were thinking, Mr. Traveler, about this behemoth creature."

"Yes?"

"You said it was benevolent and not a predator, but as with all things in the magical lands, there is good and evil."

"An evil behemoth that devours entire caravans whole?"

"Yes. Is it so implausible?"

"Mr. Lyre, you are not the first to suggest that the mystery of the Great Forest was due to some giant, ancient beast. But I remember the words of your great elfin wizard, Druil. His far more powerful wizard father was lost along with an entire elfin caravan of tens of thousands, including wizards, knights, and noble animals. Even a behemoth of evil would move without great speed, and any attack would be slow and someone, something would escape. The mystery of the Great Forest is that no one survives, and there is no trace at all, nothing to be revealed with even the most powerful magic spells. It could not be a behemoth."

"Then what?" Taylos asked.

"We do not know," Traveler said. "Don't trouble yourselves with it. Your duty is to protect Titan's Caravan. My duty is to ensure our caravan gets out of the Great Forest, across the oceans, and steps into the fabled kingdom of Atlantea."

"Have you given this mystery considerable thought, Master Traveler?" Chief Ethor asked.

"I have, chief, as has every single caravan master who leads a ground caravan through the Forest. We have thought about it and discussed it. The seasoned caravan masters each map their own paths through the Forest, but we all stay within established safe regions across the Trail."

"The disappearances of caravans have been mapped?" Lyre asked.

"Yes."

"Of course. Such a thing would have to happen, or none would ever enter the Forest."

"I must be honest though. Traveling to our true destination to leave the Great Forest will mean crossing into one of those uncharted areas. It is narrow, and one can see from one end to the other, but it is still considered separate from the safe regions we caravan masters have established over the centuries."

"Are you the only human among this clan of caravan masters?" Chief Ethor asked.

"I am now. There were two others, but they have since died."

"Speaking of death, crossing into this region, no matter how narrow, puts us in jeopardy?" Lyre asked.

"Yes, but we are in jeopardy every step we take in the Forest. Know this. The moment I decided to change course, I began to make preparations to minimize our risk. Our transport will be waiting for us on the shore once we march out of the Forest. We will arrive, and no 'mystery of the Great Forest' will thwart us."

Traveler finally turned in for the night, but it was not his last visitor. The dog woke him, as it had done so many times in the past, by tapping its nose to its master's chest.

The caravan master sat up. The dog took a slightly humanoid form and opened the flap of the tent. All sixteen of the kilmoulis stood outside.

The moon elfin night sentries guarded the western half of the caravan's perimeter, the drows, the eastern. Brownies did their duties of tidying up the camp, ensuring all the men were tucked away in their giant–slippers, animals were rested, and all the campfires were fully ablaze to last the night. They sat around the campfires on their own vigil as they gossiped silently to human and fae ears in good spirits, as was their perpetual nature, but every one of the sprites were armed with weapons. If the night camps were attacked, they would come to the aid of the moon elves or drows before anyone else.

The barrier created by the circle magic that covered the entire camp prevented sounds from penetrating, but brownies could rest an ear on the barrier and hear most sounds. More than a few had heard groaning animals within the darkness of the Forest. The sound was unfamiliar to all of them and was the chief topic of their campfire conversation.

At the northern edge, both drow and moon elf sentries saw lights in the distance. Ghostly lights hung some five feet from the ground and floated to the perimeter, at first appearing as large fireflies. Moon elves had already drawn their moon swords. The drows had their two-blades in hand.

"A night where we wished Master Traveler's phookas were on night watch running about, and they're absent again," a moon elf said. "Find Shadu-mun."

One of the moon elves ran off as they all watched the lights draw nearer.

"Are those will-o'-the-wisps?" a drow asked aloud. "Ghostly lights seen by night travelers?"

"Are they not seen only near marshes and bogs?" another drow asked.

"The air is cold, and the land damp. There are so many explanations for what will-o'-wisps are, but those are legends of Faë-Land not the Great Forest."

The floating lights flickered then evaporated. In the distance, new lights appeared, but they weren't ghostly in any way. Between floating torches and their elfin or drow eyes, they could make out the silhouettes of a humanoid party with what appeared to be horses.

"Is it another caravan?" a moon elf asked.

"Traveling at night?" another asked.

"Follow me, Maiden Gwyness."

The young woman looked strikingly similar to Gwyness, only her attire was long, flowing, and white in color. Gwyness looked down to examine her own dress—short black garments, no armor, no weapons.

"Maiden Gwyness, we must go."

The woman moved quickly down the hallway. Gwyness looked around. The hallway was large, wide enough for a five-column army to pass through. The ceiling was high, possibly fifteen feet. Sunlight peered through the open window, giving the white stone surface of the castle's interior a warm glow. The woman held the train of her dress and began to descend the winding steps.

"We must hurry, Maiden Gwyness."

"Hurry to where? Hurry for what purpose?"

The young woman stopped her descent with a distressed expression. "You are needed, maiden. There are many victims of the spectral attack. We are blessed to have you amongst us, as you're the only one who can save them."

"Do you not have a healer in a castle such as this?"

"Our healer and wizard was the first one stricken by the spell."

"You intend for me to follow you down this staircase?"

"Yes, maiden."

"I know this is a dream. The reality of it is quite remarkable. Very powerful magic, but for what purpose? What do you want from me? You need not play games or appear in forms and shapes not your own."

"But this is not a dream, maiden."

"Tell me what your reason is for this ruse, or I will awaken myself. Listen."

"I can speak."

"Yes. I know I'm in a magical dream and I have full control of my body outside of its realm. All I need to do is call Lady Aylen, and she will do the rest to awaken me from your magic. I would use your time wisely."

The young woman's expression changed to a cold sneer. As she retraced her steps back toward Gwyness, her attire transformed to be an exact match.

"Why not show your true form?" Gwyness asked.

"Do you think you're powerful enough?"

Her twin had reached her. The whites of her eyes disappeared to be wet pools of blackness. Gwyness stared without fear even as the twin grew in height slightly. Gwyness smiled, and her dress began to turn to metal—covering her torso, legs, arms. A gauntlet covered her hands fully.

"Your dream is nice," Gwyness said. "We have equal power in it."

"Why do you believe it's my dream?"

"What do you want?"

"Go back."

"No."

"Is that final? Because we wait for you ahead."

Gwyness's eyes darted side to side. She could feel a coldness crushing her body outside in the real world.

"Oh, I lied. We already have you."

Gwyness screamed.

All went black as she felt herself forcibly pulled up and away. The blackness was replaced by a blinding white light she turned her head to the side, wincing in pain. The light penetrated even her eyelids.

"Stop yelling, Gwyness." It was Lady Aylen's voice.

The elfin princess rested her on the ground. Gwyness sat up straight in shock then jumped to her feet.

"Stay here," Lady Aylen said, grabbing her wrist to restrain her. "We're under attack!"

"What is that?" Gwyness stared in disbelief.

Within the night of the camp there was a ball of white light. The camp's own elfin archers fired volley after volley at what Gwyness could only describe as misshapen, grotesque, living shadows. Then the white exploded and disappeared, startling Gwyness. She lost her balance and dropped back to the ground.

King Aereth felt the cold mud on his bare feet. He gazed across a mirrorlike lake.

"Father, you've returned for me."

The startled king turned to see his dead son facing him in white sleeping clothes identical to his own.

"I'm dreaming again."

"No, father. You're here to help me after what you did to me."

"I did nothing."

"You sent me to my death."

"I did no such thing. I forbade you to confront the Four Kings. You disobeyed me."

"Father, you did not do all you could."

"I did everything I could, but you were a man not a child. I could not imprison my own son in Helm Earldom's dungeons as its sole occupant. A man, even a king's son, must be allowed to make a wrong decision."

"You let me die, father. But now you're here to help me."

"I don't wish to continue in this dream."

"It's not a dream, father. You can help my soul rest in peace at long last. All you must do is ask the question."

"I have no question I need answered by a dead son."

"You do, father. We must kill the Four Kings and avenge my death."

King Aereth felt a pain in his chest, and he clutched near his heart.

"They're dead."

"Dead but they walk. Tell me where the man Traveler is. I will give him all the power I have gathered from this dream realm and make him more powerful than all of them combined. He will be able to destroy them and be your avenger to erase the stain of my death that weighs so heavily on your heart."

"This dream is nothing but dark magic."

"Father, your heart grows weaker."

"Make up your mind, whatever you are. Is it to learn of Traveler's whereabouts or to bring about my death?"

"Help me, father. Tell me what I need to know. Ease your pain. All you have to do is whisper it in my ear."

Aereth's son suddenly stood inches from Aereth, and he turned his head and his ear closer.

"Whisper it, father. Make the pain go away."

Aereth felt his body shaking outside the dream.

"Tell me, father, or all will die within your caravan—man, woman, boy, beast. A whisper will save them all and make your pain go away forever."

None of them knew how many there were. Women with skin glowing as if illuminated by the light of the moon ran at the circle, bounced off, then ran at it again. From above, ghostlike humanoid forms flew at the skyward top of the camp's barrier. The magic repelled them, but they kept coming. Arrows from elfin arrows flew through the barrier, striking each woman, but with each strike, the arrow disappeared.

"What are these women?" a moon elf yelled.

"They must be witches," Shadu-mun answered, "with wraiths as their untouchable fighters."

"We have no effect on them!"

The brownies had gathered up in columns, waiting with their weapons. However, not everyone in the camp had woken.

"They're weakening the circle," a brownie said to the moon elf leader.

"Where is everyone?" Shadu-mun asked, surprised that he had not been joined by his elfin questing knight comrades.

"They remain in a magic sleep. We cannot wake them."

"How many?"

"All of the humans and day fae."

An explosion of noise swept through the camp. The groaning sounds from the Forest were louder and all around them.

"The circle is weakening," a brownie said.

Shadu-mun looked at the drows and brownies. "Mr. Traveler is afflicted too or he would be here. I am open to any suggestions."

"Will you surrender?"

The voice startled them all. A woman hung in the air directly above them outside the barrier. Light beamed from her skin. Her long gray dress had sleeves that covered her arms and hands, and her feet, too, were covered.

The groaning sounds came from shadowy humanoid beasts ambling to them on all fours. Their eyes were also illuminated as if by an inner light. The groaning beasts came to them from every side of the camp. Elfin arrows and drow two-blades merely passed through the creatures. Through it all, most of the men of the camp, and even their animals, were asleep, many wincing from the nightmare spell that gripped them.

Lady Aylen reached out her hand to Gwyness.

"Gwyness, we must fight them!"

The maiden was about to reach out, but her hand would not move.

"What's wrong, Gwyness?"

"My arm won't move! What is...?" An expression of shock came over her. "I'm still in the dream. You're not the princess."

"Of course, I am," Lady Aylen said.

"No. Something is wrong."

"We must join the attack. They are creatures of evil."

Gwyness's kirin appeared from behind the women out of nowhere. It charged Lady Aylen. Her war tridents appeared in her hands, but she had no time to throw one, as the beast gored her with his antlers.

Lady Aylen screamed. Her face contorted and became the same as the woman's from the dream before, only she remained dressed identically to Lady Aylen. The kirin tossed her body to the side. The amplified sound of breaking glass was so loud, Gwyness had to grab her ears, gritting her teeth. The dream had shattered.

Lady Aylen lay in her trussing bed with her own kirin next to her. The blue kirin touched the princess's chest with his unicorn horn. Lady Aylen's eyes instantly opened, and she forcibly inhaled. She sat up, and the women looked at each other. In the tent, all the female half-elves and the tiny owl griffins were asleep, but their faces were pained.

"Gwyness, outside."

They could hear the growing groans and commotion. Gwyness jumped onto her black kirin, and it galloped forward, moving on the air itself. The camp was under attack by women with glowing skin running at the circle and a single one floating above it all. But it was the growing number of wraiths flying down from the night sky at the barrier that frightened Gwyness.

"My weapons!"

"Gwyness!"

The maiden turned. From the back of her blue kirin, the princess had her two war tridents in one hand, Gwyness's war hammers in the other. She tossed them to the maiden.

"Everyone is sleeping!"

"Gwyness, it's up to us. The moon elves, drows, brownies, and us."

"It's not enough."

"Yes, it is." King Aereth rode out of his tent, too, on the back of his golden kirin. "It must be. How should we engage the battle?"

The kirins suddenly flew forward, not waiting. The black kirin air galloped at the wraiths gathering at the top of the camp.

"The circle is cracking!" they heard one of the brownies yell.

Gwyness swung at the first apparition she reached. The wraith screamed as if it were a flesh-and-blood being and disappeared. She continued to strike at them as if by instinct. Her black kirin mount galloped in mid-air where she needed to be.

Lady Aylen's war trident hit its mark. The floating dark nymph touched the trident's handle protruding from her chest.

"Your aim is true, though you've been an elf for such a short time," the nymph leader said.

"Withdraw, witch," Lady Aylen commanded.

"We are not witches. That is a human thing. We are lampads of the sacred Necropolis."

"Withdraw!"

"Two cannot defeat us."

Lady Aylen grabbed onto her flying blue kirin as it raced forward at the dark nymph. The beast spun its body and kicked the lampad with its hind legs. Lady Aylen barely had time to see the nymph sail into the sky toward the night's full moon before, even with her elfin eyes, the lampad was beyond sight.

King Aereth had no magic weapon, but his golden kirin struck at each lumbering groaning beast with its powerful forelegs, literally ripping their shadowy bodies apart. The lampads at the circle retreated into the night, as did the remaining groaning beasts.

"Quickly, we must ensure nothing has breached the circle!" Shadu-mun yelled to everyone.

"We will attend to all who are asleep," a brownie said. They sheathed their daggers and ran to check each man and beast in camp.

"We will check the east side," a drow said.

"We the west side," Shadu-mun said as he turned to his men.

"What can we do?" King Aereth asked the moon elf leader.

"M'lady," Gwyness said.

Lady Aylen raced on her blue kirin to Mr. Traveler's tent.

"The hope is that we have lost no one to this evil night attack, especially our caravan master," Shadumun said.

CHAPTER SIXTEEN

Back to Titan's Walk

The sun rose, but there was no joy within the camp. The scene of unconscious men and animals reminded them all too vividly of King Oughtred's teleportation spell attack upon the fledgling caravan so many months ago in the Lands of Man. The evil Xenhelmian king left their, then all-human, caravan by the side of the river to die. Some did perish as they fell into a raging river to be swept away.

King Aereth surveyed the area with Lady Aylen and Gwyness, all three of their kirins trotting behind them.

"We must rouse Mr. Traveler and his dog first," Lady Aylen said.

"No, Lady Aylen. We must assume that other adversaries will arrive to finish what the witches and their creatures started. The power of the moon elves is at their lowest point with the rising of the sun, and with our brownies being primarily night fae they too, will not be at their strongest. We must wake our magic-casters first, then all our fae warriors and berserkers."

"What of Mr. Traveler, sire? And the dog?" Lady Aylen asked.

"Unless we can wake Mr. Traveler before the dog, we should not risk it. Remember what happened that last time such a thing occurred? Besides we cannot get to him at the moment with whatever creature the dog has taken the form of. Who are our magic-casters?"

"Mr. Frog-Dor, and that mole man fae is supposedly a sorcerer too."

"Him?"

"Yes, sire."

"Our kirins saved us, Lady Aylen. Mr. Traveler did say they come from magic lands far from here, and because of that fact, their magic is unique to this region. Though no less powerful, they can do what other magic-casters cannot. We must communicate with them somehow and have them free both men from their nightmare slumber too."

"Yes, sire. The—"

King Aereth's kirin and Lady Aylen's ran from them. The beasts went in different directions.

"They are running to Frog-Dor and that fae," Lady Aylen said.

"These beasts are utterly amazing in their intelligence and powers," the king said.

Frog-Dor had been reduced to a whimpering mass in his nightmare. Green bullfrogs were trying to eat him alive. He felt them gnawing at his flesh. The golden kirin appeared, standing on the water, beside his submerged body in the center of a black lake. The beast stomped its front forelegs on the water, and a blast of lightning set the frogs ablaze and the black water to a boil. The kirin grabbed Frog-Dor in its mouth and flew with the man into the sky.

A sweating Frog-Dor slowly opened his eyes.

"We have you now, Mr. Frog-Dor," King Aereth said. Gwyness helped the king use their own cloaks to wipe the sweat from the man's face. "You're free of it," the king said.

The blue kirin rescued the mole-like fae from his dream. The animal man's chief sorcerer was in a perpetual falling dream, mile after mile, when the blue kirin emerged from a cloud and grabbed the fae with its mouth. The kirin used its unicorn horn to pierce the reality of the dream. The mole man fae found himself back on his giant cocoon-like bed.

"You're safe," Lady Aylen said to him.

The mole-man rose to his feet and shook his head many times. He straightened himself and nodded. She and the blue kirin led him directly to Frog-Dor's tent.

"Very good," King Aereth said. "Men, our first task is to free all the caravan's magic-casters."

Frog-Dor rose to his feet. "Yes, sire. Your magic beasts can enter these nightmare spells without harm. Have them free Dr'amal, the drowess, and Zefea, the fauness, next. Where are the Tree Shepherds and fae-bloods?"

"We're not sure," Lady Aylen replied. "We cannot enter their realms, nor the väki's."

"We must, m'lady," Frog Dor said. "We need them all, including yourself and Maiden Gwyness. I believe our time is short."

"What do you suspect, Mr. Frog-Dor?" King Aereth asked.

"We must find these dark nymphs before nightfall. If we do not, they will likely place us all back into their nightmare spells, and we will never wake up. Your magic steeds will be all alone against untold numbers of these women and their evil beasts."

Little Root was the youngest of the caravan's four Tree Shepherds. Most times, the men never saw him. His task was to mind their realm containing their soul tree—a magic tree of immense power—and to occupy the hyper-active fairy sisters. The opening to their realm opened, and the younger Tree Shepherd stepped out. His face was drawn, and his white skin was pale and sickly rather than vibrant.

"Our soul tree," he said to Lady Aylen and Dr'amal, who had been trying to open the realm's magic door by repeatedly knocking.

"Mr. Little Root, what happened? Where are your comrades?" the princess asked.

"Is your soul tree dead?" Dr'amal asked.

Little Root stared down at the ground. He was younger than the other Tree Shepherds but always appeared taller. Lady Aylen noticed his hoofed feet, reminding her that leshies were closer in species to fauns and centaurs than elves and humans.

"The soul tree was drained of all magic. My fellow Tree Shepherds used their own life force to sustain it as long as they could. They lie unconscious within the realm."

"Mr. Little Root, what does this mean?" Lady Aylen asked.

"Our crawling trees will be without magic and thus are no longer alive. We Tree Shepherds will waste away, as we're unable to connect with the magic of the Great Forest. It does not talk to us. Any circle we create for the caravan will not be able to withstand even the weakest of magical attacks."

"These lampads knew what they were doing," Dr'amal said. "They seized me unaware because I slept. How did they do this to you?"

"Our soul trees sleep too," Little Root said, "as do we. We dream, as do you. The soul tree lives for its dreams. It had no defense against their dark dream magic. It did as it was told. It surrendered its magic power. We were helpless to stop them."

"What do we do, Mr. Little Root?" Lady Aylen asked.

"Master Traveler is our only hope. He may know what to do as he knows much of our kind in our own lands and beyond and the Great Forest itself."

"Yes, we must wake him, but you must rest. You look like you will collapse even now," Lady Aylen said.

The Tree Shepherd nodded. "I will return inside and wait for you to release Master Traveler from the spell."

Little Root slowly moved back inside, and the door closed.

"How can this spell continue even in daylight?" Dr'amal asked loudly.

"If the kirins can wake you, they can wake him. But the men, can you wake them?"

"Zefea and I will see to it. If Mr. Frog-Dor is correct, we may be in full battle by nightfall," Dr'amal said.

Traveler opened his eyes. At first, he couldn't move. The blue kirin looked down at him, standing beside his sleeping form. The caravan master was covered in his thick fur blanket. Something jumped on his chest. The dog was a third of its usual size and had a sleepy face, its eyes bloodshot. Gwyness's large black kirin also stood near them.

"Good of you to return to the land of the living, Mr. Traveler," Lady Aylen said. She knelt down beside him. "Should I ask what dream they had you trapped in?"

Traveler's gaze darted around for a moment. "My horrors are many with all the many caravans I have been a member to and all the men I have seen killed or who died. They had much to work with in creating their magic nightmares for me."

"We awoke the magic–casters first, Mr. Traveler," the king said. "We cannot find the fae-bloods, your darklings, or those kilmoulis sprites, for that matter, or get into the realm of the väki. The Tree Shepherds are in a bad state. Their soul tree is drained of all magic. Mr. Little Root holds out hope you know how that to restore the tree and them. Dr'amal and Zefea are using magic and potions to wake the men and animals from their spells."

"With limited success," Lady Aylen said.

"More importantly, Mr. Frog-Dor believes these...lampads? He believes they will return at nightfall."

"They will. They planned for this attack, sire. A spell for everyone, but they did not know of our kirins."

"What are these lampads, Mr. Traveler?" Gwyness asked. "They had ghostly creatures with them, attacking the circle, and these horrible, moaning shadow creatures. Giant, moving on all fours."

"We must find them before nightfall."

"Mr. Frog-Dor said the same," King Aereth said.

Traveler sat up quickly but then held his head as his eyes closed.

"Mr. Traveler, if you're planning on doing something, you might want to reconsider and rest more."

"Princess, unfortunately, we do not have that luxury. Maiden Gwyness, the ghost creatures, wraiths, did you and the princess fight them?"

"Yes, my weapons were able to pierce their ghostly forms and make them evaporate."

"Die, maiden. You killed them. Good. Princess, your war tridents?"

"I was not able to strike at any. My focus was on the lampads. What are they?"

"Evil nymphs from the Nether-Lands. They can summon and command creatures of the night, have the power dreams. They can drive men to madness with light."

"Light?" Lady Aylen repeated incredulously.

"Yes."

"Before they attacked, Mr. Shadu-mun said there were will-o'-wisps," King Aereth said. "I doubt they were the same as what we call will-o'-wisps in the Lands of Man."

"Sire, the will-o'-wisps were likely lampads in the form of lights scouting ahead, confirming who was awake and who was asleep. Why did I not realize it before?"

"Realize what, Mr. Traveler?"

"These lampads are also part of the Kings' Caravan. I know what he was doing. Oughtred. All these races, including humans, elves, dark fairies, the lampads, dryads, dwarves, the war wizards, goblins, all the weapons from across Faë-Land, the second Xenhelmian city in Faë-Land, the magic beasts, the creatures—he did what we did, but long before. We created a caravan of light. He created one of evil. We are his opposite number. I know the true reason why the celestial elfess helped us, helped Lady Aylen and Maiden Gwyness. I believe Oughtred means to march right into Atlantea and have them close their doors to all humans and fae forever."

The tent was in complete silence. Dr'as, the drow leader, and his daughter had entered, as did Frog-Dor. Others were gathering.

Traveler looked at the drows. "You do know that the night drows are also allies to the Four Kings."

The expressions on the drows' faces were of shock and rage.

"Then, Mr. Traveler, nothing on Pan-Earth must prevent us from getting to Atlantea's gates," Dr'as said. "I am not just a leader of the D'Shar. I am the king of the drow kingdom of Nightfire. We are sworn to secure the Atlantean alliance no matter the cost. Drows, not night drows, must speak for drow-kind."

"What is this D'Shar, Mr. Dr'as?" the king asked.

"Despite what the elves may say, our clan has the ancient knowledge and experience fighting practitioners of dark magic, which has also included, from time to time, demons. The night drows are their allies!"

Our four elfin leaders stood in the tent listening. Pangolin and the Cut-throat leaders also entered.

"Then, King Dr'as, you should have your men dress as Nightfire drow citizens and carry the weapons of D'Shar warriors. Since you have revealed your true nobility, I am certain the elves will follow, then all the other fae. Mr. Frog-Dor?"

"Yes, Mr. Traveler."

"When I'm able to stand—"

Hobbs entered the tent with a large mug in his hand. He handed it to the caravan master. "The strongest tonic we could mix, sir. After you drink it, you will be able to take on an army of elves, drows, giants, and groaning beasts by yourself."

Traveler laughed.

"Giants? I heard someone talking about us. What are you saying?" Grakdar bellowed from outside the tent.

Traveler stood. "Mr. Frog-Dor, I will leave the camp with the Tree Shepherds."

"Mr. Traveler, we spoke of this," the king said.

"We have no choice, sire. Mr. Frog-Dor will assemble his team to find the lampads and kill them. Do you understand? If you don't, they will return and kill us all with their nightmares. The kirins will not be able to save us."

"Yes, Mr. Traveler, I understand."

"I will lead the Tree Shepherds to a place to restore their soul tree. Mr. Hobbs, get the men ready to march."

"March, sir?"

"We cannot stay here through the night. Too many know we're here."

"Whether Mr. Frog-Dor and his team are successful, or the Tree Shepherds and I, Mr. Pangolin must march the men from here to safety, back to Titan's Walk. Again, we have no choice, and we're only days away from the oceans."

"So close, Mr. Traveler?" Lady Aylen asked.

"Mr. Hobbs, Mr. Frog-Dor, you have your work to do. I have mine. Sire, take charge with the princess while I'm gone."

"Mr. Traveler," Pangolin said. "We would all cheer, if you weren't also saying we'll possibly be dead tonight or in the next few days."

"You can still cheer, Mr. Pangolin. But there is much work to do, and you all look half-asleep."

"Before we begin, may I ask you about the person in your dream, Maiden Gwyness?" Frog-Dor asked.

Frog-Dor and Gresham had moved through the camp, listening to the men's accounts of their dreams. The caravan's healer recorded everything they said in his book. They gathered in the women's tent.

"I had control of the dream. Their mistake. I fashioned a hand mirror to capture the true form of the one who spoke to me. I can explain her."

"No need," Frog-Dor said as he touched her forehead. A shard of glass appeared in his hand.

Traveler slowly walked on the moving green surfaces without boots. A dog-like monkey sat on his shoulder, holding his neck with its arms and tail. The four Tree Shepherds walked behind with Mossberry leading them. In Little Root's hands, he carried a shriveled tiny white tree.

Before them, pushing through the green surface, were several trees, staring at them with stern humanoid faces. Traveler was able to peer downward. They were walking on the tops of a sea of trees. The ground lay hundreds of feet below. Traveler returned his attention to the tree lords and stopped at the first one. He said nothing. He waited until each tree could examine him thoroughly and then the Tree Shepherds.

"Why do you disturb us again?" the first tree lord said, a voice echoing around them.

Little Root joined Traveler and simply lifted their soul tree in his arms.

"Why should we grant this?"

Traveler turned to Greenwig. The Tree Shepherd joined them. His head only grew in size until it matched the tree lord's.

"I am Chief King Greenwig of the Tree Shepherds of the Green Druid Forests in the young lands of Faë-Land. We are a good people—leshy, tree people, sprites, and nymphs living in harmony with flora and fauna. Our ancestors were born in the Great Forest. Our power was born here. We have never forgotten, though we live apart. We have already tried to speak to you, our ancestors, but you have never heard us. We thought you were angry with us."

"We were angry with you younger ones for a few eons, but we have gotten over it. We will grant your wish. You young ones should begin to take on more responsibilities of the natural world, as there will be a time when we are gone, and you will be the old ones."

"Yes, that is true. The cycle of life."

"The cycle of life."

"Your magic was quite powerful," Frog-Dor said to the darkness.

An image of the dark nymph leader appeared.

"I am able to see you, though you are not here in the cave with us," she said. "What is this magic called? The ability to project your likeness across distances."

"Mirror of the mind."

"You are like a ghost in form but not. Solid but not. I must learn this magic."

"You know much magic."

"Your three beasts from far away magic lands were unfamiliar to us and are immune to our dream magic. No matter."

"What name should I call you?"

"Call me Hecata, man of frogs."

"What is your power of dreams called? I am sure you were chosen by the Four Kings because your power is far above others of your kind."

"Lampads are the nymphs of the nether world. We haunt the night. We can drive men and beast to madness like our siren sisters."

"But you are more."

"Some can catch dreams."

"But you can kill with them."

"We are nightmare mongers who can pull the fears from your essence trap you in a nightmare and kill you, should we wish."

"Why do you do this? Why do you do this for the Xenhelmian humans?"

"The Four Kings are much more. They offer what we cannot refuse."

"To betray nymph-kind."

"Nymph-kind betrayed us long before humans set foot in the magic lands. You have escaped our grasp, this time, but we will return at night with forces far more vast. No dreams or nightmares. Death is all there will be for you all."

"Yes, I told them that."

"Is that why you're here, visiting like a ghost?"

"I came to reason with you. Do not return tonight."

"When a circle has a crack, no matter how small, breeching it is but a simple thing for anyone gifted in magic."

"I am sorry."

"Sorry for what, man of frogs, being punished for deeds unforgivable?"

"You left me no choice."

Hundreds of lampads and many more of their groaning beasts waited at the bottom of a giant underground cavern in the valley of caves Titan's Caravan had bypassed. Dark clouds of wraiths far larger than those below hung above them all. Hecata sat in a floating magic throne in the center of her nymphs.

"You think you are powerful, man of frogs, but you're a distant wisp of a shadow of your former self."

"True, Hecata. That's why I brought others."

The images of Lady Aylen and Gwyness appeared. Then the mole-like fae and Dr'amal.

The lampads laughed.

"What are you going to do here? Your images can observe and communicate and nothing more," Hecata said. "If you were here in the flesh, you would have been killed on sight by our beasts."

Gwyness watched the lampad leader. Even as she stared, the dark nymph's face magically changed. It was the same one who had been in her dreams, as Frog-Dor had said. Gwyness marched up to her.

"Do not try to change your face! I know you were the one in my nightmare."

Hecata's eyes lit up like torches. "You will fail."

"Fail at what? Why was it important to be in my dream?"

"Neither of you recognize me."

"Recognize you?"

"You should. I was the mid-wife to your mothers."

"Gwyness, she lies! Do not listen to her!" Lady Aylen screamed.

"Why do you suppose the great kingdom of Rivermouth would have Nether-Land nymphs within their walls?"

"Why do you live and they do not?" Gwyness moved closer to the lampad.

"Because others made me an offer I couldn't refuse."

"Rivermouth will be reborn."

"It will have to be reborn without you."

"It will be reborn, but you won't be here to see it."

The images of the caravan's committee of magic disappeared except for Frog-Dor.

"It is done," he said. "The power of the lampads is of the night. Therefore, we must bring in the power of daylight."

The few cracks and holes to the surface began to glow with intense light. The cloud of wraiths stirred like a cyclone, but they had nowhere to go. The roof of the giant underground cave shattered. The cloud of wraiths was obliterated in a flash. The groaning beasts, exposed to the giant fire balls crashing down on them, also vanished. Screams rose from the lampad army. Hecata attempted to fly away, but Frog-Dor held her tight.

"Let go! You're only an image!"

"I am magic."

The fireball crashed and vaporized everything in its blast.

A weakened Frog-Dor opened his eyes. Lady Aylen and Gresham helped him up.

"It's done," the sorcerer said. "The dark nymphs will trouble us no more."

"What did you do?" Lady Aylen asked.

"Something terrible," Frog-Dor said. "But they had no less planned for us tonight."

Traveler and the Tree Shepherds returned well before nightfall, and the caravan immediately marched on. Before the sky darkened, the vanguard noticed giant footprints. They had returned to Titan's Walk. However, the footprints were not of the legendary ancient Titan.

CHAPTER SEVENTEEN

Troll Forest

Several brownies joined the vanguard as the caravan marched into the night. But it was not for long as into a new pocket-realm they marched. The magic realm was unlike any they had ever seen, with a forest of orange-and-yellow giant trees and bluish long grass surrounded by rolling hills and billowy clouds that hung no more than fifty feet above them.

The men were given extra time before turning in for the night. The chance to simply sit and converse was welcome after so many days. At the realm's entrance, the moon elves were taking no chances. In full battle armor, with swords that glowed with great moon magic, the elves watched through the threshold into the night of the Great Forest for any signs of life. Even their falcons and axexs were on guard in battle armor. No disturbances occurred, and the camp had a much appreciated night of sleep free of nightmares, normal or magical.

Hobbs felt it immediately as he made his predawn rounds. Most of the men were already up and dressed to march. Word had spread. The leg of the journey through the Great Forest was almost at an end. The steward could not believe that nearly six months could pass so quickly. His memories of Caravan Row, where he became the caravan's first hire under Traveler, seemed like a distant memory. He, too, was excited. Undoubtedly there would continue to be dangers traveling along the oceans of these magic lands, but they would be onto the gates of Atlantea at least.

The caravan had only just begun its march from their pocket-realm when Mr. Bragg, the dwelf, neared the caravan master with his metal golem, Mr. Glogg.

"Mr. Traveler, may I have a word and a question answered?" he asked, reaching the front of the column.

The caravan master glanced back. His dog, at his side, turned to growl at the dwelf.

"Yes, that is much better. Growl at him rather than me," Lady Aylen said with a grin. The royals and

Gwyness marched on Traveler's other side, their guardsmen and kirins following.

"Yes, Mr. Bragg."

"It would seem I am not held in very high regard any more from your human men and Mr. Pangolin and the Cut-throats only glare at me."

"Why do you think that is, Mr. Bragg?" Lady Aylen asked.

"Even your elfin princess holds me in low regard," the dwelf said with a smile.

"I never held you in high regard, Mr. Bragg," she said.

"Your main problem, Mr. Bragg, is that a caravan is a family. It is not a hunting party. Yes, the bond you have with your fellow elfin hunters and your beasts has been earned over many years of hunting as one in close quarters, depending on each other to stay alive. Here, in a caravan surrounded by continuous danger, members of a caravan must be given that same respect and regard without hesitation, even if none ever has to lift a finger to save your life. Because here, on Titan's Trail, it is known that all will lift that finger, draw their weapon, and possibly even die, at any moment to save your life."

"I do understand, Mr. Traveler. I should not have revealed your exceptional language abilities in regards to goblins so publicly. If I had a concern, I should have brought it to you privately."

"Selfishness and recklessness are not noble traits," Lady Aylen interjected.

"Yes, you should have, Mr. Bragg, but we are past all that, and I have already forgotten it. What is your question?"

"I had to ask now that our own sorcerers have destroyed these evil magic nymphs. They hid in the very underground caves that the dwarven caravan surreptitiously tried to lead us through. We know as fact, no longer a suspicion, that they were sending us into a trap. The lampads may not have been there at the time, but we can assume such. You are better traveled than any in the caravan, fae or human. Have you ever seen any dwarf behave with such treachery, such malevolent intent?"

"It is clearly not in the nature of the average dwarf, but we both know there are always exceptions."

"Were they coming from Atlantea or are they still traveling there?"

"That is the question, Mr. Bragg. That is the question of all the caravans we have encountered. We shall know more, though, as we get closer to the fabled kingdom. We will know clearly what awaits in the waters outside the city, outside its walls, and every step to its gates on the ground and in the sky."

"If we reach Atlantea's walls, Mr. Traveler, no one could prevent us from entering. Isn't that so?" King Aereth asked. "Even agents of the Four Kings."

"Yes, sire. That is true, or that has always been true, but we're not to let our guard down for even an instant until we cross into the fabled city. I would not let our guard down, even then. We've had too much subterfuge and schemes surround our simple quest."

"Simple, Mr. Traveler?" Lady Aylen asked.

The humanoid's face was not visible, hidden by the hood of his cloak. His hands were large with black nails, grayish skin. He stood in the clearing looking around then lifting his head and holding for a moment.

"He's sniffing the air for a scent," Pangolin said.

Traveler had joined the caravan, and the men stared through their telescopes to spy on the humanoid many miles in the distance to their rear. King Aereth and Lady Aylen had also joined the viewing line. Mr. Elman did not need a telescope. At the caravan's rear guard, the elves and animal men had a similar viewing line.

"What race is he?" Grakdar asked, barely able to hold the telescope in his hand it was so small for him.

"There are goblins with gray skin and races similar to them."

"Goblins again. I thought we were rid of them," the giants' leader said.

"Should this concern us?" Pangolin asked Traveler in almost a whisper.

The caravan master hesitated as he studied the distant stranger. "He is dressed as a nomad native to the Forest, same markings, but none would be so far away from their common paths and alone. And none are of the race he appears."

"Goblin?"

"Gray goblin or goblinoid."

"What do we make of this?"

"I don't know. Only that I don't like it. It's as if we travel a path that everyone knows we're using."

"If you feel that, should we not heed your instincts? You are the only one among us who knows the Trail."

"And do what? Mr. Greenwig may have said it but turning back is out of the question."

"The reason you had the caravan leave the Atlas turtles was because you feared we were walking into a trap," Pangolin reminded Traveler.

"Oh, I'm certain there's a trap waiting for us at Titan's Fall. I spoke to other caravan masters at the merchant realm. Many other caravans, or armies, have traveled ahead of us."

"But it seems we have pursuers following in our steps, which may mean others wait ahead."

"We're too close to seek another path. It's also where our sea transport awaits. We cannot go elsewhere. Soon we'll be smelling the ocean ourselves and feel its mist in the air. Titan's Caravan can be an army if it needs to be. We need this tracker—if that's what it is—to go elsewhere."

Traveler looked at the elaphine hunters. "Shoot your special arrows to send our friend in a direction far from us."

The deerlike fae nodded. Two of them pulled arrows coated with a thin fur similar to a woolly caterpillar. They fired the arrows high in air, and the arrows seemed to fly on their own.

"He moves," Pangolin said, his eye fixed looking through his telescope.

"Mr. Pangolin, let's quicken our pace a bit."

"This region of the Forest is different again, Mr. Traveler," Lady Aylen said.

"Yes, princess. It is called the Troll Forest."

"Trolls? Again?"

"We should be through it before nightfall. Trolls even here in the Great Forest only come out to hunt at night. Though there is a peculiarity about the Troll Forest. It offers one of the few dangers to any flying caravan high above, which is why they avoid it."

They came across one, another, and many more giant footprints. All were already overgrown with grass, flowers, and brush, but the indentations of the giant trolls were apparent even to the untrained eyes of humans.

"This one was at least fifty feet," Pangolin said as they led the caravan forward.

The march moved quickly through the giant trees, but even a day out, in the distance, they could see a region of trees so tall that they reached into the sky through the clouds and disappeared into the heavens. At the same time, the land was sloping downward.

They progressed from the giant trees they had passed for most of their trek to what they had thought were trees but were a forest of...

"Beanstalks!" young Quillen yelled out, pointing.

The boy had not been himself for a while. His wide-eyed bewilderment of the Forest, as with most of the magic lands, had been replaced with a formidable fear of it. He had been put on edge from the giant insects, but it was the attack of a flying spider that did the most damage to his nerves. The boy had fallen and hit his head on rocks trying to escape from it. He still wore the bandages that Gresham, the healer, had wrapped his head in. However, he stood there smiling.

"Is there not some story of giants coming down giant beanstalks from magic lands to human lands to steal people, or was it chickens?" Lady Aylen asked Gwyness.

"Lies!"

The four giants, all marched directly to face the princess. For a moment she was aghast.

"The story is fiction," one giant said. "Made up by no-good humans."

"Giants don't live in the sky," another said.

"And they don't travel by beanstalks," said another.

"And they definitely don't steal animals, let alone chickens or geese or anything from humans," Grakdar said loudly. He pointed to the top of the beanstalks in the sky. "Trolls! Not giants."

"Well, thank you, Mr. Grakdar. Giants. Thank you for correcting my error," Lady Aylen said.

The giants made huffing sounds, turned, and strode back to the vanguard.

Lady Aylen and Gwyness looked at each, stifling laughs.

"Never confuse giants with giant trolls," a smiling King Aereth said.

"Yes, indeed, sire," Nirgund, his guardsman, said. "Or you will surely get a mallet to the skull."

Titan's Caravan stopped at the base of the giant beanstalks to allow men and beast a chance to look up as far as they could see into the sky and clouds.

"We're safe here, aren't we, Mr. Traveler?" the elves asked. The four leaders joined the vanguard along with other fae leaders.

"Yes. Trolls stay out of the daylight, but up there is its own realm, an endless plateau where they can sit and observe all below and decide on their hunt for the night. It is always night in that realm."

"They observe us?" Pangolin asked.

"Yes."

"Can we really make it through this Troll Forest before nightfall, Mr. Traveler?" King Aereth asked, looking ahead.

"With a steady pace, we can, sire."

"What about at night, Mr. Traveler? Will not the trolls seek us out?" Pangolin asked.

"They will, of course, so we must make sure our realm's opening is where they can never find it."

Traveler sat at the entrance with a low campfire behind him, the dog lying on its belly next to him.

"I will join you, sir." Hobbs had his pipe in his hand. "Am I able to smoke?"

"You have nothing to fear, Mr. Hobbs."

Hobbs sat nearby. He glanced back for a moment. Moon elves camped on one side, drows on the other farther back in their pocket-realm. The camp was quiet, with men and animals fast asleep. In addition to their usual night duties, the brownies spent the night magically sewing the older pocket-realms that had been destroyed or damaged. To the eye, it looked like they were sewing sacks made of simple fabric. Everything else was normal. Traveler had told the night watch there was no need for additional security or battle gear. Though they were in the heart of the Troll Forest, it would be a quiet night.

Hobbs held his breath. He saw glowing eyes descend down a beanstalk. They had all seen trolls before. They were grotesque humanoids, but small trees and other foliage grew out of every part of this one's body. Its face was long. A long, fat nose hung just above its mouth, and a thick beard of foliage ran down its belly. The forest troll landed, and its head was just below the bottom edge of the realm's entrance. The top of the troll's head disappeared.

"Are trolls intelligent or not too much, sir? I know what our stories say but not what the truth is."

"Not too intelligent, which is why they are often mesmerized by others who use them for their own purposes."

"Are they evil, sir? I ask because you've already shown me that there's a much more nuanced view to be had of goblins."

"They're predators, and the extent of their evil considerations is to grab their next meal. It's no different than a wild wolf, bear, or cougar. They just can talk too."

"We are close aren't we, sir? I heard the women speaking earlier. Lady Aylen said she can smell a massive body of water in the distance."

"We are close, Mr. Hobbs."

The steward smiled.

"We've come a long way since that first night in Hopeshire, Mr. Hobbs."

"We have indeed, sir."

"There's another one."

Outside the realm's entrance they saw another shadowy humanoid with glowing eyes sliding down a giant beanstalk. The creature moved in a different direction.

"Should I say anything to the men, sir? The gossip is feverish."

"Let them gossip. No need to say anything. We may be close, but we can never let our guard down."

"Yes, sir."

"Tomorrow, we'll be out of the Troll Forest and on the final leg of our march to the shores to meet our icarian ship seller."

"I forgot to tell you, sir."

"What, Mr. Hobbs?"

"I can't swim."

Traveler chuckled. "I think I can overlook the one imperfection, Mr. Hobbs."

The caravan was unable to leave before dawn. Outside the realm, trolls still prowled. The creatures did not scurry up the giant beanstalks until the sunlight fully bathed the land. The caravan marched out of their magic realm in formation.

Hobbs had the men formed up. Pangolin and the vanguard surveyed the path ahead. The rear guard peered through their own magic telescopes to look for any trace of life approaching.

Traveler noticed those at the front slightly recoil. He turned. The group of kilmoulis stood nearby, waiting quietly.

"You sense them again?"

The sprites with the giant noses taking up most of their faces nodded. "Yes, Master Traveler."

"How?" the caravan master asked himself. He grabbed his telescope. "Mr. Elman!"

At the rearguard, Traveler and the half-elf joined the elves, Cut-throats, and animal men.

"How did we not see them before?" Lyre, the high elf, asked angrily. "They weren't there before."

"Look," one of the elves said.

All saw the approaching caravan led by a bearer holding a white flag. They could not see who or what race the members of the caravan were. Voices called out in their direction.

"What are they saying?" Traveler asked.

"They're calling us," Hax, the lionoid fae berserker, replied.

"Calling us?"

"Titan's Caravan. They call us by name. Titan's Caravan, please stop."

"They called your name too," Taylos the desert elf said. "They know your name."

"Can they see us?" I'wulf asked, panicking.

"No," Dr'amal, the drowess, said. "Impossible."

"The crawling trees place an obscuring sight spell around us," Mossberry said.

Traveler looked at their vanguard leader. "Mr. Pangolin—"

"What if they're in trouble?" one of the mouse men asked.

"They fly a white flag," a rabbit man said.

"Are you suggesting we stop?" King Aereth asked.

"Absolutely, not!" Pangolin said loudly.

"But if they need aid," a fox man said.

"We don't know who they are," Pangolin said.

"But they know us," Mossberry said.

Traveler looked at Pangolin again. "Mr. Pangolin, lead the caravan away from here. We will move as quickly as possible. I want us to leave these strangers and the Troll Forest far, far behind."

"Master Traveler, the big-nosed sprites," a pech said. "Did they smell them before?"

"The kilmoulis sensed this party back in Fae'el."

"Fae'el!" Lyre said. "They have followed us all the way from that elfin city in Faë-Land?"

"Yes, Mr. Lyre, they have."

"How?"

"That was the question I was asking myself before, but I'm content to leave the answer here in the Forest with them."

"Men, we march on immediately!" Pangolin said.

CHAPTER EIGHTEEN

What Is at the Top of Doom Peak?

"Both parties are nearby, Master Traveler," one of the kilmoulis said to Traveler just as the caravan began to march. The sprites were all together.

"Both? The one you said is like us but not as well?"

"What does that mean, Mr. Traveler? What are they saying?" Lady Aylen asked.

"We cannot understand it. I know you said it could not be a party of doppelgangers," the kilmoulis said.

"No, doppelgangers, like changelings, are never more than one. But we have no time. Run. We can ponder this later."

The caravan marched at a quickened pace. Those who could not run jumped in the pull-carts manned by the pech. Others returned to their small-realms.

Even the giants took such long strides that Pangolin had to increase his own pace to keep up. The five of them alone were ahead of the vanguard.

"We near a ridge," the vanguard leader said.

"The land is sloping downward even more," Grakdar said.

"Look!" Barg said, pointing.

"We did not see that before."

The dark peak had been shrouded in misty clouds but became visible as they moved forward down the path. Once again, they passed into another region of the Forest. The trees and foliage were not unlike Faë-Land and the Lands of Man, tall, huge but nothing compared to those of most of the Great Forest. Also, the new forest was not as dense.

The dark mountain, however, was massive, rising into the sky, and lay directly in their path. It was part of a mountain range, though all the small mountains on either size grew progressively smaller the farther they got from the chief mountain.

"What is that on the top of the larger mountain?" Pangolin asked. He looked to Elman and stopped.

The half-elf was vigorously rubbing his eyes. He was walking forward blindly, as his eyes were shut and watering.

"Mr. Elman, what's wrong?" Pangolin asked worried.

"My eyes," Elman said.

"Something's wrong, Grakdar," Barg and the other giants said.

All four of them stopped. Pangolin looked at them.

"We have no connection to the earth," Grakdar told him.

"What does that mean, Mr. Grakdar?"

"We have a magic connection to the earth as long as our feet touch it. It is the power of the Antaean giant race. We have never experienced this before. There is nothing. No connection. It's as if we're floating in a void."

"The earth beneath is what then?"

The caravan slowed, and the front of the caravan watched the vanguard.

"Something is wrong with Mr. Elman's eyes," Lady Aylen said.

"Mr. Traveler." King Aereth noticed the caravan master's gaze fixed on the mountain.

"That is Doom Mountain."

"Doom Mountain," the king repeated.

"That is not possible. If that mountain is here, then we're not where we're supposed to be."

"What is that at the top of the main mountain, Mr. Traveler?" Gwyness asked. "It looks like—"

They heard yells behind them. Everyone looked. All three of the kirins were gone into the sky, as if a giant invisible hand from the heavens had grabbed them. Traveler saw the caravan's glowing white caladrius bird flying away. The magic bird never left its pocket-realm of the Tree Shepherd's. Horror came over the caravan master's face.

None of them, human, fae, their beasts, had another thought or sensation. All had blanked out into dark unconsciousness. Death would soon follow.

Pangolin lay face-first on the ground. All four of the giants, the two dozen of the elaphine archer-hunters, and Mr. Elman lay around him, unconscious. Behind the royals, Gwyness, Nirgund the berserker, all thirteen of his reptilian fae hounds, all seven of the female half-elf royal guards, Mr. Hobbs, and his two bodyguards, Mr. Tyfer and Mr. Oeric lay unconscious. Every human, drow, elf, and their beasts, the pech, and all the sprites—fenodyree, gnome, gnomoid, kilmoulis, faun, elaphine, cervid, rusine, giant lizard and their human minders, every Cut-throat and all their chamroshes, all the animal men and their beasts were unconscious. Mr. Gresham and Mr. Frog-Dor, even the three crawling trees, were sprawled about the ground.

All that was standing was the metal golem, Glogg. It had Bragg, the dwelf, in its hands, and it slowly walked forward, even as its magic drained.

Traveler's eyes flickered. His eyes opened for a second. Giant black giraffes with smiling human mouths and extra snakelike arms carried him away.

"We will get you to safety, Master Traveler," one of them said. "Your dog too, but I do not think we will make it. The magic is too powerful. We feel ourselves drifting into darkness."

The giraffes stopped. Traveler could see his dog in the arms of another black giraffe creature. He was in a dreamlike state. His dog was but a fleshy armored ball growing smaller. The darklings began to stumble and fall to the ground. They shrank and transformed into black slugs.

"We will try, Master Traveler. We will try to get far down into the earth. Perhaps beyond its magic."

The darklings were specks and disappeared. Traveler lay there, his eyes open, unable to move, fighting to stay conscious. The ground he lay upon was wet. He felt the ground move. He felt them. He thought it was worms, but they moved as a collective unit pulling him into the moist earth. Traveler realized what it was. How could he not have realized only a few moments sooner? The valley was the giant tongue of a creature so large to be unimaginable. He struggled, but he was helpless. Tears streamed down the sides of his face.

The ground rumbled. The unmistakable guttural roar of a griffin pierced the air then the eagle shrieks of hippogriffs.

King Oughtred stood, looking down upon Traveler. The tall Xenhelmian warrior king stared at him with a cold expression of simmering rage but restrained. He wore his crown on his head and full knight's armor with a red cloak. His red hair, mustache, and beard were brighter than Traveler remembered.

"Lift him up so he can see," Oughtred commanded.

The hairy creature that lifted Traveler's body up by the neck was a cross between a baboon and reptile—a beast man. Their nearby portal was a size he had never seen before. A spinning vortex, its opening rested on the ground. Ahead if it was the Xenhelm caravan—a war caravan, an army.

Immediately behind the Four Kings were grayish goblins on dire wolves. Every warrior wore a blindfold over their eyes, but their eyes glowing shone through. Behind them were formations of battle elves. Their helmets covered their full faces, but the sides were open for their ears to move freely. Each helmet had two peepholes. Glowing eyes also shone through. The beast man was one of hundreds, possibly thousands, in formation behind the elves.

Traveler recognized the Gaean party, led by the same tall green-skinned dryad on a large stag with a crown of thorns. Dressed in wood armor, as were all her dryad warrioresses armed with slender black-tipped spears, she was surrounded by packs of large green fae dogs.

With them were the male centaurs with crowns, three in all, their upper torsos were fully armored in fae metal, their heads fitted with crowned helmets without faceplates to allow both their faces and hair to be free. Six-foot-tall gnomes and large satyrs with their herds of giant bison and boars stood behind them. He could also make out the party of fae-bloods, all in black, with sparkling stones around their necks.

Another party was the iguana male warriors—ten feet tall, clad in green armor with long axes on their belts and a quiver of javelins. They held thick pike weapons in their clawed hands. A row of elongated yellow scales ran from the top of their foreheads to their backs. Their tails were green, like the rest of their bodies with a bright-yellow streak. There seemed to be thousands of them.

Then came a dwarven caravan of several hundred in thick nonreflective dwarven armor and armed with metal war mallets or piked double axes, hundreds of lindworms, hundreds of humanoid, ugly kobolds draped in hooded cloaks.

Before all of them, an elfin sorceress floated in the air. Many hooded humanoids with strange yellowish eyes stood in formation behind her.

"I am told your caravan killed the morgens and lampads who were to be part of my Kings' Caravan," Oughtred said. "Show him. Yes, Mr. Traveler, I retrieved my son from where your beast sent him."

The beast walked to show the king's three prince-king sons on their hippogriffs. Prince Wuldricar the Savage was huge and bulky, his beard still dyed orange, but his blond hair was silver white. His eyes were pale. Prince Renfrey the Wily glared at Traveler, almost shaking from rage.

"I must kill him!"

"No," Oughtred said. "You must learn to savor horror."

Last was Prince Gervase the Fair. He alone wore black armor covering his entire body. No part of his face or skin showed.

"Our magic armor is indestructible, but the place where your beast sent my son Gervase managed to pour a creature inside. The thing ate much of him. I destroyed everyone and everything in their lands, but my son still lives.

"Never have I crossed one to bring so much destruction to me. But it ends here, guide, trail master, caravan master, healer, magic swordsman, master of the other-worldly shape-shifting beast, traveler of human birth. Your death will be fitting for someone who has accomplished so much against me. However, I must thank you. Years ago, I had a vast flying army, larger than even my land caravans. It set out across the Great Forest never to be seen again. I thought it was my enemies. I killed all the ones I remotely suspected. It seems as if they were telling me the truth after all. You, Traveler, have uncovered the mystery of the Great Forest. The creatures are called landvættir, the living land. They are the forebearers of troll-kind and the like. They are almost extinct but I encountered one appearing as a whole island. Never had I seen one the size of an entire human empire. Likely it is the last of its kind here in the Great Forest. Your Titan's Caravan will be its latest victims. I will tell no others, so those attempting to create their own land caravan can suffer the same fate. You have another fate, however. I created a teleportation spell for you alone, but with a twist."

King Oughtred gestured. A strange man approached dressed in a long white robe. His exposed face and hands changed. He was young. He was old. He was middle-aged.

"He is a time elemental. Almost the rarest of all elementals. I saved him for you. You will learn of his powers directly. Your caravan came closer than any other to defeating me. Your fabled quest ends here. The Kings' Caravan alone marches to Atlantea. At last, I have amassed the power and army. We march not to visit but to conquer. Good bye, Traveler. You did well. You almost made it through the Great Forest, almost to Titan's Teeth. You were correct to believe a trap awaited you at Titan's Fall, but I know you are a crafty one, so we set a trap there, and we're the ones here."

Oughtred nodded, and the beast man dropped Traveler to the ground.

"Do not let him lie there as a jumbled mess. Lay him properly on the ground, hands at his sides, so he can stare up at the sky," Oughtred said.

"King, we will not be able to hold back the power of the landvættir much longer."

"You do not need to hold it back much longer." He looked at the humanoid demon. "Attend to him and meet us at the Eye."

Oughtred mounted his griffin and raised his hand. His griffin took flight, and his sons followed on their hippogriffs. The Kings' Caravan followed them into the giant portal. When the last man and beast entered the portal closed and disappeared.

The time elemental stepped to Traveler and stood over him.

"We go to the lands where you sent the king's son, Prince Gervase. To the Nether-Lands. There, creatures will torture you. Will you be an infant or an old man when they do so?" A crystal staff appeared in the humanoid man's hand. "However, before we go, we will watch your caravan be consumed by the landvættir."

"Ahh!"

Traveler's eyes opened. He looked at his leg, and an arrow of light was embedded in his left thigh. He yanked it out.

The humanoid stepped back from him. "This will change nothing." The time elemental raised the staff in the air, and a new portal began to grow behind him.

An arrow flew straight for the staff but suddenly stopped, moving so slow that the wizard moved the staff away, laughing.

"No ally can save you from your fate."

A metal fist hit the back of the wizard's skull. He fell, and his staff rolled from his hand. Glogg, the metal golem, marched to the wizard. The man scrambled on the ground and seized the staff. Suddenly, he was attacked by elves jumping out of invisibility. They were Bragg's elves. Other mountain elves fired arrows from their long bows or threw their long axes. The forest elves fired volley after volley of arrows, and the savage elves grappled with the wizard and tried to claw and stab him with their daggers.

The wizard laughed. All of them moved in slow motion, their arrows and axes sailed through the air, floated so slowly that the wizard watched it all. He had almost freed himself from the clutches of the savage elves.

"You're not leaving!" The dwelf joined his metal golem, crossbow in one hand, the golem's war hammer in the other.

"My magic is too powerful for you!"

Bragg dropped the weapons to grab at the wizard's throat. "You may have robbed us of our speed but not the fortitude to kill you with our bare hands," the dwelf said, gritting his teeth to push forward with every fiber of his being against the wizard's magic.

One swipe and the wizard was without his staff-wielding arm. Traveler moved to strike again. The wizard waved his hand, and Traveler was blown back. The staff flew to the wizard's other hand. Bragg charged the wizard and tried with all his might to push his war hammer down the wizard's throat, but the dwelf, too, was caught in the slow-motion spell. Glogg charged and threw itself at them.

Traveler got up in time to see them all sucked into the portal and disappear in the blink of an eye.

There was no time to mourn or wonder where Bragg and his men were. Traveler did not dare step any closer. Within a secret pocket, he clutched the glowing gemstone. He quickly ran back then forward to get as much momentum as he could and threw it.

A flash, and an invisible wave hit him and knocked him off his feet. He coughed as he crashed back to the ground. Fear came over him as he realized he was not feeling the earth around him shake. It was moving. The landvættir had been lying on its back and was rising to its feet.

The doorway of one of the caravan's realms shattered. Väki tumbled out. The fire elementals' eyes were still swollen shut. They vomited. One rose to his feet first and began slapping his fists together violently over and over. The invisible crystalline cocoon around him broke apart. The väki's hand caught fire. As his eyes burned with fire, too, he shot flames at all his comrades. All were ablaze and freed from the magic. The väki began to grow in size as they shot fire from their hands and mouths at the lands. Soon they were giants tens of feet tall.

The Tree Shepherds were also free and grew to giant size. They struck at the ground with their staffs which were as sharp as swords. Their crawling trees shot out in every direction and pulled every human, fae, and animal from the titanic creature's tongue covering the entire valley.

However, the giant väki and leshy were losing their footing as the creature continued to rise to its feet. The earth was breaking apart all around them.

Traveler looked over his shoulder. He could hear the sounds. He could see the panic. The Great Forest's land animals were stampeding away. Flying ones took to the sky, and already the sky was black with them. Giant trees in the distance were pulling themselves out of the ground to run. He could see giant leshies running. The sky above the Troll Forest rained giant trolls, falling to their deaths in the sun as beanstalks broke and fell.

"No one can anger the Great Forest and live," Traveler said to himself.

A giant flying dog-headed griffin with humanoid hands grabbed the caravan master before he fell through the disintegrating earth.

The landvættir's form took shape. It rose onto its four legs, ancient earth and trees. Its single eye was what they observed on the top of Doom Peak, the mountain itself was the eye stalk. It had a giant hanging sheet of a green tongue, every inch covered with fleshy fingerlike protrusions.

Thunder boomed in the skies. Thunder rumbled on the ground. Traveler watched on the back of his dog as the Great Forest, through its giant trees, birds, insects, and animals, attacked the landvættir. Flocks of birds and flying creatures created lightning cyclones around it. Swarms of insects engulfed it, each grabbing a piece of its earthen body. Vines and snakelike branches shot up from the ground all around it, entwining its legs. The walking land mass crashed to the ground from the violence of the attack. The Great Forest against the landvættir turned day to night. Lightning flashed, illuminating it for mere moments. As quickly as the violence began, it was over. Nothing remained of the creature but a chasm in the earth and a crater around it all that stretched far into the distance. It was a lifeless black spot at the edge of the Great Forest. But the Forest would reclaim the land, as it always did so that in a year, or years, there would be no trace of the battle between the Forest and the creature—a battle of ancients.

CHAPTER NINETEEN

The Lost Warriors

Lady Aylen rested on the ground on all fours, vomiting like every other member of the caravan. Most were still prone on the ground, conscious, but so sick they could barely move. The dog landed on the ground in its flying form. Traveler got down from its back. Lady Aylen watched him, trying to smile but shivering. He managed a grin then collapsed to the ground.

"Mr. Traveler!" she yelled.

She tried to get to her feet but fell flat. Something lifted her to her feet. It was the dog in a humanoid form. He pushed her toward the caravan master.

"Yes, yes, miserable dog. You only talk to me when you want me to help him."

She reached him and picked the man up in her arms.

"Lucky for you I'm an elfin woman, otherwise I could not manage. But where am I supposed to go? Look at us!"

The Tree Shepherds' crawling trees had managed to rescue the caravan from their fate, but even the Tree Shepherds and väki, back to their normal size, looked exhausted and sickly.

"Someone approaches!"

She did not know who yelled out, but she could see the caravan running to them and saw that one of them held a banner with a white flag.

"Mr. Traveler, I will leave you here." She set the caravan master down. "Where are my weapons?"

She was startled. A sickly Gwyness tapped her with her war tridents.

"Gwyness, sit down! You're about to collapse."

"I'm fine, as fine as you are."

Gwyness pointed at the approaching caravan.

"We weren't able to escape them after all."

Lady Aylen grabbed a war trident in each hand, took a deep breath, and marched to them.

The caravan was made up of elves, humans, and humanoids. They stopped advancing as Lady Aylen and Gwyness neared them.

"Wait," someone called out.

The two women looked back. Pangolin walked to them, barely able to hold his axe-mace. Berserkers, pech, and even Hobbs with a wooden staff held like a sword followed.

Lady Aylen turned her attention back to the strange caravan.

"We may not be at our best, but after surviving that creature, I'm not about to be killed by a band of strangers. Is that understood, Gwyness?"

"Yes, m'lady."

"We've come too far."

The three members of the caravan reached them—an elfess, a human, and a humanoid fae with antenna.

"We're allies," the elfess said.

"Allies?" Lady Aylen asked. "We know you've tracked us from Faë-Land."

The three of them looked at each other. They noticed the princess's war tridents and looked at Gwyness and her weapons.

The elfess stepped to Lady Aylen alone.

"Are you and the human female, the lost warriors of the kingdom of Rivermouth?" the elfess asked.

"I am Lady Aylen."

"Aylen? You mean Faylen. Queen Faylen, the mage mother of Rivermouth. The training kingdom of the great warrior clerics of all lands. You are the slayer, and the human is the seer."

"No, they are both slayers and both seers," the humanoid fae said.

"Who are you?" Lady Aylen asked.

The elfess smiled. "We found you. We have searched for years. Many tried to stop us. We had many obstacles, but we are united."

"United?"

"Yes. You are the last of Rivermouth and destined to rebuild the kingdom and its mage clans. Under your training and leadership, we are to be the first of your warrior clerics. Elves, humans, fae, and faoladh."

"How do you know this, know about us or anything?" Lady Aylen asked with a pained expression.

"We will explain all. I promise, Lady Aylen. As the last of Rivermouth's royals, you are our queen."

"Queen? I'm a princess, not a queen."

"You are our queen," the elfess said. "The lost warriors of Rivermouth have finally been reunited."

The party of nearly a hundred all bowed their heads in unison.

CHAPTER TWENTY

Titan's Teeth

Any human who had ever seen Oceanus Omnis, the great oceans of the magic lands, felt like an ant floating in the void of the heavens. Even from a distance, hundreds of miles away, one could feel the magnitude of its power slamming against the shore.

From the oceans, the land mass known as Titan's Teeth appeared as a giant screaming skull without eye sockets and a mouth of an elongated cavernous opening mostly above the water line. The teeth were the stalactite columns from the roof of the caves. The stalagmites rose from the sea.

The blind seer knelt on the ground, her hands pressed against the deck.

"Are they dead yet?" Princess Ilirora the elf asked.

The kneeling woman with in her hooded cloak lifted her head.

"I continue to feel their presence of life," the witch said. "It was waning to nothingness but has reversed and grows."

The elfin princess rose from her chair.

"King Oughtred will think this to be unbelievable. Can this caravan not be killed?"

"He was right to keep us here," the winged humanoids said from her group of attendants.

"It would appear so."

The elfess stepped from the room onto the open deck of the flying ship off the coast of Titan's Teeth and looked up with a slight smile. Above the ship circled dozens of giant lion-headed eagles, thick yellowish manes of hair, and large clawed talons. She moved to the side to observe the land mass.

"We cannot remain in these waters for long," the flying ship's gargoyle captain said. He was exquisitely dressed, as were all of them, but his skin was gray and earthen, his face reptilian with a horn above each brow, and his large bat wings were folded behind his back. "Lookouts have already spotted what may be finfolk. They hunt in these waters."

"They are nothing."

"They are more than nothing. They are shape-shifters and magic-makers who can afflict much damage on our fleet from their boats."

"All I am concerned about is if the underwater lookouts sight any mermaids, merrow, or sea centaurs. Do not trouble me with any other matter. Sail the fleet onto the shore and open all cannon ports to prepare for attack."

The gargoyle nodded. "Yes, queen."

She glanced at the winged humanoid attendants. "Seed the shores with them all."

The flying black ships of the fleet—each the size of a human kingdom—without sails or flags, slowly moved forward, above and just out of reach of the ocean's giant waves. Long cannons emerged from the hulls of the twelve warships, two on each side.

Doors on the side of the ships lowered, and hundreds of boatlike pods with black wings flew out. The boat-pods quickly flew toward the shore. In a flash, one of the pods exploded, spilling its cargo of seeds into the great ocean.

"Who fires on us?" the elfess yelled.

"There is no life on the shore," one of the winged humanoids said.

"There!" she yelled.

All of them rushed to the hull to look. With their fae eyes, they could see the giant ten-foot-tall automaton marching forward, firing magic arrows from a giant crossbow. It continued to fire and blast the boat-pods out of the sky and into the waves.

"Fire on it!" the elfess yelled at the gargoyle captain.

The metal golem could not fire fast enough to defend against all the flying boat-pods. One crashed to the ground spilling its seeds upon the ground. The seeds, opened and rather than plants, humanoids grew from it.

"I do not know where the attackers came from, queen, but there are many living things running to its aid—men," the eye-less witch said.

"Let them come. Let them come and be destroyed by our sprouting army."

Traveler sat up in the trussing bed rubbing the sides of his face to wake himself up. He inhaled and exhaled loudly with his eyes closed. When he opened them again his eyes locked on his dog. His head rested on Traveler's leg under the covers.

"Do you sleep in this contraption, sire?"

King Aereth sat on a stool next to the bed. He laughed. "Contraption, Mr. Traveler?"

"I prefer simplicity, sleeping on the ground with my bearskin blanket."

"Mr. Traveler, we know you're not a commoner no matter how much you pretend otherwise," Lady Aylen said.

"Princess, I have vague memories of you carrying me around like a sack of food."

"I was getting you out of danger. Ask your dog."

Traveler noticed that he lay in a tent filled with people. He looked around smiling.

"Mr. Hobbs, are we having a meeting?"

The steward smiled. "Yes, sir. We were waiting on you."

The group laughed.

"What happened to me?" he asked.

"You were poisoned, Mr. Traveler," Gresham said, stepping forward. "But you've been cured of it."

"Did anyone die in the caravan?" Traveler asked somberly.

"We may lose some, sir," Gresham said. "Men and animals who remain deathly sick. We are doing everything to restore them."

"Food, provisions, and weapons?"

"Food, water, and provisions were undamaged, sir," Hobbs said.

"All our weapons were undamaged as well, Mr. Traveler," Estus said. "The creature's magic seemed to coat them with a crystalline cocoon to keep one from wielding them, but my men have broken all our weapons, armor, and supplies out and returned them to new."

"It was not weapons and armor alone that were encased in the magic crystal in their realms," Greenwig said. "We were also restored."

"Have we seen the fae-bloods?" Traveler asked.

"They have awoken from their hibernation," a hooded Dr'amal said from the back of the crowd.

"That was our first indication that we ignored," Traveler said.

"The creature's magic put them into hibernation," Dr'amal said.

"Our kirins, Mr. Traveler, have not returned," King Aereth said sadly.

"The creature magically repelled them because they are of magic different than these lands and were probably immune to its effect. They will return, sire, and we will wait until they do."

The spirits of the royals and Gwyness visibly lifted.

"What of the caladrius bird, Mr. Traveler?" Gresham asked.

"The magic bird knew what was about to happen. The enormity and the magnitude of death alone would have caused the beast to die from sheer grief. We can find it. It will not have gone far."

"I will take charge of that task," the fauness Zefea said. "We have been fortunate not to need its gifts, but we are its home. A simple seeker spell will reveal its location."

"My kingdom will celebrate. The creature that murdered so many over the ages is dead and gone," Lyre said. "All our fallen elves are avenged."

"Mr. Lyre, the creature did not murder anyone, or act out of malice or sport. We were food. It was an animal eating its food, as it has been doing for centuries. It needed to die, but do not trouble yourself with hate for it. Your emotions are best used elsewhere."

"No one will be its food ever again," Lyre said.

"No. The Great Forest has seen to that."

"But you knew, Mr. Traveler," Chief Ethor said. "You did prepare for this mystery of the Great Forest that has baffled fae for generations."

"I prepared as best I could not knowing what we faced. All I knew is that all before us had been defeated, including wizards more powerful than any in our own caravan. I reasoned it had to be a means of magic that was far more powerful. I had the darklings stay within a maze of small-realms, one within another within another. I had them wear magic armor too. They would observe us at all times.

The magic of the creature still overwhelmed their realms but they moved quickly.”

“We lost Mr. Bragg and his men,” Pangolin said.

“We did, but they saved my life from what Oughtred called a time elemental.”

King Aereth jumped to his feet as commotion broke out in the tent.

“Oughtred?” King Aereth asked.

Traveler recounted the appearance of the Four Kings and their new Kings’ Caravan. All were incredulous of their reappearance and most disgusted and angry at the fact that fae were part of his caravan.

“The poison you were afflicted with,” Gresham said.

“It was Prince Renfry. I’m sure of it.”

“It was made to transform you into something,” Frog-Dor said.

“Yes, Renfry would defy his father, but he would not do something vicious enough to interfere with his father’s plan for me.”

“A plan that has been thwarted,” King Aereth said.

“Oughtred said he planned to conquer the fabled kingdom itself.”

“He told you that he planned to conquer Atlantea?” Lyre asked.

"Madness!" Dr'as said.

"He said lots of things. I'm not sure I believe it all."

"Why would he lie?" King Aereth asked.

"It could have been a boast or deception. Why tell me? I was about to die at his hands. What did the information matter to me? Maybe he was saying it all for the benefit of his new Kings' Caravan."

"What are you suggesting?" King Aereth asked.

"No one can conquer Atlantea, sire. It has been tried many times before. Look around."

The king did and noticed the discomfort from the fae.

"Is that why the Atlanteans like humans but not fae?" Lady Aylen asked.

"Yes, but that past is of no interest to me. We are Titan's Caravan now, and we will arrive at Atlantea as Titan's Caravan."

The fae assembled in the tent nodded.

"Whether the Atlanteans care for humans or not or are indifferent toward fae, the fact remains that neither human nor fae can get to Atlantea alone along the Trail. We have seen that, and the journey is not over."

"You got to Atlantea alone, Mr. Traveler," Dr'amal said. "Without either your dog or sword."

"I did, but I would never repeat the ordeal ever again or wish it upon an enemy. They travel to Atlantea ahead of us. Oughtred did say they would be at a place called the Eye."

"I know of it," one of the bird men said. "It's an island. They say it looks like the eye of a Titan."

"What exactly was this creature, sir?" Hobbs asked.

"A landvættir, and the Great Forest killed it before it could destroy its ancient lands."

"Good," Lyre said.

"How did you affect it, Master Traveler?" Greenwig asked. "You did something to break its iron grip of magic at least upon us Tree Shepherds and the väki."

"A gift I kept from the celestial and star elves."

The revelation made the elves' and drows' ears perk up.

"I threw a star fragment at the creature."

"A magic item, Mr. Traveler?" King Aereth asked.

"The legend is that it was the only element fae could use against a Titan. I doubt the legend, but its power against magic beings cannot be underestimated. It may not kill them, but it will do severe damage."

"Where did you get this from, Master Traveler?" Chief Ethor asked.

"I stole it from the star elves, chief."

The chief smiled. "I am sure one of the many quarrels they had with you."

"One of many, chief. But I didn't care then, and I don't care now."

"I would say our caravan master more than earned his pay for the journey as much to this point as to the fabled kingdom," Nirgund said proudly.

"Hear! Hear!" The Cut-throats applauded.

"When do we leave, Mr. Traveler?" Pangolin asked.

"We must wait here until we recover, the kirins return, and if we can, retrieve our caladrius bird. We could be here days. Correct, Mr. Gresham?"

"Yes, Mr. Traveler. We would need at least a few to save the men and animals still afflicted."

"Here at least we have a safe place to rest. Nothing can follow us through the devastation left by the Forest's destruction of the creature. We should take advantage of this. We should only move forward when we are all whole again, or as close to it. The Four Kings may be gone, but he knew we were headed to Titan's Teeth. He may still have allies there waiting, as a precaution."

"Won't he think we're dead?" Lyre asked.

"I doubt that seriously. He'll know we live."

"What is a time elemental, Mr. Traveler?" a Cut-throat asked.

"A demon. Another demon," Dr'as said.

"You know much of demons," Lyre said.

"Because my people have fought them."

"What does it do, Mr. Dr'as?" Traveler asked. "It is one elemental I do not know of even by story."

"Its magic is related to time, but I am not familiar with its specific abilities, only its existence."

"I doubt it was simply going to make me younger than Mr. Quillen or older than our fairy sisters."

"Let us hope Mr. Bragg and his men were able to destroy it," King Aereth said.

"Yes, sire." Traveler turned to Pangolin and said quietly, "Hold on to Mr. Bragg's and his golem's weapons on the march."

The vanguard leader nodded.

"But we have new members of the caravan, Mr. Traveler," I'wulf said with a big smile. "They guard our portal's entrance even now."

"New members?"

"The caravan we fled from with the white flag," Pangolin said.

Traveler looked at Lady Aylen. "They are here for you, and Maiden Gwyness."

"Elves, humans, humanoids," Lady Aylen said.

"And werewolves."

"Faoladh are not werewolves, Maiden Gwyness," Nirgund said. "Werewolves are evil. These are of light."

"Are these newcomers going to accompany us on our quest?" Lyre asked.

"Of course, they are," Lady Aylen said.

"Do you know anything about them? Where they come from? How they came to know you and your maiden? How they were able to find us on Titan's Trail? Does nothing of this seem too convenient to be true to you?" Lyre asked.

"What are you trying to say?" Lady Aylen asked.

"I'm not trying to say anything. I am directly saying they cannot be allowed to remain with the caravan. Now is not the time to take in strangers, especially knowing that the Four Kings are alive and well with a more powerful caravan. Does anyone disagree with me?" The high elf looked around the tent.

"Send them away? Into the Forest alone?"

"They reached us alone," someone said.

"Mr. Traveler, what do you say?" Lady Aylen asked.

"I agree with them, princess. We cannot take them on, but the solution is a simple one."

"What solution, Mr. Traveler?"

"Do not be saddened, princess," Traveler said. "If they are who they claim to be, you are not sending them away. You are sending them to begin the construction of the new Rivermouth to be the home of the new warrior clerics. To serve all the lands of humans and fae. The new sister city of Sirnegate and all the kingdoms of the Kings Elder."

Lady Aylen and Gwyness looked at each other. King Aereth patted the caravan master on the shoulder, nodding in agreement.

"It's settled then," Traveler said.

"We survived it all to this point, Mr. Traveler. The mystery of the Great Forest is solved and will trouble no living thing again. Titan's Caravan survived a creature countless others before us through the centuries had not. I would say the Fates have spoken," the elves said.

"Perhaps."

"Mr. Traveler, do not revert to your dour self," Lady Aylen said. "We like you much better when you offer uplifting words of inspiration and hopefulness rather than your usual tales of terror in the magic lands."

"Princess, after what we all endured, I will never, ever have to say another word about how dangerous these lands are. I was saying to our elfin comrades that we're not in Atlantea yet."

Lady Aylen and Gwyness barely slept at all. Long before dawn, they met with the ones who called themselves the lost warriors.

"Lady Aylen, you can rely on us. We will find a suitable site for the new Rivermouth," the lead elfess said to them.

"When we return from Atlantea, we will have riches enough to rebuild a worthy castle, training grounds, and library to be at its center."

The lost warriors looked at each other with glee, some on the verge of tears of joy.

"How will you return?" Gwyness asked.

"Maiden Gwyness, our challenge was tracking you to the Great Forest. Returning home will be no burden," one of them said.

"How did you find us?" Lady Aylen asked.

"Someone told us where you would be, but we were sworn to secrecy. You will meet the person soon."

"Someone we know?" Lady Aylen asked.

"Oh yes, m'lady."

Lady Aylen and Gwyness bid them each goodbye. Both women wondered if they would ever see them again.

Hobbs had the men out of bed hours before dawn. Lady Aylen sat in the women's tent at the open entrance deep in thought.

"Lady Aylen, am I disturbing you?" King Aereth asked as he came from his tent.

"Not at all, sire."

"Our caravan master stepped out of the circle and returned with the darklings."

"He has a history with those creatures, sire."

"Many stories our caravan master has. I heard your lost clan has already left for Faë–Land under the cover of night. I would think that to be a dangerous thing in the Great Forest."

"I would, too, sire, but they were unconcerned. I would assume most of their party are strong with magic of some note."

"Yes, that must be true, Lady Aylen."

"Is it strange, sire, that I miss a group of people I just met, these lost warriors. I almost feel it is comparable to you missing the company of your Kings Elder comrades."

"You miss what will be, Lady Aylen. After our quest ends, you'll have the journey of life. We all do."

"Yes, sire. Our fabled quest has been far more than anything we could have imagined."

"And we have not even reached our destination."

"But we'll have completed this leg of our journey, leaving this Great Forest behind, sire. Unlike our Mr. Traveler, I do not wish to ever return."

The kirins returned at dawn's light. Each beast stood on its own cloud hovering above the waiting caravan. Lady Aylen waved at her blue kirin.

Frog-Dor walked to the royals and Gwyness. "Permit me." With a wave of his hand, they rose in the air and were set upon their mounts. The men cheered.

"Thank you, Mr. Frog-Dor," Traveler said.

The wizard bowed.

"Do you sense the army?" Traveler asked to the group of kilmoulis.

The sprites nodded. "Yes, Master Traveler, but there is more."

"More?"

"We can hear them. There are two armies engaged in battle at the shore," Strag said. The elaphine leader had never joined the front, but today he did. Every elaphine had their longbows ready to fire. Every cervid was armed with small shields to protect the elaphines, and the rusines wore armor and wielded weapons to protect the cervids.

"Two armies?" King Aereth asked. "Mr. Traveler, why do we march into them?"

"Because one of the armies will need our aid, sire."

Traveler turned to face the waiting caravan. Every man, fae, and animal was in battle-armor and wielded their weapons.

"Mr. Estus, General Estus, you will lead Titan's Army."

The caravan's weapons forge was in full knight's armor himself. "Yes, Mr. Traveler."

Estus lifted his right gauntlet and gestured the caravan forward as he marched. Wave after wave of armor golems marched behind him. Each automaton held a sword, battle axe, pike staff, or war hammer. Estus magically commanded two thousand of them.

Strag followed with his army of archers. Following them were the elves, drows, and the Cut-throats with their eagle hounds. The king's heavy weapons teams and pech followed last.

Pangolin with the giants, half-elves, Nirgund, fae-bloods, and animal men would guard the rear to protect the caravan's nonwarrior laborers and domestics, the giant lizards and their minders, and their small-realms, hidden in sacks and carts. The fenodyree sprites had charge of Bragg's Diomedian Mares, still restless after the loss of their masters.

The Tree Shepherd leader, Mossberry, appeared next to Pangolin.

"Master Pangolin, it would seem that we can no longer restrain our two little beings."

"No, Mr. Mossberry. Is there anything to be done?"

"Fairies can only be restrained for so long. Even leshies have their limits."

"We can restrain them!" The darklings appeared, jumping over each other in the form of black goat-headed humanoids with human mouths of grinning white teeth.

"Why did Mr. Traveler have to find you?" Pangolin asked.

The darklings cackled. "Why do you say that? Don't you like us?"

"No!"

The darklings cackled louder.

Something spooked the Diomedian Mares. The beasts bolted as a pack away from their fenodyree minders. They galloped hard ahead of the caravan and over the ridge toward the sounds of battle.

Estus realized that he was alone as he led the caravan forward. He had an army of armor golems, but he was still the only living thing at the vanguard. He glanced over his shoulder to see Traveler circling on a winged, iron-like snake in the sky, but the caravan master wasn't looking towards the battle. In the distance, several black shapes flew toward them.

The members of Titan's Caravan who heard him, realized what the caravan master meant days ago as they marched into the open mouth of the landvættir. "We're not where we're supposed to be." The creature's magic made them smell the ocean and feel the ocean mist even though it was not there, but now they were at the oceans of the fae's magic lands. The intense battle was almost drowned out completely by the pounding of the giant waves against the ragged shore. The waves seemed to be on top of them even though they were many miles away.

Estus's eyes could barely take in everything he saw as he walked over the ridge with his armor golem army. On the black sands of the shore was an army of humanoids so emaciated they were no more than animated skeletons, clad with iron helmets, and fighting with a sword in each hand.

The party fighting them was led by a metal golem ten feet in height firing magic arrows from its giant crossbow. Behind him, hooded archers fired an endless blitz of arrows, but the skeletonoids still advanced, and more ran to them from the distant shoreline. So tremendously outnumbered, they would soon be overwhelmed.

None of that was what made Estus freeze in his tracks. Three flying ships hung in the sky, slowly floating toward them. There was a flash. The cannonball exploded in the center of his armor golem army blowing many apart and damaging many others. Estus was blown onto his back.

The skeletonoids saw them and charged, wildly waving their swords. Their long skeleton-like faces had long black opal eyes. Estus jumped to his feet.

"Charge!" he yelled.

The armor golems rushed around him and engaged the skeletonoids, creature versus golem. Estus jumped at the sight of a black shadow that whisked by him. His eyes followed it, and he turned. An elf reached him and kicked him to the ground. Another black shaped barely missed him. A giant lion-headed hawk had almost carried him away. The anzu roared as it circled the caravan.

"Human, it would be best if you focus your attention on your armor golems before a sparti thrusts its sword through your face!" the woodland elf yelled.

"Sparti? The skeleton-like humanoids?"

"Yes! They are sparti! Turn around!"

Estus turned and barely had time to react to a skeletonoid about to strike him with its sword. Instead it was cut down by a hail of arrows. Woodland elves joined him at his side as they fired arrows at any sparti that got past his armor golems. The weapons forge wasn't happy. His armor golems were no better than a sparti in fighting ability, so they did not defeat their adversary, but they did sufficiently occupy them. Golem and sparti could conceivably battle on forever.

More anzu hovered above them. One roared, and Estus, even with his armor and a distance away, could feel the heat off their breath.

"Fire!" King Aereth yelled.

Catapult team after catapult team launched their magic projectiles but not at the growing sparti army. The first flying black ship was their target. Next, the pech aimed at the catapult, and the human men loaded the payloads. Projectiles hit their specific targets—the forward cannons first began to shower the deck.

The king did not think it possible, but the elves' bows grew longer. They arched their bodies back and fired their magic arrows. Their arrow volleys hit their mark, the second floating ship.

The giant lion-headed eagles—anzus—fell from the sky as faun archers fired at them. The faun archers noticed that a single remaining anzu was impervious to their arrows as it flew around the caravan in a fury.

Two points of light flew through the caravan toward the sparti hordes. Following them were a virtual sea of insects. The swarms flew into the sparti, picking up the creatures from the ground and carrying them away to the oceans. In an instant, not one sparti remained.

Estus gave his armor golems the command to march forward to the ocean. A group of woodland elves walked with him.

"Who was the party fighting them?" Estus asked.

The woodland elves stopped. "It cannot be," one said.

The party approached them with their giant metal golem. Estus realized that the Diomedian Mares were with them. It was Bragg and his men.

"Mr. Bragg?"

"Yes," a smiling dwelf answered.

Estus looked at them—Bragg and his elves, woodland, mountain, and savage. Every one of them was older. He could see the gray hairs in the savage elves' and Bragg's hair.

"What happened, Mr. Bragg? I mean, you survived."

"Of course, we did." He slapped Mr. Estus on the back, but the dwelf's focus was elsewhere. "Excuse me, Mr. Estus, but I have a manticore to kill."

Estus and the elfin questing knight archer looked to the sky.

"Manticore?" an elf asked. "There's only the lion bird in the sky."

"That, my fine elf, is my manticore. He is a crafty one. More so than any I have encountered. Let me attend to it before our caravan master gets himself killed."

"Mr. Bragg! Who is in the attacking flying ships?" Estus asked.

"Do not allow them to land, Mr. Estus. The Four Kings have a fondness for murderous races. Sparti are mindless. What's aboard those ships are not."

Pangolin saw him approaching but could not believe it.

"Mr. Pangolin, it has been a long time," a grinning Bragg said. "No, actually. For you it must be a few days."

"You look older, Mr. Bragg."

"More distinguished, the women have said. Ah, you have my weapons. And Glogg's, though I had a new magic crossbow forged for him. He can keep the old one for posterity's sake."

The dwelf's eyes fixed on the flying shape.

"Why does the giant lion-headed eagle concern you?" Pangolin asked.

"Because of what lies underneath its skin." Bragg took his war hammer. "I wager it's the same manticore we encountered before in Faë-Land."

"Manticore?" Pangolin's grip tightened on his axe-mace.

"This is my hunt, Mr. Pangolin. This is what I do. I have even added to my kills since we last met. I believe it was only nineteen then. This will be my twenty-sixth."

"You do this alone?"

"I rid my people's lands of these dark creatures, and I do so wherever I see them. It is a hunt I am sure you approve of."

"Do not get yourself killed, Mr. Bragg."

"That I won't allow to happen. My men and I have been traveling and have waited years for you. I have much news to share. But after."

Pangolin began to piece together what had happened to the dwelf and his men, but the conversation would have to wait. "Why hasn't it attacked? It circles the caravan with no purpose."

"It has a purpose, Mr. Pangolin. It's hunting too."

"Hunting who?"

"Our great caravan master, these creatures hold grudges."

"How could it track us?"

"It did not track you. We knew where you were going and waited. It tracked me, and my men. You all are just the additional prize in its dark eyes."

"Where is Mr. Traveler?" Pangolin asked, looking around. "He is gone, and his dog. It was in the form of a giant flying snake. No!"

The giant manticore came at them like a hurricane wind, moving at the speed of lightning, but Bragg was ready. He blocked the brunt of the creature's force with his weapon. The creature's triple row of gnashing razor teeth were unable to devour him, blocked by Bragg's walking staff weapon, its axe blade end cutting into the creature's face.

As the manticore flew away, clutching Bragg, the dwelf smiled. The creature stared into his eyes. Bragg could see the growing confusion as to why a man would smile before he was about to die.

Bragg had the manticore's tail firmly gripped in his other arm. The creature was unable to free itself or sting him with its giant scorpion tail. The creature screamed in his face to shock him. Bragg pressed a button on his staff. The manticore reacted by releasing the dwelf. The staff shot multiple spiked chains into the creature's body.

The manticore found itself impaled and wrapped in the spiked chains and erupted in a panicked fury. All that did was rip its wings, and it fell.

Bragg was already falling back to the earth many feet away. The creature could see the large smile on his face and reacted: firing poisonous barbs from its tail. Bragg swatted them away.

"I'm immune to your poison, creature!"

The creature screamed and aimed its body at an angle to fall faster and in the dwelf manticore hunter's direction.

A snaking hand yanked Bragg away. His body was placed on the back of a giant flying snake. Traveler and Bragg watched the screaming manticore violently crash to the earth.

"The ground must be thoroughly burned to destroy every piece of it. Its skin, saliva, and blood are poison to living things."

"Mr. Bragg, if we had not saved you, how were you planning to survive your fall?" Traveler asked.

"You didn't have to rescue me, Mr. Traveler. I didn't tell you, but dwelfs can fly."

Traveler shattered a bottle on the ground. A miniature boat rested on the ground but began growing. Dr'amal, Frog-Dor, and the mole-like fae were within the tent. All had their eyes closed.

The three giant city ships moved faster across the land, firing their cannons. The rest of the fleet hung back in the distance. The shores were thick with sparti and were overwhelming the caravan's metal golem army.

Estus disappeared, then the men, women, and beasts of the caravan. The weapons and armor golems remained. Bragg's giant metal golem, elves, and Diomedian Mares disappeared.

The grand illusion began to waver as the three flying ships flew closer. The illusion changed in hue then became a dark-bluish cloud larger than the three ships combined.

The gargoyle captain had no chance to react. Another, larger flying ship of stone emerged from the bluish smoke and rammed the lead flying black ship. The black ship shattered as it fell to the ground and its passengers who could not fly fell to their deaths. Ship fragments and bodies fell, crushing sparti fighters on the ground.

The stone ship fired its own cannons manned by humans and pech, at the farthest of the remaining two ships. It rammed the second one, trying to turn.

The leadership, hidden behind their invisible doorway in a pocket-realm, saw the elfess floating in the air, yelling orders at her winged humanoids and the flying gargoyle warriors escaping the ships.

"Do I need to say it?" Traveler asked to the elves.

"You do not," Chief Ethor said.

The chief and his rustic woodland elf archers, accompanied by the elfin questing knight archers, emerged from the pocket-realms to deliver their volleys of magic arrows. The dark elfess, her winged humanoids, and gargoyles were cut down in seconds. They fell to the earth, disappearing below. In the distance, the rest of the flying black ship fleet turned and rose into the sky to escape.

The caravan abandoned their stone ship on a secluded part of land between the Forest's plant-rich soil and at the threshold where the dark sand beach began.

The being descended from the sky, the humanoid with large eagle-like wings, large bird eyes, and feathers for hair, dressed as a royal. The icarian, with his upper and lower lips as pointed as a bird's beak, cawed his ear-shattering greeting. Traveler nodded. The icarian handed him a silver key. Traveler handed him a bag that looked to contain coins.

"Our business is concluded, once again," Traveler said.

"I thought you chose an unwise departure point, but the fact that we conclude our business proves me wrong."

"We were not without unwelcome guests."

"A mistake those unwelcome guests will never make again, I imagine. The Forest is already speaking of your deeds to those who can hear its words. Since you have done a service for the Forest, I will do a small one for you, free of payment."

"I thank you in advance, then."

"Be very careful of your ocean journey. Your ship may be invisible to most but even an invisible ship leaves a trail in the great ocean, one that can be seen by mermaids, tritons, ocean fae, or sea serpents. The sirens may be the least of your dangers."

"Maybe we will be able to do business again in the future."

"Maybe I will join you the next time on an adventure. You are either lucky or know what you're doing—for a human."

Traveler smiled. "Good journeys."

Caw! The winged fae shot up into the sky and disappeared.

Traveler lifted the silver key in his hand and turned to the caravan.

"We made it through the Great Forest, the Giant Forest, the Forest of the Ancients, or what I called as a lad, the Great Forest of Horrors. The rest of Titan's Trail to Atlantea is covered by water. Shall we continue on?"

"What of Mr. Bragg and his men, Mr. Traveler?" a man asked.

"They have returned, but they are different," another fae said. "They have aged."

"We will have plenty of time to speak about it and much more. Our ship awaits, and so does our sail through the Sirenic Seas."

He turned and marched forward with his dog, as the entire caravan followed. He extended his hand with the silver key into the air and turned it. The doorway to the magic realm opened. Titan's Caravan entered, and after the last human, fae, and animal marched in, the doorway vanished. In its place was a splendid flying fish.

The fish flew through the air, across the black sand beach, and dove in the great ocean.

The Fabled Quest Chronicles continues in Book Five: ***Siren Storms of Madness***.

REVIEW REQUEST

Dear Reader,

I hope you enjoyed *The Forest of Ancients*.

Can You Write Me a Review?

If you enjoyed *The Forest of Ancients (Fabled Quest Chronicles, Book 4)*, I'd greatly appreciate an honest review on one or more of the following sites:

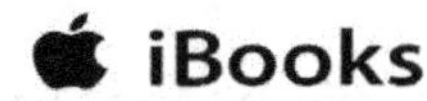

Reviews are the best way for readers to discover good books. My writer's motto is simple: "Readers Rule!" Thanks so much.

Always writing,

Austin Dragon

JOIN THE CLUB!

Don't forget to Join My Exclusive **VIP Readers' Club**!

My fiction universe includes Epic Fantasy, Sci–Fi and more. Your benefits include free books, the latest announcements, special offers and fun giveaways. You can unsubscribe at any time.

Sign up Today and get FOUR of my full–length novels **FREE!** Join at http://www.austindragon.com

Always writing,

Austin Dragon

CONTINUE THE ADVENTURE

Get Your Next *Fabled Quest Chronicles* Books!

- ***Through Titan's Trail*** (Fabled Quest Chronicles, Book 1)
- ***In the Shadow of the Kings*** (Fabled Quest Chronicles, Book 2)
- ***Comes the War Wizards' Wrath*** (Fabled Quest Chronicles, Book 3)
- ***The Forest of Ancients*** (Fabled Quest Chronicles, Book 4)
- ***Siren Storms of Madness*** (Fabled Quest Chronicles, Book 5)
- ***Kingdom at Titan's End*** (Fabled Quest Chronicles, Book 6)

- ***Fabled Quest Chronicles Box Set*** (Books 1-3)
- ***Fabled Quest Chronicles Box Set 2*** (Books 4-6)

Prequels

- ***Quest Master*** (Prequel to the Fabled Quest Chronicles)

Also by Austin Dragon

See all my books in fantasy, science fiction, and horror: http://www.austindragon.com/books

GLOSSARY

Quillen's List of Races, Beasts, and Monsters of Myth and Magic

Ant-lion (or Myrmecoleon) – a creature of varying sizes with the head of a lion and body of a matching giant ant. The creatures hunt as swarms and build elaborate habitats in giant trees. They hunt mammals, humans/humanoids, or predatory or carnivorous insects.

Atlas Turtle – the splendid and benevolent prehistoric race of giant turtles existing before the birth of fae or humans and living in the Great Forest. Standing hundreds of feet in height, their massive dark green are patterned with golden, greens, and earthen spots depending on the seasons. Their exposed skin is more like smooth rock and their giant turtle heads have a horn on the tip of their noses. Virtually indestructible as an adult alone, they always travel single-file in groups.

Beast Man – a race of violent hybrid humanoids that are part simian, part reptile. Often, their heads resemble baboons, as are their upper torso and arms. Their eyes, clawed hands, and feet are reptilian, along with a lizard tail.

Behemoth - a race of ancient beasts of tremendous size existing before the birth of fae or humans and living in the Great Forest. There is no clear description of the beasts other than they look like a hybrid of insect, crab, and earth with many, many elephant-like legs. Also, incredibly, they can fly by magical means, rising into the sky and moving without sound.

Cyclops - a sub-race of giants with a single eye in the center of their forehead. There are any different clans, both civilized and savage. Some are gifted builders, craftsmen, and merchants. Others are scholars and artisans. Rare ones are seers and oracles, able to see what cannot be seen with the normal eye or the future. There are also savage clans known for their ferocity and cannibalism.

Drow - or dark elf (not to be confused with a night elf) is a member of an elfin sub-race characterized by dark bluish skin, most often white hair—though some have black hair, and their eyes often have irises of a bright color, such as blue or purple. Drows wear only dark colors like black, dark blues, and dark purples. The original Drow sub-race had separated from high elves due to embracing dark magic. Drows abandoned the practice long ago but remain enemies to all elves, and most fae.

<u>Night drow</u> - sub-race of drows, and historic enemies, characterized by their dark purplish skin. They are mostly a nocturnal race and their magic is strongest during the night.

Elefantagriff - are hybrid beasts, part griffin and elephant. They have tough grayish skin covered with feathers—mostly around their joints, back, and rear, tusks growing from either side of their beaks, elephantine ears, elephant feet-like talons on thick legs.

Firedrake - a dog-sized orange lizard impervious to heat or fire. It can breathe fire or fiery gas to defend itself.

Gargoyle - a humanoid reptilian race with a tall and elongated body, gray, earth-like skin, and large bat wings they fold behind their back when not flying. They live and nest in the highest mountain domains in the region with or near flowing water.

Groaning Beasts - Ever-groaning shadowy humanoid beasts that walk on all fours and have glowing eyes. They kill by engulfing their victims with their shadow bodies and absorbing their life force.

Haltija - a sub-race of sprites that guard, help, or protect something or somebody. Haltijas appear as frowning full-bearded halfling men with pointy hats.

They are nocturnal sprites like brownies, coming out at night for their daily tasks. They are ill-tempered, rude, surly, and hate being talked to directly. They are also shape-shifters. A clan of haltijas is called a väki and there are many different clans in Faë-Land. (See Väki)

<u>Hedley Kow</u> - imp-like fae shape-shifter able to transform itself into almost any shape for the sake of mischievous pranks. They sometimes appear as cows to bedevil farmers or horses to trick riders, but mostly inanimate objects; all to bring a laugh to the creature. In humanoid form they appear as an ugly large-headed being with large facial features but both its hands and feet end in cloven hooves.

<u>Howler (Monkey)</u> - a sub-race of giant howling monkeys with green fur and four arms in the Great Forest.

<u>Kelpie</u> - shape-shifting water creature in the form of a horse, but can take human or humanoid form. They inhabit rivers and streams primarily. They prey on road travelers by attacking, dragging and drown them, then devouring them, and throwing what remains of the corpse onto the water's edge.

<u>Kobold</u> - a race of shape-shifting sprites who can take the form of an animal, fire, a human being, and a candle, or become invisible. In their humanoid form, they appear as figures the size of small children, little, wrinkled old men wearing caps. There are three major types of kobolds. Most commonly, the fae are house sprites of ambivalent nature. They sometimes perform domestic chores, but can play malicious tricks if insulted or neglected. Another type of kobold haunts underground places, such as mines. A third kind of kobold, the Klabautermann, lives aboard ships and helps sailors. Those that live in human homes wear the clothing of peasants; those who live in mines are hunched and ugly, and sometimes are said to have black skin. Kobolds who live on ships smoke pipes and wear sailor clothing.

Though harmless to the benevolent, when angered kobolds have been recorded as cutting victims to pieces and eating them.

Mine kobolds are expert miners and metalworkers, often drilling, hammering, and shoveling dirt to claim metals or precious stones. Evil ones are blamed for accidents, cave-ins, and rock slides that upon human or fae miners. A favorite kobold prank was to fool miners into taking worthless metal ore or gems, or, sometimes even, when smelted, could be deadly poisonous. Benevolent ones warned miners not go in a dangerous direction, led miners to veins of metal or richer ones.

<u>Landvættir</u> - another race of ancient beasts of tremendous size often described as "walking land masses." The smaller ones are as large as a mountain or even an entire mountain range. The largest ones, existing before the birth of fae or humans, can literally be as large as a continent in perception. Regardless, their size is so vast that a precise description of their form is difficult. They are beings that protect the lands they inhabit, or they feed off the flora and fauna of that land.

<u>Lampads</u> - are a sub-race of nymphs of the Nether-Lands, land of demons. They are fond of enchanting and haunting travelers in their path. Their glowing skin is also a reflection of the power of their inner light; magic they use to create torches to drive men to madness.

<u>Land Kraken</u> - a giant squid-like creature than moves through the earth and attacks with multiple giant tentacles pushing through the ground, ripping apart or crushing victims.

<u>Lindworm</u> — a wingless snake-like creature with two clawed arms in the upper body the size of a horse. Some can breathe fire, others smoke or toxic gas. They are often used as guardians or beasts of burden.

<u>Manticore, land (or crawling)</u> – the rare, wingless sub-species of the evil beasts. The creature walks on the earth with humanoid arms and are double-jointed, each with black-clawed hands. They move at incredible speeds when attacking prey.

<u>Morgens</u> – are a race of evil water nymphs who lure men to their death with their own enchanting beauty. They also have the power to cause heavy floods to destroy.

<u>Mushroom Men</u> – a race of humanoid sentient mushrooms living in forest of the magic lands. Most of peaceful but there are warrior clans. For defense they use javelins or spears, but can shoot poison or spores at attackers.

<u>Nemain</u> – a female demon creature that looks like a old humanoid woman with long, tangled hair, white eyes, and black, unsightly nails. When it screams with its battle cry, it causes all who hear it to be gripped with a murderous lust to kill all around them by any means, or kill themselves.

<u>Nemean Lion</u> – a vicious gigantic lion beast with claws sharper than most human or fae swords and able to cut through most armor. Their golden fur is impervious to the attack of human or fae metals.

<u>Owl Men</u> – a race of humanoid owls. They are adept at flying without sound and are used as trusted and confidential messengers by many fae races. However, there are also sub-races of evil owl men, who are no more than marauders and robbers.

Rat-bats - the swarming flying rat creatures used in battles by goblins and other dark fae.

Redcap - are a sub-race of evil, murderous goblins. They appear as short, old-looking humanoid males with coarse, graying hair down their shoulder, long prominent teeth, skinny fingers ending in talons like eagles, large fiery red eyes, and grisly hair streaming down their shoulders. They wear iron boots, carry pikestaff weapons, and, more prominently, wear red caps on their heads, said to red from soaking it in the blood of their victims.

Sparti (or Spartae) - skeletal-like beings with some type of a weapon and military attire imbued with the malevolent spirit of violence. They are magically grown from the teeth of evil creatures or magic seeds from the Dark Lands.

Trows - they are small, ugly, human-sized, nocturnal troll-like dark fae.

Väki - a clan of haltijas. Besides the tulen väki or väki of fire there are also väki of specific trees, forests, mountains, water, precious metals or gems, underground lands, etc.

Väki of forest (metsän väki). They possess the magical powers of the forest.

Väki of water (veden väki). They can use their magical power of water to make people sick or heal them.

Väki of woman (naisen väki). Clan of female vaki known for their nurturing and restorative magical powers.

Väki of death (kalman väki). Rarely seen clan whose power comes from ghosts and spirits.

Väki of fire: (tulen väki) the clan of haltijas who wear charred brown and orange fabric clothing. They are a race of guardians with the elemental magically ability to conjure and control fire and use warm air to heal or burn.

Väki of mountain (vuoren väki).

Väki of wood (puun väki). The haltijas of trees.

Väki of iron (raudan väki).

Will-o'-wisps – are the atmospheric ghost lights seen by night travelers, especially over bogs, swamps or marshes, of unknown origin and purpose. Witches and other dark fae have also transformed into these lights to spy, follow, or escape.

Wraith – a ghost or ghostlike image of someone, often as an omen of death. Also, the ghost-like henchmen of various dark fae, especially witches and evil nymphs.

Wyvern - like a lindworm in appearance, but the bipedal serpentine creature has large black, bat-like wings and its tail often ends in a diamond- or arrow-shaped tip. Like the ancient and extinct dragons, they are the most powerful of the remaining fire-breathing creatures in the magic lands.

ABOUT THE AUTHOR

Austin Dragon is the author of over 20 books in science fiction, fantasy, and classic horror. His works include the cyberpunk detective *LIQUID COOL* series, the epic fantasy *FABLED QUEST CHRONICLES*, the international epic *AFTER EDEN* Series, and the classic *SLEEPY HOLLOW HORRORS*. He is a native New Yorker but has called Los Angeles, California home for more than twenty years. Words to describe him, in no particular order: U.S. Army, English teacher, one-time resident of Paris, ex-political junkie, movie buff, Fortune 500 corporate recruiter, renaissance man, futurist, and dreamer.

He is currently working on new books and series in science fiction, fantasy, and classic horror!

Connect with Austin on social media at:

Website and blog: http://www.austindragon.com
Pinterest: http://www.pinterest.com/austindragon
Goodreads: https://www.goodreads.com/ADragon

See all my books at:
http://www.austindragon.com/books